The Trinity Signs

By
Scott M Sullivan

DIGITAL INK
PUBLISHING

This book is a work of fiction and any resemblance to persons,
living or dead, is purely coincidental. The characters were born in
the author's imagination and used fictitiously. Most of the
locations used throughout are real. However, the author has taken
the liberty to embellish them wherever necessary.

ISBN-13: 978-0-615-69312-5
ISBN-10: 0615693121

Also by
Scott M Sullivar.

IMPETUS
IMPERFECT INSIDE

Prologue

Early 11th Century, England

Galen clung to his mare's outstretched neck as she galloped across the stormy English countryside. His broken ribs stabbed at his flower-petal-soft lungs with each stride she took. He was lightheaded and weak—a direct result of the savage wounds inflicted upon him—but he was still fiercely determined to see this through to the end. He had come too far to stop now. His Brotherhood counted on him—as did the world, albeit unknowingly.

He ignored the blinding pain that seemed to worsen as the seconds passed and reached up with his bloodied hand to brush the wet tuft of hair from his eyes. He then peered over his shoulder at the rapidly approaching evil army that crimsoned the night sky. Carried on the blustery winds, their clicks and gurgles were much louder now. They whispered his name—teased him to give up in their unmistakably cruel way. What they were too simple to understand, however, was that he would never relent to something so completely vile. He would never give up. They would never accomplish their sinister goal.

"Come on, girl!" he shouted, slapping his mare's rump.

Even with visibility next to nothing, they raced unabatedly through the night. His mare galloped like she never had before, passing through forests and fields like a comet through the sky. The enveloping, unnatural darkness made it nearly impossible to see a thing, but he trusted her instincts—she knew the land well and had always carried him safely. If it weren't for her, his mission would have ended in failure hours ago.

They rode through a shallow river—a frigid splash of water doused Galen's tattered robe—and into a small grouping of trees. No sooner had they exited when the sky blew apart from a bright flash of lightning, silhouetting a world on the brink of annihilation beneath its luminous glow. A crashing boom of thunder soon followed, bowling its way far into the distance as if warning anything in its path to turn around and run the other way. Galen knew that if the storm could think—even an iota of thought—that it, too, would flee from what neared.

As his mare rumbled on, he reached into his simple rope belt with his mangled right hand to steady the jostling Crux. The relic was mankind's most valuable possession—its one bright beacon in an otherwise hopeless situation. And, as such, Galen knew it was therefore his foe's most sought-after prize. He swore the Crux would never fall into their possession while even one drop of blood remained in his beaten body. He knew that if mankind were to lose the Crux, then all possible hope would go with it.

His mare scaled the side of a large hill, pushing her muscular body with whatever energy remained after their nightmarish ride. She crested the hill's peak purposefully and skidded to a stop on the soupy earth. She then reared back and neighed triumphantly at what Galen, too, thought he had seen. Even surrounded by the tempest's unnatural darkness, Galen recognized this hill instantly. This is where his Brotherhood prayed on the first of every new month. It was where he married his wife and taught his children to forage. Being atop it meant the castle was near—as was mankind's possible salvation.

Then, like a coordinated sign from the heavens, a feathery strand of moonlight pierced the thick storm clouds and softly brushed the castle in the distance, illuminating its towering white walls and pointing the way home.

Thank the Lord.

His mare bolted down the far side of the hill of her own volition.

Garbled trumpets sounded into the darkness as they rumbled closer, mixing with the repeated claps of thunder that now seemed more frequent. Torchlight spread in succession along the castle walls. They had seen him. He was no longer alone. Simply knowing that felt like the warmest hug on the coldest day. But the warming feeling quickly dissipated, tossing Galen violently back to reality. Their voices — those seemingly protected within the thick walls, men he'd known for most of his life — would never be heard again if he did not succeed. Some part of him wanted to keep riding — away from the castle he finally found and the battle he brought with him. It was not out of fear, as the only thing he felt for his pursuers was a seething hatred. But if he fled, maybe they would follow. The lives inside would be spared. Lillian, his wife, may live to see another day.

It was a fleeting thought — one quickly pushed from his mind. He knew better than most that there would be no refuge from what approached. He had seen their savagery firsthand. Unbridled pain and a tortured death were the two things he could assure those inside the castle of. And, from what he had seen, one did not necessarily occur before the other.

His mare rumbled up the sloping grade of the castle's hill, bounding over obstacles in stride. Tall, storm-ravaged trees blurred to the right, with the thick stone walls of the castle to the left. She pushed, with what little energy she had left, through the arching stone entryway and into the frantic courtyard. The large iron portcullis slammed down heavily behind them, sealing them in and hopefully keeping the Evil that approached out. Galen then slid from his mare's unsaddled back and onto his wobbly legs. His first instinct was to topple over and die, but there was no time for such selfishness.

He touched his mare's head with his own. "Goodbye, girl," he said, patting her for the final time, thanking her for what she had done for humanity.

She had bravely done her duty.

Now it was time to finish his.

Knights clad in glimmering armor rushed around him in an organized chaos. These were the Guardians, the fearless protectors of Galen's Brotherhood. Their commanding officers screamed orders to anyone close enough to listen, preparing them for what approached. Their combined voices were strained and fearful, but when the battle commenced, he knew they would fight to the death. They would fight for something far greater than themselves.

"Archers," one of the knights yelled, "take your positions atop the walls." His words were a catalyst, igniting the valor of the soldiers as they hurried up the surrounding stairways. The clanking of their armor echoed in the courtyard like a rhythmically beating drum.

Galen pushed through the commotion with the little energy he had left. Each painful stride brought him closer to the towering doors of the sanctuary, towards his ultimate goal. Seeing him approach, the scruffy knight standing guard froze in shock. His Guardian armor bore an insignia — a purple-hued, wavy-armed cross intersected by two swords.

"You are alive," the Guardian said, his eyes wide with amazement as Galen limped closer.

Galen patted the knight's shoulder and flashed a reassuring, but forced, smile. "For now," he said. "Where is Joseph?"

The Guardian pushed one of the heavy doors open and nodded inside. Joseph was within the inner sanctuary, no doubt praying for a miracle. Galen hoped there was still enough time to give him one.

He stepped forward to enter, but a shooting pain crippled him to a stop. Doubling over, he reached out and held onto the wall for support, smearing a bloody hand print on the white stone. It was imperative he get to the inner sanctuary with the Crux, as there was not a second to spare, but the same wounds that were stealing his life cried out to be noticed. He had purposely ignored them for too long.

The Guardian braced him at the shoulder with his gauntleted hand.

Galen looked up, grimacing. "The battle nears, Commander." He gulped, but found no saliva to swallow. The pain was almost unbearable. "Are your men prepared?"

The knight, compassionate, yet hardened, surveyed the commotion within the castle. "While we are drastically outnumbered, each of us will fight to our last breath. You know that to be true, Brother."

Galen turned to the Guardian. He felt his eyes well with emotion. "That I do, Commander." He knew this would be the last time he saw any of them again. "I pray, however, that our darkest hour is soon to be shown the light."

With that, he straightened his posture and broke his stare. He quelled the pain, and, with a determined push, stood tall.

It was then that the monstrous army arrived at the castle's walls.

"Loose!" screamed one of the knights.

Hundreds of taut bowstrings released, arching a volley of arrows from high atop the crenellated walls. A slew of piercing whines filled the air as the projectiles darted away and vanished into the darkness.

The evil army rammed into the castle's walls like a mile-long ocean wave crashing upon a rocky, unwelcoming shore. The castle reverberated, tossing some from the high walls and onto the courtyard below, while sending a few unfortunate others tumbling into the lava-like flow of Evil outside.

"Fire!" screamed another Guardian. Large boulders sprang into the air from a nearby battery of catapults and hurled out of sight.

The Guardian bracing Galen broke from his position, commanding the knights closest to him into action. "Form a defensive wall…"

Leaving the Guardians to do what they did best, Galen pushed his way through the crowd and into an expansive, table-filled room. He was met with a wave of surprised faces. Gasps and cheers filled the air. He had been gone for so long that they must have feared him dead. Now he returned at the last possible moment to see his duty through to fruition.

He stumbled off to the right and into a smaller side room. Fiery metal sconces decorated the white walls and cast a dancing amber glow all around, highlighted by distinct purple hues like that of the Crux.

Across the way, a group of Guardians stood huddled at the far end of a long table. They surrounded Joseph, the very man he needed to find.

"Thank the Lord you are safe," Joseph said as he hurried over to meet his pupil. He took Galen's hand in his. "I feared we had lost you, my son."

"Not yet," Galen said, looking down at his abdomen, "though that time is near, I'm afraid." A bloody patch darkened his drenched robe, branching out further as time passed. "The Guardians entrusted with my protection valiantly gave their lives…" He winced in pain and instinctively brought his hand up to his stomach. "Thanks to their bravery, I was able to find my way before you now."

The nearby group of knights bowed their heads in memoriam.

"Then it is complete?" Joseph said. "The first two Trinity Signs have been activated?"

Galen nodded and winced.

"And I pray you still have the Crux?"

Reaching down, Galen removed the cross from his waist; it was smeared with his own blood. The purple-hued Crux flickered in the torchlight. Its preservation had cost too many men their lives. He was sure Joseph would see to it that hope flowered from their deaths no matter the cost.

An earth-shaking explosion suddenly knocked the men from their mesmeric stares. The entire castle rattled again— this time with more force than before. The thick stone walls bowed inward as the weight of the castle above diminished their might, spitting loose debris into the air.

Joseph toppled to the floor.

Galen fell to his knees in pain before crumpling to the ground, near death. The loss of blood had weakened his extremities to a point where he could no longer fight the inevitable.

Quickly righting himself, Joseph reached down towards his fallen pupil.

Galen held his hand up in defiance. "My time is at an end," he said, grinding his teeth in pain. "I pray, however, that humanity's is not."

With an endearing gaze, Joseph seemed to accept the situation for what it was.

There were no alternatives.

There was no time.

"Prepare the final Sign," Joseph shouted over the noise.

The group of men scattered through a large door in the

back of the room.

A prisoner to the ground, Galen watched from the cold floor as a Guardian burst into the room. The knight's armor was smeared with blood, his face pale and battle-scarred. Galen met his gaze for a moment. A mix of fear and anger was buried deep within his eyes, shrouded by the collect demeanor of the loyal knight. He felt proud for even knowing such men, for being part of something greater.

"Joseph," the Guardian said. "The walls have been breached. There are too many of them. Our men are being slaughtered."

Another loud explosion rumbled nearby. The entire castle shook once again with unprecedented force, as if rattled in the hand of a giant. The clang of steel echoed from the nearby courtyard as the Guardians tried to beat back the Evil that had come to extinguish them.

Then a bellowing roar overtook all the other sounds and drove itself deep into the very fiber of Galen's soul.

Everyone looked towards the courtyard.

That guttural sound could belong to only one thing, Galen realized. It meant their time was up.

Joseph anchored himself to the table, grasping its sides, and rode out the turbulence. "It is imperative we have the time to activate the third Trinity Sign, Commander," he shouted above the commotion. "Please, do what you must."

Another explosion erupted, followed by tortured, agonizing screams from somewhere close by.

Galen watched the knight soak in Joseph's words. The Guardian stiffened his posture and left with a newfound fire in his eyes. He knew the knight bravely marched to his own demise. And, if he'd still had the energy to do so, he would have grabbed the nearest sword and stuck to his side. That choice was no longer his to make, though. His life's story already had an ending, albeit not the one he would have chosen.

The men who departed on Joseph's orders rushed back into the room, carting the final Trinity Sign in front of them.

The air thinned as more debris clouded his vision. Galen's breathing slowed. Each painful gasp seemed harder to come by than the last.

Suddenly, the sanctuary door ruptured from the thick stone wall, splintering pieces of wood in every direction as it blew apart. A repercussive boom popped Galen's ears and caused a high-pitched ringing to drown out all else. Those seeking refuge inside the castle's sanctuary halls were scorched to death in an instant as fire engulfed the hall outside. Thick smoke then billowed through the gaping hole in the wall, shrouding everything within its masked blackness.

Unable to move, Galen gazed at the worst that the Evil had to offer as they slithered and crawled into the room. Their glowing red eyes hovered within the charred skin of their sunken faces. Their ghastly chatter of clicks and gurgles sent shivers racing down his spine. They moved with jerks and spasms—never fluid, never staying in one place for more than a second. Some had humanistic features, while others were the furthest thing from human. A mix of the vilest creatures was gathered in one place, and Galen knew this was just the beginning.

In an instant, a blur of steely Guardians rushed by him and towards the invading army with their swords raised high. Their fierce and determined battle cries echoed off the walls. Their bravery was unquestionable, their purpose resolute.

It was at that moment, when all seemed lost, that another thunderous boom filled the room, followed by a blinding white flash so brilliant that Galen was forced to shield his eyes. He felt the light pass through him. It tingled with warmth and purity. All of his pains vanished, and his impossibly frigid body warmed. That light was a good light, he realized, significant beyond words.

Thank God, Galen thought as a numb smirk grew on his face. Joseph had done it. The third Sign had been activated.

Galen found the thought comforting as the last breath escaped his lungs. The cheers of those who survived were the final sounds he would ever hear, but he died grateful that they could be heard at all.

Chapter 1

In the ear-popping quietness of the private jet's cabin, Tobias held the cell phone in his lap and watched the familiar number scroll across the screen, debating with himself before reluctantly tapping the green button to answer. "Come right away," he was told. "It's an urgent matter." But it was always *urgent* when the Vatican was involved—according to them, at least. They had a propensity to exaggerate when it served their needs—something Tobias had gained a firm understanding of over the years. That call was hours ago. Now, having unwillingly traded the air-conditioned comfort of the jet for the stifling and insect-ridden heat of the jungle, Tobias regretted his decision infinitely more.

It seemed like each swipe of his dull machete stirred something new into the air—something with an automatic hatred for him buried deep in its genetic code. In hindsight, Tobias wished he had taken the main road from the airport. It certainly would have been faster and far less aggravating, but he preferred the path less traveled. He had been around the world too many times to count, opting to stay out of sight whenever possible. The tingle of exploration is what he loved feel in his bones. But now the only thing tingling was his hair. He was sure something had fallen onto his scalp.

Tobias stopped momentarily and sheathed his machete. He ran his calloused hand through his sweaty salt-and-pepper hair and itched so hard that streams of sweat rolled down his neck and tickled his back. *Damn bugs.* They were useless creatures. He then reached into his backpack and removed a canteen from within that felt unfortunately light. Unscrewing the cap, he angled the canteen over his head and tapped its bottom, trying to force any water that might have permeated the plastic back out into the open. A single drop raced down the slick green plastic inside and hung precariously from the rim before falling into his mouth, proving to be nothing more than a tease. *God forbid we meet in a normal place for once,* he thought, angrily shoving the canteen back into his pack. *We wouldn't want that.* Yet despite his yearning, Tobias knew better than anyone that normality was not in his cards. Not while he hunted what he did—creatures that were better left unimagined.

The tall trees surrounding him were motionless. No breeze to be found amongst the dry, inescapable heat. Tobias figured it was around two o'clock, which meant he'd spent the past two hours hiking through this godforsaken jungle, much longer than he had anticipated. The hike should have taken at most an hour—maybe less if he found an old militia path—but he never expected it to be so thickly overgrown this way. Not only did his legs beg for respite—the path being far from even ground—but his arms burned from the constant hacking. At forty years of age, he wasn't the spry man he once was, but he still had more in the tank than anyone twenty years younger would, of that he was sure.

Thankfully, Tobias felt like he was close to his destination. The trees were sparser ahead; they seemed far less claustrophobic than what he had become accustomed to trudging through. And as the jungle thinned, the howls of the monkeys and the rustling of whatever else stalked him from a distance began to fade. They were telltale signs that the animals' greatest enemy, mankind, lurked nearby.

Much to Tobias' relief, he soon came upon a muddy clearing that seemed oddly situated out in the middle of nowhere. He peered across at what appeared to be a newly-constructed wooden hut. Leaning haphazardly against its right wall was an aged canoe. Tobias figured it was for the river that flowed nearby, maybe fifty yards or so, past the hut. Red and black paint had chipped and fallen from the canoe's sides and dotted the muddy ground beneath it, as if an army of ladybugs had gathered to welcome him.

Each sinking step he took across the clearing burped a rank waft of decomposing flora into the air, clinging to the cilia in his nose like a frightened child would its mother until a few powerful strides brought him to within arm's reach of the hut's flimsy door. He reached up and grabbed the makeshift door handle, nothing more than a simple knotted rope, and pulled the door open with more force than he had intended.

The startled priest inside turned as fast as he could from the table where he was busily reading. "Mr. Ramsey," he said, his plump face jiggling. "You scared me half to death." He let out an exhaustive sigh and then dabbed his forehead with a white handkerchief, collecting himself briefly before saying, "It is good of you to come on such short notice."

"It's what I do, Father," Tobias said, exiting the mud and squeezing through the narrow entry, the door flopping shut behind him.

Father Fenn adjusted his posture, though the mountainous priest had little room to move. The seams of his black cassock appeared only moments from bursting apart. His pale British skin was wrinkled and slightly sunburned, showing not only his age, but a wisdom that Tobias had come to admire over the years. The priest then tapped his half-smoked cigar with his chubby fingers, setting a small ash cloud on its way towards the ground. Several wisps of smoke rose ethereally into the air before the cigar was casually stubbed out.

Tobias sat on a rickety chair to Fenn's right. "Care to tell me why we couldn't do this over the phone?" It felt good to be off his feet, if only for a moment.

"Sorry about that, chap. I realize you were on your way home when I called, but it was imperative we meet in person this time." He gazed at Tobias with the look a teacher would give his student. "And since you were already airborne in a nearby Vatican jet, it seemed like the most efficient path to take. I would have come to you, of course, but I'm afraid my presence is required here a bit longer." He then paused and looked at Tobias with his brow raised, waiting for a follow-up question.

It was a question Tobias didn't plan on asking, but he knew it didn't matter. Fenn would explain *why* he needed to remain beneath the oppressive sun, and Tobias would listen. It was a give and take relationship that had developed over the past eight years—ever since the oversized priest took over as Tobias' handler. Fenn was the best at what he did, and with Tobias being the Vatican's most valuable asset, it only made sense for the two to be paired together.

"The reason I am here is actually quite interesting," Fenn began, as Tobias expected he would.

Tobias stopped him before he could get going. He suddenly had the thirst of a thousand men. "You mind?" he said, eyeing a pitcher of water on the small table. The thought of his empty canteen ran through his mind, punctuated by the pasty feeling left by the last of his saliva.

"Of course," Fenn said following his gaze. "How rude of me not to ask."

Before Fenn could even finish his thought the glass was full. Tobias quickly downed the warm, yet refreshing, water. Albeit a small comfort, the water somehow made a crappy situation seem less crappy. He didn't realize just how much he needed a drink until right then. He then poured and sloppily downed another glass. "You were saying?" he said, wiping his mouth with his shirt, gathering the stray drops.

Fenn thought for a moment before seeming to find the mental bookmark. "Ah, yes," he said. "A few days back, a young boy supposedly died not far from here."

"Supposedly?"

Fenn nodded. "They even buried him that night, as is their custom, but when the *dead* boy wandered back home the next day covered in dirt, babbling on about his visit with God, the village elders proclaimed his return a miracle from above." He then waved his hands out to his sides and said, "And here I am."

Tobias had been around long enough to understand that it was in the Vatican's best interest to make sure God was only accessible through them. It helped anchor their purpose in an ever-changing religious landscape. So-called miracles were dealt with quickly and quietly. Fenn just so happened to be uniquely suited for that task. A former college professor, he was one of the few Vatican investigators that had as much scientific background as he did religious. The Father tended to be more pragmatic in his investigations—a somewhat difficult task for a man of the cloth, given his beliefs—and he was, therefore, dispatched across the globe to disprove miracles with practicality on a regular basis.

Curiosity, however, got the better of Tobias. He let his body sink deeper into the uncomfortable chair.

"Another miracle, huh?"

Fenn smiled. "There are times like these when nature can work in the most devious of ways." He looked out the hut's tiny window and to the nearby river that snaked through the trees. "This area has been saturated by rain over the past months—more than they've seen in decades."

That explains the damn mud outside, Tobias thought, eyeing his crusty boots.

"I believe all that extra water forced the acidic river

16

nearby to overflow and settle in places it was never intended to. After walking its banks, I came upon one particular spot near the tribe's settlement that was overgrown with Flame Lilies. They are a captivatingly beautiful plant," Fenn motioned to a small cup of water capped by a red and yellow Flame Lily, "but apparently highly toxic if ingested."

Tobias apathetically gazed over at the flower as Fenn continued his spiel. "I believe the acidic river water caused the Lily to excrete a bit of its toxins, and the boy must have stopped to drink from one those toxic pools. While the amount of poison wasn't deadly, I suppose it interfered with his body just enough to put him into a mild coma, of sorts."

"So they buried him alive?" Tobias inferred.

"It would appear that way," Fenn said, nodding. "Fortunately for the boy, he woke before his supply of oxygen ran out. I suppose he then dug free from the shallow grave he was prematurely buried in. I cannot even imagine what a horrifying experience that must have been."

"At least the kid's got a story to tell."

"Indeed he does, Mr. Ramsey." Fenn said, laughing ever so slightly. "While miraculous he survived, I'm afraid an actual miracle was not involved. I will say, however, that I am surprised by the size of the Lily patch I found. I thought of sending a few back..."

Here we go again, Tobias thought. Fenn, as usual, was about to continue on his tangent of details that Tobias found too digressive, wishing the priest would just stick to the facts. But he knew that wasn't the Father's longwinded way of doing things. Tobias decided it was best to stop him before he got rolling.

Tobias cleared his throat. "So tell me, Father. What's so important that I had to divert my flight home to come see you in person?" Not that it really mattered much. All that waited for him there was an empty refrigerator and stark

17

walls.

"Right then," Fenn said. He coughed and then dabbed his forehead with a handkerchief. A few beads of sweat rolled down his balding head shortly after and disappeared into the black of his cassock. "Forgive my abruptness, Mr. Ramsey, but how familiar are you with the prophecy of Armageddon?" Fenn must have considered it more of a rhetorical question—a lead-up to his explanation—as he didn't wait for an answer. "I'm sure you know the basics— end of the world, destruction of mankind, and such?"

Tobias nodded. *Such cheery topics.*

"Well, as it turns out, the *prophecy* is actually more *history*, albeit factually skewed. Over time, the powers that be thought it best to let the truth remain blurred for the sake of mankind, as having it out in the open would do nothing more than cause utter chaos."

Tobias grinned. "You're joking, right?"

"The Vatican never jokes, Mr. Ramsey. I would think that, after all these years, you would know that." Fenn leaned back in his chair a bit. "While most believe in evil, few actually know it exists in a very real, very un-human, form. Evil's master made an attempt at our destruction roughly one thousand years ago. Should it have succeeded, our world would be very different today, if not entirely destroyed. It is a tale not often told and little known, even amongst the most knowledgeable of religious scholars."

The priest looked placid—worried. Tobias couldn't remember a time when Fenn appeared so suddenly distraught. While far from a jovial man, Fenn still had a dry sense of humor—something that seemed to be missing from the conversation.

"If it were not for the efforts of the Brotherhood of the Sealed," Fenn continued, "under the protection of the Guardians, your ancestors, we would not be discussing this right now. Unfortunately for all of us, the Brotherhood's numbers have dwindled to dangerously low numbers. Their best defense, in this case, was to disappear—to hide from the reach of evil and try to rebuild, but rebuilding was not something they had time for. And, to make matters worse, the Keeper of the Crux Signate, their most prized relic, is now on the run." A sad look overtook the Father's face as he paused for a moment. "And only he and one other remain. We find ourselves unprepared and desperate, Mr. Ramsey, victims of a continuously evolving world."

"Okay," Tobias said, drawing the syllables out. It all seemed a bit farfetched, but Fenn rarely exaggerated. Tobias knew, from experience, that the line separating reality and fiction was razor thin.

Fenn had a sip of water and then neatly dabbed the corners of his mouth. "The Brotherhood successfully stopped its attempt sometime around the eleventh century. By activating the Trinity Signs, they cast back into the shadows that which should never have escaped." Fenn leaned in closer to Tobias. Stale cigar smoke clung to his breath. "But, over time, evil has slowly seeped back into everyday life. Wars, famine, and greed are all part of its plan to weaken mankind. And, although our population is many times greater than it was during its last attempt, I'm afraid our resolve is but a fraction of what it needs to be."

Tobias stopped the priest. "Wait," he said. "You keep saying *it*. You aren't talking about the devil, are you?" Tobias wearily held each of his index fingers up to his head and pointed his pseudo horns at Fenn. He'd heard stories here and there over the years—most too farcical to believe—but he couldn't just dismiss the notion that the devil did exist. He had seen more than enough to give the thought validity.

"Mr. Ramsey," Fenn said. "You, of all people, should

understand the magnitude of what I am now telling you. Over your countless years as a Guardian, you have selflessly protected mankind from the worst this world has to offer—man and beast alike. That is something you know all too well. It is your Guardian bloodline that has forced you to see these unfortunate things. And, as the last of your kind, that duty falls to you more often than it should. For that, I am truly sorry. The world owes you a debt of gratitude it will never know existed, let alone that it would be able to repay, but everything must have its source, and evil is no different." Fenn looked past Tobias and stared at the hut's wall. "Vatican records tell of a towering behemoth—one so large the clouds parted in fear, and the ground shifted to avoid it." He slowly turned back. "It may be embellished history, and it may not. Regardless, we believe the darkest Evil is amassing its army from within the shadows of the globe. Its spies are undoubtedly already in the open, which is the very reason you needed to meet me in person. There are many ears listening, but not all of them should be." Fenn again dabbed his forehead clean of the newly formed perspiration. "The Keeper of the Crux has been forced from hiding. He assures us he can elude whatever now chases him, but not for long."

Tobias nodded, soaking in what he just heard.

"Thankfully, we believe the devil is too weak to rise up yet, but with each passing day, his strength grows. It is imperative that the Brotherhood activate the Trinity Signs before the devil and his spawn overtake them. If they do not...," Fenn paused. "Well, sadly, this may be our last conversation."

Tobias pushed his disbelief aside for a moment. "If these Trinity Signs are so important, why haven't I heard of them before now?"

Fenn kept his eyes locked on Tobias. A palpable sense of

immediacy filled the tiny hut.

"Very few know of the Signs' existence, Mr. Ramsey. No living soul has actually seen them. It is said that, once the Trinity Signs have been activated, the devil and its evil army will be sent back to hell—failures once again. However, words tend to change when copied by different hands. For our sake, I pray the tale of the Trinity Signs is everything we need it to be." Fenn stopped for a moment and took a breath. "As for their locations, I'm afraid that remains a mystery to us all."

It's always a damn mystery.

Fenn handed over a black, unmarked folder. "The Keeper is headed here."

Tobias flipped through the contents. A name, John Benjamin, accompanied by an address in Connecticut, immediately caught his eye.

And so it begins, Tobias thought, standing from the rickety chair. There would be no rest for the weary today.

"See you around, Father," he said, walking back out the doorway.

"Good luck, Mr. Ramsey," Fenn said, tripping over his own words. "And Godspeed."

Tobias laughed to himself as the door swung shut. He realized he would need a lot more than luck if what the Father said was true.

Chapter 2

John slouched on his wicker chair and stared up at the underside of his porch roof, which had blackened over the years from willful neglect. Regardless of how it looked, though, the dilapidated roof still protected him from the downpour the storm brought, and that was really all he cared about at the moment. The Grateful Dead's *Touch of Grey* CD spun inside, looped infinitely, with *I Will Get By* playing for maybe its fifth time that day. John left the screen door open so the music could spill outside, but when the drizzle became a downpour—which seemed to happen more often than not—the eclectic sounds became nothing more than an unperceivable hum in the background.

He dangled a bottle of Bud Light Lime by its neck and swished the remaining gulp into froth. For the past three hours, the alcohol, coupled with the rain's rhythmic patter, had helped ease him towards the brink of sleep. It was another lazy day, and with nowhere to be and not a soul wondering where he was, his life of complacency could remain unquestioned. His inheritance dwindled over the years, but not enough to force him to work like the rest of the poor bastards around him. But even if he had to work, it would be some menial job that paid just enough to get by and required little to no thought. The house was paid for, and his beat-up Volkswagen bus still ran, albeit slowly and occasionally, which was fine by him as he'd prefer to stay out of sight and reclusive. He found people to generally suck, and the less interaction he had with them, the better.

Aside from Rusty, his aging German shepherd that was perched next to him on the porch, John was a loner in most respects. That was the way he wanted it—needed it—but Rusty's unexpected and throaty growl forced him down a road he never could have imagined.

"What is it, buddy?" John slurred. "That squirrel harassing you again?"

Rusty picked his head up from the knotted deck and growled again. He stared into the thick brush that had slowly eroded any semblance of a yard in front of the cabin. Rusty rarely made an effort to do anything but sleep and eat, much like his master, so the fact that he was upright, let alone growling, was cause for concern.

John brought the beer to his lips, gulped the remaining froth, and placed the bottle on the deck's railing. It wobbled off-kilter before falling into the wet brush below. As the bottle fell, as if on cue, a blinding flash of lighting ripped through the sky, illuminating the brush with an iridescent bluish hue and prompting a crack so shocking that John jumped from his seat.

Rusty barked louder, fiercer. His ears were tightly pinned back, his upper lip retracted, exposing his teeth in anger.

John, his ears still ringing, attempted to listen past the barking. He heard something else. It sounded like splashing. It was distant...faint. He strained to listen, but the pounding rain made it difficult to discern.

He wasn't expecting anyone.

Another splash...this one sounded closer than the last.

Rusty bolted from the deck and quickly vanished into the brush.

"Rusty," John shouted. "Get back here."

The barking trailed off.

"Rusty?"

Seconds after losing sight of his dog, John saw a figure emerging from the rain-obscured distance. He squinted, attempting to identify the blurred shadow that seemed to move towards him with an unnatural speed. *What the hell is going on?* It didn't look to be anyone he knew. The figure was closing in on him quicker than he imagined it should have. Maybe he was just too many beers deep. That was certainly a possibility. Or it could have been just another hallucination like the one he had a few Sundays back, courtesy of some magic mushrooms he was able to acquire. But this seemed more real. His body revved up.

"John," the figure yelled. "Please move inside. We are in grave danger."

Each breath escaped John's lungs quicker than the last. *How does this guy know my name?* He involuntarily balled his hands into fists. His mind screamed for him to flee, but his legs felt as if they were cemented in place. His pulse raced to a point where he felt like his heart might burst.

"Who are you?" John said. His voice crackled.

The man neared the rotted steps of the porch. He wore a brown monk's robe, concealing his thin, tall frame. His height forced him to duck beneath the overhang and up onto the deck, inches from John. His cleanly shaven head dripped with rain, the drops beading down the sides of his face.

"All will be explained, John, but we must move inside quickly. Our time together is assuredly very brief." The monk motioned with his head toward the clearing and shot back a look of urgency to John.

More sounds came from the woods. They sounded faster, heavier. The monk wasn't alone.

Grabbing John's arm with surprising strength, the monk seemed to lift him up off the deck and cautiously shove him through the door of the cabin. He then spun around and locked the deadbolt in one swift motion with uncanny precision.

"Quickly…," the monk said, taking hold of John's arm

again, ushering him towards the stairs.

John's instincts seemed to grip him oddly, causing him to retract his arm and put a few feet between him and the monk. A minute ago he was happily wasting another day away, but all that was ruined now. "What the hell do you think you're doing? Get out of my house, man."

"I'm a friend, John." The monk's voice was disturbingly calm, yet stern. "What chases me is not." He stared and then, seeing little register with John, he pleaded, "Please, we don't have much time."

John, for lack of a clear thought in his alcoholically-dulled mind, rushed up the stairs. Quickly reaching the apex, they turned left and headed to the master bedroom. Once again, John was pushed through the open door.

The monk closed the door behind them and moved behind a tall oak dresser. "Help me move this."

John instinctively jumped to the other side of his dresser and pulled until it came to rest solidly against his bedroom door. He didn't want to, but things were moving too fast. He didn't have time to think.

"Okay. I've had about enough of this, man," John said. "What's going on? Who are you?"

"My name is David Ethos. I am one of the two remaining descendants of the Brotherhood of the Sealed."

"The Brotherhood of what?"

"The Sealed, John. The Brotherhood of the Sealed," David said, staring at John like he should know that. He reached into the front of his robe. "You must take the Crux and guard it with your life." He removed a wavy-armed cross from his neck and attempted to hand it to John.

John pushed it away. "Did you forget to take your meds today or something?"

"I assure you, John, I am perfectly sane. What I hold, and have held for many years, is something too powerful for words to properly grasp. What I offer you now is something you cannot reject. Life, as we know it, rests on your acceptance."

John stared at David, his brow raised. The monk's robe dripped water and formed a shallow puddle on the scuffed wooden floor. John wouldn't exactly call what he was just told *sane*. It sounded like one of those fantasy books he read when he was a kid, except John was no hero. He was the furthest thing from it, and he had no real desire to listen any longer. Something inside him kept him where he was, though. He didn't know what it was—fear, loss of balance from the beers, or just the utter shock of the past few minutes—but some invisible force made him listen despite his desire not to.

"Please, John. Time is a commodity we do not have." David once again held out the cross for John to take. A fearful sincerity filled his eyes. "You must."

John grabbed the large silver cross. He found himself staring at its mesmerizing purple tint. He'd never seen a cross like this before. Its wavy arms made it clearly different from anything he'd ever come across. The more he stared, the more unable he was to look away.

A loud, piercing screech echoed from outside the cabin. It was followed by the sound of breaking glass and a thump John felt through the bedroom floor.

David looked towards the barricaded bedroom door. "They're here." He turned back towards John, whose face clearly registered a mortified questioning of who "they" were, and added, "You are humanity's last hope, John. You must go to Reverend O'Brien at the Trinity Church in Boston. He'll be able to guide you further."

"Wait," John said. His mind scrambled. "What are you talking about? Is this some kind of joke? Because if it is…"

David interrupted. "Your father never told you about

the Brotherhood—about your calling?"

John started to speak, but he couldn't find the words. The subject of his father hadn't been brought up in a very long time. The last John remembered of his father was the deep depression he sank into after his mother passed. Less than a year later, his father had died. It was sudden and unexpected. The authorities ruled it a suicide. John never fully believed that, but he came to find out that life rarely went the way he thought it should.

He looked back at the monk and shook his head. "We didn't really talk all that much when he was alive. He was always away on business." He paused. "How did you know my father, anyway?"

"Oh, dear," David muttered, looking away from John. "We are in a far worse position than I had anticipated." His face was drained of all color.

A furious pounding on the stairs captured the men's attention. They both hushed and looked towards the improvised barricade. The sound of raspy panting came from the other side of the bedroom door. Something sniffed around out there, something big.

David continued in a whisper. "As I said, we are the last of the Brotherhood of the Sealed. I fear, however, that our numbers are soon to be shortened once again."

Another shrill cry echoed, this time with only a door separating it from them. The decibel was next to unbearable. The fact that John heard the noise through the thick insulated walls was almost as disturbing as the noise itself.

"I will hold them off for as long as I can, but you must go before they break through."

David stood before John could speak, mumbling what John thought to be a prayer under his breath. He then moved silently towards the windows. As quietly as he could, and with noticeably trembling hands, David opened

27

the closest window and nodded for John to climb out.

The rain had lessened slightly, but a strong wind had whipped up and pushed it sideways.

The dresser bulged, alerting the men to the immediacy of the threat. The sound of splintering wood solidified it. The door only had seconds left.

John's survival instinct took over. Leaving logic behind, adrenaline bore itself deep into his being, and he placed the chain around his neck. It chilled his skin.

"Who's after you?" John asked, looking towards his bedroom door. "Who's out there?"

"Not who," David said, "but what." He stared deep into John's eyes. "Now, please, you must go while you still can. Don't stop running. They are much faster than you, and they will find you, of that you can be sure."

John extended his full body length out of his second story window to try and lessen the impact. The rain drenched his meager clothing in only a few seconds' time. Releasing his grip, he impacted the wet ground below with a squishy thud, forcing a rush of air from his lungs.

With fear as a driving factor, John sprinted into the woods behind his cabin. No sooner had he reached the tree line when his footing gave out, causing him to skid along the wet ground for several feet before coming to a stop on his back. He turned in time to see David lifted into the air. A fine mist of blood shot from his back as what appeared to be a large claw ripped through his torso, coating the window red. David then slumped to the bedroom floor past John's view.

Two pairs of glowing red eyes stared out from behind the open window and then faded away.

Another piercing scream scattered the birds from the tops of the trees.

Instinct took over. John turned and ran as fast as he

could, away from the safety of his reclusive life and from whatever now hunted him.

Chapter 3

Tobias pulled the rental car to the side of the Connecticut dirt road, exited in a rush, and ran into the nearby trees. He knew that a swelling bladder was one battle he couldn't win, no matter how long he fought. With no one in sight, he went about his business. A tingle of relief passed through him as the pressure released and gravity did its job.

It was then, with his eyes closed in momentary bliss, when he heard a sound come from deep within the Connecticut woods and echo amongst the trees. It was a shrill cry. One he hadn't heard in many years. One he hoped to never hear again.

*

John ran until his lungs burned and his vision blurred. The terrain in front of him seemed to bounce in a surreal fashion. The slight fog in the woods created a hazy view, and the forest around him seemed to move and sway with each step he took. Fear pushed him to continue, but the years of alcohol abuse had taken its toll. His breath came in frequent segments, and his legs beckoned him to halt. His limbs, heavy with booze, caused him to run in a diagonal motion. His feet slid over the brush without ever quite making air. Looking for a soft place to pass out in a drunken stupor was the most exercise he got on a regular basis, but now, giving in to his physicality, he stood gasping, his heart pumping beyond a safe zone of effort as a pain sharpened up his side.

With his hands on his knees, John stared down at a

blanket of decaying pine needles and mud. It was near impossible to understand what had just happened at his house. The glowing red eyes still burned bright in his memory. *What where those things?*

Water pooled within the indents of the uneven ground. His pale, unhealthy reflection stared back from the puddle below. Regaining some of his lost breath, he stood, removed the cross from beneath his shirt, and held it at arm's length. It turned slowly at the end of the chain. Its purple body seemed out of place surrounded by the brown and grey nothingness of the forest. The sun had set, but the cross still seemed to gather an extra amount of light from nowhere, refracting it in an unnaturally beautiful way.

A large drop of water, be it sweat or rain, slid down the cross's side and fell into the puddle below, causing ripples to echo outwards. John watched as the ripples flowed from the inside out. But, rather than fade away as he thought they would, the ripples increased in intensity. His reflection vanished in a blur.

It felt as if a thunderous freight train was headed for him. The hairs on the back of his neck stood tall when the chilling screech echoed through the air. John sucked back in some of the drool that had exited his mouth during his attempt to recalibrate. He knew they were close by. He felt them coming.

Shit.

His heart pumped the adrenaline-rich blood throughout his body. His weary legs found new energy despite their pain. If his lungs were to burst, they would do so while he ran for his life, but his high top Chuck Taylors, having lost their tread long ago, made the coating of wet pine needles feel like ice. No sooner had he started to run when he lost his footing and sloshed face-down onto the wet ground.

Another high decibel screech pierced the air.

Whatever made it was closer now. It was louder, closing in around him like a black shroud.

While John understood this was no dream, he still felt the limitations of one imposed upon him. Fear kept him firmly planted on his stomach. He closed his eyes tight and hoped they'd fuse shut forever. He'd wish the monsters away like he had when he was a child. If he couldn't see them, then they didn't exist or—at the very least—they couldn't hurt him.

Then, as quickly as the thumping began, it stopped. The forest seemed hushed, save for the patter of the lessening rain.

John's eyes shot open, and he scanned the greater periphery. He knew from countless B-rated movies that silence always came before the kill. Slowly shifting his head, he pushed himself up into a plank position. Water beaded into his eyes, stinging, and causing a blur in his gaze. The discomfort in his mouth, dry from panting, was rivaled only by the swelling knot in his throat. He could taste the salt on his lips. Quickly, he raised his left arm and wiped the wetness from his eyes with the back of his t-shirt sleeve, pushing his wet, sticky bangs off to the side of his face. With a gulp, John slowly, unwillingly turned around.

He went to gasp but was too frightened.

Two doglike creatures stood before him, each poised on four muscular legs that brought them chest high to John's six-foot frame. They scanned the area from no more than thirty feet away. Their blood red eyes were coated in a filmy white pus and moved loosely about their sockets like slowly spinning billiard balls. John couldn't move—not an inch. He watched silently as their black hides, which were spotted by coarse yellowish hair, rose and fell with each raspy breath they took. The beasts snarled and sniffed in the air, causing thick saliva to drip from their jagged teeth onto the mucky ground.

The beast closest to John suddenly stopped in its tracks. It stared through him like an x-ray. Then, without even a hint, it screeched again. John wanted to cover his ears, but the weight of his arms anchored him to the ground. His skin felt as if it would coil and loosen from the very tendons that attached it to the bone. A shiver traced his spine. He closed his eyes as tightly as possible and grasped the cross beneath his shirt. *Please go away. I promise I won't be so lazy.* All of his faults began to run through his mind. *Just give me another chance. Oh, God, please.*

*

Tobias ran through the sloppy environment the best he could. The high decibel screech he heard belonged to a Hell Hound. That was a certainty. He had dispatched a few of them in the past but hadn't seen them in years, not since Romania. *Or was it Japan?* Regardless of where they *were*, they were *here* now. Tobias was not a fan of loud noises to begin with, and the Hound's screech was nothing short of unbearable. Aside from being an earsplitting annoyance, though, Tobias knew it served a purpose. The Hounds were mostly blind. They used their screech much like a bat would, sending out waves to see what bounced back. It made them lethal hunters so long as their target was moving.

Thankfully, with the leaves off the trees, it was easier to find things amongst them. Tobias was relieved to see a man in a green t-shirt ahead. A pair of Hounds inched closer to him. John Benjamin, he figured. That or the baddies were after the wrong guy. Either way, this needed to be dealt with now.

Tobias slowly leaned out from behind a large tree. "Don't move," he said to John as quietly as he could.

"They…"

Before Tobias could instruct him, John spun around in a flash.

The Hound must have sensed him move, as it dug its claws into the ground and screeched again.

So much for that, Tobias thought.

As the Hound coiled back on its hind legs, Tobias darted from behind the tree and in-between John and the beast. With the built-up energy released, the beast propelled itself through the air with an unnaturally graceful agility towards Tobias.

Tobias pushed aside his long black trench coat and swept one of his modified Glocks from its holster. The world around him slowed. His attention was absolute. Pulling the trigger, he released a bullet that had no trouble penetrating the beast's hide. It dropped from its arching trajectory and landed heavily on the ground, skidding for a few feet and kicking waves of leaves and dirt into the air.

Tobias knew that one bullet was never enough.

As the Hound began to rise, Tobias lined his gun up with its head and fired another round. The bullet impacted its skull and kicked up a spray of black blood. The beast flopped to the ground, dead. Acidic green smoke seeped from the motionless corpse.

"Drop to the ground," Tobias said, taking his eyes from the smoking carcass and shifting them to John.

John didn't budge, apparently cemented down in fear.

Tobias held his gun towards John's head. "Get down!"

John instinctively fell like a bag of rocks just as the second beast lunged forward. The mass of evil barely missed him, its large claws ripping out a few of his hairs along the way. It hit the ground and turned to relocate its prey with its screech, which was rivaled only by John's flamboyant moan.

Tobias wasn't going to give it another chance. He

sprinted towards the creature. "Over here," he said, waving his arms over his head. Hell Hounds were fearsome hunters, but feebleminded, at best. Tobias knew it wouldn't take much to steal its attention. "Come on," he said, moving side to side. "Over here." The Hound stopped. It then bolted toward Tobias at an alarming rate of speed.

He fired off two quick rounds. The first bullet barely missed and disappeared into the trees to the left. The second round splintered a sapling in his line of fire. Before he could fire a third, the beast was on top of him. The impact knocked the gun from his hand and the breath from his lungs. The Hound's crushing weight pinned Tobias' chest to the ground.

The Hound snapped and snarled at Tobias. Its rancid, warm breath washed over him like a burst septic tank.

With no time to spare, Tobias grabbed the beast's upper jaw to stop it from closing around his head. As he did, one of the Hound's shark-like teeth pierced the palm of his hand and caused a bright flash of light to burst in front of his eyes. The pain ripped through the entirety of his body in a matter of seconds. Warm blood trickled from the newly formed gash onto the ground, a few drops falling onto his cheek.

Lightheadedness crept in, but Tobias' brewing anger quickly wrestled it away. He was no stranger to pain and was about to give the Hound its own dose.

He kneed the creature in the side with as much force as he could muster, and then struck two more blows in quick succession. With its thick bundles of muscles it was like kneeing a rock, but it was just enough to throw the Hound off balance and knock it off to the side. Tobias wasted no time and quickly palmed for his backpack that had fallen during the collision. Reaching in, he removed a small vial of liquid wrapped in thick rope. A mixture—mostly holy water—ironically worked to dispel more things than it should have. It paid to be prepared.

The Hound shot from the ground and back towards Tobias. It was on top of him in less than a second. Like dropping an egg into boiling water, Tobias flung the vial into the Hound's snapping mouth with care for his hand. The vial was instantly crushed open and poured its contents down the Hound's throat.

The Hell Hound spastically convulsed as smoke poured from its mouth.

Tobias drew his second gun and emptied the entire clip into the Hound's soft underbelly. With a thump, the Hound fell dead atop him, its full weight further compressing his lungs. The same green acidic smoke that rose from the first beast now clouded Tobias' position.

He attempted to push free from the smoking carcass, gagging at the overpowering stench, but it proved to be too heavy. His body was at its limit of exhaustion.

Tobias looked at John. "Help me get this thing off." His breath was hard to come by with the evil paperweight atop him.

John stood frozen, staring back, petrified.

"Come on, already," Tobias yelled. *What was with this guy?*

With a look of disgust, John finally bent down and helped heave the smoking remains to the side. The Hound's body sloshed on the wet terrain. John then turned and wretched out what little remained in his stomach.

Tobias sucked in a deep breath and pushed himself upright. He looked to his hand, mangled and covered in blood. His fingers still moved, which was a good sign that it was fixable.

He reached into his backpack and removed a shirt, which he then ripped into a makeshift tourniquet.

"Are you John Benjamin?" Tobias asked, wrapping the

thin cloth around the wound and tying it off with his teeth. He hoped it would stop the bleeding for now.

John stood there, silent, but still panting to recover his breath. He was noticeably shaken from what just went down.

"My name is Tobias. I was sent to protect you." Tobias could only assume that, since John was alone, the Keeper had succumbed to the Hounds. He realized that the odds of him completing his already ridiculous task were now cut in half.

John shook himself back to reality. "Sent to protect me?" He laughed nervously. "Who sent you to protect me? Why do I all of a sudden need protection? What the hell is going on?" John grabbed a tuft of his hair and walked away anxiously.

"It's complicated."

John paused after walking a few yards from Tobias and shook his head. He exhaled a deep breath and then turned back, eyeing the readily decaying Hound at Tobias' feet. His nervousness turned to anger. "What's complicated?" he said. "The fact that I was almost eaten by Cujo over there?"

"It means that this is neither the time nor the place to discuss it," Tobias said. His voice was stern, yet compassionate. "Do you have the Crux Signate?"

John stared back, a blank look on his face.

"A big silver cross. Do you have it?"

John nodded and removed the Crux from around his neck. "Here," he said. "Take it."

Tobias grasped the relic. The purple hue was slight, but clearly noticeable in the moonlight. He had a hard time believing that he now held the Crux Signate in his hands, as so many Guardians had lost their lives protecting it over the years. He'd seen the drawings and heard the stories, but he never thought he'd hold the actual Crux.

"It's imperative that you keep this on you at all times." Tobias said. He grasped the chain and placed the cross around John's neck. It fell behind his mangled t-shirt. "Do you understand, John?"

"Actually, no. I don't understand." John backed up a few steps. "I don't understand any of this. I didn't ask for this, man. I don't want this stupid cross."

"There are things in life we just need to do, John. This is one of yours."

"Says who?"

"Right now, me. But I'm like you in one regard." Tobias doubted there were many other similarities between them just by looking at John. "We both have an obligation that we never asked for. Like me, you, too, will need to accept this. The more you fight it, the more powerless you'll feel."

John put his hands on his head and paced nervously around the clearing, eyeing the dead carcasses, and Tobias, in an erratic manner.

"I realize this is a lot to handle right now, but I'm obviously here to help. You're going to have to trust me."

"Trust you?" John again laughed nervously. He stood and stared into Tobias' eyes. "I don't even know who you are, man." John then walked over to one of the smoking Hounds and hesitantly nudged the carcass with his foot. "What the hell happened to these dogs, anyway?"

"They're not dogs. They're Hell Hounds, vile offspring of Cerberus." John didn't reply, so Tobias added, "guardian of the gate to Hell."

John looked back at Tobias like he had just been told the Tooth Fairy was real. This was now John's reality, but Tobias understood it would be impossible for him to accept what he had just seen as anything more than some whacked-out nightmare. Tobias understood, probably more than most, the position John was now in. He knew that, in time, John would be forced to live in this new reality regardless of whether he accepted it or not.

"And why are these things chasing me?"

Tobias wanted to tell John it was because of the Crux hanging around his neck—that the ancient relic was like a tracking beacon when out in the open—but he figured telling John the whole truth would be counterproductive to what he needed to accomplish at the moment

"Listen, we don't have time to debate this here and now," Tobias said. "Let's get to somewhere safer, and I'll explain in more detail."

John just stared back, eyeing Tobias disdainfully.

This was going to be more difficult than he first thought it would be. No surprise there. Nothing ever seemed to come easy nowadays.

Tobias flexed his fingers and watched the blood-soaked cloth slide in his palm.

"I need to clean this up." He held his damaged hand up. "Is there any place we can go that's nearby? I'd rather we be out of the darkness."

John looked up from the dead Hound with an empty look on his face.

Tobias knew that expression well. It wasn't the first untrusting glance he'd ever gotten, and he doubted it would be the last. He knew, if the situations were reversed, that he'd have a hard time understanding what had just happened, but Tobias realized he would need to be a bit more aggressive to move things along. It was his job to dictate to John what needed to be done, not the other way around.

"You have two choices, John. You either trust me, the guy who just saved your ass, or you can trust them." He nodded quickly at one of the dead Hounds. "Your choice."

John paused. "This whole scene is really messed up,

man."

Tobias stared silently. He couldn't argue that.

"Fine," John said, shaking his head. "Whatever." He rubbed his eyes and then looked around. "I think we're near Sam's house." He scanned the trees before turning right and walking away. "This is so messed up."

Tobias gathered his pack and followed John through the dripping landscape. This wasn't how Tobias envisioned it, having to rescue John from certain death so early, but at least John was now safely under his protection. Why this lazy hippie was the last of the Brotherhood of the Sealed was another story, but Tobias knew it was going to make his task exponentially more difficult. *One step at a time,* he thought, flexing his hand again. Despite being lightheaded from the loss of blood, he kept his senses peaked. He feared another attack would come soon and in far greater intensity.

Chapter 4

Tobias followed John silently through the trees. He knew John probably had an infinite number of questions bouncing around in his head; he just didn't have the energy to explain everything right now. Even if he had, Tobias sensed that John wouldn't listen. Why would he? His world had just been turned upside-down and inside out.

"It's right up here," John said, pointing through the trees to a dirt road.

A short trip up the road led to Sam's humble cabin, which sat on a good-sized clearing surrounded by the same thin oak trees they had just spent the past twenty minutes walking through. A steady column of thick smoke rose from within a chimney that pierced the cabin's sloping roof, disappearing into the inky night sky.

Tobias closed his eyes and took a deep breath of the chilly autumn air. Hickory. It reminded him of his childhood—of his parents. He rarely had time to think about them, but when he did, they were always good thoughts. He missed having someone to share parts of his life with. His father, also a Guardian by blood, would have been the only person to understand what it meant to do what Tobias did. The years had forced Tobias to accept the secluded way of things, but his memories—no matter how deeply buried— always found a way back to the surface at the most inopportune times.

John stepped onto Sam's small front porch. A spiraling wind chime of hollow metal tubes dangled from an eyehook next to the door and clanged gently in the chilly air.

John gave a quick rap on the door and waited. No reply.

He knocked again, more forcefully.

"Sam." John cupped his hands next to his eyes and peered through the window to the left of the door. Sheer curtains obstructed the view inside. "You home?" He knocked again.

Moments later, the interior of the cabin lit.

Soft footsteps traveled over squeaky floorboards. The deadbolt shifted to the unlocked position, and the door creaked open. The light from within the cabin spilled onto the darkening porch and illuminated the two men in its soft glow.

Wow, Tobias thought as he gawked at the leggy woman who stood blocking their entry. This wasn't the Sam he had expected. He thought, for sure, that the name belonged to some forest-dwelling hermit with a dark bushy beard and a raspy voice. He was overjoyed to be wrong.

A tight ponytail kept her long, silky black hair in place. She wore snug-fitting blue jeans and a grey, hooded sweatshirt, which hung loosely on her thin, yet curvy, physique.

"Hey, John," she said, annoyed.

Her attention shifted from John to Tobias. Tobias looked back stolidly and directly into her soft blue eyes. He wanted to convey that he meant her no harm, even though his rough appearance suggested otherwise.

She looked Tobias over, and then looked back to John. "What's going on, John?"

"You wouldn't believe me if I told you." John walked past her, uninvited, into the cabin.

"Come on in," she said, rolling her eyes.

Tobias remained where he was. He wasn't about to follow John and invite himself into her house. He decided it was best if he allowed her to make any decisions she needed to, but that an introduction might help speed things along.

"My name is Tobias. I assume you're Sam?"

She nodded and looked down at his bloodied hand.

"Looks like you have a mess there."

He did his best to hide the wound, not wanting to give her any more reasons to turn him away.

"Let's get it cleaned up before it becomes infected." She stepped aside and gave Tobias a clear path.

Not what he had expected. He thought for sure they'd need to find another place to hide. Tobias smiled politely and brushed past her into the cabin. He noticed her soft, flowery scent hanging in the air as he passed. He took a few extra seconds to revel in the moment. Most of his time was spent with creatures that, on a good day, reeked of trash.

John sat on a stool at the tiled divide that separated the kitchen from the living room. He then buried his head in his arms and mumbled to himself, shaking his head every now and then.

Tobias stopped a few feet into the house and turned around to face Sam. Several drops of blood dripped from his wound onto the aging hardwood floor. It couldn't be helped. The bandage was no more than a waterlogged dam at that point, but while it could no longer soak up the blood, it did lessen the amount that could escape. Without it, he feared a mop and bucket would be necessary.

The hickory scent was much stronger inside. The fireplace across the room crackled fiercely as the fire overtook the newer, untouched logs. The cabin was small, but it felt warm and inviting. His body silently begged for sleep.

Sam walked past Tobias and continued through the main room, into a small half-bath. She rummaged around briefly, opening and closing a few drawers, before flicking off the bathroom light and walking back towards the men.

Tobias pulled up a seat next to John as Sam entered the

kitchen with a roll of thick gauze and a brown bottle of hydrogen peroxide. She moved with a purposeful stride and sat opposite Tobias at the divide. She then skillfully put on a pair of blue latex gloves, gently grabbed his hand and, pinching the bloodied rag in her fingertips, slipped it off. Sam leaned to her right and tossed the blood-soaked t-shirt sleeve into the trash without a word. It landed with a wet splat.

"Okay," she said, surveying the damage. "We're going to need something a little more heavy-duty than gauze. You should really go to the hospital."

"Can't do that," Tobias said. He wasn't prepared to answer her, though, if she asked why.

She looked at him for a moment. "Okay then."

Sam then stood from the divide and walked to the closet in the living room. She pushed things aside carelessly until she apparently found what she was looking for. She removed a large, thin needle from a sewing box and held it to the light. Without so much as a word, she went out the front door and onto the porch. A gust of the chilly autumn air rushed in. When she returned she held a roll of thin fishing line.

Tobias realized what it meant.

"I don't have any pain meds," she said, "but I can offer you a shot of vodka, if you like." She nodded over her shoulder to the kitchen cabinets. "It might help take the edge off."

She then walked over to the stove, lit the front burner, and heated the needle over the flame.

"I don't drink, but thank you. I'll deal with the pain."

She smirked at his bravado. "It's your choice, cowboy."

When the needle glowed red, she removed it from the flame and threaded its eye with the fishing line. She then took Tobias' hand and placed it on the table, palm up.

Unscrewing the bottle of hydrogen peroxide, she doused the open wound with it. The clear liquid quickly transformed into a white, bubbling pool as it disinfected the gash. After a minute or so, she dabbed it away with a clean rag. She repeated the process a few more times before getting to work.

"I need you to be as still as possible. I don't want to stick you any more times than I have to."

Tobias nodded and locked his jaw. He would have stitched the wound himself had it been in a different location. His hand, however, was one of those precarious body parts that was better tended to by someone else.

John looked up briefly before hiding his head once again in his hands.

Tobias kept his hand firmly planted on the tiled divide as Sam pushed the needle through the skin, meeting some resistance at first. His resolve, especially in the presence of a good-looking woman, had never been stronger. Each flesh-piercing stroke was precisely accurate and equidistant from the last. The wound made his hand numb to the needle's journey through his skin.

This couldn't be her first time stitching someone up, he thought.

Ten minutes and twelve improvised stitches later, the job was complete. Sam held the long end of the fishing line in her teeth and reached over to her left. A quick snip from the scissors, and the job was complete.

Tobias looked down. In certain morbid circles, her handiwork could be considered art.

"I was going to become a nurse," she volunteered.

Tobias looked back and grinned. With her hair pulled back and her silky complexion, she looked all of twenty-five years old, though Tobias figured her to be a youthful thirty-something.

"Why?" he asked.

"Why what?"

"Why didn't you become a nurse?" He looked down at his hand again. "It seems to me you would have made a good one."

His hand was still numb, but it felt better already. Stopping the loss of blood was his main concern. Time would take care of the rest.

Sam put the fishing line and needle on the divide. She then removed her gloves and put them atop the soggy rag in the trash.

She looked down at the ground. "It's not a story I tell a lot." She looked directly into Tobias' eyes. "Especially with people I've just met."

"Fair enough." Tobias shrugged. "The world's loss, I guess." He liked her already. She had spunk—a solid quality, as far as he was concerned.

Hiding behind an innocent smile, Sam paused. "All right," she said, "screw it, if you really want to know. Not like it's some big secret."

Tobias was surprised she opened up that easily. Then again, he was used to questioning far less kind things— things that didn't want to be questioned.

Sam paused and then continued. "I was in the middle of my nursing internship, working overnights at the hospital. It was early in the morning, and I was about to get off my shift when the call came in. A drunk driver crashed into someone while he was driving wrong way down the highway. Both drivers were killed. The sole survivor was rushed to us with critical injuries. The surgeons operated for hours, but in the end they weren't able to save him." She paused as her eyes welled ever so slightly with tears. "He was just a little kid, no more than six years old. He had his whole life ahead of him, and some idiot went and took it away. I remember the surgeon having to tell his parents what had happened. It's one moment I make myself remember, even though it would be easier to forget."

Tobias bowed his head but kept his sight trained on her. Death was an everyday part of his life, but when the innocence of a child was wasted for some stupid thing, it was never easy on anyone, including himself.

Sam quickly collected herself. "I just couldn't deal with that on a daily basis," she said, putting away the medical supplies. "When I thought about becoming a nurse, it was the noble idea of saving people that appealed to me. I never thought about the people that couldn't be saved." She sighed. "So I became a bartender. The worst thing that happens on that job is someone passes out." She looked at John. "At least I know they'll wake up."

Tobias watched her walk away out of the corners of his eyes. A small smirk hid amongst his scruff.

"So what are *you* doing here?" she asked. "And what the heck happened to your hand, anyway?" She walked back into the kitchen and leaned on the divide. "That's a pretty serious gash you got there. I'll say it again; you should probably head to the hospital. At the very least get yourself some antibiotics."

"He's here to protect me," John said, abruptly lifting his head from the divide and pointing at himself with his thumb. "Lucky ole me." John stood. "You got any beer, Sam?"

She shook her head. "Nope, but like I offered to your friend here, there's a little bit of vodka in the kitchen. Don't overdo it, John. You remember what happened last time."

Last time?

John waved her off and walked into the kitchen. He rummaged through a few cabinets before finding the bottle. He poured a glass and sucked it back. The burn of the vodka

47

shriveled his face for the briefest of moments. He then poured another glass and walked to the window over the sink and peered out catatonically.

"Protect you?" Sam asked with a nervous smile. "Protect you from what?"

"Talk to him about that," John said, nodding towards Tobias.

Sam turned to face Tobias with her brow raised.

Tobias figured there was no use trying to make up a story. John would probably just squash the lie anyway. "I'm here to protect John from the devil." It sounded absurd when he said it, but absurd was their reality now.

A muffled laugh escaped John's obstructed mouth. His second glass of vodka slid down his throat.

Sam tried to stop a giggle before it came out.

"You won't be laughing for much longer," Tobias said, turning his attention back to John. "Things are going to change quickly. You need to be prepared for those changes, John."

Tobias stood from his stool and made his way over to the window by the front door. He parted the curtains and peered outside. It seemed quiet enough out there. "Did the Keeper say anything to you before he died?"

John looked over. "I don't know, man." He closed his eyes and thought. "Yeah, yeah. Actually, he did say something about some Trinity Church in Boston. I'm supposed to see some guy there." He paused for a moment. "Reverend O'Brien or something."

Sam looked on curiously.

"Then that's where we need to go," Tobias said.

John snickered. "Have fun."

"I don't think you understand, John."

"I understand just fine, man. I understand that I'm not going to Boston because some monk told me to. No way, no

48

how. This is just some bizarre bad dream."

Tobias held up his newly-stitched hand. "What did this to me will do a lot worse to you, and they will never stop coming. Wherever you are, they'll find you. The Hounds are nothing more than the devil's pets. Trust me when I say that there are far worse things to come." He trained his stare dead into John's eyes and said, "Things you can't un-see."

Tobias peered out the window again. It was now apparent that this was going to be more difficult than he'd first thought.

"Listen," Sam said, "why don't you guys try to sleep it off? You both look like you could use some rest."

John shook his head. "No way I'm going back to my place. No way."

"I meant stay here," Sam said, holding her hands up to placate John. "I have a spare bedroom, and the couch is nice and soft. I've spent a few nights in front of the fire there myself."

Tobias thought about it. Urgency was the pushing force, but he realized sleep deprivation could lead to death on their next encounter. He didn't know when, if ever, they'd get another chance to rest.

"I think that's a good idea," Tobias said. He looked at Sam. "Thank you." He found it strange that she could remain so calm and unquestioning, especially after all the talk of the devil. It was not what he had expected.

John placed the empty bottle of vodka and the used glass down in the sink. He looked at both Tobias and Sam, paused to say something, but said nothing before silently walking into the guest bedroom and closing the door behind him.

Tobias bowed his head. He couldn't just drag John around to the Trinity Signs. He needed to come willingly to understand the magnitude of what the world needed from him. The question of how to accomplish that was what perplexed Tobias beyond a comfortable level of aggravation. He was good at fighting monsters—probably the best—but he was no babysitter.

"I guess you get the couch," Sam said with a smile after watching John sulk away. "I have to get some sleep. I was up way too early this morning." She nodded towards her bedroom. "I can trust you, right?"

Tobias nodded. "Thanks again for the hospitality. ..." He held up his stitched hand. "...and for this."

"Any friend of John's...," she said, walking past him. She casually glanced back before closing her bedroom door and locking it.

Tobias grabbed two small pieces of wood from the stack to the left of the fireplace and tossed them atop the burning pile. The wood fell with a thump and kicked up a small cloud of embers that rose like a fleeing colony of fireflies. He leaned back against the couch as the wood crackled soothingly. The warmth seeped deep into his bones. With his hand resting on the handle of his gun, Tobias slowly drifted off into a half sleep, knowing he'd need to be ready for anything, at anytime.

Chapter 5

The air shifted slightly when Sam opened her bedroom door. Tobias felt it, but he kept still. He'd hovered in a restful state for the past few hours. It was a much needed reprieve for his tired bones. His legs were shot and his hand still throbbed, but he had felt much worse in the past, and the rejuvenating heat from the fireplace felt wonderful. Yet, while his body gladly accepted the rest, his mind wouldn't allow for a full sleep, not with so many things bouncing around in there. How was he going to explain everything to John? Where were the Trinity Signs? Did they have enough time to find them before the devil grew too powerful? These were questions without answers.

Sam walked quietly, almost gliding from her bedroom into the kitchen. She fished a glass from one of the cabinets and poured herself some water from the faucet. She took a couple small sips and turned towards Tobias.

"Oh," she said, surprised. "You're awake."

Tobias nodded. "Is everything all right?"

Sam placed the glass down in the sink and walked towards him.

"Yeah, everything's fine." She looked away with a touch of embarrassment. "It's just the wind. It's got my imagination going. I'm sorry if I woke you."

"You didn't," he said with the slightest smirk.

She seemed relieved. "Well, how are you feeling?" She fell to the couch like a drifting feather, soft and graceful. "Your hand must be killing you now that the booze has worn off?"

"Like I said earlier, Sam, I don't drink."

"Sure you don't." She grinned. "It's okay. We all have our vices. I'd have coffee on an intravenous drip if I could."

"I promise you. I've never had a drop in my life." And that was the truth. It made him easier prey for the things he hunted, or so his father had told him many years ago. There were times, though, when he longed to be free of his normality for even a few moments, to feel what it would be like to escape reality and have life lighten even the slightest bit.

Sam studied him for a moment. "You're serious, aren't you?"

He nodded. "Completely."

"Huh," she said, taken aback. "I just assumed you were an alcoholic like John."

"John's an alcoholic?" Tobias said, louder than he'd intended. That explained some things.

Sam shushed him. "How can you be his friend and not know that?" she whispered. "He's always drinking. If he's not at the bar with me, then he's on his front porch. Sometimes he sits out there for hours, drinking away the day with his dog."

"John isn't my friend."

She smiled. "Oh, that's right. You're his protection from the devil. Gotcha."

It didn't matter who believed the story. All that mattered was that John survived; but, for whatever reason, Tobias wanted Sam to believe him—to know that he was a moral guy. He felt a need to convince her. It was a feeling he didn't like. Tobias had never felt the urge to convince anyone of anything. He did what he needed to without looking back, but it was different with her.

Before he could speak again, he was forced into action by John's guttural shout from behind the closed bedroom door. Tobias shot to his feet and darted past Sam in a blur.

He tried the doorknob—locked. Without so much as a second thought, Tobias lowered his shoulder and pushed through the thin bedroom door like a wrecking ball, knocking the door off its hinges.

John sat upright on the bed with the blanket pulled tight to his chin. He shivered uncontrollably, and his skin was white with fear. Beads of sweat dotted his forehead, yet the room was eerily cold. The temperature had gone from warm to that of a walk-in icebox in no time, chilling even Tobias' breath into quickly vanishing clouds.

"John," Sam said, rushing in behind Tobias. "Are you all right?" She sat on the edge of the bed and stroked John's cheek with her hand. "You're freezing."

John's jittery eyes frantically searched around the room, looking for something. His mouth was pursed tight, his lips white.

"John. What happened?" Tobias said. *Whatever scared him did a good job of it.*

"Some…something's here," John muttered through shivers.

Tobias drew both of his guns. "What was it?"

John shook his head. "I…I don't know. One minute, I was a…asleep, and then the next…," he shivered and closed his eyes. "I didn't see anything, but I felt it. Something wanted me dead. I wasn't alone, man." He looked at Tobias. "I wasn't alone."

Tobias realized that their time here had just run out.

"Stay here," Tobias said.

He flipped on the lights within the cabin and looked around. He then walked to the window beside the front door, parted the curtains, and glanced out. The full moon cast the outdoors in an eerie glow, silhouetting the trees like thin stick soldiers waiting for their command. Nothing seemed out of the ordinary, except for the wind chime that had fallen from the hook and was now strewn across the porch. It could have been the wind that knocked it off. Then again, it could have been something else.

Tobias turned around and glimpsed Sam and John as they sat in the bedroom, staring back at him, frozen in fear. "I'll be right back." It went against his better judgment to leave them alone, but he couldn't just sit inside the cabin and wait for whatever it was to come back. That wasn't his style.

Tobias holstered one gun and ripped open the front door.

A gust of cold air raced into the warm cabin, blowing across his face as if howling a warning. He passed through the doorway and gave his surroundings a quick once-over. While he couldn't see anything, he trusted what he felt. His senses never lied. Something unnatural was definitely there, lurking in the shadows and watching him. It was a feeling he'd become accustomed to over the years.

An owl's hoot bounced off the trees from somewhere nearby.

The gusting wind came in spurts, dragging dried leaves across the ground, crackling as they vanished into the darkness.

Tobias feared whatever was there would get the jump on him. It not only had the cover of darkness, but also the element of surprise. Bullets would do little if he couldn't get a shot off. It was that realization that made him change tactics. He holstered his other gun. He needed something a little more personal.

With his un-bandaged hand, Tobias reached over his shoulder and withdrew a large glimmering sword from the darkness. The blade gleamed like polished silver as the full moon bore down upon it. The Guardian's Blade, a remnant from days gone by, was hidden from sight while in its sheath by powers he didn't fully understand. It was those powers that allowed him to travel armed at all times. The blade was more powerful than any bullet ever could be. It had been forged long ago, hundreds of years before Tobias was even born, in a ceremony that was never talked about and was always denied if the subject was brought up. Over the years, it had bested everything it had come in contact with. Its only limitation was its range.

Tobias firmly grasped the ornamental hilt in both hands and crept forward. He breathed slowly and quietly, listening to everything.

He was only a few steps away from the cabin when Tobias realized something was wrong. His hair tingled, and his ears rang softly. His senses peaked, but it was too late. Tobias turned in time to see the cabin door slam shut and the lights go dark.

Sam's piercing scream soon followed. He rushed through the darkness and back onto the small deck.

Sam screamed again, and then Tobias heard a thump.

He hammered his foot into the door, breaking it off the hinges and sending it flying into the kitchen. The interior of the cabin was dark—ominous. He flipped the switch to his right, but the lights remained off. The fire had been extinguished. Only its dwindling embers remained. It was just enough light to see Sam lying motionless on the floor and an eerie glow emanating from within John's room.

Tobias ran to Sam's side and held two fingers to her neck.

Thank God. She's still alive.

He then stood and ran into John's bedroom.

There, hovering over John, was a Phantom like a ghostly black transparency. It hummed and clicked like a cicada bug in the heat of summer, while wispy trails of white smoke traveled upwards from John's body.

Tobias knew it was consuming his soul.

John's body arched at his lower back, while his head and feet remained firmly planted. With rolled-back white eyes, John gasped for air that he couldn't seem to find.

Conventional weapons had little effect on Phantoms. Tobias had found that out the hard way. They were born in darkness and thrived within it. The last time he'd met up with one was in the Australian bush. Damn thing got the jump on him then. If it hadn't been for the headlights of the poacher's truck, Tobias might not have been able to fight back.

Headlights. That's it.

Tobias ran to the kitchen. He tossed open every cabinet until thankfully finding what he was looking for below the sink—a large flashlight. Simple, but effective.

He broke for the bedroom and rushed past Sam's unconscious body. He quickly shined the light on the Phantom.

No reflection.

No shadow.

But apparently it did cause some kind of pain.

The creature screeched and turned to Tobias. Its vibrantly red eyes peered from within the light and through his soul. Tobias thought of his parents' deaths, of having to watch his father die in his arms. He thought of the innocent lives he hadn't been able to save—the woman in the small Russian town that was taken as she slept in the room next to him, the young girl savagely ripped apart in Brazil, and the three brothers that had been turned *dark* from a pagan ritual gone horribly wrong.

Tobias shook himself back to the now as John fell limp to the bed. The Phantom clicked and gurgled. Its face moved spastically from side to side. At least, Tobias thought that was its face. Stopping at times, as if it was a photograph, the face would then shift into some aberration Tobias chose to forget.

But the light was working.

He moved closer, now only a foot from the blackness that still hovered over John.

The creature wailed again, dark and empty, and shattered the small window above John's bed.

Phantoms were hateful creatures, but they were not overly resilient. They worked better as thieves. Their loot was a human soul, and Tobias was not about to give John away to this one.

"Get the hell out of here…," Tobais said, bringing the flashlight closer and quickly realizing his ironic choice of words, "…and tell your master that he'll need to do better than you."

The Phantom wailed again and then lunged towards Tobias. It passed through his body in an instant. His cells felt frozen at the molecular level, causing him to shiver uncontrollably. Then, with a trailing screech, the Phantom vanished.

The lights flickered briefly, popping, before again lighting the house in its mild glow.

John opened his eyes, still shivering. "What happened?"

"How much do you remember?" Tobias asked.

"I remember you opening the front door. Then it slammed shut, and everything went dark. After that, I don't remember anything until now."

Sam moaned and pushed herself back upright.

"Are you hurt?" Tobias asked, passing through the door and kneeling down beside her. He braced her back with his muscular left arm.

"No," she said, shaking her head. "I don't think so." A look of fright rushed into her eyes as she seemed to remember.

Tobias felt her heart rev up through his supportive

grasp. Sam stared into the bedroom, wide-eyed. "Is it gone?"

"For now," Tobias said, helping her off the floor.

"What was that thing?"she asked.

"It was a Phantom," Tobias said, not offering more. "Are you sure you're not hurt?"

She nodded. "Just a bit shaken, but I'll be fine." She shivered. "I remember seeing these beady red eyes next to John. It's like they just appeared out of nowhere. Scared me to death." She took a breath. "I guess I must have passed out after that."

Tobias glanced out the broken window above John's bed. Icy air howled in from the dark outside.

"With the sun rising in a few hours, I don't think it's coming back, but we can't stay here."

"So you really weren't kidding…," Sam said, "…about the whole *devil* thing?"

"I'm afraid not, Sam. I'm sorry you were dragged into this." He touched her arm gently. "I think it would be best if you came with us. You'll be safer with me."

"Go where? To Boston? I can't leave. What about my job?" She then sat on the bed next to John. "So all this monster stuff is real? These things actually exist?"

And there are a lot worse things out there, Tobias thought, nodding.

Sam paused and then buried her head in her hands.

It was hard for Tobias to put himself in others' shoes, considering he'd grown up knowing about the darker things. However, seeing the look on Sam's face made it a little easier to understand her well-placed fear. Realizing that monsters existed outside of movies and books was a lot to soak in. A reality changer, as Tobias would put it.

"The devil knows you mean something to John now," Tobias said. "It will do everything possible to accomplish its goal, and that involves going through you to get to him."

Unfortunately for Sam, he meant that both literally and figuratively.

That was apparently all he needed to say. Sam turned and left the bedroom, shaking her head as she did.

The situation had escalated far quicker than Tobias thought it would. He'd hoped they, too, could move in the shadows and be hidden from Evil's view, but that was no longer an option. He worried that the battle might be lost before it had even begun.

Chapter 6

Their travel time increased exponentially once they exited the highway and came into Boston proper. Forty-five minutes of maddening traffic and randomly placed one-way streets brought Tobias to the brink of a mental breakdown. He'd go down one street, only to find a giant orange detour sign at its end that pointed him in the opposite direction of where he needed to go. A frequent visitor to Boston, he knew what to expect, but the city's infrastructure was nothing more than paved lunacy as far as he was concerned.

He pulled the car to the side of the road, a few spaces down from Trinity Church. With the glass-filled Hancock Tower to its right, the Romanesque architecture of the church seemed out of place where it was. The church was built on a patch of lawn, neatly nestled amongst all the concrete and steel of Boston. Varying shades of brown splashed its stone exterior, only to be interrupted by the dark red of the pyramidal roof.

Tobias hoped this would be easy, but he knew from experience that it never was. They exited the rental car and followed the cement walkway leading up to the church. Tobias pulled open the heavy wood doors and ushered Sam and John through. He scanned behind them, looking for any signs of a tail before following them through.

Wafting incense, coupled with a scent he could only describe as "churchly", filled the vast, open interior. A rich crimson carpet rolled down the entirety of the center aisle. Dark wood pews ran the carpet's length to either side, each coated with a shiny lacquer that helped to protect them from the cruelty of time. Hymnals—some horizontal, others vertical—rested within the confines of the shelving attached to the back of each bench. A few scattered parishioners went about their business, unaware of anything but their prayers.

Tobias never had been one for prayer. In an ironic twist, and after all he'd seen, he still didn't fully believe in the idea of a supreme being. It wasn't that he purposely rejected the thought. He'd simply seen too much pain and suffering over the years to accept that one creator could allow such things to happen. He left worship to those who embraced the idea.

An organist practiced her craft on a landing above them as they walked down the crimson path towards the altar. Tobias recognized the tune, but he couldn't place it. After a while, they all seemed to blend together.

Tobias gazed upon the myriad of stained glass that hung high on the towering walls. Each of the intricately formed pieces depicted a different colorful scene from the Bible. The walls below them were splashed with vivid murals.

Ironically, churches were something Tobias tried to avoid. While most people found them to be a spiritual sanctuary, he thought of them as an extension of his work. When you were employed by the Vatican, churches were just satellite offices, but sometimes, like today, they couldn't be avoided.

The altar spanned a wide area beneath a large domed ceiling at the end of the aisle. Tobias stepped onto its elevated platform and moved towards a reverend who sat on a small bench off to the right. His eyes were closed, and his hands were locked tight on his lap. A string of rosary beads snaked out from within his fist and fell off the side of his leg.

As the group neared, the man's eyes creaked open. "Hello," he said, a bit startled. "Sorry about that. Sometimes when I communicate with the Lord, I tend to go a little too deep." He rose from his chair with a smile and brushed some temporary wrinkles free from his pants. "May I help you with something?"

"We've come to speak with Reverend O'Brien. It's important."

"I am O'Brien," he said apprehensively.

Tobias stepped forward and pushed up his right sleeve. The Guardian's Mark, the Crux intersected by two swords, was burned into the skin of his inner forearm. It was a Guardian tradition that would thankfully die off with him. Tobias realized flashing a strange burn to most people would warrant nothing more than a look of curious revulsion. They were, however, directed to find this man; therefore, he hoped the reverend would recognize the legacy behind the mark and that a certain level of trust would be bestowed in Tobias because of it.

The reverend leaned in closer to Tobias. He looked around before speaking. "What business do you have here, Guardian?"

Good, Tobias thought. He knew what the mark meant. It would have been an odd starting point for their conversation if he hadn't.

"Not in the open," Tobias said, looking around. "Is there somewhere more private?"

The holy man stood up straight and took a step back. He nodded and waved for them to follow.

While the noble past of the Guardians was something cherished by the Vatican, not every person in the know thought so highly of them. Some viewed the Guardians as nothing more than evangelical thugs, doing the Vatican's dirty work with a blessing from above. It wasn't always monsters that Tobias was forced to hunt, but whatever he did hunt had it coming—that was a certainty. Being the last of his kind, Tobias now held that distinction all unto himself. He hoped Reverend O'Brien was not one of the misguided individuals. He needed to get information and would prefer to get it the civilized way.

They made their way to the right of the altar, through a white ornate door and into the back of the church. The same pristine architecture that ran throughout the entirety of the church flowed down the hallway through which they now walked. The reverend held open the thick door at the end of the hall until they had all passed through.

"Now," O'Brien said, turning from the door. "What is this urgent matter?"

Tobias turned his sights to John. "May I see the cross?"

John removed the relic from around his neck. He handed it to Tobias who, in turn, handed it to O'Brien. Tobias wanted to get right to the reason of their arrival. They had lost too much time already.

The reverend grasped the cross tightly, bringing it in close to examine. He furrowed his brow and removed a pair of half-circle glasses, pushing them snug to his face. He rotated the cross in his hands. It only took a moment before the reverend's eyes grew wide, and his jaw dropped.

"It can't be...," O'Brien said.

Tobias nodded. "It is. That's the Crux Signate."

O'Brien looked down again at what he now held. "Surely this is nothing to jest about, Guardian."

"I assure you, reverend, this is no joke. That's the real deal."

The reverend's hands trembled. He looked as though he might faint. Tobias took him by the arm and helped ease him down into a nearby chair.

"Then it has begun," O'Brien said, in the most serious of tones. "The end of days is upon us."

A proper response for such a heavy statement escaped Tobias, so he again nodded.

O'Brien peered over at John with a crazed look on his

face. "And since the Crux hangs around your neck, I can only assume that you are a member of the Brotherhood of the Sealed?"

John shrugged. "That's what I'm told."

And he's the last one, Tobias thought. He figured that information would be best unspoken at the moment. No need to further worry the reverend and upset John.

The reverend was well-versed in the lore of the Crux. Tobias quickly realized there would be no need for convincing here. O'Brien obviously knew what was at stake.

"And it is the Trinity Signs you now seek?" O'Brien said.

Tobias again nodded. This was going better than he'd expected.

On shaky legs, O'Brien rose from his chair and placed the Crux on a nearby table atop a lush velvet pillow. He then walked a short way to the bookshelf nearest to the door. Scanning the shelves, he removed a book from the second highest shelf. Miniscule particles of dust flickered down from years of neglect and glinted in the sunlight, cast through the stained glass window to their right.

Hustling back to the others, O'Brien sat on a chair at a small table in the center of the room. He placed the book down and flipped through the pages with great care, eventually stopping about a quarter of the way through. "Yes, yes," O'Brien said. "Here we are."

The left page was covered in strange text that Tobias couldn't make out. *Latin, maybe,* he thought. The right page was splashed with a dreary picture depicting a horned beast rising from a giant rift in the ground. Fire burned all around it. People ran from the rift, fire engulfing them. At the top of the picture was a representation of God in the heavens, His back turned on the events depicted in the scene.

"This book has no name, nor an origin," O'Brien said, "but I believe it may help show you the way."

O'Brien stood from his chair and rummaged through some rolled-up, worn parchments that occupied a nearby desk. He moved like a man possessed. Finding the one he wanted, he made his way back to the group.

"Can you tell us where Trinity Signs are?" Tobias asked.

An unexpected smile appeared on O'Brien's face. "I was just getting to that, Guardian." He sat down on an old wooden stool. "There are three signs—The Sign of the Father, The Sign of the Son, and The Sign of the Holy Spirit. Each Sign can only be activated by one of the Brotherhood of the Sealed." O'Brien looked towards John.

"How do you know that?" John asked out of curiosity. "Why does it have to be me?"

The reverend loosened the ribbon that held the rolled, time-stained parchment. Centered on the page was a small collection of words. He held his finger on the page and slowly traced the lines as he read. "Yes, here we are. *And God gave unto his children the means to live free from evil for all eternity. A Brother's blood, and only a Brother's blood, holds within it the power to preserve that which He created.*"

The reverend moved his finger faster over the next few lines, slowly mumbling to himself. He stopped a bit further down the page and read aloud again. "*If the day cometh that the Brothers have been removed from this world, then the devil shall rule over all within its reach, free from the thought of its own destruction.*"

The reverend rolled the old parchment and retied the thick ribbon.

Typical religious story, Tobias thought. "How does John activate the Signs?"

The reverend shrugged. "That I do not know. I'm sorry. Very little was written of the Signs. I wish there was more to tell, but like I said, this book may be of some help." He handed the nameless book to Tobias. "It mentions the first of the Trinity Signs. Hopefully it will guide you to it."

Tobias took the book. It felt surprisingly heavy for such a tiny piece of writing. Its cover was rough, worn from time, but its binding was surprisingly well-maintained.

"What was that?" Sam asked, a look of concern plastered on her face.

The group looked, in unison, towards her. She leaned against the door to the hallway, her ear tight against it.

"What was what?" Tobias asked. She'd been so quiet that he'd forgotten that she was even there.

A second blood-chilling scream shot them all to attention. This one was clearly audible and haunting.

"That," she said, jumping back from the door.

Tobias shot past Sam and ran from the room, back up the hallway. He quickly reached the end of the hall and ran back through the white ornate door into the open hall of the church. There, in midair, was a woman held aloft by a ghastly creature, trapped in one of its clawed feet as it hovered above the altar. Its head jerked from side to side like a bird's, as its two large fleshy wings beat feverishly to keep it afloat. Its proportionally small head, crowned by a circle of protruding bumps from beneath its skin, seemed out of place when compared to the rest of its body. Its ribs pushed from within its emaciated body and gave it the appearance of a skeleton wrapped in grey shrink wrap.

Reverend O'Brien stopped short behind Tobias and gasped. "What in God's name is that?"

"Gargoyle," Tobias said, reaching for his guns. "And God had nothing to do with it."

"Did you study the big book of monsters or something?" John asked.

Tobias kept his eyes on the beast. "I've been doing this for a long time." He motioned to the group. "Stay here."

He slowly crept towards the altar. He knew it was best

to close the distance between them first. Gargoyles moved quicker than he could naturally track. His efforts, however, were in vain, as the Gargoyle noticed his approach. It jerked its head and trained its dead eyes on Tobias. It then released a shrill, ear-ringing cry. The stained glass above them shattered. Tobias turned back and dove at the group, pushing them out of the way as the multicolored shards came crashing down.

The woman held within the monster's grasp screamed again, but this time the cry was softer. Tears streamed down her face. "Please, help me," she whimpered.

Tobias pushed himself off the floor. With one fluid motion, he aimed and fired. The beast disappeared, causing the bullet to crash into the stone arch of the church. Moments later, the gargoyle reappeared.

Tobias sneered at the beast. *Cheater.*

The Gargoyle beat its wings and rose until it reached the top of the high-arching ceiling. It jerked its head down at the woman and then released its grasp. Tobias watched in horror as the woman fell to her death on the altar below. The crack of her neck abruptly ended her screams.

"No!" O'Brien yelled, breaking for the altar.

The beast pulled its wings back and dove. It disappeared again, leaving only a trail of black, wispy smoke behind. Seconds later, it reappeared next to O'Brien and swept him into the air before Tobias could react. The Gargoyle circled the rows of pews below like a vulture circling a dead carcass.

Tobias removed both his guns and unloaded a few rounds at the beast. Same results as before. The beast turned into black smoke and disappeared.

"Save yourselves," O'Brien yelled in pain, helplessly beating on the Gargoyle's leg.

The monster reared its head back and let go another

fierce cry. The remaining stained glass shattered and fell, one of the larger pieces smashing against the organ near the entrance. It bellowed an ensemble of unmelodious notes that echoed within the church's large interior.

The beast shrieked again, but this time in pain. Its grasp on the reverend released. Sam screamed as O'Brien fell to the floor with a thump.

Tobias turned to John. The last thing he wanted was to endanger him, but there was little choice at that point. He needed an extra pair of hands, and he figured now was as good a time as any to break John into the man he would need to become.

"John, I need you to get to that organ and mash the keys."

John looked back. "Seriously?"

"Yes, and do it quickly. I'll cover you."

John stared hard at Tobias, as he had when they'd first met in the Connecticut woods. Seconds later, driven by what Tobias assumed was adrenaline, John sprinted towards the small door beneath the organ's overhang. The monster swept down with John in its sights.

Oh, no you don't.

Tobias holstered his guns and reached towards his right leg. He removed a micro-shotgun from the bracket holding it tight and pulled the trigger. Two scattershot shells exploded from the barrels. The beast didn't have enough time to react as the thousands of micro-needles punctured its skin. It shrieked again, but seemed unfazed. Tobias knew one shell wouldn't be enough to end the Gargoyle from that distance, but it would be enough of a distraction.

John reached the small stairwell unscathed. He dashed through the open door, up the small winding staircase, and onto the landing. He ran to the organ and slammed his fists down on the keys as Tobias instructed. The organ coughed the most unharmonious sound Tobias had ever heard, bouncing off the high-reaching walls and reverberating throughout the cavernous church.

The Gargoyle shrieked in pain again. It covered, what Tobias believed to be, its ears with its stringy hands.

Again John slammed his fists down on the ivory keys. The beast flailed about in the air, clutching its head. Wisps of smoke jutted off in every direction as the Gargoyle blinked in and out of solid form.

Tobias made his way up the center aisle with his shotgun drawn. His eyes never left the hovering beast. He knew that it would only take one lapse in concentration to ensure his quick death. The Gargoyle was far quicker than he was, but Tobias had more toys.

As Tobias came within ten feet of the monster, the notes stopped in some kind of cosmic middle finger.

He looked up. "John?"

"I'm trying," John yelled, banging on the keys. "I think it's busted."

Tobias inched backwards as the monster lashed out like a snake turning on its charmer. What Tobias assumed was a smirk grew across the beast's dead face.

The creature's eyes bulged, as it was now free from its musical prison. Another screech bellowed from its open mouth. It then shot towards Tobias like a kamikaze coming in for the kill. Tobias clenched his jaw and readied for the impact.

John picked up the organ's bench and slammed it down on the keys. The notes once again filled the air, forcing the monstrosity to stop in midflight, inches from Tobias' face. Its pointed, razor-sharp teeth were bared and ready to dig into his flesh.

Not today, he thought, staring into its ghoulishly red eyes while plugging the shotgun barrels with new shells. He pointed the weapon at the Gargoyle's head, next to no space between it and the barrels. *Nighty-night.* Tobias squeezed the trigger and sent the shells on their short-lived trip. The Gargoyle's cranial cavity blew apart like a watermelon being dropped from a forty-story building. Its smoke-ridden body fell from the air and crashed onto the crimson carpet, dead. Moments later, the beast vaporized into a pile of dust.

Tobias looked up at John. "Good job."

John stared past him, towards the altar. Tobias turned to see Sam kneeling and crying beside the motionless body of Reverend O'Brien.

Chapter 7

Sam sniffled and wiped a tear away as she knelt beside the reverend's broken body. Seeing him bleeding on the ground conjured up memories of why she left nursing. She was quickly reminded of the boy that couldn't be saved and the misery that came along with it. It would be nearly impossible to avoid tragedy for the rest of her life—she knew that—but she never expected it to hit her from out of the blue like this. It was as if the world she knew was slowly eroding away into something she couldn't grasp—didn't want to believe was true.

Everything Tobias had said suddenly became more real. The devil was coming, as crazy as it sounded. No one was safe anymore. She thought of her parents in Colorado and her brother in California. There was a part of her brain that kept everything in perspective, but now that perspective had changed. Her reality had changed. All of her worries and hang-ups seemed so unimportant now.

O'Brien's eyes were closed. A trickle of blood seeped from a small laceration on his forehead and pooled onto the marble floor beneath him. Sam thought, for sure, he was dead. The L-shaped contortion of his right leg was far from natural. He could never have survived that fall. Not from that height. A slight quiver of his lip, however, suggested otherwise.

The reverend's eyelids fluttered and tried to open. It was a miracle he'd survived. His wounds were severe and needed immediate attention, but he still had a chance to live. That small bit of hope filled Sam's heart until it felt like it might burst. Something good had finally found a way through the darkness from the past twenty-four hours.

She turned to Tobias, who stood, looking silently over her shoulder. He surveyed O'Brien, nodded at Sam, removed a cell phone from his pocket, and walked away.

"I didn't see that coming," O'Brien coughed.

"Lie still," Sam said. "We'll get help." She caressed his cheek with the back of her hand.

John ran from behind, gasping for breath. "How is he?"

Sam turned to give John a better view. "Oh," he said quietly, bowing his head.

Tobias flipped his phone shut and walked back from the corner. "Help's on the way."

"We need to stay with him," Sam said.

O'Brien forced a smile, but his pain was obvious. "You can't, my child. You need to go. There are greater things at risk than an old man's life."

Sam saw the truth in his words, no matter how hard they were to accept. She squeezed her eyes closed, forcing a reluctant tear out, and then stood. Tobias put his hand on her back, but comfort was something she couldn't find at the moment. To leave someone in need went against every fiber that wove throughout her body. She knew this, like the boy who died on the operating table, would haunt her dreams for a very long time to come. She felt cursed to have to endure so much pain and yet be so powerless to change it. For all intents and purposes, she was captive to her own reluctance.

Tobias bent to one knee beside the reverend. "They've dispatched a medical team for you. They should be here within minutes." Tobias had called on a team of specially trained medical personnel the Vatican had in place in every state. It just so happened that the closest team was in Boston already, preparing for a papal visit early next month, so they were only a short way across town. These teams knew

72

enough to not be shocked by what they found once they were called. "I'd call for local help, but you know that would be impossible to explain."

O'Brien nodded. A drop of blood snuck from his mouth and down his pale cheek. He propped himself up on his elbows. The tip of his tibia created a small bubble of cloth as it pushed against the inside of his pant leg. His eyes rolled loosely upon seeing his snapped limb, as if he might faint. He then slowly descended back to the ground with Tobias' help.

"You need to leave now, Guardian. You're wasting time staying here with me." He glanced towards John. "Take care of him. I don't need to tell you what he means to humanity."

Tobias nodded softly. He understood all too well.

O'Brien coughed again. "Would you mind handing me my rosary beads before you leave?"

"Of course."

Tobias reached into the reverend's breast pocket and removed the glassy string of beads. He placed them in O'Brien's hand.

"Thank you for the help, reverend." He gave O'Brien one final look and then stood.

Tobias gathered Sam and John from nearby. "He's going to be fine, Sam," Tobias said, guiding them back towards the front door.

"I was going to be a nurse, remember?" She appreciated Tobias trying to ease her mental pain, but his words couldn't change reality. She feared this was only the start of things. What was she going to have to endure tomorrow, or the next day? Maybe she should have just kept on down her nursing path. If she had, then she wouldn't have met John at the bar all those years ago, and undoubtedly, she would not be at the Trinity Church in Boston right now.

They exited through the large double doors and walked

back into the chilly Boston air. A group of people had gathered outside the church's main entrance directly in front of them. The pavement below their feet was littered with stained glass debris, and several people were consoling a woman off to their right who was crying hysterically.

Tobias surveyed the crowd that was growing by the minute. He realized that exiting the church had drawn unwanted attention to his small group. He now looked for a quick exit from the chaos.

Piercing sirens echoed off the tall buildings as the emergency vehicles stopped in front of the church. Firefighters scrambled from three doors on the first ladder truck to arrive on scene. They equipped their oxygen tanks and helmets. Two of them headed directly past the large group of people and hustled by Tobias' position into the church. Their heavy equipment jostled against their yellow fire-retardant suits as they lumbered past.

The Fire Chief pulled up in a red Chevy Suburban and immediately began to direct the arriving police officers to push the crowd back. He then made his way up next to Tobias and stopped.

The Chief communicated with his men inside via a shoulder mounted radio. "I need confirmation on possible accident victims. We got a report of some kind of giant bat in there."

A static-filled reply hissed back. "Chief, this place is a mess, but there ain't nobody in here."

The chief paused. He leaned over his shoulder towards Tobias. "You guys see...?" was all he got out. They were long gone.

Chapter 8

They came to the church for answers, but left with none—no known locations for the Trinity Signs, no knowledge on their activation...nothing. All they got was a little blue book, and instead of helping, as O'Brien had hoped, it just seemed to further complicate things.

"What happened to the other Guardians?" Sam asked abruptly from the back seat of the parked rental car.

Tobias snapped from his thoughts and looked in the rearview. "Some died of old age. Others died of...," he paused, trying to think of the best way to put it, "...unnatural causes."

He looked from the mirror and down to his lap. He didn't offer any more. There were seven Guardians when he was old enough to join their ranks. Now it was only him. What he wouldn't give for their help right now. He needed someone to turn to for guidance. That wasn't going to happen, though, and Tobias understood it was up to him alone to figure this mess out.

Tobias reached into his jacket pocket with his bandaged hand and removed the small blue book O'Brien had given him. He fanned through the pages, forcing an aromatic waft of old parchment past his face.

"Either of you happen to read Hebrew?" he asked rhetorically. That was what the writing looked like.

"I do," Sam chimed in.

Tobias turned in surprise.

"Long story," she said. "But the short of it is that I grew up with an Israeli stepbrother." She held her hand out. "I'm not completely useless, you know."

He grinned and handed the book to Sam.

She, too, thumbed quickly though the pages. Paging to the front, she scanned through until she came to a drawing.

After a few minutes of silence, she spoke. "Well, from what my rusty translation skills are telling me, the Sign of the Father is protected by some kind of spell. It says here that the Sign can only be activated by the ancestry of the Sealed. Then there are some scribbles that I can't really make out."

"Sounds like some kind of biblical fairy tale to me," John said, somehow still in denial.

"There's also a drawing." She held the opened book towards them.

The black and white drawing showed what appeared to be a small fountain, surrounded by a moat of water. A ring of, what Tobias assumed was, a light source was sketched above it.

"This must be the Sign," Sam said, pointing to the page.

Tobias looked out his window. "Does it say anything else, Sam?"

She flipped back one page and then forward two. "Not much. It makes mention of a cave, if I translated it right, but the words are really faded." She looked up. "I can't be sure."

Tobias sent his mind into retrieval mode, trying to fetch anything having to do with a cave with religious meaning. A few came to mind, but it wouldn't be something obvious. The Signs were a secret, not something ordinary historians would be able to record so easily, and so their resting spots had to reside in ambiguity.

The weather had quickly soured since they left the tattered Trinity Church. Several sheets of improperly discarded newspaper whipped through the air and down the street. One piece, the first page of the *Boston Globe* sports section, enveloped the rental's antenna before being sucked away to continue its solemn duty as litter.

Tobias knew what he needed to do. "I need to make a call," he said. "I'll be right back." He opened the driver's door and raced out. It was better to make this call in private. He didn't know what he'd have to discuss, and he'd rather not have to answer extra questions from either John or Sam.

He walked to the sidewalk, flipped open his antique of a cell phone, and dialed a rarely-used number. It rang two quick times, and the call was picked up on the third ring. "How can I direct your call?" the woman asked with a soothing voice.

"This is Tobias Ramsey. I need to speak with Cardinal Rathady."

"Hold please."

Tobias looked around while holding the phone to his ear. The Vatican, for all its publicly visible flaws, was a well-oiled machine in private. He waited no longer than a minute before being greeted by two quick beeps, followed by another ring.

"Tobias?"

He was relieved to hear Rathady's voice. The trustworthy Cardinal was one of the few people, not only in the church, but in the world, that seemed to actually care about another person's wellbeing. Tobias appreciated that. It was something he noticed the world was losing as the years went by. He also considered the Cardinal a sort of father figure. He was well-aged, but not too old.

"Cardinal, it's been quite a while. How have you been?"

"I live a humble life, Tobias. I don't need much to fulfill my duties to the Lord. He rarely asks me to do anything, anyway." The Cardinal laughed softly. "A simpler life leads to simpler problems. In short, I am well. And you?"

"I've had better days."

"So I hear." Tobias knew the Cardinal would be updated

on their latest doings, but he was surprised at how quickly the bad news traveled. "I just received word on Reverend O'Brien." Tobias was just about to ask. "The doctors assure me he will live, though he won't be walking anytime soon."

The news on O'Brien was very much welcomed, as the last thing Tobias wanted was another death on his shoulders."This is going to sound rude, but… ."

"You won't be able to speak with him for quite some time, Tobias," the Cardinal said, stealing his thought before he could finish it. "However, maybe I can help you?"

Tobias was so set on talking to O'Brien that he lacked the sense to see what was right in front of him. "Of course, any help you can lend would be great."

The Cardinal would be up to speed on what had transpired. His knowledge of the Church's past was also extensive, especially in lesser known areas—areas the public weren't privy to.

"Very well, Tobias. How may I be of assistance?"

"Reverend O'Brien gave me a small book before we were attacked." Tobias looked over his shoulder to the rental car. Sam and John remained where they were. "It mentions the Sign of the Father."

"Yes, I am familiar with the story."

"It also has a drawing of what appears to be a fountain surrounded by water. Above the fountain is some kind of glowing circle. It looks like it might be a light of some kind."

The Cardinal answered without skipping a beat. "The light is said to signify the path to the second Sign."

A strong wind whipped by, hampering the audibility of the phone.

"We think the book also mentions a cave," Tobias said when the wind died down a bit. "But the words are faded, so we can't be sure."

The Cardinal wasn't so quick with a response this time.

A heavy silence hung on the line. Tobias turned around to face the street and to keep the ever shifting wind at his back. For all its beauty, Boston was nothing short of a brick wind tunnel at the moment.

"I am hesitant to even mention this to you," the Cardinal said, "as it has been passed down by word of mouth throughout time, but there is said to exist a cave where a fountain eternally flows. It may just be coincidence. Then again, it may not be."

The stories of the Church never failed to entertain Tobias.

"So, say this cave existed. Where would it be?"

"I wish I knew. For what it is worth, though, a prevalent part of the story makes mention of the Crux Signate." Tobias' thoughts drifted to John. "It is said that the Crux points the way to the first Sign."

Tobias shook his head in disgust for failing to see it before. *Of course.* The answer had been dangling around John's neck the whole time. He felt stupid for not thinking of that himself, but the thoughts in his head were becoming more difficult to wrangle.

"Are you still there?" Rathady asked.

"I think you just pointed me in the right direction, Cardinal. Thanks."

"You're welcome, Tobias. Please keep me apprised of your progress. As you know, this is our number one priority."

"I will, Cardinal."

Tobias ended the call and walked back to the car with one thought on his mind. The wind kicked up as he went to close the door, slamming it with more force than he'd planned.

"John, can I see the cross again?"

John removed the cross from around his neck and

handed it over.

Sam looked on eagerly from the back seat. "You have something?"

"Just a hunch," he said, placing the Crux in his open palm and surveying its simplistic beauty. He followed the Crux's raised edge with his eyes, looking for a clue. The purple hue gleamed across its surface. He flipped it over and inspected the back. It was unspectacular and lacked the raised ridge the front had. At the top of the cross was etched *Zubar Island on the Sea* in very small, almost illegible hand-carved letters. Above and below the line were more carvings, each in a different language, Tobias assumed.

"Zubar Island on the Sea," he said, more to hear it out loud than to fill the others in. He stared out the windshield.

Sam leaned forward in her seat. "What?"

"Zubar Island on the Sea. That's what's engraved at the top of the cross."

Sam looked over Tobias' shoulder at the carvings. "Look there," she said, pointing to another grouping of Hebrew characters. "It says the same thing in Hebrew. I think, anyway. And that's Spanish below that. They must have carved it in a bunch of languages."

John rubbed the back of his neck. Then, with a quick twist, he cracked it. "Never heard of Zubar Island."

"That makes two of us," Sam said, sitting back.

Tobias nodded. That made three of them.

He handed the Crux back to John and turned the key.

"By the way," Tobias said, looking back over his shoulder at Sam. "I got word that the reverend is going to make it."

Sam's face lit up. It was nice to see after all the tears.

Checking the surprisingly empty Boston road, Tobias pulled out and headed to the one place nearby that might hold some answers.

Chapter 9

"Where are we going?" Sam asked.

Tobias stopped as if on cue. "Here," he said.

He looked to his right at the Boston Public Library. Tobias had spent a brief stint in Boston with his parents before they died. His mother took him here on cold winter days, of which there were many. He loved being surrounded by rows and rows of books. There was so much knowledge just waiting to be uncovered, but unfortunately there was so little time to find it. He shied away from technology whenever possible, preferring instead to pry open some long forgotten book and devour it. The times when Tobias could actually sit down and enjoy a book were few and far between as of late. His day job kept getting in the way.

They entered through the middle of three tall doorways. The library's interior was architecturally much different than its uninspiring outer shell. With its high-arching, rainbow-like ceilings and ornamental windows, it seemed like a hidden oasis tucked away in a desert of modernization.

The inside was warm and bustled with commotion. Tall bookshelves filled every inch of the inside not occupied by long tables.

It was just as he remembered it. Each of the dark wood tables held court with a row of green-shaded lamps. They resembled the Scales of Justice, with their overhanging arms to either side.

They no sooner had started down the main aisle when Sam darted off to their right and vanished among the sea of Bostonians.

"Be right back," she said, quickly disappearing in the

crowd.

"Where is she going?" John whispered.

Tobias shrugged. He'd have to talk to her about wandering off like that. While she was a grown woman, and could therefore make her own decisions, it was difficult to protect someone that was out of reach. He put the thought away for now and motioned for John to follow.

A short line stretched in front of them, ending at a large semicircular desk. Two elderly women sat rigidly behind it and methodically checked books in and out. Each had short white hair and a determined look on their face. The one in command of his line seemed younger than the other. Maybe it was her mannerisms, as she moved with more ease, like her joints weren't as worn down from age.

The line shortened quickly as the women did their work with the utmost efficiency.

When his turn came, Tobias stepped up to the desk. He met the librarian's eyes. She peered out from the upper part of her horn-framed glasses, which hung low on her nose.

"May I help you?" she asked.

"I'm looking for any information you may have on... ."

"Excuse me for a moment," the librarian interrupted. She looked over Tobias' shoulder at a group of boys sitting at a table behind them. "Shhh." She held her bony index finger to her mouth.

The boys looked back and stopped talking in an instant. When she looked away and back at Tobias, the boys giggled to each other—not loud enough for the librarian to hear, but loud enough to bring a silly grin to Tobias' face as he remembered the carefree ways of boys.

"I'm sorry. Can you repeat that?" she said.

Tobias cleared his throat. "We're looking for any information you may have on Zubar Island."

She looked away, recollecting. "Mildred," she said,

turning her head to the older-looking librarian to her left, "have you ever heard of a Zubar Island?"

"Zubar Island, eh?" Mildred paused with a book below the scanner. She was missing one of her two front teeth. It caused a tiny whistling sound as she spoke. "I've never heard of a Zubar Island, per se." Tobias slumped. "But zubar is the ancient Sumerian word for copper, if that's any help." She smiled with her remaining teeth. "Funny you bring that word up. It was five down in the *Globe's* crossword puzzle last month. Tricky one. Had to look it up."

Tobias smiled back and nodded his thanks. He hadn't really expected to get an answer so quickly and easily. Somewhere inside of him he felt a long, arduous fact finding mission was headed their way, but now at least there was a semblance of a clue. He exited the line to his right just as Sam reappeared from within the crowd, skipping the last few steps.

"I think I've got it," she said. A smug smile beamed across her face.

"Sam, you can't run off like that," Tobias scolded. It came out harsher than he had intended it to. While he didn't want to lecture her, he felt it was necessary. She needed to understand what the implications of her disappearing could be under different circumstances.

"Sorry about that," she said holding up a piece of paper. "This, I think, is Zubar Island on the Sea." She handed the paper to Tobias. It was a small print out of a map.

"Cyprus?"

She nodded. "That's my best guess. Zubar, as it turns out, is the Sumerian word for…"

"Copper," John volunteered with a smile on his face.

Sam whipped around like she had just been slapped.

John motioned towards the librarian who was busy checking in books. "She just told us It's not like I have that info bumping around in my head." He paused. "Or do I?"

Silently mouthing an "Oh", Sam moved on with her story. "Anyway, Cyprus can, in a roundabout way, be boiled down to Zubar Island because of the large amounts of copper ore found there."

"And Cyprus is on the Mediterranean Sea," Tobias added. "Well done, Sam." It was an impressive piece of detective work given the short amount of time—one that would hopefully shed some light on the location of the first Sign.

Sam looked pleased with her work.

"How did you figure that out, anyway?" John asked.

"There's a bank of computers over there with Internet access," Sam said, pointing.

A white sign with a blue arrow pointed down. It read: COMPUTERS – PUBLIC ACCESS. Tobias had missed that when they entered. He was too focused on getting to the librarians to realize a quick Internet search might have yielded the same results.

"There's nothing you can't find on Google," Sam said, smiling.

Tobias made another mental checkmark for her. Looks and brains. She had it all.

Now that they had a sliver of hope to go on, he made a quick call and had the Vatican arrange for a flight to Cyprus. He prayed their hunch was correct, as time would assuredly not afford them a misstep.

Chapter 10

The private jet rolled to a smooth stop on the tarmac after an uneventful flight to Cyprus. Tobias used the time to go over the recent events in his head and grab some much needed rest. The past day-and-a-half had gone by in a flash. He hoped, for the sake of the world, that they neared some answers, but something told him it wouldn't be that easy. It never was.

He dragged his weary bones to the jet's door and peered out the small circular window. Tranquility stared back at him. Activating the mechanism to his left caused the door's airtight seal to break and the door to swing out on its hinges to the side of the jet. The stairs unfolded and locked.

A relaxing blend of autumnal coolness and Mediterranean warmth greeted him. In Boston yesterday, he'd noticed the bite of winter starting to rear its ugly head. Now, at least for a moment, Tobias soaked in what the rest of the world had to offer in the otherwise dreary month of November.

He removed his trench coat and tossed it to the side before exiting the jet. He wouldn't need extra layers here beneath the invigorating sun. With both feet back on solid ground, he arched his back and raised his arms to the sky, forcefully stretching out the tiredness he knew would linger.

Sam and John soon followed him off the plane.

Tobias had gotten them to the island. That much was done, but now he was left without a direction to follow. He hoped something—anything—would present itself, but walking up to the locals with the Crux Signate in hand and asking questions wasn't what he had in mind. It would be best if they could search for the Sign unnoticed.

No sooner had Tobias begun to develop a plan of action when a disheveled man approached from their right. He pushed a cart full of what looked to be ancient Greek statues, each about two feet high. They appeared to be nothing more than cheap plastic trinkets. A mouth full of dirty teeth arched a crooked smile across the man's shiny face.

Tobias made eye contact, but the man seemed unfazed by his piercing stare. *What the hell does this guy want?* He felt the aggravation grow inside him. He had neither the time, nor patience, to deal with this right now.

"Hello, friends," the islander said. "Do not go home without one of Damon's authentic Cyprus replicas." He held one of the statues up for them to see. It lacked arms and any form of authenticity.

"We're all set," Tobias said, not breaking stride.

Damon dropped the statue on his cart. A hollow plastic sound echoed as it hit the others. He ran up next to Tobias and turned. Walking backwards with his arms extended, he begged them to stop and listen to his pitiful spiel.

Tobias adjusted his backpack and rolled his eyes. He felt like he could snap at any moment.

"Okay, okay, you do not want souvenirs. No problem. Maybe you would be interested in some…," he leaned in closer, "…companionship, then?" His brows arched to the sky. Tobias could only assume he was referring to some of the island's less prudish women.

I could knock this clown out with one punch, Tobias thought. He doubted Damon would be missed, but reason got the better of him. He pushed the slimy islander aside with a look of disgust and continued on his way.

Damon then turned his sights on Sam and gave her a wink. "Something for the lady, then?" Her face contorted in revulsion.

That's it. Tobias stopped and turned around. Harassing him was one thing, but Sam was another. Two purposeful strides, and he was in the islander's face.

"Back off." He stared, stone-faced, into Damon's eyes. "Do I look like the type of person you want to harass?" he asked, staring down at Damon. "This is your last warning." What little patience he'd had was now completely gone. At this point, Tobias needed an outlet for his frustration, and it might as well be this guy.

Damon shrunk back a few feet and held up his hands. "I apologize, but you must need something? Everyone needs something."

Tobias was seconds away from giving him another hole in his already airy head. "I need you to get away from us, for your own sake."

"Okay, okay," Damon said, holding his hands up once again, relenting. "But if you should need anything—a tour guide, directions, maybe a list of the best places to eat, just let me know. I run a special on those during the week."

Tobias stopped in his tracks. John, who followed too closely behind, bumped into him and pushed him forward. He then removed a folded twenty-dollar bill from his pocket and handed it over to the dirty native. He figured it was worth a try. "Do you know where we can find a fountain within a cave?"

Damon took the twenty and grinned. "There are many fountains on Cyprus, many indeed." He paused. "But I do not know of any fountains within a cave." His face lit up. "Of course, that is not to say that one does not exist. I will take you to Nikitari Village. The local priest there knows the island better than anyone." Damon bit his lip and looked away, appearing distraught. He thought for a moment before looking back and nodding. "Yes. Let us go to Nikitari Village." He lowered his head and mumbled, "I am sure he has forgotten by now."

Tobias wondered what he meant by that, but it didn't matter to him enough to ask.

Damon held out his hand with his palm up. His unhygienic smile once again cut across his greasy face.

"I already gave you more than enough to get us there," Tobias said. "If we arrive quickly, I may consider giving you a bonus." His lip twitched as he waited for a response. *One punch is all it would take.*

Damon nodded. "Of course. One moment, while I take care of my valuables."

Damon pushed his jalopy full of *valuables* off the tarmac and into a small, shaded alcove off to the side. He then hung a sign off his cart that read *GONE FISHING* before grabbing a walking stick from amongst his other belongings and running to a position in front of the group.

"Follow me."

Chapter 11

They followed Damon on the dusty road en route to Nikitari Village. Three hours of tedious travel drained Tobias further than he had been in a very long time. The overtired energy he felt when exiting the jet was now gone, and the exhaustion that permeated his bones felt impossible to shake.

Tobias considered having them stop and take a rest, but fate, as it were, intervened before he could make that decision.

"This," Damon said, holding his arms open, "is Nikitari Village."

Before them was a small gathering of crude huts. A fire burned in the center, surrounded by several of the villagers. The area was quiet except for a few squawking birds held within a simple metal pen to their right. Dinner, Tobias figured. He had expected more, but if the answers they sought rested here, then that was all that mattered.

The group followed Damon into the village. The low chatter all but stopped, replaced by silence and the branding stares of the entire village. Most of the eyes were trained on Damon, accompanied by the unmistakable look of anger.

"I told you to never come back," yelled a man of the cloth as he rapidly approached the group like an attack dog.

Where'd he come from? Tobias thought. It was like the priest had appeared from out of thin air.

He was a tall man, standing taller than Tobias' six-foot-two frame, but rail thin.

Damon held up his hands and backed away slowly. "I am just showing my friends here the way to your village, nothing more."

The priest stormed by and stopped inches away from Damon. He peered down his long, thin nose. The two men not only differed in stature, but also in character. The priest was forceful and confident, while the greasy Damon pitifully slithered back, as Tobias expected he would.

"I warned you the last time, you lowly slime." The priest made a fist.

Tobias didn't enjoy Damon's company, but he had brought them this far. As much as he wanted to let this go for his own enjoyment, they didn't have the time.

"I asked him to bring us," Tobias said.

The priest peered hard at Damon and clenched his jaw before turning his attention to Tobias. "I am sorry. There are no tours today." He looked back at Damon. "And you had better leave now before it is no longer an option." His eyes boiled red with anger.

The priest turned and marched back to the hut he had come from.

"We're not here for the tour," Tobias said. He hurried up next to the priest. A small distance divided them from the others. "I'm here on Church business." He rolled up his sleeve and once again revealed the Guardian's Mark.

The priest turned his attention to the Mark. Tobias waited for it to sink in, but the priest looked back up and then continued to walk away.

"Wait," Tobias said. He had a feeling it was a long shot, but he had to try. Nothing was out of the realm of possibility now.

"As I said, stranger, there are no tours today, even for those with strange markings on their arms."

"And, like I said, we didn't come for the tour." Tobias looked to the others before continuing. "We're looking for something very specific, a fountain hidden within a cave.

Our guide said you may know of it."

The priest scrutinized his unflinching expression. "And who sent you to find this fountain?"

"Like I said, we are here on Church business — a mandate from the Vatican."

The priest laughed a small laugh. "You are telling me that the Holy See sent you to Nikitari Village to find a fountain?" The priest then laughed again, this time more boisterously.

"Well, in a roundabout way, yes. We could use your help to find the Sign. It's of the utmost importance." Tobias instantly realized his poor choice of words. He meant to say fountain, not Sign, but he was too tired to filter his words.

The priest's eyes grew wide. His mouth parted with a small rush of air. Ushering Tobias closer, he scanned the villagers in his sight.

"Please, come with me. I dare not speak about such things in the open amongst all of God's creatures." The priest turned and continued his march, albeit now softer and more accepting of his new visitors.

Tobias followed the holy man towards the largest structure in the village. His team followed a short distance behind, Damon in tow.

The priest shot around. "Your services are no longer required," he yelled at Damon, somehow sensing him. "That is your very last warning. Do not make me look past my passive nature, worm."

Damon looked to Tobias for help. He shrugged. His allegiance had changed.

The greasy islander reluctantly turned around and kicked a nearby tree. He then headed back down the path away from the village and disappeared down the sloping road they had just walked along.

The priest stared angrily until he was out of sight. "I

apologize for my behavior." He signed the cross. "It is unbefitting a man of God to act in such a way, but that heathen is not welcome among us." The priest spat on the ground.

Tobias was not surprised. "What did he do?" he asked, following the priest to the hut.

"He is a thief—a scoundrel—lower than the lowest form of life." The priest spat again as if to rid himself of the words and the thought of Damon. "A man passed through our small village last year. He was on some sort of expedition. We fed him and gave him a place to rest his head for the night. He appreciated our hospitality so much that he donated a large sum of money to our village. A week later, a large portion of the money had mysteriously vanished. And our *friend* there had a new supply of cheap statues. Trust me when I say that coincidence was not to blame."

Damon was exactly the person Tobias thought him to be. He could spot an unsavory character from a mile away.

The priest motioned them inside. Tobias ducked his head under the low-hanging entry. Sam and John followed closely behind. The priest waited for them to pass and then closed the wooden door.

He swept his hand towards the aging table at the far wall. "Please, sit."

A faded green vase sat in the middle of the table with a single white flower rising gracefully from its thin glass neck.

The priest walked past the two windows and closed their rickety wood blinds. The room grew darker. But the sun, not willing to be shutout, shone through the many cracks and crevices available to it.

"I apologize for all the secretiveness," the priest said, sitting down next to Tobias. "My name is Venedictos. Most know me as Vene."

He seemed genuine enough. They shared a mutual

dislike for derelicts like Damon, so his character was sound. Tobias wanted to trust him—it would just be easier that way—though to let his guard down prematurely could be their undoing. He needed to keep a certain distance to ensure he maintained the upper hand.

"Thank you for helping us," Tobias said.

"I wish I could help you, stranger, but what you seek is as much a mystery to me as it is to you."

Tobias reached into his backpack and removed the blue book. Opening it to the drawing of the fountain, he handed it to Vene.

The priest looked over the picture. "This is what brought you here?"

"Well, that and this," Tobias said, looking over to John. John once again reached in and removed the cross that hung around his neck.

Upon seeing the defined ridge and skewed arms of the Crux, Vene bowed his head and signed the cross.

"I take it you know what that is?"

The priest raised his eyes, but kept his head bowed. "It cannot be."

"So you do know?"

Vene took a deep breath and rose to his feet. He then walked over to a pantry near the door.

If Vene was indeed their enemy, Tobias felt he would strike now, knowing they had possession of the Crux. The devil had far more than monsters at its command. Man was easily enough turned to serve his needs. Knowing this, Tobias understood the need for an extra amount of caution. His hand rested atop his gun, his thumb on the hammer.

Inside the pantry were several sagging shelves filled with used white candles of varying lengths. Below them was a rusted metal box. A slight orange tinge forced its way from beneath the oxidization.

Vene picked it up carefully and walked back to the table. He sat next to Tobias and quickly opened the top. Reaching in, he removed the container's sole content, a blue book. It was similar to the one Tobias had. In fact, it was almost identical. Fanning quickly through the pages, he arrived at a drawing.

Déjà vu set in. Tobias looked down at a black and white sketch of a cross. Its arms angled like the Crux.

"This," Vene said, pointing to the drawing. "This is what you just have just shown me, no?"

Tobias nodded. "It would appear that way." They were in the right place. There was no doubt about that now. It was nothing close to coincidence that the priest had a sketch of the Crux. Whether warranted or not, Tobias felt a minimal sense of relief. It appeared, thankfully, that this village was not a dead end and that there were actually answers to his questions out here. Cyprus was, no doubt, where they needed to be at that moment.

Vene reached into his shirt. He removed a small cross and gave it a kiss. "Father in Heaven, you being here can only mean one thing. The devil has come."

Tobias nodded again.

Be it blind luck or fate that brought them there, he was grateful that things seemed to be going their way for a change, but he knew it wouldn't remain that way for long. They couldn't waste any more time than necessary sitting there rehashing what was already known.

"This book," Vene said, pointing towards his blue book, "tells of the first of three Signs."

"As does ours," Tobias said. "That's the reason we're here. We believe the fountain is the first Sign."

The priest collected his thoughts. "There is a church deep in the Troodos Mountains. I travel there to pray when time permits. I find it relaxing." He paused. "During one of my visits, I was drawn to a certain mural on the wall. There, through what I can only assume was guidance from above, I discovered a sealed off substructure." Again, he paused. "Sometimes, when the world is especially quiet, I can hear the faint sound of trickling water down there, but I've never been able to locate its source. The Asinou Church is less than five kilometers from here. I will take you there immediately."

Vene hurried toward the door. A wash of sunlight shined through as he opened it. Tobias, John, and Sam stood and followed him out, heading for the old Byzantine church and what they hoped to be the first of the fabled Trinity Signs.

Chapter 12

Vene led them up a narrow trail along the west side of the island, farther into the Troodos Mountains. The path cut unevenly through rows of thick, well-rooted trees. The trees closest to the path bent out of the way, as if they tried to avoid the procession of man through time, but froze in mid-leap. From their right blew a warm, steady breeze that danced through the treetops to their own private song.

Left to his thoughts, Tobias found himself focusing on Sam. He worried about her mental wellbeing. He could send her home, but that would only put her back into harm's way. She was better protected by him. Plus, he realized that a break in the group dynamic now might cost them later. It was better to leave things the way they were. If the situation became worse, which he assumed it eventually would, then he would reassess and go from there.

The path eventually spilled into an open field. The Asinou Church stood alone on the mountaintop; a backdrop of lush vegetation and a blue sky helped to frame its simplistic beauty. Vene had gushed about the small, twelfth-century church during their hike. Its structure, though slightly worn, looked no more than fifty years old. The temperate climate no doubt played a large role in its preservation.

"It is one of many churches hidden amongst the trees of the Troodos Mountains," Vene said, walking closer. "It, like most of the others, is dedicated to the Virgin Mary." He again signed the cross on his forehead.

Dark wood doors broke up the monotony of brown and grey stone. An intricate web-like pattern, an artistic inlet for the sun, was carved above each entryway.

Vene removed a black skeleton key from his pocket and unlocked the door nearest to them. It begrudgingly opened with a creak. The priest pushed it aside and invited them in with a casual wave of his arm.

The artistic craftsmanship within the church was breathtaking. Well-maintained frescos decorated the walls and ceilings. It seemed like every square inch was, at some point, a blank canvas to showcase an artist's piousness. The main room's silent beauty was enriched by the multitude of paints. Men—some dressed in colorful holy robes, others wearing nothing more than simple white garb—adorned every wall.

Tobias felt like he was on stage with a thousand pairs of painted eyes waiting for the show to begin. He could swear the eyes followed him as he moved farther into the church.

"These frescos are regarded as some of the finest of their kind," Vene said, a proud smile on his face. "Very few people, outside of select historians, have looked upon their beauty with their own eyes."

Vene led them through a small archway. It, too, was covered completely in religious frescos.

The priest then stopped in front of one of the colorful walls and rummaged through his pocket. He withdrew an unsharpened pencil. With a gentle push, he fit the pencil into a miniscule hole, hidden ironically within a painted lock.

Vene removed his improvised key after a soft click. The wall swung open, revealing a waist-high opening.

"This church holds many secrets. I hope we discover another today." He removed a torch that hung to the right of the stairs. He pulled a book of matches from his pocket and lit it.

Slinking down was a short, narrowly-winding staircase that led into the hidden belly of the church. Tobias turned sideways in order to fit without scraping his shoulders. It was a confining descent he didn't care for, but one he knew needed to be made.

Vene stopped close to the bottom of the stairs and turned. "I believe the section I am about to show you is much older than the church above."

Tobias stepped off the last step and into a sizeable room. The carved-out understructure was nearly quadruple the space above. Frescos lined these walls, too, although they were more scattered and considerably more difficult to make out. They appeared to be much older. These paintings also depicted men, but only one color was used for their clothing—white. Each painted man had his right hand raised to his forehead.

Tobias took a whiff of the air. It smelled like any other basement would, musty and stale.

"Watch your step," Vene said, pointing down towards the uneven earth beneath their feet. He made his way farther into the basement, towards a rounded alcove straight ahead of them. "This is as far as I have ever ventured; however, it is not for lack of desire." He brought the torch in closer to reveal a stone wall with a large cross carved in the center.

Tobias looked at the carving and then back at John.

"The Crux," Sam volunteered. Tobias was relieved to hear her voice.

"Exactly," Vene said. "In my version of the blue book, it is written of the one true key. This key allows entry to the first Sign. The carving in the wall, the drawing in the book, and now the actual cross all lead us to this very spot, at this very moment."

It does resemble the Crux, Tobias thought. There was no doubt about that.

Tobias stepped closer to the wall and traced its outline. The carving was the depth of the actual cross and painstakingly detailed. The edges were smooth to the touch, as if they had been sanded down for a hundred years.

He turned to Vene. "What now?"

Vene shrugged. "I was hoping we would find out together."

"John," Tobias said, turning, "the Crux, please."

John removed the cross from around his neck and politely pushed his way past Sam. He handed it to Tobias. The chain slithered over the side of his hand and dangled free.

Tobias reached towards the carving but paused before fitting it in. He realized that this could be a trap. Unfortunately, he knew there was only one way to find out. As much as he disliked sidestepping caution, he realized that he didn't have much of a choice. He fit the cross carefully into the wall that bore its shape.

He looked around. Nothing happened. He then backed the cross out and tried again, this time using the other side. Again, nothing happened.

Vene's expression was one of despair.

Tobias removed the Crux from the wall, looked at it, and then handed it back to John. "There must be something in this room we're missing. Look around for anything that might help, but be careful."

Tobias knew that this could be an elaborate deception created to throw off anyone getting too close to the actual Sign. And, if that was the case, it was working to perfection.

Sam and Vene moved away and looked at the surrounding walls and ceiling. John, however, stood transfixed. He stared in silence at the carved wall. Then, as sudden as a sneeze, he thrust the Crux into the carving just like Tobias had before. The clink of metal hitting stone made the others turn in surprise. A searing white light traced the outline of the Crux and then vanished.

The ground beneath them shook. A cloud of dirt shot from the center of the room like an erupting volcano.

Sam leapt to the outer edge of the room and leaned against the wall.

Tobias coughed as dust filled his throat. "Hang on," he yelled.

Vene covered his mouth and shone the torch towards the center of the room. What was uneven earth seconds ago was now another descending staircase. Dirt fell from the edges and into the darkness below.

Moments later, the grinding stopped with a loud thud.

John removed the Crux from the wall.

"What just happened?" Tobias asked, looking down the dark hole in the earth.

John shook his head. "That was weird, man. It was like someone whispered in my ear to do that."

Tobias walked up to the wall. "What did I do wrong?"

Vene seemed to have the answer ready. "I do not believe you did anything wrong. If I had tried instead of you, I would have been met by the same results. It was not just the act of placing the cross in the wall. It was also the placer."

Of course. John was the last of the Brotherhood of the Sealed and the holder of the Crux Signate. In essence, John was a living key. The cross was just his tool. It explained why the relic was passed down within the Brotherhood. They were the only ones capable of using it.

Another tremor shook the ground. Its intensity was much greater than the previous one. Tobias turned to John. "What did you do?"

John shrugged. This time, it was not his doing.

Chapter 13

The air in the basement thickened with dirt to the point where it felt soupy. The shaking was far worse than before, and this time it seemed to come from above, rather than below. It felt like the Earth had split in two, and each side battled the other for dominance.

Tobias wiped his tearing eyes. The dirt stung and made it difficult to see. He took a few well-placed steps on his way to the base of the ascending stairs.

Another tremor hit. He tried to remain upright, but the erratic shaking proved to be too much. He lost his balance and fell.

A large piece of the ceiling broke free. It crashed inches behind Vene and kicked up another cloud of dust that completely enveloped him and extinguished the torch.

In an instant, the room's dirty air was sucked up the stairs. The fine grains of ancient dust picked at Tobias' exposed skin like a sandstorm of bees as it passed. It lasted for only seconds, but it felt like hours.

Visibility returned as the last of the dirt was vacuumed away.

Tobias checked on the rest of the team using the dwindling light from above.

Vene was frozen in place, still on his hands and knees. The ceiling fragment lay inches behind him. It was much larger than Tobias had initially thought. Thankfully for Vene, he wasn't beneath it when it fell.

Sam and John were huddled together at the far end of the room. Their hands were above their heads, and their eyes looked to the floor.

Fragments of the church's mosaic-covered walls trickled down the stairs. Several of the larger chunks rumbled past him and into the newly-opened second stairway in the center of the room. Their fall ended with a loud splash.

Tobias met eyes with Sam. "Are you hurt?"

She shook her head.

"Are you guys okay?" Tobias asked, looking over to John and then at Vene.

They both nodded.

Tobias wiped the dirt from around his eyes and spit to clear what he could of his mouth. Crossing his arms, he reached down and removed both guns.

"Stay put," he coughed. "I'm going to find out what's going on."

With grace unbefitting a man of his size, Tobias made his way up the steps. He was stunned silent when he reached the top. Instead of the church's painted ceiling, he now looked at the open sky. The stars, which seemed close enough to touch, shone like tiny, illuminated pinholes through the fading daylight.

Where the hell is the church?

He exited the stairs and swept his guns from left to right.

If he hadn't seen the Asinou Church with his own eyes, he would have had a hard time believing it had once stood there. The old stone structure, along with its precious art was gone, swept away into nothingness. Left behind were several scattered rocks from the foundation, but little else.

Tobias looked and listened. An unnatural silence abounded. It was as if the world had been hushed. Like it, too, couldn't believe what just happened.

"Are you all right up there?" Vene asked from the bottom of the stairs.

Tobias ignored him. He felt something watching him. His body tingled.

"When I did not hear you reply, I feared the worst," Vene said, exiting the stairs. He looked around in awe.

Tobias turned to tell the priest to go back down when he noticed it. Behind Vene lay a steaming crevice in the Earth's crust. It divided the ground twenty feet from where the church once stood. The gap was fifty or more feet wide, with no visible beginning or end.

A heavy cloud of steam erupted from within the chasm and rapidly cooked the air. It caused a thick fog to roll in, surrounding them like an airy tsunami.

"We must leave this place," Vene said, slowly backing away. He took a position next to Tobias. His face grew pale. His hands trembled.

Tobias shifted his sight to the priest and then back to the crevice. Something was coming.

"Please," Vene begged once again. "Being here makes my very soul want to die."

The fissure completely dematerialized as the fog solidified further. The humidity of the air made Tobias break out in sweat. Dirt-filled droplets slid down his face and into his eyes. He quickly wiped his brow.

"Tobias?" Sam yelled, still within the understructure of the recently departed church.

"Stay there, both of you." He noticed his words had no echo. "Priest, I think it's time you went back down as well."

The fog parted ahead of them as a figure cut through it.

Tobias squinted, trying to determine if his eyes were playing tricks on him. Damon, the bumbling statue salesman, hovered over the ground like a specter in the foggy air.

Damon's mouth hung open. His lips were still, yet a constant string of incoherent mutterings drifted from deep within him. His stringy arms hung limp by his sides. Cloudy, red orbs floated in place of his once brown eyes. His previously tan face was now whitewashed and morbid. Sparsely planted tendrils stood where his full head of hair once had. Yellow and decaying fingernails spiraled from his fingertips.

Vene dropped to his knees, cross in hand. He closed his eyes and bowed his head. "Our father, who art in heaven...."

Tobias looked down at the priest and then back at Damon, his guns at the ready.

Damon's head cocked back. His arms spastically rose until they were positioned straight out, forming a T-shape. The mumbling stopped.

"What's going on up there?" John yelled.

Damon whipped around in the direction of the stairs. He stopped hovering and dropped to his feet. Like a zombie, he walked towards the church's secret underbelly, one lumbering step at a time.

Dammit. Tobias fired both guns. Each bullet punctured the back of Damon's knees. The abomination stopped but stayed upright. Black ooze flowed instead of blood. Tobias realized he was nothing more than an annoyance to the skulking creature. It was after John.

Tobias fired again, this time multiple shots into Damon's back. Damon jerked forward but kept walking.

"Amen." Vene stopped praying. He rose to his feet, turned, and fled into the fog behind them.

Tobias holstered his guns and sprinted forward. He reached the aberration as it began to descend. He dropped his shoulder into its bullet-ridden back and tumbled down the short flight of stairs. They reached the bottom and fell from the last step. Momentum carried his head into the side wall. It brought stars to his eyes. Seconds later they came to rest on the dirt floor.

"Is that the statue salesman?" John asked.

Damon burst from the ground and flung Tobias into the low ceiling. Tobias crashed back to the ground with a thud. Pain ripped down his spine. "Down the second stairway. Quickly!" Tobias shouted, wiping dirt from his eyes. His whole body ached. It felt like he'd broken a rib.

Sam and John hurried down the stairs as told.

Damon was already halfway down before Tobias could get to his feet.

Tobias rushed to the stairs and felt his way down. He jumped off what he assumed was the last step and into shin-high water.

"Sam! John!"

Sam screamed. Damon had apparently gotten to them first.

"Tobias!" Sam yelled. "Hurry! He's got John."

Blinded by the dark, Tobias felt his way along the wall. He sloshed through the water as rapidly as he could. John's muffled gasps came from somewhere up ahead.

The situation was spiraling out of control.

Tobias soon reached the three of them. His eyes had acclimated to the tiny amount of light enough to see John held off the ground by his throat. Damon was choking the life out of him.

Tobias reached up and tried to pry Damon away. Damon's free arm, like a retracted tree branch, swung around. The blow knocked Tobias back into the wall. He slid down the damp rock and into the pool of dark water. Dazed and wet, he blinked, trying to regain his senses. The slime they knew as Damon was no longer. Whatever stood in front of him now was far more powerful.

Another loud splash came from the direction of the stairs.

"Are you all right?" Vene asked.

Tobias moaned and grabbed his bruised chest. "I've had

better days, priest." He thought for sure Vene had fled.

Two quick snaps, and the cave filled with an eerie green hue. He watched as Vene snapped and tossed several more glow sticks around the room. They provided enough light to discern the true severity of the situation. John was close to suffocating.

Before Tobias could stand, something unexpected happened. He watched as Sam's fright transformed into rage in the ambient green of the glow sticks. It was like a second, more aggressive personality had shown itself. She darted towards Damon in a mad rush. With the nimbleness of an Olympic gymnast, she dropped to her knees and ducked beneath his grabbing hand.

Crouched below him, she picked up a jagged rock from the muddy ground. She eyed it for a moment as if second guessing herself before grasping the improvised dagger firmly in her hand. The first attempt wasn't hard enough, merely breaking Damon's skin. The second, however, got the job done with precision. She shoved the makeshift stone dagger deep into the base of Damon's spine. The thin edge sliced through his flesh and came to rest between the sacrum and the lower lumbar vertebrae.

No longer having impulses travel to the brain, Damon dropped John from his grasp and then fell to his knees. John fell to the ground like a rag doll, limp.

Sam released her grasp on the stone. A small amount of black ooze stained her hand. She dragged John off to the side and immediately started to perform CPR.

Tobias stood and walked over to the partially crippled aberration. It twitched spastically on the wet ground. He picked up a large, jagged rock from the ground and held it high. He then forcefully rammed it down on Damon's head. The hollow sound of a cracking egg echoed throughout the cave. Again, he brought the stone down. The gap in

Damon's skull opened wider. Tobias raised it above his head for a third strike, but it wasn't needed. Damon's mangled body stopped convulsing in the murky water. Black liquid oozed from within his broken cranium.

Vene splashed through the water towards them. "Sorry for my sudden disappearance." He was out of breath. "There is an abandoned military base near here. I went to find weapons, but it had long been stripped of anything valuable. The glow sticks were all I could find."

"The light ended up being more valuable than any weapon would have been," Tobias said. "I'm glad you came back."

Sam continued her CPR. "One one-thousand, two one-thousand, three one-thousand." She pushed down below John's diaphragm rhythmically. At the end of each sequence, she took a deep breath. Pinching his nose shut, she breathed oxygen into his deflated lungs. She then put her cheek to John's mouth and felt for any hint of life.

Tobias looked on in despair as Sam repeated the process. She did her routine three more times before John's body suddenly jerked up and gasped for air.

Tobias kneeled on the wet mound of dirt beside John and braced his back. Sam's face beamed with happiness. She threw her arms around John.

"Careful," John said, voice raspy and close to a whisper. He brought his hand up to his bruised throat. "You don't want to take back the air you just gave me." He painfully smiled before succumbing to a small coughing fit.

Sam laughed out of happiness with a rogue tear in her eye.

"Glad to have you back," Tobias said, rising to his feet. "Humanity came awfully close to ending right there." He lowered his hand and helped John up off the ground.

Vene stared at the motionless body of their attacker. "I

fear the devil will stop at nothing until…," the priest cut himself off abruptly.

"Until I'm dead," John finished, rubbing his neck.

Vene nodded.

"It's all right. I realize now that I can't change that. But we sure as hell can fight it."

Tobias grinned and patted him on the back. The doubts he'd had about John had just been squelched. Apparently, John would now stand up to what wanted him dead. He would not let the devil win without a fight, and it was a fight that Tobias would give it.

"And where," Tobias said, looking at Sam, "did all that come from?"

Sam looked back. A smile beamed across her face. "I don't know, really. I guess I was just tired of seeing people suffer when I could do something to change it. Tired of letting the fear of what could happen keep me away from doing what I needed to."

Sam was proving more useful than Tobias could have ever imagined. He went to tell her just that, but the sound of Vene stumbling through the water stole his attention. He looked toward the priest.

There, illuminated in the eerie green hue, rested a small fountain on a raised patch of dirt. A thin moat of murky water surrounded it.

With everything that just went down, the fountain went unnoticed. Tobias reached into his pack and removed the blue book Reverend O'Brien had given him. With a quick fan, he opened to the marked page and held it out at arm's length. The drawing on the page mimicked the fountain that stood only feet away. The only difference that he could see was the shining light depicted in the book that was absent from the room.

Chapter 14

Tobias stepped over a small moat of water and took his place beside the rest of the group.

The fountain appeared to be carved from a single block of grey stone. It resembled a large goblet around three feet in height. A continuous stream of crystal clear water overflowed its rounded edges and fell into a small pool below.

Tobias handed the blue book to Sam. "Can you see if there are any instructions to this thing?"

She grabbed the book and turned to the page with the drawing. She looked over the pages for a moment. "It doesn't say all that much, really." She read the same passage as before. "Just mentions the ancestry of the Sealed."

"Nothing on its activation?"

Sam checked again and shook her head.

Tobias was afraid of that. They'd found the Sign, but had no idea how to use it.

"All these years," Vene said, standing in awe before the Sign. "All these many years this lay in wait right beneath my feet." He reached out with his right hand, but hesitated, pulling it back before touching the water.

Tobias surveyed the rest of the room. It, too, looked to be very old like the cavern overhead but had stark, damp walls with no form of noticeable art. He figured the space above must be an entryway, with the Crux being the material key, and John being the spiritual one. And, if that were true, then the Asinou Church, he surmised, must have been built as a landmark for those with enough information to find their way—a sort of sign post. But even if someone was to find their way to the basement, as Vene had, they wouldn't be able to access the Sign beneath it.

"I may have something," Sam blurted.

She held the blue book open a couple or more pages beyond the drawing. Words ran across the left page, while nothing was on the right.

"There was one part of the book," she said, skimming the line with her finger, "that I couldn't read because the words were too faded, but now they look like they were just written." She looked up, confused. "It's like someone just rewrote them."

"What does it say?" John asked, turning around from the fountain.

Sam read it again to herself before answering. "Roughly translated it says, *to cleanse the soul of original sin is the path that one must follow to be reborn.*" She shook her head. "Or something along those lines. Again, I'm no expert."

Vene remained eerily mesmerized at the Sign. "To cleanse a soul of original sin, one must be baptized in the eyes of the Lord." His rippled reflection stared back at him.

John turned to the priest. "But I was baptized."

"While that may be true," Vene said, still captivated, "I have a feeling this water is unlike any other."

Tobias peered at the priest through the corners of his eyes. "Something doesn't feel right," he said. "What do the words, *'to be reborn'*, mean?" Sign or no Sign, he wasn't about to take any undue risks, especially at John's expense.

"I believe it to have more of a spiritual meaning than physical," the priest answered. "Once baptized, John will be free from all sin. For the briefest of moments, he will be untainted by the world around him. He will, in essence, be reborn." Vene turned to face John. "If you wish, I can perform the baptism."

John nodded. "Let's get this over with. What do I need

to do?"

"Please," Vene said, sweeping his hand at the Sign and cuffing his sleeves, "if you would kneel before the fountain."

"Hold on," Tobias quipped. "Are you sure about this?" He feared the wrong move could prove fatal.

"I am not sure, no," Vene said, "but I see no other solution presenting itself."

The priest was right. It just felt like they were risking too much. Then again, this whole journey was one giant risk, and this was nothing more than a part of the larger picture. Tobias didn't like it, but he realized there were no alternatives.

He nodded for them to continue.

John slowly went down to one knee. After steadying himself on the uneven ground, he lowered his second knee and faced the flowing water.

Vene gently raised John's chin, tilting his head back so that his forehead was directed towards the ceiling. Vene then took a deep breath and closed his eyes. Slowly, almost hesitantly, he plunged his hands into the fountain. The shimmering surface enveloped his touch and sent ripples to the edges. More of the water slopped into the pool below with a splash. He then paused.

"Is something the matter, priest?" Tobias asked.

"It is nothing," Vene said, shaking his head. "All the excitement must have dulled my senses." He nervously smirked and looked back at the shimmering water. "It is strange, though. I cannot feel the water."

Tobias looked at the rock chalice. Water clearly still flowed over its edges.

"I am not crazy," Vene said. "Come and see for yourself."

Tobias walked over and stood next to John. He looked down at the water. He now understood why the priest's stare was unrelenting. The water had a hypnotic quality to it. The ripples seemed to carry the unspoken words of the fountain to his mind, pleading with him to interact. Tobias shook the feeling and rolled up his sleeve. Decisively, he plunged his hand in. *What the hell?*

"See what I mean?" Vene said.

He now understood what the priest had felt, or actually hadn't felt.

"This defies logic." Tobias said.

Vene laughed. "Logic and faith rarely see eye-to-eye, my friend."

His hand was clearly still submerged, yet he felt nothing. Staring, absorbed in thought, he forgot about John.

"Are we going to do this, man, or can I get up?" John asked. "My knees are starting to hurt."

Tobias removed his hands and backed up. "Sorry about that."

With his hand up in front of his face, Tobias watched the water drip down his arm. He still couldn't feel it. He wiped his hand on his jacket. No wet spot formed.

This keeps getting stranger by the minute.

Vene stepped forward and proceeded with the improvised ceremony. Cupping a small amount of the water in his hand, he slowly craned it over John's uplifted forehead.

"John, will you renounce Satan and all that is evil?"

Tobias left the irony of the statement alone.

"Yes," John said.

"Then I baptize you in the Name of the Father, and of the Son, and of the Holy Spirit."

Vene allowed a few droplets to slip over the side of his palm and onto John's forehead.

John cried out in pain the instant the drops hit his skin. He fell to his side on the muddy ground and writhed in agony. A burning white scar appeared on his forehead where the drop hit.

Sam dropped the book and knelt beside him. She reached out to help, but a searing heat pushed her away. That same heat forced Tobias and Vene to retreat as well. But almost as quickly as it began, it ended. John stopped moving and lay motionless on the dirty ground. Short, raspy breaths escaped his lungs.

The sound of running water ceased and cast them into a nervous silence. The fountain had dried up in an instant. It was as if all the water evaporated at once, leaving no trace of its existence.

A hazy white outline traced the entirety of John's figure. He then rose from the ground, lifted into the air by some unforeseen force. His arms and legs dangled over the sides of some invisible, uplifting hand.

John, surrounded by the white aura, rose until he reached the top of the Sign. Hovering there, dangled like a puppet, he completed the picture in the blue book. John was the missing light.

As the moment approached surreal, the blinding light diminished, and John floated back to the ground, placed gently on his feet. His mouth was shut, and his eyes were closed. Tobias' first instinct was to reach out for him, but he thought better of it. The glow still remained. There was no telling what it might do to anyone but John.

The group remained as they were, on their knees in awe.

Another few seconds passed before John's eyes shot open. The white haze surrounding him diffused into the artificial green light of the glow sticks. The wound on his head had vanished as if it was never there.

"It's done," John said suddenly, looking blankly out into space. "The first Sign is complete."

"How do you know?" Tobias asked.

"I just do." He paused. "Whatever it is, it's now a part of me. I can feel it in me. It's a weird feeling, man." He laughed. "Very weird, but loving at the same time. I really can't explain it."

The situation left Tobias a bit unnerved. What if he made a mistake?

One thing was for sure. Tobias was going to need help. What they faced was the devil at its weakest. Possession of a mortal man was like playing with a puppet. It was toying with them, like a child holding a magnifying glass over an unsuspecting ant. Tobias had the skills to defend John. If it came down to it, he would give his life to ensure that John's continued, but he knew this time was different. He could feel it in his bones. Something was brewing within the shadows of the world—something he couldn't defeat on his own.

Tobias had made certain acquaintances over the years. Two of those, in particular, stood out in his mind.

"Priest," Tobias said, looking at Vene. "I need you to do something for me."

Vene nodded for Tobias to continue.

"I need to go somewhere, but I can't risk taking you or Sam with me. I'm going to have the Vatican send transport for the two of you back to the nearest safe house."

Vene nodded. "And John?"

It would be easier, and ultimately much safer, to send John to the safe house as well, but Tobias couldn't risk being away from him for even a minute. He knew the devil would be waiting for the perfect opportunity to strike.

"John will come with me."

Chapter 15

Tobias pushed open the dented metal door of Hathaway's Machine Shop and stepped into its dimly lit, grimy interior. An unexpected sense of nostalgia washed over him. It was just as he remembered it. Overhead were two long rows of fluorescent lights, more than half of them burned out. A few of the lights' casings were open as if someone—Rupert, he assumed—had begun to change them and then got distracted.

The shop was a mess, with its oil-stained concrete floor and random pieces of cut metal tossed about, but Tobias had seen it look much worse. That was years ago, though, and things were different then. He didn't know what to expect this time around. He wondered if the people he left as friends now considered him an enemy. Deep down, he knew their divorce wasn't his fault, But could he have done more was a question that frequented his mind.

From the far right corner of the shop arched a fiery plume of sparks, accompanied by the sounds of grinding metal. He motioned for John to stay put near the entrance. It would be safer for him there until he could assess the situation. At this point, he wasn't going to take anything for granted.

Like a jungle cat stalking its prey, Tobias crept silently through a small maze of scrap metal. Some of the piles reached well over his head, obstructing his view, but he knew where he was going.

The sparks stopped. The shop became eerily silent in an instant.

He heard muted shuffling from his right. It was nearly

impossible to make out anything from the shadows. The hairs on the back of his neck stood tall. Someone was trying, but failing, to sneak up behind him.

Going on instincts, despite an urge to resist, Tobias spun around and dropped to one knee, barely avoiding the muscular hand sweeping towards him.

Tobias punched. The massive figure groaned in agony and dropped to his knees. It was at that moment Tobias realized his mistake. He had just punched Rupert in the balls. *Oh crap.*

A moment of uncomfortable silence passed before Rupert stood back up to his full, towering height. At six-foot-seven and three hundred and ten pounds the man was not someone to take lightly. His freshly shaved scalp reflected the crude lights overhead. To offset the lack of hair on his head, Rupert grew a coarse, bushy beard that began at his sideburns and filled in the rest of his sculpted face. His bright green cat eyes punctuated his determined, pissed off stare.

Rupert took a step towards Tobias. Tobias tensed up. *Here it comes.*

In that instant, when Tobias feared the worst, Rupert began to laugh. Tobias looked on, confused. If someone had punched him in the nuts, even accidentally, the last thing Tobias would do is laugh. But Rupert was laughing, hard and loud. It soon became infectious, as Tobias, too, began to laugh. While he didn't find the humor in the situation, he nervously followed Rupert's lead.

Before he could react, Rupert reached out and captured Tobias between his giant, muscular arms. Tobias' limbs flailed about. The air rushed from his lungs like a quickly deflating balloon.

"Damn good to see you, Tobias," Rupert exclaimed in his deep baritone voice.

A few gasps escaped Tobias in place of words. His depleted lungs were unable to muster anything more.

John came running from the door and stopped as he came upon the two men. He stared in awe at the mass of man that now held Tobias.

Rupert released his grasp and held Tobias at arm's length. Tobias reached up to his now sore chest. Out of breath, he held up his index finger and signaled for Rupert to let him regain his composure.

"It's good to see you too, old friend," Tobias said. He coughed a few times, half-expecting to see blood. "This is John." He pointed.

Rupert nodded with a grin. "How long has it been, Tobias?"

Tobias rubbed his chest. "About four years, give or take."

Rupert seemed genuinely happy to see him. It helped remove some of the doubt in Tobias' mind. He considered very few people to be friends. His line of work didn't allow for it. Rupert was different. Tobias had saved his life once. Damn near got himself killed in the process, but it was something Rupert never forgot. Tobias thought maybe the painful split from Tia would have clouded those memories, but he was glad to see that wasn't the case.

"Listen, big fella. I'm sorry about that whole… ." He motioned towards Rupert's crotch, but his apology was cut short.

"No need for apologies." Rupert threw one of his massive arms around his shoulders and led him through the scrap and over to the workbench a few feet away. "Man, it's good to see you."

On the bench, held firmly within the grasp of two vices, was an exquisite sword. Tobias recognized the blade instantly. He looked at Rupert. "Hey, isn't that… ?"

117

A smile cut Rupert's face. "Yup." The sword belonged to his ex-wife, Tia. It was one from a twin set of blades handcrafted by Rupert many years ago. They were his finest work.

"But I thought you two split?"

"It's a long story, Tobias." Rupert said, "but it has a happy ending. A lot can change in four years, you know." He smiled.

Apparently. This was going a lot smoother than he had anticipated. A small sense of relief allowed him to back down his guard for the time being. He knew he was safe here.

"Tobias?" A familiar female voice chirped from behind.

He spun around and was greeted by a giant wet kiss on the lips. Tia was never one to beat around the bush.

"You're a sight for sore eyes, sweetie," she said.

A glowing white smile of perfect teeth beamed across her face. She was average height, but far from average. She was one of the few women on the planet that could actually pull off the giant pigtails that hung from either side of her head. Her body was rock solid, a gift from genetically superior parents and not from extensive exercise.

He glanced down at her taped hands.

"I was just getting in a few rounds while the old man sharpened my blade."

Tia walked over to Rupert and gave him a big kiss. She gently stroked his bushy cheek while looking into his eyes and then slapped him hard. Rupert sneered and then gave her a quick pat on her perfectly toned butt. She looked towards Tobias' bandaged hand, but didn't question it. The Hell Hound's work, while no longer throbbing in pain, was still evident by the small bloody patch of gauze Sam had placed over the stitches.

"I can't tell you how good it is to see you," Tia said.

"What brings you out this way to see little old us?"

"What, I can't stop by to visit friends?" He was overjoyed to still be able to call them that.

Tobias rubbed his chest again. Rupert didn't know his own strength.

"The art of deception isn't your strong point, honey." Tia smiled and then shot a glance at John. "I don't believe we've met."

"This is John," Rupert offered. "Tobias' friend."

She grinned. "Then you're a friend of ours."

John smiled.

"Listen, before we get into why I'm here, can we discuss you two for a minute?"

Rupert and Tia looked into each other's eyes. If one was to look at them for only this moment, they would be fooled into believing these were passive people. Nothing could be further from the truth. Each of them could disarm a small army in a matter of minutes. Together they were next to unstoppable, and that was exactly what Tobias needed.

The last time he'd seen them they were going through a painful divorce. Neither of them wanted to see the other. Words were exchanged in front of Tobias that made even him cringe. Eventually, it became so uncomfortable that he left the two of them, and their friendships, behind. His life was complicated enough. Now he stood before the lovebirds he wanted to remember and not the hateful people he chose to forget.

"I know it must seem strange," Rupert said. "The last time you saw us we wanted each other dead. If it wasn't for you," he paused and looked lovingly at Tia, "well, that may have happened."

"If it wasn't for me?"

Tia gave Rupert a loving smile. "We just kind of found each other all over again," she said, giving him another kiss.

"After you disappeared, we realized it was because of us. We put you in a tough spot, hon. The fact that you kept trying to fix us despite the crap we were pulling really made us think. If you loved us enough to try, then we owed it to you to do the same. You know what they say. Absence makes the heart grow fonder. Your absence gave us something to start talking about. And, luckily for us, the talking didn't stop. We talked our way out of divorce and back into each other's hearts, as sappy as that sounds."

Tobias was genuinely happy to see them together again. They were meant for each other in every way possible. The fact that they were together also made his job of rounding each of them up much easier. Now all he needed to do was convince them to risk their lives for the good of humanity. Before Tobias could get a word out, Rupert spoke. "We're in."

"But I didn't say anything yet."

"It doesn't matter, hon." Tia said. "We're in. Now why don't you fill us in on all the details?" She arched her left eyebrow and smiled the sweetest of smiles.

Tobias waited fifteen minutes while the dynamic duo packed their weapons of choice.

Tia was the first out of the shop. She had removed the sword from the workbench, along with its twin, and sheathed them both. Tobias knew the swords' beauty was a deception that masked their deadly accuracy once wielded in her hands. The swords were merely extensions of her power. Mastering any form of martial arts she could find, Tia had become one of the most deadly combatants on the planet.

Rupert lumbered out the door a minute later, locking it behind him. He dropped two hockey-sized duffle bags by his side. A metallic clink sounded when the bags hit the pavement. His weapons of choice were less subtle and more explosive. His trademark weapon was one based on his trade—a giant graphite mallet, three feet long, that he carried in his right hand. He used it to smash anything that got in his way.

"What's with your friend?" Rupert asked, looking over Tobias' shoulder.

John, who up until a minute before was fine, swayed catatonically. A continuous, but very soft murmur flowed through his slightly parted, quivering lips.

Something was happening to John—something Tobias couldn't explain.

Chapter 16

Tobias walked past the old rusting gas pumps of the abandoned truck stop and up to the diner's entrance. Above the door hung the remaining white letters of the word diner, *I* and *R*, the rest of the letters long since gone. With a casual nudge, Tobias pushed open the decrepit glass door of the safe house. He'd been here before, a few years back. The Vatican had many of these places scattered throughout the globe. They were bastions of absolute refuge and known only by a select group of people.

The shifting wood of the doorframe displaced a small cloud of dust that wafted across Tobias' face as he entered, causing him to sneeze.

"Bless you, hon," Tia said.

He thanked her with a smile.

Time had not been kind to the interior. The old black-and-white checkered linoleum floor beneath his feet was covered with caked-on grime. Variously-sized pieces of broken glass plates and bowls littered the ground like delicate landmines. The shards stood as reminders that life had once been there, but had long since departed for greener pastures. Or, at least, that's what it was made to look like.

A thick coating of dust covered what used to be the diner's counter. One stool remained as a sentry, affixed to its anchor in the rickety floor. A slice ran the length of its blue cushion, revealing its inner cotton padding, which had yellowed over time. It was all part of the illusion.

Tobias made his way behind the old counter and stood in front of a dusty, broken-down register. He punched in a six-digit code on the large, and surprisingly clean, circular buttons, followed by the quick tug of the register's metal arm. Satisfied, he walked back to the rest of the group and waited.

Before they could ask, a loud grinding echoed from within the walls. It lasted no more than five seconds before it stopped. A loud click followed soon after, and the door leading to the kitchen area swung open.

Tobias took hold of John's shoulder and guided him forward. John's condition—whatever it was—hadn't worsened during their trip. For that, Tobias was thankful. He wondered, though, how long it would last and, more importantly, what he could do to fix it.

"This way," he said to Rupert and Tia.

They walked behind the counter and proceeded through the newly opened door and into the back.

The back room mirrored the front for thickness in dust.

Having reached the back wall of the old building, Tobias stopped at a tarnished metal square on the floor. He waved the married couple in closer until they all stood grouped together. Rupert made the small space seem even smaller. Looking up to his right, Tobias gave the hidden surveillance camera a quick nod. Four metal gates rose from the ground and surrounded the group, stopping when they reached waist height. Another grinding sound, and the floor they stood on began to descend into the bowels of the old building.

"I wasn't expecting that," Rupert said, looking up at the disappearing light of the old kitchen.

Tobias grinned. The church had many tricks up its proverbial sleeve. The amount of money it had scattered throughout the world was staggering. Generations-old wealth mixed with present-day collections to form an impressive financial portfolio that would make even the wealthiest oil sultans envious. Nothing was out of reach that had a price tag, and those things that didn't have a price were acquired by other means. The Vatican constantly preached of dwindling bank accounts, but Tobias knew it was nothing more than a public ruse. Money was never an object, nor would it ever be.

They slowly descended for another fifteen seconds before stopping with a jolt. The metal bars lowered and disappeared from sight. As they exited, the wall in front of them rolled to the right and revealed a brightly-lit, barren room. Tobias guided John forward with Rupert and Tia in tow. No sooner had they passed through than the door rolled shut behind them. In an instant, the room went completely dark.

"What the...?" Rupert said.

None of it worried Tobias, though. He knew it was all part of the Vatican's overzealous security measures. He looked over his shoulder, not in an attempt to see, but to direct his voice towards Rupert. "Can you hold John for a minute?"

He heard Rupert's large hand feel around until securing John's shoulder. Tobias then let go. With nothing to obstruct his path, he walked towards the wall without fear of tripping. A click echoed through the room, and a small, glowing instrument rose from the ground to his right. This part always seemed like overkill to him, especially since the surveillance camera saw them get on the elevator, but he knew it was better to be safe than sorry, especially with human possession being one of the devil's tricks.

As the instrument neared him, a thin, gangly arm extended from the rear of the device. It was a retinal scanner. He leaned into it as he had done in the past. A blue outline traced his head, both up and down and side to side, followed by a muted beep.

A soothing female voice poured from hidden speakers.

"Tobias Ramsey. Verified."

"What the hell was that thing?" Rupert asked from somewhere behind him in the dark.

"That's where the collection money goes from Mass."

Rupert laughed. Tobias wasn't joking.

They didn't have to wait long before the wall slid aside, revealing the unexpected.

"Cardinal," Tobias said in surprise. He thought another call to Cardinal Rathady might be in order, but he never expected him to come out to the field. While Rathady was not the run-of-the-mill Cardinal and liked to roll up his sleeves, this kind of act was never seen amongst the higher order. They had people for this kind of thing. Tobias had expected to see one of the safe house keepers.

Cardinal Rathady met Tobias' outstretched hand and grasped it firmly with both of his.

Tobias turned around. "These are my two closest friends, Ru... ."

"Rupert and Tia," the Cardinal interjected. "They need no introduction, Tobias. Their selfless work for the Church in the past by your side has earned them, at the very least, recognition." Cardinal Rathady smiled.

Tobias stood, surprised. "Well then, Rupert, Tia, this is Cardinal Rathady."

"Pleased to meet you, Cardinal," Rupert said.

Tia smiled flirtatiously, obviously catching Rathady off-guard. The holy man blushed. It became difficult to distinguish between his face and the red robes he wore. She always found a game in the tougher men, especially those sworn to a life of celibacy. She could disarm even the most proper of them with only the bat of her eyes.

"Did Sam and Vene make it here ok?" Tobias asked.

The Cardinal nodded. "Yes, Tobias. They are in the main room."

John swayed in place with Rupert's hand still firmly planted on his back.

"Cardinal, this is John, the last of the Brotherhood of the Sealed."

Rathady's his eyes widened. "Is he all right?" He took a step back.

"Honestly, I don't know. The first Trinity Sign did something to him."

"I think it best we show him to a bed," the Cardinal said, "and hopefully let whatever is affecting him run its course."

Tobias hoped it would be that simple. He realized that they were stuck in a holding pattern, waiting for the next clue to present itself. That is, if there was a next clue at all. It was a maddening game of hurry up and wait.

With a wave of his hand, the Cardinal motioned for them to follow. He led them through a thick steel door which slid open as they approached, like something out of a science fiction movie.

"Tobias," Sam said, running over and flinging her arms around him. "I was so worried."

A warming aura emanated from her and filtered deep into his body. He felt rejuvenated simply by her touch.

Tia stood behind them, scowling.

"I'm glad you made it here safely," Tobias said.

Cardinal Rathady led John into the small alcove off to their left.

"What's wrong with John?" Sam said.

Tobias shrugged. "Something must have happened when he activated the first Trinity Sign. He appears to be fine, just kind of zoned-out. He keeps mumbling something, but I have no idea what."

Sam nodded and then directed her attention up at the towering Rupert. Her eyes bulged at the sight of the behemoth.

"Sam, these are my friends, Rupert and Tia."

Rupert dropped his bags on the ground and reached out. Her tiny hand became lost in a blanket of calloused flesh. "Pleased to meet you," he said.

"You too," she said slowly.

Sam shifted her attention to Tia, who was eyeing her up and down. Sam held her hand out, but Tia kept her distance. She just gave a quick nod. Sam awkwardly retracted her hand and backed away a few steps.

Tobias glanced back at Tia. She shrugged with the slightest of grins on her face. She knew what she was doing. Tia had always been protective of him, especially when it came to the pretty girls. Although her heart was with Rupert, Tia's sisterly love for Tobias was just as strong. It was enough to keep her cattiness ever present.

"Where's Vene?" Tobias asked. He hoped maybe the priest from Cyprus had been able to find something in his absence.

Rathady waved for them to follow. He led them through another door and into a larger main room. Vene sat on a metal chair with a notepad on his lap. He had a well-gnawed pencil in his hand and an intense look plastered across his face. Several open books, some large and some small, were strewn about the table. He looked like a college student cramming for finals.

"Hello again, priest," Tobias said, startling Vene from his concentration.

Vene stood from the chair. The notepad slipped from his lap and onto the floor. Its pages lay fanned open like a winning hand of poker. He removed the pencil from his mouth and put it behind his ear. Looking past Tobias, his eyes grew wide at the hulking sight of Rupert. He then looked over to Tia, who winked.

"I have been attempting to find any information that

may help us locate the second Sign," Vene said, "but so far it has been a lesson in futility. How am I to find that which does not exist?"

"I have a feeling John has the answers we need," Tobias said. "Something's going on with him." He just had no idea how long it would take.

Shifting his attention from Tobias, Vene tilted his ear towards John, who now lay down on a bed within the alcove. The mutterings had become slightly louder since they arrived, now more of an understandable whisper than simple a sound. Whether it was the acoustics of the enclosed bunker they were now in or something else remained to be seen. It was apparently enough of an audible increase for Vene to pick up something he recognized. He walked over to the bedroom with a purposeful stride, passing the group in a blur. Bending down, he leaned in close to John's barely parted lips. His eyes moved from side to side as he collected the words.

"It's Latin, I believe," Vene said, picking up a nearby piece of paper and removed the pencil from behind his ear.

"I think so, too," Rathady said from behind the group. "It was too faint to tell before."

Vene listened for a full minute. "Three repeating sentences, if I am not mistaken." He feverishly scribbled down the words.

"What is it?" Tobias asked.

Vene held up his index finger, signaling that he needed more time. He checked the three Latin lines scribbled down on the paper and shook his head. Scribbling out the second line, he rewrote it and then reread all of them again. A slight nod gave Tobias hope.

"It appears to be some form of riddle, if I am not mistaken." Vene peered down at the paper and started to read the lines aloud. *"Amongst sand and sun the Sign awaits.*

The watcher of the three holds within it the path. The touch of the Sealed shall reveal that which is not."

Tobias brought his index and middle fingers up to the bridge of his nose and tried to rub out a strengthening headache while the rest of the group stood in silence.

"Aren't riddles supposed to rhyme?" Rupert asked.

"Apparently not, sweetie," Tia said, leaning up against him.

Tobias took a position behind Vene and looked at his scribbles. "Are you sure that's the correct translation?"

Vene nodded. "I am certain of it."

It baffled Tobias why he needed to not only hunt for the damn Signs but also solve stupidly perplexing riddles while doing so. It had been too long since the devil's last attack. They had taken themselves off the map the best they could, but it wouldn't last forever. Sooner or later, they'd have another run-in. With the Vatican unsure just how powerful the devil had grown, Tobias couldn't help but feel that everything they were doing right now was all for naught. He couldn't let the group sense his frustration, though. Hope and faith were two things they still had on their side.

"Well then," Tobias said. "I guess we need to figure out what John is trying to tell us."

Chapter 17

Aside from being led in, John hadn't moved since arriving at the safe house. He lay motionless atop the bed. The thin grey blanket covering him rose and fell with each breath.

Tobias sat across from him in silence. He wondered if John was aware of what was happening. It seemed like he might be, but Tobias couldn't be sure if it was misplaced optimism on his part. Regardless, he doubted that any of it was coincidence. The fact that his mutterings stopped only after Vene translated them seemed preordained in some way, like it was all part of some master plan. It was as if John understood that he gave them what he needed to, even though he was still in the trance.

Tobias couldn't help but feel bad for John. In less than twenty-four hours John had been jolted out of his life of relative normality and had been thrust into the role of Savior of Man. The fate of humanity rested in his hands, and he had no say in that matter. That, alone, was enough to shut down anyone for good, let alone an alcoholic deadbeat.

"You better come take a look at this," Rupert said, startling Tobias back from his thoughts.

The big man sat in front of the LCD TV that hung on the far wall in the main room.

Tobias swung his feet around in the chair, stood, and headed out of the smallish bedroom. He gave one final look over his shoulder to make sure John would be all right.

Tia sat on the arm of Rupert's cushiony chair and stared at the screen.

Vene and Rathady sat engaged in a heated, but friendly,

debate. The table between them was littered with opened books and crumpled pieces of paper.

Tobias glanced over at Sam. She sat quietly in the back of the room with a cup of coffee in her hands. She was nestled on a padded bench and had her knees up to her chin. She shot him a sincere, yet tired, smile before taking a careful sip from the mug. This woman, who he had known for less than two days, had a way of lighting up his soul. Her innocence helped to fortify his belief in what they were trying to accomplish. There were millions more just like her, albeit far less beautiful in his eyes.

The ultrathin television display that hung on the wall was tuned into the news and showed a passing aerial shot. Sections of the hilly terrain below were blacked out by the shadow of a helicopter as it hovered. The cameraman kept his lens focused on the centerpiece to the current news story—a giant fissure that split the ground below them. Several trucks could be seen parked, and dwarfed, along its edge. Red steam seeped from the open gap and into the waiting air. Below the image, a stationary tagline read: *San Paulo Earthquake?*

Tobias picked up the remote and hit a blue button. The blinking mute icon disappeared from the lower right corner, and the TV's volume engaged.

The newscaster's monotone voice spit from the speakers, "...that San Paulo has experienced a tremendous earthquake. Its cause is thought to be a shift in the tectonic plates deep beneath the ground. What you are now viewing appears to be an enormous crack in the Earth's crust. We are being told that the red cloud emanating from within the gap is what scientists refer to as Magmatic Steam. Until now, it was only theorized to exist."

He flipped the TV back onto mute. *That's not good.*

"That is like the crevice that appeared on Cyprus," Vene

said, looking up from his debate with Rathady.

Tobias had hoped the incident was local, relating to John being there at the time. Now he feared his estimations fell far short. The devil's strength was increasing and apparently much farther reaching than he thought. The imaginary countdown clock in his head just sped up.

Placing the remote back on the armrest, he walked over to the two men of the cloth. They sat, divided by the metal table and their differing opinions.

Tobias eyed them and the open books. "Have you found anything?"

"Nothing of substance," the Cardinal replied.

Vene shook his head. "I beg to differ." He cursed the Cardinal with his eyes.

The Cardinal looked disdainfully at Vene and huffed just enough to be heard.

Tobias looked at Vene. "You think you have something?"

Vene flipped through some pages of a thick, red book that lay on the table in front of him.

"We were debating the first line John spoke: *Amongst sand and sun the Sign awaits*. I do not believe it to be a riddle, but more like a map of words."

Tobias nodded for him to continue, but Cardinal Rathady chimed in, stirring their debate once again. "I just do not think the Brotherhood of the Sealed would place the second Sign in such a well-known place. It doesn't make sense."

Vene rolled his eyes. "And, like I was saying, it was not so well-known back when they placed it there. It makes perfect sense."

Tobias interrupted the two men. "Hold on, back up. Where are you talking about?"

"Egypt," Vene said, pointing to a glossy color map

within an atlas. "To be more precise, Giza." And, when he said that, he looked directly at Cardinal Rathady. "It makes sense. *Amongst sand and sun the Sign awaits.* Sand – check. Sun – check."

It makes sense, Tobias thought. But that description could fit a hundred places throughout the globe.

Cardinal Rathady spoke up after appearing to read Tobias' mind. "And like I said, that does not necessarily point us to Giza. Sand and sun could mean anywhere."

Vene grinned and held up his index finger. It appeared he had another part to his thinking. "Which leads me to the second line."

Rathady looked surprised. Apparently Vene had not shared this part with the Cardinal yet.

"*The watcher of the three holds within it the path.* If we are talking about Giza, then what could the three be in reference to?"

"The pyramids," Sam volunteered. She was now standing beside Tobias, listening.

"Exactly right," Vene said. "And if we are, indeed, talking about the pyramids, then there can only be one watcher of the three."

Silence fell upon the room.

"The Great Sphinx," John said.

The room looked as a whole in John's direction. He was now awake, upright, and speaking normally.

Sam rushed over and gave him a hug.

"Are you all right?" Tobias asked, relieved.

"I'm fine." His voice was groggy but strong. "How long have I been out?"

"About sixteen hours," Sam answered.

"I guess I really needed that sleep. I feel good right now. Better than I've felt in a long time." He stretched his arms to the fluorescently-lit ceiling. "Vene's right. Something inside of me is pushing me towards Giza."

"Well done," Cardinal Rathady said, looking beaten. A trace of animosity lined his words.

Vene humbly bowed his head in recognition of the Cardinal's subsidence. "I have yet to determine what the third line references, however."

Tobias looked down at the notepad. The third line, *the touch of the Sealed shall reveal that which is not*, was underlined twice. It was obvious to him the priest was having issues with this line. But at least they now had a reference point.

"All right, it looks like we are headed to Egypt. Cardinal, can you have arrangements made?"

Cardinal Rathady nodded. "Of course. For how many?"

Tobias looked around the room and took stock of who he had. "The four of us," he said, pointing to Rupert, Tia and John.

Sam cleared her throat.

He glanced back. "Sam, there is no reason to endanger you if we don't have to. You'll be safer if you stay here."

"I don't want to be safe, Tobias," she said, the slightest bit of anger in her voice. "If I wanted to be safe, I most certainly wouldn't have opened the door the other night and let you in, and I definitely wouldn't have stitched up a stranger's hand out of the kindness of my heart."

Tobias looked down at his bandaged hand.

"I'm a part of this whether you like it or not," Sam said, "and I refuse to be treated like delicate flower."

Sam shifted her eyes to Tia, the only other woman in the room.

Tobias realized he didn't bring Tia's abilities into question, albeit for reasons obvious to himself. Regardless, he knew Sam was right. She'd ended up being invaluable in the cave below the church. If it hadn't been for her quick thinking, John might be dead. She had already proven her worth. Tobias was letting his emotions get in the way of good judgment. He wanted to protect the woman who had already shown she needed no protection.

"You're right, Sam. I'm sorry." He shifted his glance back to the Cardinal. "Make that five."

Sam grinned satisfactorily.

Tobias introduced John to Rupert and Tia before they readied themselves to depart.

Tia checked her blades and attached several small daggers to straps beneath her pant legs. Rupert donned a black trench-coat, much like the one Tobias wore, except the sleeves of his were torn off. His giant arms protruded from the black cloth like sequoias bursting from the ground.

With everything in check, the team departed the safe house and went back into the changing world. Nothing Tobias had faced in all his years would be able to help them now. He knew they were in uncharted territory. Everything rested on him making the right calls at the right time. He knew all too well that a foul-up could cost them all their lives.

Chapter 18

Tobias slouched in the high-back leather chair aboard one of the Vatican's custom Gulfstreams. Each time he shifted, another ache screamed for attention. He tried to get some rest—slow his mind down enough to collect his thoughts—but it was no use. With one Sign activated and the second one within reach, he wondered if there was still enough time to get the job done. He purposely kept the news off. He'd bask in ignorance for now.

Sighing in frustration, he casually glanced over his right shoulder to the rear of the plane. Sam sat in one of the plush leather seats, curled up and sleeping. John sat a row over and stared placidly out the window.

The interior dimmed as the jet cut through a patch of clouds. Tobias turned back and reclined in his seat.

Across from him, diagonally to his right, were Rupert and Tia. They sat divided by a small polished table and spoke softly to each other. He thought about the last time he'd seen them together. He was barely able to duck the thick glass vase intended for Rupert's head. Before they ripped each other apart, Tobias had been forced to intervene and physically separate them. That, in itself, was no small feat considering who they were. For whatever reason, that moment in time had been erased completely, replaced by what they were meant to be, in love.

While hearing their banter was warming, it also brought his feelings of loneliness to the surface—feelings he quickly suppressed once they arose. Tobias hated downtime for this very reason. Born an only child, he started his life alone. Because of his parents' deaths, he was destined to end it the same way.

"How are you doing?" John asked as he sat down across from Tobias. Tobias was so caught up in his own thoughts that he failed to hear him approach.

"I'm fine," he said, shifting in the seat. "Why do you ask?" The words came out sounding defensive, but that wasn't their intent. After all, it wasn't John's job to look after Tobias.

"No reason, in particular," John said. "It's just...well, I didn't ask for any of this to happen to me, but now that it has, I'm glad to have you on my side, is all." He paused and looked out the window. The jet whipped through another ghostly cloud. "I guess, what I'm trying to say, is thanks. Thanks for watching out for me." John smiled and patted Tobias' knee, before standing and walking back to his seat.

Something in the pit of Tobias' stomach churned. Emotions he rarely acknowledged started to vie for attention. He was rarely, if ever, thanked for what he did. Of course the Vatican would occasionally throw a hollow compliment his way, but John's was heartfelt. He meant it. Tobias forced the feelings back down, deep within his soul where his brain could never find them. It was better for everyone that way. The less he soaked in, the less he felt, and the easier the difficult decisions were to make.

"You okay, Tobias?" Rupert asked from across the way.

Tobias pivoted in his leather chair to find both Rupert and Tia staring at him.. "Why does everyone keep asking me if I'm okay?"

"I don't know. You just seem a little off."

"I'm fine, really." Tobias repositioned himself in the chair, fixing his slouching posture. "Listen, I wanted to thank you guys again for agreeing to help. I have a feeling things are going to get nasty, and I couldn't think of two people I'd rather have by my side."

Tia leaned forward and grasped one of his hands across the aisle. "Honey, listen. We would do anything for you. We owe you everything."

"You owe me nothing."

Rupert smiled at Tia and then looked at Tobias. "If it wasn't for you...well, we probably wouldn't be sitting here right now, at least not together."

"I think you're exaggerating."

"No, honestly...," Rupert paused in mid-thought as the pilot unexpectedly exited through the cockpit door and walked by with a nervous smile.

He nodded at Tobias and then carried on towards the lavatory in the rear of the plane. A light coating of sweat clung to his forehead beneath his cap. Tobias watched him disappear through the hardwood divide that separated the main cabin from the kitchen and lavatories in the rear. The pilot closed the heavy door behind him with an air-sealing whoosh.

Tobias rested his head against the back of the seat and thought nothing of it. Everyone needed to obey the call of nature. It was one of the many reasons to have a copilot. But no sooner had the thought entered his head when the copilot exited the cockpit. He, too, walked by the group, smiled nervously, and entered the divide. It again shut with a whoosh.

Tobias sat straight in his chair and twisted around. After a moment of thought, he turned and faced Rupert, confused.

"Is it just me, or does that seem strange to you?"

"Don't seem right. That's for sure." Rupert said, standing.

Tobias stood and made his way to the back of the plane when a sudden, turbulent jolt knocked him from his feet. He jammed his shoulder on the way down to the ground. A shooting pain ran down his spine. He tried to stand, but the jet's dive made it too difficult to regain his balance.

Oxygen bags dropped from the overhead compartments. Anything loose quickly became an airborne projectile.

They were going down. Fast.

The cabin flooded with a deafening mix of alarms.

His mind raced. *What the hell happened?* The pilots must have done something. He should have been more alert, trusted his instincts. This was no time for self-pity, though. Things needed to be righted, starting with their angle of decent.

With the jet in a nosedive, Tobias flipped onto his back and let go his grip on the seat base. Gravity carried him down the hardwood aisle, past the rest of the group, and sent him crashing into the closed cockpit door. He braced his feet to the right and pulled it open. A new wave of blaring alarms flowed out. Climbing in as best he could, Tobias fell into the pilot's seat, bumping his head on the way down. He had a yearning to get back into the cockpit as a pilot, but this wasn't what he had in mind.

The flight controls jittered like an epileptic ghost sat behind them. Alarms buzzed throughout the cabin as a wash of red and yellow lights lit up the overhead panels. The gauges, of which there were many, spun out of control. Digital readouts counted down from the high thousands at an alarming rate.

The cabin door budged open again. Sam made her way into the copilot's chair.

"What's going on?" she yelled. Her face was white as a ghost. She was obviously scared. The varying alarms made it very difficult to hear. "Where are the pilots?"

Tobias grabbed the controls, but the plane was in too steep of a dive. A large red warning light flashed on the center console. Its label confirmed his suspicions—the door below had been opened, no doubt by the fleeing pilots, and caused the jet to dive. He flipped the switch and waited. The light went out, but the multitude of others remained. He knew if he couldn't pull the jet out of the dive that their journey ended here and now.

He pulled back with every fiber of his being. His arms felt like they might snap off at the elbow. Closing his eyes, Tobias locked his jaw and stiffened his body.

"What can I do?" Sam yelled.

He looked over at Sam. His face painfully contorted."Get...Ru...pert."

Nodding, she stood and climbed her way back up the incline through the cabin door. Seconds later, the hulk of a man appeared.

Tobias looked over his shoulder. Rupert understood. He grasped the headrest of the copilot's seat and eased down into it, like a giant sitting in an infant's highchair.

The altimeter spun around frantically as they descended through the last of the clouds. The expansive sands of the Sahara Desert quickly filled the jet's windshield.

The collision alarm echoed throughout the cabin. "Warning," repeated a female voice over and over.

Rupert grasped the co-pilot's handle and pulled with everything he had. Tobias felt his burden lessen the more Rupert pulled. The sound of the twin turbines roared, and the jet began to level off. Blue sky replaced the golden sand in front of them. Moaning in pain, both Tobias and Rupert reached their arms' limits. More of the view became blue. One by one, the alarms turned off until they started to climb.

Tobias glanced at his old friend in the copilot's seat.

Rupert had a big grin on his face. He started to laugh. "Looks like we escaped another..."

Sam screamed.

She stood with the cockpit door open and her hand over her mouth. She pointed out to the left of the windshield.

Tobias looked through the clear glass with enough time to see a red and black blur shoot by the jet. A huge pocket of turbulence jostled the aircraft. More alarms rang out.

"What the hell was that?" Rupert asked.

"I don't know." Tobias said. He could have sworn it was a dragon. "Sam, I need you to go back into the cabin and take a seat. Tell the others to hold on."

Sam darted from the cockpit.

Tobias throttled down the jet. He realized that maybe staying in the air wasn't the best idea. He was going to try to bring the jet down, sans runway.

Another turbulent jolt knocked the plane to its left. Tobias leveled it off quickly. "Whatever it is, it's tailing us."

"It looked like a dragon," Rupert said. He hung onto the sides of his seat. The turbulence bounced him around. "Big wings and stuff."

"That's what I thought, too, but dragons aren't real."

Rupert gazed over at Tobias. "You're kidding, right? I guess we'll just file dragons away with the devil in the *aren't real* category."

"Point taken."

Tobias took the cabin microphone in his hand. He flipped the switch labeled *internal* and spoke. "Hang on, gang. This is going to get a lot rougher." He placed the speaker back and grasped the handles tight.

After checking some of the instruments above, he banked sharp right with the jet. It cut the turn with precision. He peered out the cockpit's left window. Darting towards them again was the dragon. Its reptilian head swiveled with ease on its scaly, elongated neck. Its powerful, yet ragged, black wings beat in unison and somehow easily caught the speeding jet. Its scaly body went some seventy feet, at Tobias' estimations, down to the end of its lengthy tail, which ended in a ball of spikes. Its long snout, the bone

141

partially exposed, was jagged and menacing. He looked closer before banking the jet once again. He could have sworn the beast had a collar of human skulls around its neck.

A loud, deep screech shot through the air, followed by a ball of flames. He banked the jet again as the flaming missile barely missed the jet's nose. Intense heat filled the cabin as the fiery orb shot past his line of sight.

Rupert and Tobias exchanged glances. "Definitely a dragon," Rupert said.

Tobias put the jet into a dive as the beast regained its pursuit. The g-forces were intense, but necessary. The alarms went off again.

"Ideas?" Tobias yelled.

Rupert shook his head. Then he suddenly climbed out of his seat and made his way out of the cockpit without a word.

Another ball of flames shot from the dragon's mouth. It engulfed the right side of the jet.

Tobias looked out the window. The right turbine was destroyed. His control on the jet slipped away with each passing second.

Tia burst through the cabin door and tripped into the center console. She pushed herself off and fell into the copilot's seat.

"He's crazy, Tobias."

"Who?"

"Rupert. I told him, but he wouldn't listen. The man has lost his marbles."

The cabin door warning began to buzz incessantly. Someone—Rupert, he assumed—had opened the exterior cabin door.

The plane again shook, this time from the resultant change in cabin pressure.

The dragon again screeched from behind them. It was

142

much closer. He knew the jet couldn't outrun the beast on one turbine. Hell, it could barely outrun it with two. It would catch them before he could bring the jet down, *if* he could bring it down.

A sudden boom echoed from the cabin, followed by a loud, screeching whine.

He looked over his shoulder and into the cabin. The flapping cockpit door obscured his view, but he could clearly see thick white smoke. Turning back, he leveled the jet off as much as he could. The sand approached faster now. The blue sky in the windshield had all but vanished. The left engine then cut out.

The sandy terrain of Egypt approached too quickly.

"Buckle up, Tia. This isn't going to be pleasant."

Tobias once again got on the cabin microphone and warned the others to brace for impact. He checked the altimeter. Their dive was too steep. He pulled the flaps to try and slow their speed as much as he could.

The alarms meshed into one deafening sound. Tia covered her eyes as Tobias pulled back on the handle. The desert sand was everywhere in his view. He again checked the altimeter—two-thousand feet and fading fast.

He used one hand to strap himself in.

One-thousand feet.

"Hang on."

The last thousand feet went by in a flash. The golden desert sand met the belly of the jet with a violent crash. The Gulfstream bounced off a nearby sand dune and shot back into the air. Seconds later, it crashed back down, splitting in two. The nose section careened to the left and smashed into another dune, halting its progress immediately. The tail section stayed the course and disappeared over a small sandy hill, rolling to its eventual stop.

The dragon crashed down moments later. Its motionless,

burning corpse landed twenty feet from where Tobias and Tia sat unconscious.

Chapter 19

The heavy electrical fire burning around Tobias forced him from unconsciousness. Its thick, smoky odor filled the entirety of the destroyed jet's cabin. He lifted his chin from his bruised chest. His eyes felt heavy, almost sedated, but he willed them open despite their desire to remain closed. A blur of sparks spat continuously into the air from the destroyed controls on the dash. It was nothing short of a tiny warzone.

He lurched. Nothing but bile found its way up his throat.

He brought his hand up behind his head and rubbed the sore spot on his neck, wincing. Somehow he was alive, no doubt thanks to his last second securing of his safety harness. He hoped the others were as lucky. Rubbing his eyes to clear the blurriness, Tobias peered through the smoke. A blanket of golden sand covered what he could see of the windshield. He remembered leveling off the jet as best he could with no working turbines and a dragon on his tail. The next thing he knew, they'd hit the sand, and then he went black.

Tia was still fastened to the copilot's seat by her safety harness. Her head slumped to the right, motionless. A small gash in her forehead produced a larger amount of blood than it warranted, or at least Tobias hoped that was the case.

The thick electrical smoke made his lungs burn."Tia," Tobias said, coughing. No response.

Reaching down, he flipped the heavy metal latch on his safety harness and wearily rose from the pilot's seat. Broken electronics were strewn about the cabin. Exposed wires dangled from seemingly everywhere. More sparks burped into the air.

Propping Tia upright, he held her against the seat and unbuckled her belt. Her harness fell with a metal-on-metal thump. With all the energy he could muster, Tobias lifted her from the chair and carefully slung her over his shoulder. A sharp pain cut through his neck. He figured he'd pinched a nerve, or worse. He'd add it to the list of things he'd need to get fixed if they made it out of this alive.

The cockpit door was gone, blown off when they crashed. The tail section was gone, too. Along with it, Tobias quickly realized, had gone the rest of the team.

He made his way out of the cabin through the gaping hole where the tail section used to be. The sand shifted beneath his feet. He looked around. The jet breaking apart during the crash was a blessing in disguise. The fuselage was in the tail section that slid away. The electrical fire that now burned out of control would, at most, leave some charred sand in its wake.

The priority was to find John.

Tobias walked a small distance from the jet and dropped onto the sand. The hot grains pressed against his knees through his pants. As gently as he could, he laid Tia down. He placed two fingers on her neck. A slow, but steady, pulse ran through her veins.

He put his hand to his forehead, blocking as much of the sun as he could, and scanned the area. As far as he could see was more of the crystalline sand. Its prismatic reflection forced him to squint while he searched for any signs of the tail section, but the near infinite amount of sand made it next to impossible to distinguish anything. It all looked the same, dune after dune of it.

While Tobias' sight was limited, his sense of smell was not. The pungent odor of burning flesh carried on the air. He lurched again. A small distance away, engulfed in flames and partially buried, was the corpse of the dragon that had downed them. He propped himself off the ground and stumbled his way through the shifting sands towards it.

Only now, as it lay on the ground before him, did Tobias truly comprehend the dragon's enormity. Its bony head remained fully intact, propped slightly on its side. The malodorous stench of death grew worse the closer he crept. A second wave of nausea hit him. His stomach tossed, causing him to dry heave a few times. It was one of the most awful smells he had ever encountered, far worse than a decomposing Hell Hound. The stench was a mix of all things bad coupled with a pungent sulfuric odor that trumped them all.

The dragon was a charred black mess, no doubt in large part because of the fire that burned in its belly. Its master was no mystery. The beast had been forged in the pits of hell. What truly trouble Tobias was the fact that he'd never seen anything like it in all his years doing what he did, nothing this big.

Two dark red horns protruded from the dragon's enormous head. Each of them spiraled out from its skull for more than six feet. Several smaller horns, each the size of his hand, encircled its giant, red eyes. The beast's mouth was agape, and its black, forked tongue hung limp from within like a fleshy carpet. Jagged teeth, as sharp as metal spears, sprang in every direction from the portion of its snout above the sand. Circled around its neck was indeed what Tobias thought he saw in the air, a collar of human skulls.

Oozing holes spilled its blood onto the sand. He remembered Tia yelling about how crazy Rupert was, and she was never like that, not that he could remember. This had to have been Rupert's doing.

I have to find them. But there was something that Tobias

needed to do first. If he didn't, it could literally come back to bite them later.

The dragon's tail slithered out of sight like an unwound firehouse behind another large sand dune. It, like the rest of the dragon, was motionless. Tobias would make damn sure it stayed that way.

He walked up to the dragon's head and removed his blade from behind his back. The Guardian's Sword, now unhidden from the protective sheath, glimmered in the hot Egyptian sun. He placed its razor sharp tip on the dragon's temple and gripped the hilt firmly within his hands. With one swift motion, he thrust it deep into its horned cranium, penetrating until it could go no further. A bone-splitting crack accompanied the thrust. He knew all too well that the devil's minions didn't obey the rules of death, but even though he couldn't be certain, he was fairly confident this one would haunt them no more.

Tobias removed the sword and plunged it into the hot sand, wiping clean the black ooze. He then placed the sword back into its sheath, hiding it from the world once more. It wouldn't be the last time he drew his blade, of that he was sure.

As Tobias turned his attention back towards, Tia he noticed an indent in the sand trailing away from his location. It was wide enough to be caused by the sliding tail section. Following the trail with his eyes, he saw that it disappear over a sandy ledge into what looked like a small basin about one hundred yards ahead. A glimmer of hope sparked within him. He ran as fast as his legs would carry him in the shifting sand until he arrived at the ledge of the sandy basin. At the bottom lay the rear of the plane. He rushed over the bank and slid down the hill. The shifting sand caused him to tumble the final few feet before coming to rest face-down.

Tobias spit the sand from his mouth, pushed himself

back on his feet, and rushed through the gaping hole in the tail section. Rupert and John were both slumped over, still fastened to their seats. A second hole was ripped from the side of the jet in the very back. His heart sank.

Sam. He made his way through the debris that littered the cabin floor until he got to John. He knelt down next to his seat and checked for a pulse. As Tobias' fingers pressed on John's skin, he awoke."What happened?" John asked. He put his hand to his head. "Oh. That doesn't feel good."

An overwhelming feeling of relief surged through Tobias. He didn't know how much more of this he could take. Tobias figured the obvious, more believable, story would suffice for now.

"We crashed," he said. "Are you all right?"

John looked around and nodded.

Tobias helped him undo his safety belts and eased him to the floor. "Do you know where Sam is?"

John looked around and shook his head.

Tobias gazed over at Rupert and watched his chest rise and fall, signaling he, too, was ok, albeit unconscious.

"Can you do me a favor?" Tobias asked John. He realized John wasn't in any condition to do favors, but then again, none of them were. John nodded the best he could. "Help the big man out of his seat." They both looked over to Rupert. "I'm going to go find Sam."

He worriedly left the tail section of the plane and looked around the sandy basin. Tobias hoped she was jettisoned during the slide and not during the crash, but there was no sign of her anywhere.

His legs burned like he had been treading water for days as he climbed the sliding sand wall of a nearby dune. Reaching the top, he shielded his eyes and surveyed the vast wasteland around him. Sand as far as he could see. The dragon still burned off in the distance to his right.

149

Waves of heat rose from the brownish-gold grains. The soupy heat, coupled with his many unfound injuries, made him lightheaded. His resolve to find Sam, though, was as strong as it could be. Doubts forced their way into his mind. He knew better than to bring her, despite her worth. He had a feeling something like this would happen. It was all his fault.

As hope began to fade, he caught a glint of something in the distance, diagonally to his left. He knew he was running, but he couldn't feel his legs moving. He was carried by emotion—by feelings he didn't know he had, by feelings he didn't know he was capable of. There, in the distance, lay Sam's seat on its side. She was still firmly strapped in. He broke out into a full sprint. His legs burned, but he fought through the pain. He dropped to his knees beside her chair.

Her head hung limp to the side. He dug his feet into the loose sand, bracing against the tilted jet seat, and pushed with all his might. *Dammit*. The metal burned his flesh, but he shook it off. He would deal with a thousand burns to ensure her safety.

He put his cheek to her mouth and felt small, hot breaths escaping her lungs. Sam was alive. Giddiness—something he rarely, if ever, felt—rushed to the forefront of his single file line of emotions. He looked to the sky and gave his silent thanks. How she survived that was beyond reason.

Unbuckling her safety straps, Tobias slid Sam free from the seat and onto the sand. With the care of a father for his newborn, he propped her head onto his lap and brushed the hair free from her face. She had a small cut below her hairline and a large bruise on her right arm, but no other injuries that he could see—hopefully nothing internal. A tattered clump of hair stuck to her bloody, sand-covered wound.

He lightly caressed her cheek with the tips of his fingers.

Her skin, even after all that had happened, was soft to the touch. The right side of her face was slightly sunburned. With her hand in his, he gently squeezed, trying to get a reaction.

"Sam." He squeezed her hand again. "Sam, wake up."

The slightest of flutters in her eyes gave him immediate hope. He traced her cheek again.

"Sam. It's Tobias. I need you to wake up."

Her eyes fluttered again, staying more closed than open.

"Hey," he said, gently moving her head to the side and away from the blinding sky. "Are you with me?"

She made a sound and tried to answer. Tobias felt a wave of relief wash over him. For a second, everything else in the world faded away. He smiled and brushed the hair from her eyes again.

"Tobias?" She looked up at him and winced. "What happened?" Her voice was soft, distant.

He laughed out of relief. "We crashed."

Sam brought her hand up to her head and moaned in pain. The laceration on her head, while small in size, was apparently quite painful. She went to stand but lost her balance and fell back down.

"Maybe you should rest here for a minute?"

She shook her head. "I'll be fine. I'm just a little lightheaded. Are the others all right?"

"As far as I can tell, yes." He looked to the nose of the jet. Rupert was now awake and caring for his wife.

Tobias put Sam's arm around his shoulder. He realized it was better to get her off her feet for a while. In fact, it was probably better for everyone to rest for a bit, considering what they had all just been through. Still, he couldn't believe their good fortune to escape from that alive. He was hesitant to even think it, but maybe something greater was somehow looking out for them.

They slowly made their way back to the tail section of the plane. Rupert had carried Tia down there, away from the smoking nose of the jet and the rancid odor of one burning dragon. She was now awake and hugging the jolly giant. John looked on with a smile. As soon as he saw Tobias and Sam, he leapt from his seat.

"Easy now," Tobias said, seeing him approach. "She's a little banged up."

John acknowledged the comment with a smile and gently hugged Sam.

"You guys okay?" Tobias asked, looking over at the married couple.

Tia reached up and gave Tobias a kiss on the cheek. "You never cease to amaze me, Tobias Ramsey."

He smiled at her and then looked over to Rupert. "I take it we owe you for that mess up there?" He pointed over the hill to where the dragon lay burning.

"That thing was pissing me off." Rupert grinned. "Nothing my bag-o-tricks couldn't handle, though."

Tia rolled her eyes. "My hero."

Tobias laughed. "It looks like you can add dragons to your list of conquests."

Rupert made an imaginary checkmark in the air before grabbing his side and wincing.

Tobias reached into his backpack and removed a GPS. He tapped a few keys. They were eleven miles southwest of Giza. He decided their best bet would be to wait until nightfall. The temperature, while ironically cold at night, was still better than the heat. In the meantime, the group could rest and heal as much as possible before making their way to the Sphinx.

He felt like chum in the middle of a shark-filled ocean, waiting to be eaten. He just hoped the devil's minions weren't hungry.

Chapter 20

Moonlight painted the sand a very light blue, masking the formidable desert in a sea-like tranquility. The searing heat of the day gave way to the chilling air of the night. While the sudden temperature change played tricks on his body, Tobias knew their trek wouldn't have been possible in the midday sun. Dehydration would surely have set in, making any attempt to find the Sphinx impossible.

For everything that had gone wrong, he realized it could have been far worse. A few bumps and bruises, but overall it was amazing they'd survived. He wondered if Father Fenn would be able to dismiss these events as anything less than a miracle, as he had those in the African jungle.

For each step Tobias took forward, it felt like he slipped half a step back. The grains of sand were the epitome of teamwork. Each grain, by itself, was nothing more than an afterthought of nature. When grouped together, however, they formed a powerfully awkward surface that slowed the team down considerably.

A little over five hours of laborious travel brought them to within one hundred yards of the Sphinx. The Great Pyramids, silhouetted in the pale moonlight, rose gracefully in the background.

The scene sprawling out in front of them reminded Tobias of a postcard. The amount of craftsmanship the Egyptians possessed amazed him. It always had. Thousands of years had passed, and these great structures remained incredibly well preserved, save for their long gone outer coating. He wondered what treasures remained hidden within their sloped walls. He swore to come back another time and find out; that is, when the world didn't need saving.

Egyptian history had fascinated Tobias since he was a child. Sal, an Egyptologist friend of his father, would visit their house once a year, usually during the summer. Tobias would watch from afar as Sal and his father sipped on beers and told stories, laughing as only friends could. Sal, as far as he could remember, failed to discover a treasure worth talking about, but he did bring back stories of those who had—stories so shrouded in mystery that Tobias had been hooked ever since.

Tobias had seen Sal for the last time at his father's funeral. He remembered standing in the funeral home, greeting the procession of mourners that came to pay their respects. He was too young at the time to really know what it meant—no longer having the guidance of his parents—but time would be the ultimate bearer of bad news.

Halfway through the service, Sal appeared. He bent down with tears in his eyes and hugged Tobias tight. With a somber tone to his voice, Sal said, "Your father was a great man, Tobias. He loved you very much, more than you'll probably ever realize. Make him proud." The look in his eyes hinted that Sal knew the family legacy. But, of course, Tobias could never be sure. Moments later, he stood and walked back out the way he came. Tobias later found out that Sal had been killed in a freak accident not long after.

Whenever thoughts popped into his head about ending his Guardian lifestyle, Sal's words echoed through his consciousness. *Make him proud*, a voice would cry out from somewhere within him. The words were inspirational in one regard, but they held him prisoner in another sense. He never felt free to deviate from the life that was chosen for him, and when he had thoughts about doing so, Sal's words crushed them dead.

Ancient Egypt, up until this point, had faded from Tobias' mind. It became a thing of the past, like so many other parts of his life. Yet now he stood like a character in his own memory, taking part in one of the stories that meant so much to him growing up.

He pushed his thoughts aside for now as the team approached the Sphinx. Its two enormous paws stretched out and grasped firmly at the ever-shifting desert sand. Atop its elongated, lion-like body rested the frozen image of some long ago Pharaoh. Time had been kind to preserve the statue as well as it had, yet devious to allow the hands of men to defame its marvelous structure at the same time.

For such an important and highly-traveled area, Tobias found it surprisingly calm and empty. He thought for sure that they would need to find a way around patrolling guards, or—at the very least—some caretakers. Now that they were there, standing among some of the greatest structures ever built, Tobias found it beyond quiet. It was like the world held its breath for the unexpected.

"Okay. We're here. Now what?" Rupert asked.

Tobias looked over with a blank stare. It was a good question. He figured something was bound to happen to help light the way forward. Now that they had arrived, and nothing volunteered itself, he was left wondering, as well.

"*The touch of the sealed shall reveal that which is not,*" John said. "I think it's fairly obvious that I have to touch something. But what?"

Tobias reached out and felt the large right paw of the Sphinx. Sand drifted free and fell to the ground. It seemed too obvious, but it was still worth a try.

"Just try touching the Sphinx, John."

Shrugging, John closed his eyes and reached towards the right paw. His hand hovered close and then pushed down slightly against the chilled limestone. He gasped.

Sam spun around, excited. "What is it?"

John opened his eyes and turned. The group waited, hushed. A mischievous grin cut across his face. He removed his hand and brushed the loose sand from his palm. "I'm just messing with you guys."

Sam grimaced, silently scolding his poorly-timed humor.

Tobias shook his head. "Spread out. Look for something... ."

Rupert interrupted, "...that has eluded Egyptologists for hundreds of years?"

Rupert was right. How could they be expected to find something so intangible? The mention of the *touch of the sealed* had to have been about John or, to a larger extent, any of the Brotherhood of the Sealed. Where to touch was the million-dollar question. Egypt was a big place.

Casually drifting apart, the group spread out around the Sphinx. Tobias made his way between the paws and stopped below the head. A large slab of stone stood propped against the chest. This, he remembered, was the Dream Stele.

Sal's passion for Egypt was infectious, but it was strongest for this single block of stone. Its carvings held frozen in time a tale of Tuthmosis, the then-prince of Egypt. It told of a promise the Sphinx had made to the prince upon visiting him in a dream. If the prince were to dig the Sphinx free of its sandy prison, he would then become the King of Egypt. The prince, so overjoyed at the thought of becoming king, put a small army of men on the task. After days of digging, the Sphinx was free. It held true to its promise and made the boy a king.

Tobias traced the age-old carvings with his index finger. He wondered if there was any truth to the story. If the boy was already a prince, then he was destined to become a king, anyway. Still, like much of Egyptian history, the more you dug into the story to try and understand it, the more confusing it became.

An out-of-place giggle disturbed the relative serenity and made Tobias turn his attention.

Sam, who stood examining the front of the left paw, looked up and met his gaze. It wasn't her laugh. That much was evident. It sounded like a small child. It sounded familiar. He looked away from Sam and surveyed the landscape. There was nothing there except the sand he'd grown to despise. He shook his head, realizing he must have been hearing things. *I need to get some sleep.*

Tobias turned back around and returned to his examination of the Dream Stele. The hieroglyphics stopped a little more than halfway down. He took a knee and looked at the sand-pocked bottom half. Nothing of interest caught his eye. He then reached to the sides of the tablet and felt for anything out of the ordinary. Nothing more than several pockets of windblown sand found his touch.

It was like looking for a needle in an infinitely large haystack.

"Find anything?" Tobias asked as Rupert and Tia come up behind him. They shook their heads in unison.

Tobias looked to Sam. She shrugged.

"What were you guys laughing at?" Tia asked. "I could use a good joke right about now."

Sam walked towards them. "I heard it, too. I thought it was just me."

As if on cue, more giggles filled the air and then stopped. Something clicked. Tobias recognized the sound now and quickly realized why it rubbed him the wrong way.

John walked around the giant paw of the Sphinx. "I didn't find anything. …"

Tobias held his finger up to his mouth, shushing John. He drew his guns from their holsters.

Rupert removed his giant mallet. Tia crouched low to the ground and drew her blades. They all looked at Tobias, waiting for an explanation.

Sam took John's hand. They inched their way farther between the outstretched paws. They stopped when their backs were to the Dream Stele.

A louder chorus of giggles came from all around them and then vanished once again.

Tobias closed his eyes and shook his head in disgust. He was sure of it now. That obnoxious giggle could only belong to one creature.

"Imps," Tobias said, opening his eyes and looking around. He figured they were most likely surrounded, though he wasn't too concerned.

Rupert turned to him. "Excuse me?"

"Imps," Tobias repeated. "Annoying little spies."

"Where are they?" Rupert asked.

"They're probably everywhere. Damn things are invisible."

Tobias detested Imps, with their tiny wings, beady eyes and sinister laugh. While they posed no real threat to the group, he worried what they would bring back once they reported to their master.

Tobias removed his backpack and dropped it to the ground. The group stood silently by and watched the Guardian do his work. Reaching in purposefully, he removed an oblong shotgun shell. He shoved the shell into the chamber of the micro-shotgun from his left leg and closed it with the flick of his wrist. A second later, he reached towards the sky and pulled the trigger. A sharp pop sounded from above, followed by a shower of shiny blue particles raining down upon them.

As the particles fell in the moonlight, the situation became clear. Surrounding them, as Tobias thought, were hundreds — if not thousands — of Imps. Each pair of their black eyes was trained on the group. Some rested on the outstretched paws of the Sphinx, while others hovered overhead, using their tiny wings to keep them stable. Each of them had a rigid tail that split into three branches towards the end, like a Cat O' Three Tails.

Tobias wasted no time. He removed the second micro-shotgun from his right leg and began blasting. The Imps fell to the sand all around. Some pests, the ones closest to the group, exploded in a burst of black ooze as the scattershot shell ripped through them.

Rupert and Tia followed Tobias' lead.

Rupert swung his giant mallet around with the grace of a samurai wielding his sword. Before the Imps could react, they were pulverized beneath the enormous weight of the mallet's hardened steel head.

"Batter up," Rupert yelled, taking aim at one near John. With the thrust of his mallet, the Imp sailed high into the air.

Tia shimmied to the top of the right paw with the nimbleness of a spider, defying gravity. With one graceful cutting of her blades, she lopped five of the Imps in half as they attempted to flee. Ten foot-long pieces fell to the dark sand with a cushioned splat. The rest of the creatures quickly vanished, flying out from beneath the umbrella of particles.

Resting on one knee, Tia kept her swords at the ready atop the Sphinx's paw. Rupert's two enormous hands tightly gripped the shaft of the mallet.

The Imps appeared to be gone.

"They're harmless," Tobias said, clicking his guns back into the brackets on his legs, "but what they bring back won't be. We better find what we're looking for soon. I have a feeling this desert is going to become very crowded, very soon."

159

"Um, Tobias?" Sam said.

He turned to find John catatonically facing the Dream Stele with his arms limp by his sides. No sooner had Tobias turned when John fell to his knees in the sand. With both hands, John dug frantically a foot or two down into the sand on the side of the Stele, revealing something that had eluded Tobias. At the base of the slab was the imprint of the Crux, the same carving they'd found below the Asinou Church in Cyprus.

Removing the Crux from around his neck, John placed it in the shallow carving like he had at the church. Also mimicking the Asinou Church was the same white glow that traced its outline. The sound of stone moving against stone churned from beneath them. The Dream Stele descended into the sand and vanished. John stood and turned. His eyes were rolled back and white.

The ground shook. The paws of the Sphinx rose towards the sky. Their bases, much to Tobias' amazement, were apparently a great deal deeper than previously thought. Continuing higher, they rose until settling above the Sphinx's head. From behind them protruded a new stone slab that trapped the group within a limestone cage. The Guardian's Mark was carved on the new stone.

That solidified it for Tobias. This was definitely the right place.

Then, in an instant, everything stopped. The silence of the desert night returned.

"What's going on?" Sam asked. Her voice was uneasy.

Before Tobias could answer, the ground beneath their feet started to give way. The sand funneled into itself and disappeared into a newly opening gap. The group crammed to the sides, backs to the towering Sphinx paws, as the black abyss engulfed everything below them.

Tobias looked at John and met his white-eyed stare. John

jumped feet first into the dark pit.

"John!" Sam screamed.

Tobias glanced at her. She looked back, confused and afraid. She tried to remain standing, but her footing slipped. She unwillingly followed John into the emptiness below. Her screams were lost among the sound of falling sand.

Tia fell and, soon after, so did Rupert.

Left with no alternative, Tobias crossed his arms in front of his chest and followed them into the unknown darkness below.

Chapter 21

The friction of the coarse stone slope tore at Tobias' clothes and scraped his back the further he slid below the Sahara. Enveloped in complete darkness, it was like some kind of sadistic amusement park ride. He heard the others sliding in front of him, carried by the landslide of sand that followed them into the black unknown. He hoped what they now hurdled down was indeed the entrance to the second Trinity Sign and not a trap. Regardless, he supposed it was too late to turn back now.

The tunnel abruptly ended. Tobias crashed down hard on his back after a second of weightlessness. The air rushed from his lungs in one collective gasp. What little breath he could muster was now overpoweringly stale. A soupy humidity closed in around him. He figured there was someone, somewhere, laughing at him right now.

Tobias coughed to clear his throat of sand. "Is everyone all right?" He coughed again.

"I'm good," Rupert said from somewhere in front of him.

Tia was next. "I'm fine, honey, though I can't say the same for my butt."

"I'm here," Sam said from his left.

Tobias then felt her reach out and brush his arm. He must have barely missed her when he fell.

He waited for John to chime in. "John?" No answer. "John, where are you?"

Where the hell is he? His response came moments later in the form of illumination. Torches that lined the walls lit in succession from farthest to nearest. The sound of their coordinated ignitions filled the air. The darkness surrounding them quickly became consumed. Before them stretched a narrow hallway carved out of the soft limestone. Tobias figured it ran for maybe fifty feet on a slight downward slope and was close to six feet in width. At the end of the tunnel was John, swaying ever so slightly like he had been before their impromptu descent. He faced a solid wall at what appeared to be a dead end.

Tobias stood and bumped his head. He looked up, frustrated, at the extremely low ceiling. He didn't think it was possible to intensify his already merciless headache, but it was.

Sam sat huddled on the ground to his left. The moodiness he felt suddenly took a backseat to the relief of knowing that she was safe. The heaviness of his pounding head seemed to lessen. *What was it with this woman?* She had the power to cure all his pains with nothing more than a look. On the one hand, he welcomed these types of feelings, though they were somewhat foreign to him. He did not like being a captive to their pull, though. He rarely felt powerless to stop anything.

Tobias held out his hand and helped Sam off the ground. "Are you all right?"

A smile of thanks blossomed on Sam's face. "I'll be fine, thanks," she said, brushing the sand from her clothes. "I think I'm starting to get used to all this." She looked around. "Whatever this is."

He looked to Rupert and Tia. "And you guys?"

"You know us, honey," Tia answered, "just another day in paradise."

Rupert grinned in agreement.

Tobias walked past the others and made his way down the tunnel. The ceiling gradually increased in height as the tunnel stretched on. The torches, each attached to the walls with two large metal rings, were evenly spaced on both sides. The flames, for the most part, were ordinary, except for the purplish coloring evident throughout. *This is definitely the place,* he thought. The Brotherhood had an affinity for the color purple. The hue of the Crux was the material proof for anyone in objection.

The torchlight, along with the tunnel, ended at John. Tobias reached out and touched John's shoulder. His palm instantly went from body temperature to frigid. John was freezing.

Pivoting at the waist, John slowly turned. His rolled-back, white eyes stared back blankly. His lips quivered very slightly like they had at the safe house, yet no words emanated from his lips. John then turned back towards the solid wall and placed his hands on the cold limestone. A sudden, quick burst of incoherent murmurings spouted from his mouth. Tobias wished Vene was there. To be where they were and to need a translator was an evil form of irony.

Everyone remained silent and waited. John's head dipped down to his chest, like he had fallen asleep while standing. His hands still braced the wall as if he supported the tunnel's weight. An exhausted sigh followed his mouth's last murmur.

The torches blew out in unison. Complete darkness captured the narrow tunnel once again.

Tobias felt Sam bunch in closer to him.

A small pulsation rumbled the floor, followed by another stone-against-stone grinding sound. The blanket of humidity that drenched the tunnel suddenly dissipated, sweeping past them in an instant. From their left came a cooling breeze. Tobias turned towards the refreshing, yet still stale, air. It felt good against the unwanted beads of sweat on his forehead. The darkness made it impossible, though, to know what — if anything — approached.

Chanting, this time louder, again flowed from John. An eerie purplish glow began to approach from the direction of the breeze. Tobias watched as torches lit a tunnel that wasn't there seconds ago. After the last torch flamed into existence, John dropped to his knees, limp.

"John," Tobias said, grabbing him beneath his arms before he could fall on his face. "Are you all right? Can you hear me?"

John's eyes had returned to normal and now looked back curiously. "What happened?" He locked down the new torch lit corridor. "Where did that come from?"

"I was hoping you could tell me." Tobias snickered in relief. "Apparently you know this place pretty well." The new corridor appeared to wind around a corner and out of sight.

"It's strange that you would say that," John said, standing, using the wall for support. He seemed drained. "For some reason, I feel an odd connection to this place. It's like I've been here before."

Odd is an understatement, Tobias thought. Whatever was happening to John was downright creepy. Tobias had no idea what to expect next. This was like nothing he had ever dealt with before, and he'd dealt with more than enough over the years. Because of that, he felt unprepared, like the team might be jeopardized at the next turn. Unfortunately, there was no time for debate. They needed to keep moving towards their goal.

"Tia, I want you to hang up here with Sam until I give you the okay."

Tia nodded her approval and drew her blades.

Sam looked at Tia and then at Tobias with confusion. "Why do the *girls* have to stay back?"

"The *girls* aren't *staying* anywhere," Tobias said, feeling attacked. His headache made itself known again. "I'd feel

165

better if we had our tail covered." He couldn't have anyone, Sam included, questioning his command. It was imperative that they follow his lead if they had any hope of finishing this.

Sam withdrew her scowl. It was easier for Tobias to lie than tell her the truth. He worried about her safety. In fact, he found himself worrying about her too much. If put in a situation where he had to choose who lived and who died, he prayed he could make the right choice for the sake of all humanity. He realized that snapping at her wasn't helping the situation.

Tobias reached to his left leg and removed one of his micro-shotguns. Walking over to Sam, he held it out as an offering. "I don't want to leave you unprotected. Have you ever used one of these?"

Sam grabbed the gun from Tobias. With a quick snap of her wrist, the gun popped open and revealed the two red shells nestled within the chambers. Another quick snap, and the shotgun closed.

Tobias' puzzled look was the strongest of the group.

"What?" Sam looked around. "I used to shoot skeet with my father when I was a teenager." She raised an eyebrow.

"Okay then," he said, handing her a small leather bag of custom shells. "The ones with black casings are scattershot and the red ones…well, only use those in times of desperation. They tend to leave a mess." He gave her a serious look. "And whatever you do, make sure none of us are in the way."

Sam looked into the bag before attaching it around her waist. "It looks like a fanny pack."

Tobias grinned and began to walk down the new tunnel.

"Give us a yell when you're ready," Tia shouted as they walked away.

He knew Tia would take good care of Sam. He wished

he could leave John with them, too, but his umbrella of protection only reached so far. While he trusted Tia with his life, he knew he couldn't trust anyone but himself with John's.

The breeze he felt earlier intensified the farther along the downward sloping tunnel they traveled. The torches that ran on either side pointed back like arrows in the breeze, as if ominously warning them to turn around.

Slowing to a stop, Tobias peered around the corner to his left. The corridor appeared to continue another forty yards or so and eventually disappeared into darkness once again.

"This place gives me the creeps," Rupert said. "Where's that wind coming from, anyway?"

Tobias shrugged. He had a feeling they would find out soon enough. It went against his better judgment, but it looked like they needed to continue forward into the darkness. Peeling himself from the corner, he continued down the hall. John and Rupert followed. If something were to attack, he would take the brunt of it.

They neared the end of the tunnel when a loud click echoed. The large portion of the wall to their right began to slowly inch across the tunnel. Quickly putting the pieces together, Tobias realized this tunnel was about to become a tomb.

"Sam, Tia, run!" he yelled.

The women bolted from the top of the ramp. Tia rounded the corner and dashed through the closing stone with plenty of time to spare.

"Where's Sam?" Tobias asked.

Tia looked back, surprised. "She was right behind me."

Darting through the shrinking gap, Tobias moved quickly back up the ramp. Sam, only feet away, was picking up the shotgun shells that had poured out of the bag when she apparently fell.

"We don't have time for that," he said, grabbing her by the arm and tugging her back to her feet like a rag doll.

He rounded the corner with Sam in tow, her feet barely touching the ground. The stone had eaten almost the entirety of the tunnel.

"Hang on," he said.

Winding up, he flung her through the opening like a human slingshot. She whipped past the stone and into Rupert's waiting arms. Tobias then flattened himself with his back to the wall. The stone was only inches from his face. This wasn't how he wanted to die. Sucking in his chest, he forced his way farther in. Now more than halfway through, his chest felt tight as the weight of the stone pushed on it.

I'm not going to make it. It was then that he felt Rupert's hand grab his shoulder with the strength of a bear. The next thing Tobias knew, he was ripped into the air like he was shot out of a cannon.

The rock stopped seconds later with a loud thump and a burp of dust. With it, went any hope of going back the way they came, but Tobias had a feeling it was intended to be that way. He hoped that this wasn't a one-way trip.

Tobias looked up at Rupert. "Thanks, big fella."

Rupert patted Tobias on the back. "You're not getting out of this that easy," he said with a smile.

John walked away from the group, towards the dark end of the tunnel. "We're close."

"Hold on, John," Tobias said, brushing himself off. "I think we should move with a little more caution." He touched his shoulder and eased him to a stop. John turned around.

"This place ain't all butterflies and puppies, you know," Rupert said.

John smiled. "You need to trust me on this. I'm telling

you, it's like I've been here before. It's déjà vu times a million."

"I do trust you, John, but it's my job to make sure you live. It's hard for me to do that when you go walking off into the dark." Scolding a grown man was not in the dossier that Fenn had given him, but Tobias felt compelled to get his point across.

John smiled with an eerie confidence. "I finally feel like I have direction in life, Tobias. There's something new inside of me that I really can't explain. I realize it's probably hard to comprehend. Heck, I'm even having trouble understanding it. But you have to trust that I know what to do. I'm not the drunk you saved in the middle of the woods anymore. I can feel myself changing, and it's something I can't, and don't want to, control. I finally feel...," he paused, "...good."

Tobias stared into John's eyes. "I don't fully understand what's going on here, but one thing is certain—you need to stay alive. Everything else plays second fiddle to that. Okay?"

John nodded in acceptance. "Understood, but just go with me on this."

Tobias sighed. He knew he had little choice. "All right, we'll follow whatever it is you feel, but I lead."

John nodded again.

Sam pulled up next to John. "What did you mean when you said there was something inside of you?"

"It took me a little while to fully understand, but what happened at the church on Cyprus was something much more powerful than any of us could imagine." His voice was calm and monotone. "When I activated the first Trinity Sign, my body became sort of... ." He looked for the right words. "Well, I guess a shared vessel is the phrase that comes to mind."

169

"A what now?" Rupert asked. He rested his hammer on the ground and leaned against it for support.

"For whatever reason, all the knowledge of the Brotherhood of the Sealed is bumping around in my head. So far it's only been spurts of information, but they've been coming more frequently now. Those pieces are starting to form into memories, leading me forward. It's like someone else is in my mind, telling me where to go and what to do." He shook his head. "I know it seems really weird, but that's the feeling I get."

Tobias realized that his control over their fates waned with each passing moment in the dark underbelly of the Sahara Desert. He had to trust that whatever was leading John forward was a friendly force. If it was not, then Tobias was marching them all to their deaths.

Chapter 22

Now that the tunnel was blocked, the air, lacking a way out, was relegated back to captivity among the curious limestone tunnels. The staleness crept back, riding atop the drops of humidity. One torch, their only remaining light source, fluttered in the small remaining draft that was still present.

Standing there was doing the group no good. Tobias realized they needed to push into the darkness and see what, if anything, lay in wait. If this was a trap, which he knew was a real possibility, now would be the perfect time to spring it. Because of that, he decided to proceed with extra caution, if there was such a thing.

With the group to his back, Tobias took a step closer and unsheathed his sword. He peered into the curtain of darkness that hung from ceiling to floor. It proved to be a useless endeavor on his part. No matter how intensely he stared, nothing but darkness stared back. His eyes began to play tricks on him, seeing shapes and objects he knew weren't really there.

He poked his sword into the black air ahead and lightly swung it around. The blade clanked against the limestone walls, but the path seemed to go on unobstructed. He realized his makeshift detection system was far from reliable but, at that point, it was better than nothing.

"Follow me," he said, stepping into the darkness, "but stay close."

It felt cooler in the shadows, like he was suddenly trapped within a huge block of ice. Small, careful strides carried him forward foot by foot. With darkness surrounding him, it would be impossible to know if the floor dropped away. It would not be the first ancient trap he'd come across, and Tobias doubted that it would be the last. Years of experience had taught him to expect everything and trust nothing. It was one of the things that had kept him alive this long.

A few steps farther, and a torch erupted in flames behind him. He quickly turned at the sound. Like the torches before, this one also had a purple hue, but it was far more brilliant than the others. The shades of yellow, orange, and red were guests on this torch, with purple being their host. The small circle of illumination provided enough light for Tobias to check his surroundings. As far as he could tell, the floor, ceiling, and walls all continued on as they had before. No visible signs of a trap. Then again, Tobias knew that the best traps were the ones you never found.

After they'd moved forward a few paces more, a second torch flamed into existence. As that one lit, the torch behind them extinguished. It was as if someone guided them towards their goal one torch at a time. Tobias wondered how much longer this game of lights would continue. For all he knew, they could be traveling in a circle that looped for miles.

The wind, more evident now, swirled around in spurts. A hollow sound, like a strong breath over an empty jug, bellowed from far below. His senses hinted that they now stood on the precipice of something extremely deep.

"Stay where you are," he said. "I have a feeling the floor drops out up ahead."

"Hang on," came John's voice from somewhere in the darkness in front of them.

How the hell did he get ahead of me? Tobias heard John clank the Crux against something. A heavyset clawed-foot urn ignited from up ahead. It sat purposefully within a rounded alcove cut into the limestone wall. A rich purple flame reached up from deep within it. Then another urn flamed into existence, and another. Suddenly, the darkened room glowed with the brilliance of hundreds of urns. They saturated the walls with their plum glow, casting the group in a discoloring ambiance. Emblazoned upon each of their metal casings was the Guardian's Mark.

With the aid of the urn's light, Tobias could clearly see a winding staircase that descended down beyond his sight, hugging tight to the wall to their left. The bursting sound of igniting urns continued far below them.

John stood in the middle of a small cul-de-sac at the end of a narrow path twenty feet away. In front of John was an obelisk around four feet in height, capped by a small pyramid covered in a shiny yellow outer coating. Below the cul-de-sac was nothing but a void of emptiness. One misstep, Tobias realized, was all it would have taken for John to fall to his death. Tobias wanted to scold John again. He had just finished telling him to stay close and let him lead the way. For whatever reason, Tobias suddenly realized, he needed to let John continue to lead them and relent a portion of his control, as much as he didn't like it.

John removed the Crux from the monument's side and nonchalantly walked back over the thin path to where the group stood in awe.

"You're starting to creep me out," Rupert said.

John snickered playfully.

"No, seriously. You're a weird dude."

"How did you know to do that?" Sam asked.

John shrugged. "Like I said, I have all the knowledge of the Brotherhood swirling around in my head. Since they helped build this place, I just kind of knew about it."

What was once solid limestone now formed a gaping cavern below the sands of the Sahara. The purplish glow gave the cavern an abnormally regal appearance. Tobias found it somehow peaceful, like small lapping waves against a beach.

"It looks like this place was manmade," Tia said, looking around. "You can see the chisel marks everywhere." She pointed to the domed ceiling twenty or more feet above their heads.

The walls and floor seemed to have been chiseled out, as well. Tobias carefully peered over the ledge on which they stood. There appeared to be no bottom, only a spiraling row of fiery urns that eventually disappeared from sight. It must have taken an army of men countless years to build, but after the past couple of days, Tobias had learned that nothing was impossible, no matter how improbable it seemed. The Brotherhood of the Sealed appeared to be far more resourceful than he'd first thought, no doubt thanks to the might of his Guardian ancestors.

"I guess we go down from here," he said, making his way over to the beginning of the winding staircase. "Stick close to the walls. If you need to stop, let me know, and we'll stop as a group." Everyone nodded in agreement.

Tobias led the way slowly down the staircase that most likely had not been used in eons. The path wound continuously around the outer edge of the subterranean cavern. For the magnitude of what this project must have been, surprising care had been taken on its details. Each step that furthered their descent appeared to be a mirror image of the others. The walls, for the most part, were chiseled smooth. It was an amazing feat of excavation that would be difficult to duplicate today, even with all the advanced machinery available.

An increasingly gusty wind tested their balance the deeper they went. The jug-like, hollow sound grew louder. The stairs, while uniform, were narrow and made for uneasy footwork. As such, the group was forced to descend with their backs to the wall. It was an unnerving thought that something as accidental as a misstep could be the last step they ever took. Sam's gasp brought the group to a harsh stop.

Tobias turned to find her right leg flopped over the edge of the staircase. She leaned precariously towards the emptiness. A loose rock bounced from beneath her foot and into the darkness below. The group stood perfectly still, in a single file line, trying to will away the unthinkable. Tobias had no room to move, to react. It was a mere second in time, but it felt like an eternity.

Sam quickly regained her balance and gave the group an apologetic look. Her chest pulsed rapidly. She took a deep breath and sighed as a second piece of stone fell from the side of the stairs. It tumbled for a few seconds before clearly hitting solid ground.

"Looks like there is a bottom to this damn thing," Rupert said, helping Sam back to her feet.

Having carefully gravitated down the stairs for nearly fifteen minutes, knowing there was an end in sight was a welcome relief. Sam seemed all right—for that, Tobias was thankful—but the stairs weren't as solid as they'd appeared. All it took was a slight fall to knock portions loose off the edge. He wondered how old this place actually was. If the stairs were falling apart, what else might? He prayed the ceiling's construction would hold, but there could be no assurances of that. It was an unnerving feeling he forced aside.

Five tense minutes later, the group emptied into an expansive, well-lit, rectangular room. It extended for what seemed like a hundred yards ahead. The same giant urns that lined the path down also sat scattered along the walls of the room. Aside from the urns, the area appeared to be a vast, empty space. There were no doors or alcoves of any kind. Above them was the same empty black air they'd recently looked down upon.

Tobias knew there had to be something here. The Brotherhood would not construct a seemingly endless flight of stairs for nothing. Whatever it was, Tobias was sure John was the key. They just needed to find the lock, as they had in Cyprus.

"Spread out," he said. "Look for anything resembling the Crux." He figured, if the first sign needed the Crux, then the second may as well also. Then he remembered what happened in Cyprus. "But stay ready. I have no idea what's coming next."

The group nodded and then fanned out to search.

Rupert and Tia walked closer to the center of the room, whispering quietly to each other. Sam smiled innocently and then brushed by him, but stayed close.

Tobias kept a watchful eye on John as he walked from the base of the stairs and towards Rupert. Slowly, John's posture began to change. His arms rose from his sides and stretched out towards the black nothingness above. He began chanting again, louder than before, and with more conviction. Rupert looked back at Tobias.

Tobias raised his hand, signaling Rupert to hold tight for now. He was not about to interrupt whatever was happening. This might be their only chance to find the second Trinity Sign, so he decided to let it—whatever *it* was—play out.

A thunderous sound resonated from within the darkness above. It sounded like a thousand lions roared in unison.

Rupert reached back and removed his hammer, grasping it firmly in both his hands. Tia unsheathed her swords. Sam fearfully ran back to Tobias. No harm would come to her. He silently swore his life on it.

Another roar echoed around the hollow cavern, this one louder and closer. Tobias realized something was coming down towards them, and it was coming down fast.

Instinct took over. He pulled Sam away just as a large piece of the limestone stairs crashed down. Dribbling remnants of the fallen stone bounced off the spiraling staircase to their right. Tobias wrapped his muscular arms around Sam, shielding her as debris washed past them. He looked over to Rupert and Tia in the center of the room. "We're not alone," Tobias said.

Rupert rolled his eyes. "You think?"

Tobias dragged Sam away from the stairs and towards the back of the room. "Stay behind this," he said, banging on the giant metal urn with his sword. Its sonorous gong rang throughout the cavern.

Sam nodded in agreement and crouched behind it.

Another large piece of limestone fell to the floor with a ground-shaking thud. This one was far larger than the last. Sediment kicked up from the ground. A purple-hued tapestry of dust filled the air. Tobias' view was obscured, but not enough to mask the two gigantic legs firmly planted to the left of the stairs. They were definitely not alone.

John's chanting continued on louder and with more authority. He seemed oblivious to what was happening. A white aura began to surround him, like it had at the Asinou Church.

Tobias turned back and peered through the settling dust. His sight fell upon something from ancient mythology gone horribly wrong. The beast was a mass of muscle with thick, red, pulsating veins running beneath its charred, bubbled, and — in some places — peeling flesh. A thick metal helmet was bolted to its horned head. A long, black tail of hair fell from a hole in the top of the helmet and down the beast's back. Its empty, black eyes surveyed the room.

At first, Tobias denied what he saw. There was no possible way it could exist. He figured their kind to be a myth, a ghost story told by his kin and passed down to scare the new Guardian recruits. The more he stared, the more he realized it was no myth. What fell from the darkness overhead was surely a Tormentor. The beast was said to have killed thousands of Guardians in the past. It was the one creature Tobias prayed he never ran into. Those prayers had apparently gone unanswered.

The Tormentor arched back and took in a deep breath, bringing its four muscular arms up above its head. With all its might, it opened its mouth and roared again. The urns nearest it blew out. The sound sent a shiver down Tobias' back, and his heart raced. For the first time in a long time, he felt fear.

The Tormentor lowered its head and rumbled towards John. Before Tobias could react, the beast was on him. With a powerful swipe of its arm, the creature flung John through the air and to the far side of the room. He bounced off the limestone wall and crashed to the floor. He lay motionless, face-down. It charged once again. Each massive stride from its stumpy legs vibrated the ground.

Tobias shook the disbelief from his head. There was no time for that now. With his blade in hand, he raced towards the Tormentor without any form of a plan. Tobias, nearing the beast, jumped into the air from the limestone floor. The creature turned and swatted him like an annoying mosquito. Tobias crashed to the ground with a thud. His sword clanged from his hands and across the ground.

The Tormentor then turned and looked at Tobias with its hate-filled eyes. It roared again. Droplets of nastiness spit from its open mouth. The Tormentor wasted no time in continuing to follow what Tobias assumed was its mission —

to destroy the last of the Sealed.

Rupert, one step ahead, had already moved into position behind it. He swung his hammer towards its legs with a might befitting Atlas. His precise swing hit its mark and knocked the creature's footing out from under it. The Tormentor crashed to the floor, kicking up a cloud of limestone dust and rumbling the ground. Part of the wall to their right crumbled and slid off like a glacier in warm waters, eventually settling into a pile of rubble.

As if in perfect synchronization, Tia landed on the beast with both her swords pointed down. Her blades pierced its chest all the way down to their hilts. The monster roared in pain before swiping her off, leaving both of her swords buried in its ashy flesh.

Tia fell inches away from Sam. Her head bounced off the floor, knocking her out cold.

The beast rose and looked back towards John. Black liquid poured from its wounds, yet the monster seemed unfazed. It was even more enraged.

Grabbing Tia's arm, Sam dragged her limp body behind the relative safety of the urn.

Tobias' disbelief vanished, replaced by anger. He fearlessly charged the Tormentor. Grasping his sword over his right shoulder with both hands, he held it like a pole-vaulter holds his pole. With a full head of steam, he plowed with all his might into the beast's spine. He felt the sword cut through flesh, muscle, sinew, and whatever else was in its path. The Tormentor spun around with the sword buried in its back.

"This thing's like a pincushion," Rupert said as he backed away, trying to catch his breath.

Diving for cover, Tobias barely escaped another swipe from its giant hand. This was hopeless. Their weapons were doing nothing but annoying it.

The Tormentor spun back around, ignoring Tobias and Rupert, and rumbled away towards the now upright John. The two were on a collision course towards the center of the room.

"Rupert," Tobias yelled, nodding towards the Tormentor's back. "Think you can hit it?"

There, half-exposed, was the Guardian's blade. With the might of a god and the accuracy of a sniper, Rupert hurled his giant hammer into the air. It tumbled end over end in the straightest of lines until hitting the sword squarely. The force of the impact drove the blade clear through the beast's body and out through its chest. It was a one-in-a-million shot, but the big man made it. Exploding through its body, the sword dug into the soft limestone wall on the opposite end of the room.

The Tormentor released a deafening moan.

Rupert looked back at Tobias. "I think that just pissed it off more."

Before Tobias could react, a flurry of whizzes shot past his ear. Tia was back upright, wobbling in place. Her throwing blades cut through the cloudy air. Each blade hit its mark and impaled deep into the Tormentor's skull, dropping it to the ground.

It pulled the daggers free with one giant handful and tossed them aside. The Tormentor pounded on the ground with both of its massive fists.

"Now that definitely pissed it off," Rupert said.

"Okay," Tobias said as the light bulb turned on, "plan B." He wondered why it took him this long to think of it. He removed the micro-shotgun from his leg and cocked it open to reveal two red shells nestled firmly in the barrels.

The Tormentor rumbled towards him. More putrid droplets flung from its mouth. This would be his last effort. He prayed the red-cased shell would do what he told Sam it

180

would—make a mess. He pulled the trigger and set loose the molten-fire rounds. The room flashed with a sudden deep red light.

As the rounds exploded, a webbed circle of molten fire cut through the beast with ease, slicing it into rounded pieces of charred flesh that slid to the limestone floor with a wet splash. A steaming pile of evil was all that remained.

Tia put her hand to her head. The adrenaline that carried her to her feet had apparently worn off. Sam eased her down to the floor.

John, back on his feet, passed the remnants of the monster in a zombie-like trance and proceeded to the center of the room, seemingly unfazed by what'd just happened to him. The aura surrounding him was now more defined. He once again held his hands up. Chanting again flowed from his mouth.

Giggles, the same type they'd heard beside the Sphinx, now echoed from overhead. Tobias figured the damn Imps had brought back the Tormentor, and they'd apparently stayed to watch the slaughter, although he doubted it worked out as they had hoped it would.

The giggles stopped. Three crashes, one after another, hammered the ground behind them. Tobias looked back to the base of the stairs. Three more Tormentors stared back. The one closest to them roared and pounded its chest.

The devil had apparently grown powerful enough to summon more than one of its fearsome hunters, and from the looks of it, there was no shortage of them in hell.

"You have to be kidding me," Rupert said, clutching his hammer for the next wave.

Tobias went to reload the gun. It was then that he realized he'd told Sam to leave them back in the tunnel after she fell. There were no more shells.

He reached over and pulled his sword out of the

crumbling limestone wall. The hot metal scalded his hand, but he was not about to let it go. He would prefer a burn over death any day, though he wasn't sure the choice was still his to make. He looked over at Rupert by his side.

"Been nice knowing you, Tobias," Rupert said.

The Tormentors charged in unison as Tobias and Rupert took a position directly in front of John, their weapons at the ready.

Pieces of the wall crumbled away as the ground shook like a herd of elephants rumbled by. Several of the metal urns tipped over sideways and spilled their fiery purple contents onto the ground.

As all points converged in the center of the room, John suddenly stopped chanting. There was less than a second of silence before the thunderous boom exploded in the open room. A brilliant white flash of light ringed out from John and engulfed the entire room.

Looking down in surprise, Tobias watched as the ring sped through him in an instant. He felt nothing as it passed. The same ring of light soon found the Tormentors, but they weren't as lucky. The brilliant ring of light seared through them, leaving nothing behind but the echoes of their parting moans.

The brilliance of the light faded, and the room was cast back into dim, purple illumination. Two urns remained upright and lit. They provided just enough light to see John sway in place and then fall to the ground, unconscious.

Tobias caught sight of something on the far wall. There, carved within the limestone, stood an entryway that had not been there minutes ago. Etched into the door, on the right side, was the shape of the Crux.

Chapter 23

Tobias searched in vain for a way into the new door. No matter what he tried—ramming it, prying it, pushing it—it all failed. He soon realized that the only person capable of opening it was unconscious in the middle of the room. Their only option, at that point, was to wait yet again.

Nearly an hour had passed, and Tobias was starting to get antsy. John's magic trick, whatever it was, had worked wonders on the Tormentors. Tobias had no doubt that it had saved all of their lives, but he knew they were just a taste of the things to come. Next time they would attack in greater numbers, and with more ferocity. The devil's strength had grown to a point where it could summon its most fearsome of hunters. For all he knew, an army of Tormentors was already on its way to them. The devil's spies would ensure it.

Giving up on the door, he walked over to the group and sat down, aggravated. John lay on his back in the center of their disorganized circle. He wasn't bleeding and had no visible wounds of any kind, at least not that Tobias could see. That, in itself, he found surprising, especially since he had been thrown across the room like a human dart, not to mention the as-yet-to-be-discussed ring of light that emanated from within him. The best he could tell, John was just in a deep sleep, much deeper than he had been at the safe house. His eyes skittered beneath his thin, fleshy lids. His chest rose and fell with each passing breath. All attempts at waking him had failed.

Tobias looked from John over to Sam. She sat next to John, cross-legged and caressed his hand caringly. Because her hair was in a ponytail, Tobias was able to get a good look at her face. He hadn't seen her cry, but her red, puffy eyes told him enough. She was the most vulnerable of them all. Her kindness back in the woods of Connecticut had opened the door and allowed trouble to walk in. Guilt is what he felt when he looked at her. In a roundabout way, he knew this was his fault. At least, that's what he kept telling himself, despite his mind's attempts to convince himself otherwise.

Rupert sat with his back to the wall. Tia leaned against him for support. Together they stared at the ground in silence. Maybe the hour-long reprieve was a blessing in disguise. Everyone could use the rest. He just wished it didn't have to be there, in the bowels of some long-forgotten vault. Tobias yearned for some fresh air. And, while he hated the heat, feeling the sun's rays again would be a welcome change.

"Tobias," Sam said, startled.

Tobias turned to find John stirring. His eyes fluttered a moment and then opened wide, like he had been shocked awake from a horrible nightmare. Sam clambered to support his back, but it was unnecessary. John rose from the ground as if cushioned by some unforeseen force. His ascent was quick and graceful. Now on his feet, he looked around the room, grinning in a knowing way.

"Are you okay?" Sam asked, rising from the ground, surprised.

John turned to her. With a smile, he took her hand in his, but said nothing.

Tobias drew up beside him. "John?"

"John is fine, Guardian." His voice was deeper than before and more confident.

Tobias arched his right eyebrow.

Rupert laughed. "Can *John* tell us what's going on then?"

John turned to Rupert. "John has stepped aside for the time being so that I may complete the second of the Trinity Signs."

Everyone gawked, unsure of what to say.

"If you're not John, then who are you?" Tobias asked. *It just keeps getting weirder,* Tobias thought.

"My name is not important, Guardian. I gave it up long ago."

The group looked at one another, baffled. Tobias eyed John carefully. He knew this could be a trick of the devil, but that wouldn't make any sense. If this was a trick, then why would he toy with them, rather than just kill John?

"Where's John?"

"He is still here, Guardian. You need not worry about his safety. I am merely using his body as a vessel to achieve what I have come to do. His consciousness is beside mine, patiently waiting for the task to be completed."

Tobias remembered John saying something earlier about his body being a shared vessel.

"And what is it you've come to do?" Tobias said.

John pointed towards the door that had appeared from the crumbled limestone. "Therein lies the second of the Trinity Signs." He looked back at Tobias. "It would not be possible for John to complete this Sign without my help."

"I'm sorry," Tia interrupted, "but does nobody else find this just a little bit crazy?"

Rupert nodded.

"Crazier than what just happened, you mean?" Sam said. "Crazier than those giant things that played ping-pong with us?"

"Tormentors," Tobias added. "Those things were Tormentors." He hoped that was the last time he ran into them.

"Whatever they were," Sam said, "they would be

included in my definition of crazy."

John continued, "The Trinity Signs have saved humanity once before. I pray this time the number of lives lost will be drastically less than it was one thousand years ago."

"And I take it you were there the last time the devil attacked?" Tobias asked.

John nodded. "I was tasked with the preservation of humanity then, as you all are now." He looked around at the group surrounding him. "The devil's minions were more powerful than we had expected and overtook Camelot after a fierce battle. They came dangerously close to capturing the Crux Signate. At the last possible moment, my understudy arrived with the Crux in hand. He had successfully activated the first two Trinity Signs." He looked over at the door and then back to the group. "The walls of the great castle had been breached, and through them poured an unrelenting wave of savage Evil. I was able to activate the third Trinity Sign just as the army of hell burst through the inner sanctuary doors."

One word stuck out above all others in his explanation.

Sam spoke before Tobias could. "I'm sorry, did you say Camelot?"

John turned to Sam and smiled again.

Tobias noticed the longing look on his face as he stared at her. He had a feeling that whoever shared John had much more to offer, but for whatever reason, he was holding back. Tobias wanted to ask questions, but he didn't know where to start.

"The glorious castle of Camelot was the epicenter for the Brotherhood. Its walls, impervious to every prior attack, fell that day. We lost a great number of our protectors when the devil's army attacked." He turned towards Tobias. "They fought with an unmatched bravery, never to be duplicated until now."

"The Guardians?" Tobias asked. It seemed he heard a new story about his long lost brethren each day. It bothered him that something as enormous as what John was now telling him had not been shared before, but he wasn't surprised.

"Yes." John sighed and looked towards the black emptiness overhead. "If it were not for the Guardians, pushing with all their might to prevent the army's advance, I would not have had the time to activate the final Sign. Many a good man was lost to the forces of evil that day, the day of the blood sky."

Tobias had spent most of his life with the knowledge he was the last Guardian. The thoughts of an army of Guardians fighting valiantly side by side made him gush with a sudden feeling of pride, a feeling that had eluded him thus far in life. He would not tarnish their memory by failing his task.

"Can we get back to this Camelot thing for a minute?" Rupert asked. "Are we talking about the same Camelot with King Arthur and the round table and all that stuff?"

John paused and eyed the ground. After a brief moment, he looked back to Rupert.

"John's memories reveal that history has spun a web of untruths. I suspect it was to protect the true purpose of Camelot as the final resting place of the final Trinity Sign."

"So, no King Arthur?" Rupert asked.

"He did exist," John said, "but we do not have the time to discuss his villainy now."

Villainy? Every tale that Tobias had heard heralded Arthur as a savior and loyal king to his people. However, sorting out who was good and bad was not imperative at the moment.

The knowledge of where to locate the final Sign was of immeasurable help, though the fact that it was located in a castle that didn't exist was troubling. Tobias did, however, feel the tiniest bit of relief knowing the wild goose chase was nearing an end. He also realized that it did him no good to know where the third Sign was without first attending to the reason why they were in the bowels of the desert.

"How do we activate the second Sign?" Tobias said.

John looked towards Sam and removed the Crux Signate from around his neck. "It is up to you, my dear, to complete the second of the Trinity Signs."

"Me?" she said, pointing to herself, shocked.

John nodded. "The Sign of the Son can only be initiated by one of the Brothers—in this case, John, with my help, but its completion rests solely on the acceptance of the Matron."

Sam furrowed her brow. "And I am the Matron?"

John again nodded.

With her back to the wall, Sam sank to the floor. "I don't understand." Her face whitened. "What does that even mean?"

"Deep breaths, Sam," Tobias said, kneeling down beside her. This was a twist he had not envisioned.

John, too, bent down on one knee beside her. He again took her hand and smiled. "My dear, you have been involved in this since the very beginning. The fact that you are under the Guardian's protection is not by chance, but by fate."

Tobias' thoughts swirled. He found it hard to grasp that this was all planned out in some preordained fable, but if it was, then the sense of guilt he felt for dragging Sam along was unwarranted. He was just doing what needed to be done. If he hadn't brought Sam this far, then it wouldn't be possible to activate the second Sign. He felt the guilt lessen, making enough room for confusion to take its place. If this had somehow been planned out, he wondered where the hand of fate would push them next. What else was written in the book of time that he wasn't privy to?

John helped Sam off the floor. He then walked to the Sign's entrance and held the Crux Signate to the carving that bore its shape. The heavy stone door slid to the right and revealed a small room.

With a wave of John's hand, four large white pedestals ignited within the room, each of them resting in a corner. Their flames shined brightly enough to discern its small size. In the middle of the room lay a large table. It appeared to be carved from a single slab of white marble, polished and elegant.

"What does it mean, exactly, that Sam is the Matron of the Sealed?" Tobias asked.

"Sam, like those before her, is a descendent of a bloodline imperative to humanity's continued survival. Her ancestors, those of my day, were the mothers of each member of the Brotherhood of the Sealed. The Matrons carried within them a gift from above. The Brothers were sent to protect the rest of God's children, using the Trinity Signs as their last means of defense. Over time, our true purpose has faded away, but now, at this very moment, the past meets the present. Both John and Sam are integral to the success of the endeavor you have undertaken. Without Sam's ancestors, there would be no John, and without John's ancestors, humanity would live under the oppression of the devil. It is a perplexing issue that needs no solution, only acceptance, for that is the way of things."

Tobias wanted to speak, to say something, but words eluded him. What could he say? What he was just told blurred his thoughts and beliefs. He soon realized *John* was right about one thing—acceptance was the only answer. There wasn't time for a full history lesson today.

John reached out for Sam with an open hand, palm up. "Will you accept the selfless task humanity has placed on you, my child?"

Sam hesitated. "Do I have a choice?"

"The choice is only yours to make, my dear," John said. "Know, though, that rejection will mean certain death for much of mankind."

"Since you put it that way…," Sam said, hesitantly.

"Why?" Tobias said. "Why must Sam be impregnated? It seems to me a rather strange way to activate the second sign. Why not just stick the Crux in the Sign and start it up?" Tobias realized it wouldn't be that simple, but it seemed a bizarre way to go about things.

"All of this is done for a reason, Guardian. John activated the first Sign so that he may gain the knowledge of the Brotherhood and, in turn, allow me to show you the path. Now the Matron must take on this duty as only she can. John is the last of the Brotherhood. There needs to be a continuation of the bloodline. The second Sign will ensure that."

Sam nodded softly at the explanation and took John's hand. She appeared nervous, yet confident at the same time. A few stray tears ran down her cheeks. She turned to Tobias."I have to do this, Tobias." She smiled. "It will be okay. Don't worry."

"So you're alright with having sex with a ghost that's taken over John's body?"

"My dear boy," John said, almost snickering. "The activation does not involve any form of physical connection with the Matron. There are many things at work here, some of which I would not be able to properly explain – forces that act in our benefit."

Tobias nodded reluctantly. Relief flowed through him that Sam wasn't about to have sex with a possessed John, but the whole situation was not something he could ever properly prepare for.

Sam brushed Tobias' arm. "I need to do this."

Tobias nodded. He realized this was their only option.

John then led Sam down the three stairs and into the small room.

Tobias stood on the top step, about to descend, when John turned around. With his hand held out, palm facing them, John signaled for the group to remain where they were. This apparently was a private affair. Tobias was dealing with things he didn't understand. He wrestled with thoughts and emotions he couldn't possibly sort out at that moment, if ever. Letting Sam and John out of his sight, especially after what he had just been told, was the most difficult thing he'd had to do so far, but he realized he had little choice in the matter.

With a wave of John's hand the door slid closed. Tobias watched helplessly as they vanished behind the thick stone.

Chapter 24

Anxiety manifested into anger the longer Tobias paced in front of the sealed door. Waiting was not something he did particularly well, this much he knew. He wondered what could be taking so long. It had been over thirty minutes since Sam followed John into the small, sterile-looking room. Since then, there had been nothing to speak of—no sound, no brilliant white light, nothing. He had seen more than enough of what Egypt had to offer and hoped to be en route to the final Trinity Sign by now. But as more time passed, it became apparent that his hopes didn't line up with those of the fate.

Rupert rose from the ground. "What's up, babe?" he said, seeing Tia walk back after surveying the damage done by the Tormentors.

She turned and nodded over her shoulder. "Those things beat the stairs up pretty good. The big rocks that fell earlier were actually large sections of the staircase. We're definitely not going back up the way we came down."

Tobias' gut had already told him that much. Even if they did get back up to the top, there were no assurances that the tunnels were now unblocked. There had to be another way out, and hopefully John knew about it.

Rupert and Tia took it upon themselves to search the chamber for another way out. They both walked along the walls, using the dim, purple light to scour the limestone for a hidden exit, if one existed in the first place.

No sooner had they stopped at the far wall than the sealed door finally slid open.

Sam was the first one out. She walked casually up the

stairs with an innocent smile on her face. John followed on her heels. The four torches blew out, and the thick door shut behind him. As it sealed, the door's outline faded away like it had been erased by the hands of time.

"The second Trinity Sign is complete," John said, in his own voice.

"Is that you, John?" Tobias said. "I mean, the real you?"

John nodded.

Tia and Rupert meandered back from their search for an exit and stood beside Tobias.

"Can someone explain to me what happened in there?" Tobias asked. His frustration showed, and he knew it, but he couldn't help it. He felt like he was losing control of the group, like everything had suddenly overshadowed his leadership. Above all, he felt a certain amount of jealousy, and that bothered him.

"I'm not totally sure, really," John said. "I mean, I was there, but I felt like I wasn't at the same time." He closed his eyes and shook his head. "It was like I was a stranger in my own head."

Tobias turned to Sam. "Are you sure you are okay with this?" Regardless of her answer, he knew it was too late to change things. He just needed her reassurance.

"Thank you for caring," she said, stepping closer. She placed her hands on his cheeks and pecked him quickly on his dry lips.

Tobias was stunned silent.

"I'm fine," she said. "I don't know how to describe it, really. I've always had this feeling I could never really grasp, like there was something missing in my life—something I knew was out of reach. But now...," she smiled and looked down, "...I feel good. I really do. I know what that something was." She brought her hand up to her belly. "Now I know my direction. I know my purpose. For the first time in my life, I actually feel whole."

He followed her hand and watched as she made small circles on her stomach. Reasoning aside, she was now pregnant, and his protection duties had officially increased again. While he would never let harm come to her, or the immaculately conceived child, he hoped the choice between who to protect—John or Sam—never came into play. He knew his heart would fight his mind every step of the way, but there was no reason to complicate matters. Not yet. The second Trinity Sign was complete. *One more to go.*

"John, you...ah, the other *you*, mentioned Camelot as the third Sign's location."

John nodded. "I remember him telling you." He snickered. "It was so strange. I was there, listening to his story, but from the inside." He paused, took a deep breath, and continued. "Camelot was where the third Trinity Sign *was* kept."

"Was?" Tia said.

John nodded. "After the devil and his army were beaten, the Brotherhood would have moved the Sign to another location. That's what I feel to be the truth, anyway."

"Moved it where?" Tobias asked.

"That's the problem. While the spirit that was with me was unimaginably powerful, he did have his limits. He died when the devil's army was sent back to hell, or, as he put it, the day of the blood sky." John froze up and looked expressionless, as he apparently dealt with something internally—something that seemed to bother him deep down. His voice became softer. He shook his head and cleared his throat. "Anyway, the sign must have been moved after the invasion. Its location is as much a mystery to the spirit as it is to us."

Tobias reached up and grabbed the back of his neck. With a quick twist, he cracked it to the left and then to the right. He sighed in frustration. *So much for catching a break.*

"So how do we find the Sign, then?" Tobias said.

John shrugged. "I don't know, but something tells me we should start looking in its last location. The Brotherhood would have left a clue behind, like directions or something."

"Not to be a party-pooper," Rupert chimed, "but how exactly do you suggest we find the legendary castle of Camelot?"

Tobias looked to John for an answer. John again shrugged. "I asked him the same question, you know, before he left my body." He shook his head like he still couldn't believe it actually happened. "He said that we will happen upon the castle because it lies directly on our fateful path."

"And that means what?" Rupert asked.

John shrugged.

Tobias looked to the rest of the group for any input. Their faces were blank.

"All right, one problem at a time. Let's worry about finding a way out of here first," he said. "Then we can try and locate Camelot." It sounded absurd even speaking the words, let alone following through with the act.

"I know the way out," John volunteered, walking away from the group. "That much the spirit did know."

Finally, some good news.

John walked to the base of the crumbled stairs. Moving out of the light and into the shadows, he put his hands to the wall and felt along until he found what he was apparently looking for. He fit the Crux into a small slit. A sudden click sounded from behind the thick wall, followed by the shifting of the limestone. The new hallway lit as the others had before, except these torches burned with the natural hues of a fire, absent of the purple glow. John looked over his shoulder to the group and waved them in.

The passage rose at a steep angle, but went straight for

the majority of the fifteen-minute walk. Limestone stairs, like the ones they'd descended earlier, ran the length of the tunnel. A wall of solid stone blocks, each of which was around three feet high, ended their ascent. John again felt along the shadows on the wall until he found another slit. He placed the Crux within, and again it clicked. The bottom slab of stone blocking their exit swung out like it was on some kind of giant, invisible hinge. A flood of sun swept in through the opening. Getting on their hands and knees, the group was forced to crawl their way out of the musty tunnel.

As he exited, Tobias brought his hand up to shield his eyes from what seemed like an overly-bright sun. They had grown too accustomed to the dark interior of the underground cavern. The rest of the group followed him out through the opening, back into the fresh, yet scorching, air. They were met with scattered shouts of surprise and rapid clicks.

"What the...?" Rupert said, still holding his hands up, shielding his eyes.

Through the sun spots in his vision, Tobias made out what looked to be a large group of Asians directly in front of them, snapping pictures.

"What the heck is going on?" Sam asked.

Shading his eyes with his hand, Tobias looked at the group of people standing some twenty-five feet away. He then rotated around and looked behind him, following their gaze. With a smirk on his face, he turned back around and nodded for the rest of the team to take a look.

Behind them the Great Pyramid of Khufu jutted high into the sky like the manmade mountain of stone that it was. They had just exited through its base and apparently into a tour group. The tourists, who couldn't take pictures fast enough, must have thought this was some kind of planned show. *If they only knew,* Tobias thought as the stone closed behind them, sealing away the second Trinity Sign. *If they only knew.*

Chapter 25

Pyramids Road bustled in a blur of tourism. Vans, taxis, bicycles, and scooters all rushed by, oblivious to the team as they waited for the next airport shuttle to arrive. Tobias found it hot, but not unbearable, thanks in large part to the shaded canopy they sat beneath. Anything, at that point, was better than the musty limestone basement they had been trapped in for what felt like days. The scent clung to his clothes like an all-encompassing, invisible stain. No matter where he looked, everything still seemed to have a purple tint to it. To say he was happy to leave the cavern behind would have been a major understatement.

No sooner had he slumped onto the bench when his pocket vibrated, alerting him to a new voicemail. Since the cell reception beneath the Sahara was nonexistent, the message must have been delayed up until now. Using his un-bandaged hand, he dug into his pocket and removed the black cell phone. The glare forced him to hold it close to his face, like an old man reading the tiny words on a pill bottle. The icon in the upper right hand corner indicated that he had one new message waiting. With the push of a button, he retrieved the voicemail.

He was glad to hear the familiar voice of Cardinal Rathady. The Cardinal informed Tobias that he had received communication of the downed jet. Not surprising, considering it was the Vatican's. The fear that the group might be lost was enough to bring Rathady overnight to Cairo International Airport. He mentioned trying to form a search party at the time of the message, but with international tensions at an all-time high, it was proving more difficult than he had expected. His message requested Tobias to be in touch as soon as possible, and said that he would be praying for them.

Dropping the phone back into his pocket, Tobias decided it was best to speak to the Cardinal in person rather than call him back. They were already headed to the airport, and there was no telling who or what could be listening in.

Fifteen minutes passed before the airport shuttle arrived. A whirling trail of sand followed the bus as it squealed to a stop in front of the group. Tobias pushed himself off the bench. His legs let their displeasure be known via a strong cramp that ran from the small of his back down to his toes.

The cooling sensation felt heavenly as he stepped up into the air-conditioned cabin. The bus was about half-full, with a mix of varying ages and nationalities. All eyes were on the group as they sat down in the front, closest to the forceful air. The benches lined the windows, with the riders facing towards the center of the bus. The other passengers looked on with a mix of curiosity and fear. Each pair of eyes that Tobias met looked down and away. He couldn't blame them for staring. After all, the group was a beaten and disheveled mess. Rupert with his large hammer, and Tia with her swords was enough to warrant a few sidelong glances, at the very least. Put them all together, and he was surprised they were even allowed on the bus in the first place. But Egypt seemed more than happy to accept them, oddness and all.

With a jerk of the gears and a loud backfire, the bus continued down the road after the emaciated driver gave it more gas. Rupert and Tia abruptly dozed off. Several minutes later, Rupert, his mouth agape, began to snore heavily. The back of his head rested against the window, directing his tenacious snores towards the roof. It garnered several looks of disgust from his fellow travelers, but Tobias didn't have the heart or the desire to wake him. These people could live with the minor inconvenience his snoring caused. He was, after all, helping to save all their lives. They just didn't know it.

John sat quietly by himself and stared blankly through the window. Ever since the ghost took over his body, John seemed different. Something clearly bothered him, and it was something that hadn't been there before. Tobias wanted to dig deeper, to help him, but it was not the time, nor the place. Anyway, he had no idea how to help him. All of this was uncharted territory.

The bus stopped again, and a small exchange of people took place. A young couple wearing safari gear stepped on and sat across from Tobias. Each had on a rounded pith helmet, light brown shirts and shorts, and brand spanking new Timberland boots. He felt an urge to tell them how stupid they looked, like latecomers to a yuppie Halloween party, but he held back. The pot and the kettle came to mind.

Another backfire, and the bus continued further down the road.

Exhausted, Tobias reached to his scalp and combed the wet tendrils of his hair back with his hand. Thin channels of sweat streaked down his face, carving clean valleys on his dirty, sunburned skin.

As disgusting as he currently was, it did not seem to deter Sam. She took a queue from the power couple and slept soundly, nestled against Tobias' left arm. Pins-and-needles quickly settled into his limb, as the positioning was poor for blood circulation, but he gladly dealt with the discomfort so that she could sleep for a moment.

As she lay there peacefully, he felt the emotions from before brew back to the surface—emotions he didn't quite know how to deal with. He successfully fought them off at first, but now it was a losing battle. The peck on the lips Sam gave him after the second Sign was activated, while small and seemingly meaningless, solidified feelings that could not be easily shunned. He was falling for her, no matter how hard he tried to fight it. Occasionally, as in this case, he thought about how much easier life would be without emotions. They just tended to get in the way of things—of his duty—but he figured those very emotions were what separated them from what they now fought.

Fifteen more minutes passed before the bus squealed to a stop. Those hoping for more sleep were rudely jostled awake as the driver let the clutch out a little too soon. The weary-eyed group begrudgingly left the cool, air-conditioned bus and lumbered back beneath the hot, yet thankfully dimming, sun.

Checking with airport services, they were directed one hundred yards down to hanger nine, the Cardinal's location. Another short walk, and they arrived at the dimly-lit hangar. The collapsible stairs of the jet were down.

"Tobias?" boomed the Cardinal's voice. He sounded more surprised than thankful. "Thank the Lord you are safe." He exited the jet so quickly that he nearly tripped himself.

The Cardinal hurriedly approached the group. He grasped Tobias tight and gave him a solid hug. Tobias patted the Cardinal on the back with his left hand. He never had been one for physical shows of emotion.

"Where's Vene?"

Rathady surveyed the rest of the group before answering. His eyes undoubtedly fell upon a haggard gathering of people who desperately needed a hot shower and a full night's sleep.

"Vene is still at the safe house. He was on to something and did not want to leave."

Tobias nodded in understanding.

"I feared the worst when we lost contact with you," Rathady said. "How on earth did you survive?"

Tobias steered the Cardinal back towards the jet. "Are we alone?" he asked.

Cardinal Rathady nodded. "Yes. My pilot just so happens to be Egyptian. He and the copilot went for a visit and for dinner. I told them we would not be leaving anytime soon, not until I was able to find you." A smirk arched across his face.

Rathady was one of the few people that Tobias trusted explicitly, yet Tobias felt like he was holding something back. His mannerisms seemed to suggest that he wasn't telling Tobias everything. Then again, maybe it was his tired mind making him think things that were not. The reiteration of needing sleep bounced around inside of him.

"I hope your pilots are better than ours," Tobias said.

Rathady arched one eyebrow. "Did they perish in the crash?"

"If, by perish, you mean left in mid-air, then yes."

The Cardinal looked confused as they stepped up into the jet.

Tobias filled in the blanks. "Our pilots bailed out during the flight. I'm assuming they were paid by some cult loyal to the devil to dispose of us."

Rathady looked nauseous. "Do you suspect anyone in particular?"

"No," he said. "And it doesn't really matter who did it, just that it was done."

"Tell him about the dragon," Rupert said, sitting down in one of the jet's high-back leather chairs.

"Dragon?" Rathady said.

Tobias nodded. "After the pilots bailed we encountered what could only be a dragon. I know, I know," Tobias said, holding up his hand, "dragons aren't real. But, trust me, this dragon was very real."

"And pissed off," Rupert added.

The Cardinal perked up. "Was this dragon covered in an ash-colored hide, by chance? With small horns around its eyes, large tattered wings, and an enormously long tail that ended in a ball of spikes?"

The group looked at one another in surprise. It was like the Cardinal was there with them. Tobias found it strange that the Cardinal had that information readily available in such detail.

Cardinal Rathady grinned and looked away. "Chapter twelve in the Book of Revelation speaks of a dragon with a fierce disposition. It was said to have waged a war with heaven. The dragon in the book was thought to be a representation of the devil, but from your accounts, I can only assume that it is just another tool of the devil and not his manifestation."

"The devil keeps some strange pets," Rupert offered from the rear of the jet. He took the liberty of opening a bottle of single malt scotch and quietly poured himself a refresher.

Tobias watched Rupert offer a glass to John, the alcoholic, but was surprised to see John refuse. He was changing more by the minute. It appeared that the Sign's power had cured him of all his afflictions, including the crippling disease of alcoholism.

"You must remember, Tobias," Rathady said, "what is awakening is the pinnacle of evil. Death itself fears what you now fight."

Sam spoke. "I don't understand how the devil is getting stronger when John is still alive." She sat slouched in one of the leather jet seats. She had taken a nearby pillow and rested it in her lap.

Tia plopped down into the seat opposite Sam and

waited for the answer from the Cardinal. Her head rested on its side, facing the rest of the group. It was apparently the most energy she could dedicate to paying attention.

Rathady was quick with his response. "The devil thrives on the misery that he inflicts on man. Plagues, disease, war, famine… all of it is meant to weaken man's resolve so we can be more easily enslaved. With each good soul that is swayed towards evil, the devil gains in strength. And, nowadays, it seems like more follow that path by the minute."

Tobias took a seat next to the Cardinal. He looked at him with tired and bloodshot eyes. "We need to go to England."

Rathady leaned in closer, a serious expression on his face. "The final Trinity Sign?"

"Possibly."

"Very well, then. To England we go," Rathady said. "I will have to call back the pilots, but that should not take too long. In the meantime, why don't you all try and get some well deserved sleep?"

Tobias nodded and looked to the rest of the team. Tia was already asleep, and Sam was drifting before the Cardinal had offered the idea. Rupert crossed his arms on his bulky chest. He took a deep breath and shut his eyes.

"I think you should try and rest, John," Tobias said.

John looked back with quarter-sized eyes. He appeared calm and relaxed. "I'm not really tired." He turned back and looked out the window. "As they say, there'll be plenty of time to sleep when I'm dead," he muttered under his breath.

Tobias was truly worried about John's wellbeing, but his own exhaustion had its limits. He found that keeping his eyes open had become a losing battle, one he stopped fighting a few minutes later.

Chapter 26

Tobias found sleep elusive during the flight to Bristol International Airport. His body begged for even a short respite, but his mind, still lingering on their last flight, wouldn't allow it. If the Cardinal trusted his pilots, then Tobias knew he could, as well. Trust, however, would not protect all of their lives. He needed to remain alert, even if it went against his internal urgings.

John also remained awake for the duration. He sat with the Cardinal across the aisle from Tobias and discussed all that had transpired over the past few days. John had questions, and Rathady did his best to answer them. Some questions, though, went beyond the scope of the Cardinal's understanding. Rathady advised John to search deep within himself for the answers he sought, for only there would he find them.

The last part, about needing to search within himself, struck Tobias as corny in a high school counselor sort of way. Yet, the more he thought about it, the more he realized Rathady was right. John, through some kind of mystical event, had been instilled with all the knowledge of the Brotherhood. He was, therefore, the only person capable of answering his own questions. Tobias couldn't imagine how it felt trying to grasp at wisps of information from days gone by.

While the jet had been on the ground for over ten minutes, Tobias felt it best to get their bearings before heading out. They had access to more information on the jet than they would in the field, and storming out blindly would do no good. Sam took it upon herself to find the answers they sought, and until then, they were staying put.

"It's getting worse," Sam said abruptly from the back of the jet.

Tobias turned to find her staring fixedly at a small LCD television propped on the gleaming hardwood table in front of her. The blue reflection of the screen made the unmistakable look of concern that much more pronounced. He eased out of his chair and walked to a position behind her. The rest of the group followed suit.

The CNN news ticker streamed information across the bottom of the screen. The headline, dramatic in its red, smeary font, indicated that a war between North and South Korea was imminent. Sam reached out and turned the volume up.

A video of soldiers, marching in formation down a long street with rifles on their shoulders, surrounded by a cheering crowd of thousands, filled the LCD.

The reporter chimed in, "As South Korea plans to defend its border against the antagonistic North, they show off their might in a demonstration through Seoul today." The TV cut to a 3D military diagram of a missile. "The North has threatened to use one of its newest and most advanced short range weapons, the Taepodong-2 missile. This has caused the United States, and much of the rest of the world, to go on high alert as it watches and waits."

"My God," Tia said, rubbing the sleep from her eyes. "It's really happening this time. It looks like the next World War is in the making."

"All of this is the work of the devil, I'm afraid," Rathady said. "Mankind has always been weakest when at war with itself, and the devil surely knows that." He looked from the screen and out through the window of the jet. "I think the world has a history of underestimating its power. The devil works in ways we could never understand. It's wondrous, in an evil sort of way." He turned back with a strange smirk on his face.

The words bothered Tobias, but he realized that opinions differed. Ultimately, he knew where the Cardinal stood. Plus, the old man was probably the most well-versed clergy member when it came to anything devil-related. Years of study and dedication would certainly bring some kind of appreciation to the subject, even if it was the purest form of evil.

The screen flashed to a breaking story. The tag banner read *Black Plague Returns?* The news anchor, a thin, blonde-haired man, sat behind a high rectangular desk and read the incoming news as it appeared on the teleprompter. "We have just received word that the World Health Organization has deployed an emergency containment unit to Alberta, Canada." The LCD showed an increasingly zoomed-in map of Alberta. When the picture reached the desired detail, a red circle appeared, showing the location of the apparent outbreak. "Our initial reports are scattered, but from what CNN has learned, there may be a new strain of the Black Plague cropping up throughout the country."

Sam nervously bit her nails.

The news anchor continued. "The Black Plague, which was thought to have started in the 1330s, cost millions of people their lives. Initial analysis of this new strain has caused so much alarm within the WHO that it has requested an emergency meeting of the United Nations. We'll keep you informed as more becomes available."

Tobias reached over Sam's shoulder and turned off the screen. It was doing them no good to watch the world fall apart when they alone had the power to change things.

"Did you find anything, Sam?" Tobias only hoped the legend was somewhat accurate and that the castle did indeed rest somewhere in England.

She opened the laptop resting on her knees. Swiping the touchpad, the screen came to life. The Vatican spared no expense when outfitting its jets. This one, like the one that was downed in Egypt, was equipped with satellite feeds for both television and Internet.

Reading the same information she had twenty minutes ago, Sam shook her head in disappointment. "From what I've been able to find, there is no agreed upon spot where Camelot stood. In fact, historians appear to be divided on whether it even existed."

"It existed," John said. He turned from the jet's window to face the group. "Trust me, it existed."

Tobias knew they had to go on that assumption. "Let's take the doubt out of the equation and go on the notion that Camelot is historical fact, rather than disputed myth. Where is the most obvious location?"

Sam scrolled down the screen. "Here," she said, pointing. "It's called Cadbury Castle. Historians believe the hilly landscape was once the perch for Camelot."

"Okay, then, that's where we're going. How far away are we?"

"Not far," Sam said, "it's about twenty miles or so to the southeast."

It was a better situation than Tobias had expected. Not too far away, and a place where some believe the castle may have existed. It was better than nothing.

"Let's gear up and get going, then." He realized they had been lucky to avoid further confrontation. He didn't want to press it.

The group packed whatever they planned on bringing with them and shuffled off the jet.

Tobias turned to Rathady. "Cardinal, I need you to stay here and monitor the world's situation."

Rathady looked saddened to have to stay behind.

Tobias reached down to the table and opened a small, black metal case. He removed two small earpieces from the cloth interior and handed him one. "Stay in touch with these. If anything new happens, let me know." Tobias had been forced to use this same equipment once in Transylvania—small and uncomplicated, just how he liked it.

Cardinal Rathady nodded as Tobias fit the communication earpiece snuggly into his ear.

Tobias then exited the jet and followed the others. He hoped the mysterious and undiscovered castle of Camelot awaited them at the end of the road.

Chapter 27

Exiting the airport, Tobias came upon two black taxis idling at the front gate, just as Rathady had said they would be. Tobias piled into the first car with John and Sam. Rupert and Tia followed in the second. The man behind the wheel of Tobias' car was of considerable weight, with a shiny complexion and a bad attitude. He wore an aging, charcoal-colored derby cap, a cheap wool blazer, and he chain-smoked unfiltered cigarettes with reckless abandon.

Before leaving the jet, Rupert had complained of hunger pangs. devil or not, Tobias was not about to deny the big man his needed sustenance. He, too, was hungry and could use a boost to his lagging energy. There was nothing he could do to prevent an attack while they ate, but he would make their stop as quick as possible. There was no reason to jeopardize their safety any more than necessary.

With Rupert in mind, Tobias asked to be taken to the village nearest to Cadbury Castle. The driver, in between deep inhales from his cigarette, told them of Spiloot Village and raved about McDonough's Pub. According to him, it was the best, and only, place to eat in town. Tobias decided to take the man at his word and asked to be dropped off there.

The road seemed more curved than straight, a direct result of the uneven landscape it cut through. For the life of him, Tobias couldn't understand how the driver swerved down the unlit A-303 with only two dim headlights guiding his way. Practice, he guessed. You do something long enough, and it becomes second nature.

Sam would crash into him on the sharp right turns, and he would repay her on the lefts. John sat in front, oblivious to their uncomfortable plight. A few times Tobias caught the Englishman's quick glance in the rearview mirror. It occurred to him that the driver may be swerving on purpose, causing them to bump and slide for his own enjoyment. It made him wonder if he'd made the right decision in taking the fat man's word on where to eat.

Ten jostling minutes later the taxis pulled up in front of McDonough's Pub. Tobias gladly exited, followed by Sam and then John.

Rupert and Tia walked up from the second car. "What was up with your driver?" Rupert said. "He was all over the road."

Tobias looked over his shoulder at his taxi. The fat man grinned and tipped his cap, as if acknowledging what Tobias had thought. He had been doing it on purpose. The driver then faced forward with the smirk still on his face and pulled away down the dark road.

He turned back to Rupert. "Apparently he was having a little fun at our expense." He opened his palm. In it rested a tiny blade. "I couldn't let him have it all by himself, though." He grinned. "A couple miles down the road, and he should find one of his tires has suddenly gone flat. How unfortunate for him."

Rupert laughed. "That's my boy."

Pocketing the blade and shrugging his pack, Tobias opened the front door of McDonough's Pub. A waft of heat and the smell of stale beer greeted his senses. He stepped in, unintentionally sneered, and looked around. Directly to his right ran a long, makeshift bar, at which sat three patrons, two of who looked up disdainfully. To his left were a few decrepit and dirty booths. The dark interior was lit by several floor lamps. The pub, from what he could quickly gather, was nothing more than an old converted house, as evidenced by the open toilet in the far corner. He hoped that was a leftover and not the bathroom.

The bartender, a round, greasy fellow, followed them with his eyes while drying a thick glass mug with a dirty rag.

Tobias walked to the far end of the room and took a seat at a rectangular table.

Muted chatter arose from two of the bar's patrons, the two who looked up when they entered. The third sat alone at the end closest to the team. He seemed less interested in their presence. Watching him sway in his seat, Tobias figured he had to be highly inebriated and therefore kept his attention on remaining upright.

The bartender broke his stare and flung the rag over his shoulder. He made his way from behind the bar and approached the team, untrustingly eyeing them the whole time. "What can I get for ya?" he asked.

Tia looked up. "Can we see a menu?"

The bartender stood frozen in shock before breaking out in a fit of boisterous laughter. Sparse, yellowing teeth filled his blackened hole of a mouth. The few greasy strings of hair he had left shimmied from side to side as the turbulent guffaw ripped through his body.

The barflies farthest from them also started to laugh. Tobias heard one of them repeat the word *menu*, which made the other one laugh even harder. Curiously, the third man picked his head up, but remained quiet. It seemed the ruckus had garnered his attention.

Tobias realized the cab driver had gotten the last laugh. He prayed for his sake their paths never crossed again.

"I'll take that as a no," Tia angrily muttered under her breath.

Suddenly, like a jack-in-the-box, the third bar patron

kicked back his barstool and spun around. He brought his arm up and wiped his mouth sloppily. His stare, directed like a laser, remained on the round barkeep.

The greasy barman let his laughter drift away. "Listen, Quincy," he said, "your mouth better remain shut, or else."

"Or else what, Simon? You gonna sit on me with yer fat arse?" He chuckled to himself, which was followed by a deep belch. His eyes seemed to bulge as the air escaped his lungs. The group laughed in unison at the drunken man's witty retort.

"I want you all out of me pub—now," the bartender said, whipping around to face the group.

It wasn't worth starting something. At that point, Tobias didn't dare tempt the fates and try whatever food they offered, anyway.

"You, too, Quincy," the bartender said, turning back around. "I want you out." He pointed towards the door.

Laughing, Quincy staggered through the dark room and over to the door. On his way by the other two at the bar, he faked a punch, making them lean back instinctively. With a laugh, he then heaved open the door.

The group stood and followed the drunk. Tia gave a look over her shoulder on the way out that made the bartender freeze. Her utter dislike was conveyed with a single gaze. He was lucky they weren't staying.

With his back to the group, Quincy stood hunched over in the middle of the road just outside the pub. He wobbled in place, trying to light a cigarette against the small wind that had kicked up. Tobias knew he accomplished the task once the white, cancerous cloud rose into the air.

"Nothing like the first puff," Quincy said, turning around to face the group. "Listen, I didn't mean to get ya kicked out, but it's probably better for your health I did." He chuckled and then coughed on the smoke.

Tobias smiled back curiously.

"From the looks of ya, though, I don't think ya need anybody's help. That's for sure." He swayed to his right a bit before catching his balance. "That fat bastard is a real wanker, anyway. Five hundred people in this whole damn town, you figure he would welcome the business." He took another deep drag off his cigarette. "Well, screw him, I say." He laughed. "Listen, I'm going home to cook me up some food, and I don't mind doing the same for you neither. I could use the company. And I could definitely use a little nippy, since Simon there...," he waved his finger towards the bar, "...so rudely tossed me out." His mouth swelled as he captured a burp.

The team looked at one another and then back to Quincy. Nobody answered. Tobias was unsure of what to make of him. He seemed harmless, and for some odd reason he found him amusing, like a cartoon character. The drunk was a needed break from all the seriousness they'd been thrown into.

"Well all right then," Quincy said, taking the silence as a yes. "Come on."

Tobias shrugged and shifted his pack to a more comfortable position. The rest of the team followed them up the cobbled street.

"Don't you worry. It's not far," Quincy said. He staggered another thirty yards before tripping over his own feet and falling down on a small patch of grass. With unexpected grace, he shot up from the ground. Wiping the residue off his now-soiled pants, he turned back to the group, smiling. "Here we are," he said, smiling. "My house."

Quincy reached the front door and fumbled with his keys several times. None of them worked on the lock. He took a step back, looked at the silver numbers on the side of the door, and then looked to his right.

"Actually," he said, pointing to the house next door. "That's my house."

Tobias shook his head and followed the drunk through a set of shrubs and up to what he hoped was the correct house. Thankfully, for all of their sakes, it was. Quincy opened the door and stepped in. He flipped the switch to his right, illuminating the room with the light from several old table lamps. "Come on in."

"Nice place you've got here," Sam said, trying to be polite as she followed Tobias through the door.

Quincy flashed a toothy grin.

In reality, the small house was minimally decorated. They all gathered at a table in the middle of the only room downstairs as Quincy knelt in front of a crumbling fireplace, trying to light it. Across from the front door rose a small flight of rickety stairs. Several vertical bars of the banister were missing.

The drunkard, unsuccessful in his attempts to light the fireplace, strolled over to the old wood-burning stove and heaved in some dry planks. He had better luck with that, as the stove ignited on the first try.

"Ah," Quincy said, wide-eyed.

He rubbed his hands in front of the fire for a moment before closing the stove's black metal door. He then reached up into the only cabinet on the wall and removed a large pot. Placing the metal container on the hot surface, he walked over to the ancient-looking white refrigerator. Tobias wondered if it could even be called a refrigerator. Icebox seemed more like the appropriate word.

"Don't you worry about a thing," he said, catching the Guardian's gaze. "They look old, but they work like the day they were made."

Tobias watched him, amused. He was like a one-man play. He just hadn't yet figured out if Quincy was a comedy or a tragedy.

Quincy reached into the refrigerator and removed a handful of ingredients. He spun around, about forty degrees too much, and put the varying foods on the cutting block to the right of the stove. He then did something that took Tobias and the rest of the group by surprise. Reaching into a side cabinet, he grabbed a dark blue apron. With a semi-embarrassed look, he wrapped it around his waist.

"I know it looks silly, but I'm a splasher when I cook." He smiled, shrugged. "Especially when I'm brewing up my special lamb stew," he continued, sloppily wetting his lips.

After seeing that, Tobias felt his hunger slip away. The recurring vision of the old man's tongue, sliding across his dry lips like an eel in murky water, replayed in his mind.

They let Quincy go about his business for the next twenty minutes. The group limited their talk during that time. Instead, they sat quietly and rested. While the house was run down, it was warm and dim enough to rest their eyes. When Quincy was done, he brought the large, steaming pot over to the table and placed it in the middle.

"Dig in," he said, taking a pull from the bottle of whiskey in his hand.

Everyone looked at one another and waited for the one brave soul to volunteer as the test subject. Tobias took the task upon himself. His hunger had returned with ferocity, and he wanted to get something down before the old man made him queasy again.

Scooping a bit into his bowl, he threw caution to the wind and took a heaping spoonful. The others watched him, waiting. Tobias couldn't believe the amount of flavor derived from every scrumptious bite. He closed his eyes and breathed slowly through his nose, savoring the stew. With one swift gulp the first bite slid down his throat and into his barren stomach.

Rupert looked over with his eyebrows raised.

"That," Tobias said, pointing with his spoon, "is one of the best things I have ever tasted." He scooped more into his bowl.

Quincy brought his hands together and clapped once. "It's a family recipe." He winked and walked over to one of the rocking chairs. Behind it rested a dusty wood crate. He bent down, slid off the cover, and removed a new bottle of whiskey to replace the empty one in his hand. He angled it towards the group, offering a taste of his master. Rupert was the only one who took the old man up on his offer.

After ten minutes of silent devouring, the group sat pleasantly full. The pot was empty, almost wiped clean. Tobias would never have guessed that a masterful cook lay beneath Quincy's grimy exterior. Not in a million years.

Rupert and the old man cheered another glass of the liquor and sat back in their seats.

Tobias checked his watch again. It was getting late, and they needed to get back on track. This little detour had taken more time than he'd wanted it to. While he was grateful for the full belly, they needed to slip away and continue on. The old man, however, spitting out slurred story after story, didn't give him an opportune time to cut in.

"I've seen your tattoo before," Quincy said, drawing Tobias out of his thoughts. Tobias looked back in surprise.

"The tattoo," Quincy said, nodding, "on your arm. I've seen it before."

With his jacket off and his sleeves rolled up, the Guardian's Mark was easy to spot. He held his arm up closer to the light. "You've seen this before? You're positive?"

Quincy nodded and then took down the rest of his glass of whiskey. "Up on the hill," he said pointing through the wall of his cabin. "It's etched onto a rock on the top of Cadbury Castle. Although, I don't know why anyone calls it a castle. It's just a giant hill." He made himself laugh. "It's more like Cadbury Hill." He continued to drunkenly laugh.

Tobias' suspicions were validated. Whoever put the Mark there meant it to be found. It had to be a marker.

"I hope you're not going looking for King Arthur and all the bollocks that goes with him, though," Quincy said. He refilled his glass with whiskey. He went to refill Rupert's glass, but he politely refused. Quincy shrugged.

John, who had remained silent until now, spoke. "Why do you mention Arthur?"

"Just trying to save you time is all." His words became increasingly more difficult to understand. "I've been up to that stinkin' hill a thousand times and never found nothin' worth keepin'."

"Can you tell us where on the hill you saw the symbol?" Tobias asked.

"Tell ya," Quincy said, standing from his stool. "I'll show ya. Follow me." He took two steps and then fell flat on his face. He was a victim of too much alcohol and not enough coordination.

Tobias bent down and turned him onto his back. He was out cold.

The information he kept, while possibly a drunken man's ramblings, could lead them to Camelot. He figured they could search the hill themselves, but it was night and they didn't know the way there, or even where to look if they found it. That process could take far longer and create even more aggravation. Tobias decided to wait for the old drunk to wake, if they had that long.

Chapter 28

Five restless hours passed before Quincy, thanks in no small part to a gentle nudging from Rupert's boot, woke from his alcoholic slumber. The haggard man rose from his bed, a single mattress on the floor, where Rupert had carried him earlier. Quincy reached for the ceiling and stretched. He then scratched his scalp through his unkempt head of grey hair. His clothes, the same as from last night, were wrinkled and twisted in uncomfortable looking ways.

Tobias watched as Quincy walked past Rupert, somehow oblivious to his hulking presence, and proceeded slowly down the stairs. The banister swayed when the old man's weight met its brittle construction—not enough to break, but just enough for Tobias to picture a nasty fall looming. Much to his relief, Quincy cleared the stairs without incident.

With slits for eyes, he walked silently past the group huddled around the table and into the pseudo-kitchen. As he bent down next to the stove, his knees cracked with the sound of bone on bone. It must have sounded worse than it felt, as the old man continued to fish around for a few seconds before removing a bottle of pills from the cabinet. After popping the cap with ease, he cocked his head back and downed a handful dry. A look of distaste washed across his face as the uncoated pills traveled down his throat, dissolving as they slid.

He cracked his neck with a moan and turned around, facing the group that sat in awe of his behavior. Upon seeing them, he jumped back and tripped over the whiskey carton he had pulled out the night before. With a cushioned thud,

Quincy hit the ground, his head bouncing off the refrigerator's door. He winced in pain before fumbling through an open drawer to his right. Removing an old gun from the clutter of junk, he held it, shaking, in front of him. Tobias couldn't tell if it was fear, or the lingering effects of last night's binge. Either way, he was the last person Tobias wanted with a gun in his hand.

Sam cringed and ducked. Tobias stepped into Quincy's line-of-sight and held his hands up next to his shoulders with his palms out.

The old man's eyes darted around the room before settling on him. "I don't know where you people are from, but around here we don't much go into other people's houses without asking." He rose slowly from the ground using his free hand for support.

"Quincy, hold on a second," Tobias said. He mentally prepared to draw his own weapon should this get out of hand quickly.

The old man cocked his head and eyed Tobias carefully. "How do you know my name?"

"You told us last night." Tobias said. "You don't remember?"

He stared at Tobias for a good minute, squinting, as if trying to discern the truth, before his face broke into a smile. He lowered the gun and put it on the stove.

"Sorry about that," he said, laughing. "Sometimes the booze drinks the man, if you know what I mean." He patted Tobias on the shoulder as he walked by. He nimbly lifted the bottle of whiskey from the table. "Nothing like a little hair of the dog to set ya straight the next morn," he said, uncorking the bottle with his teeth and taking back a deep swig.

Rupert's face took on a sickish green color.

Tobias noticed. "Are you all right, big man?"

"The possibility that I," he swallowed dryly, "drank his

backwash just doesn't sit right with me."

Quincy looked over and waved his hand. "There're far worse things." He wiped his mouth with his sleeve and turned back to the group. "I never did catch your names last night."

Tobias introduced the group again. Despite his decaying mind, Tobias still found the old man amusing.

"Ah, yes," he said, looking at Tobias' arm. "Weren't we discussing your tattoo last night?"

Tobias nodded. "Before you passed out-"

Quincy interrupted. "Who passed out?"

Tobias looked stoically into the old man's eyes and realized he wasn't toying with them. He must do this all the time to have a memory like he did.

"You did, Quincy. You were out cold. Remember?"

The old man reached up and scratched his head. He then nodded in what Tobias could only assume was acceptance.

"Fair enough," Quincy said. "So what was it we were talking about?"

"You said you could take us to the rock with the carving."

"Ah, yes, up on the hill…Cadbury Castle," Quincy recollected. He took another swig from the bottle of whiskey. "I guess it wouldn't hurt if I went to work a bit late today, now would it?" He walked past the group. "Let me put on some clean clothes, and we'll be on our way," he said, walking up the stairs and into his bedroom.

"What did you say you did for work?" Sam asked with morbid curiosity.

He popped his head out from his bedroom with a green sweater half on his torso. "Oh, didn't I mention it last night? I'm the town constable." He smiled and disappeared back into his bedroom.

Sam glanced over at Tobias, shocked. He shrugged. The

irony was too thick for him to even try and figure out. Thankfully, he didn't have time to contemplate the welfare of the rest of the village as Quincy stumbled down the creaky steps. He threw on a thick jacket, donned a ragged derby cap, and headed out the door without a word.

Tobias, with the group in tow, hurried after the old man. The foggy English morning brought a quiet stillness that hovered over the entirety of the village. Sounds of livestock came from somewhere nearby, hidden amongst the fog, but there was not much sound than that. He wondered how different a life these people must lead. Nestled away, seemingly untouched by the world. He knew that wasn't the case, of course. He'd seen Quincy's television tucked into the corner of his house, but he found the old age charm pleasing compared to what most of the world had become.

They walked down the main avenue leading out of the village and then cut across the grassy plains towards the hill.

"You also mentioned King Arthur last night," John said.

Quincy glanced back, but kept on walking. "Yes. I did. Didn't I? Did I get into it with ya?"

John looked for the best way to put it. "That's when you," he paused, "went to sleep."

The old man grunted. "I'm sure you've heard the legends of King Arthur and his Knights of the Round Table, and blah, blah, blah…." He held his hand up over his right shoulder and waved it around in circles. Well, around here we have our own tales of the legendary *Arthur*, but they aren't as noble as the ones you may know."

John raised an eyebrow. "What do you mean?"

"What I mean is this—the man was a vindictive and jealous heathen," he said, spitting on the rocky soil. "Gives us proper Englishmen a bad name."

He led them over a small brook to their right and out of the thick grass. Before them stretched a small dirt road, which they made a left onto.

Quincy continued. "Legend tells of a group of knights that Arthur desperately sought to join. Back then, he was no more than any other man—just another vagabond with no real power. Apparently, much to Arthur's chagrin, the order of knights was not accepting new members. In fact, all of the knights were descendants of the men before them. They all shared some kind of common bloodline, and it was the only way in."

Tobias felt like he had just been slapped. *Knights of a common bloodline? Not the Guardians.*

The old man continued on his way down the road, oblivious.

"Do you know the name of the order?" Tobias asked.

Quincy stopped and turned. He shrugged. "Don't know. Just know it was an order of knights is all." He removed a small flask from within his right pocket and unscrewed the top masterfully. With a deep breath, he took a long swig. Like before, he offered a sip to the rest of the group.

Rupert held his hand to his stomach and looked like he might throw up.

"Suit yourselves," he said, pocketing the flask. "Now where was I? Ah, yes, the order of knights. Anyway, Arthur felt shunned by their rejection. He amassed a huge army thanks, in large part, to a sizeable amount of gold left to him from some relative. With the manpower in place, he set out to find the most sought after of holy relics. He hoped that, once he located it, the knights would have no choice but to allow him in. In fact, he grew so powerful that he changed his sights from joining the knights into ruling them." He arched his brow. "Funny what power can do to a man."

Thoughts swirled through Tobias' mind. Holy relic could mean almost anything, but one in particular stuck out—one that held the most meaning.

"When you say relic, do you mean the Holy Grail?"

Quincy nodded. "The Grail indeed, but his search was destined to fail from the start, you see. The very knights he wanted so badly to join already had possession of the relic, locked away in their holy castle of Camelot." Quincy waited for the words to sink in. "But Arthur's army had grown to a size where it could easily challenge the smaller numbers of the knights linked by blood."

"So what happened to the Holy Grail?" John asked. "Since it's not locked away in some museum, I assume it was lost?"

"I was getting to that," Quincy said, scowling at John. He turned and started walking again. "The order of knights feared they would one day be attacked with all of Arthur's might. While their castle was strong, or at least they thought so, they couldn't risk losing the Grail. Arthur became so caught up in finding the Holy Grail that it took over his life. The thought of joining the knights drifted away and was replaced by the thought of the unprecedented power the Grail would bring."

Cadbury Castle materialized from out of the fog ahead. Its banks rolled with dark green grass. Tobias noticed the tiered walls that cut its slope and disappeared into the thick, milky air above.

"In order to protect the Grail," Quincy said, "they sent it away to a distant land where Arthur could never find it. You know, they say within the metal was mixed drops of Christ's blood." He laughed again. "I think that part was added later to give the story more oomph, if you know what I mean." He laughed with a raspy gurgle stuck in this throat.

The group neared the hill. It rose to a plateau above their heads.

"Well, here we are then," Quincy said, turning around at the base of the hill.

The group hung on his words, waiting for him to finish the tale.

"Where did they send the cup?" Tobias asked, eager for an answer.

Quincy lifted his head. He realized he left out the end. "Oh, sorry 'bout that. Well, I don't know where the Grail went, but I can tell you it was no cup. No, the real Grail was in the shape of a cross."

A chill ran through Tobias.

"They say it had funny lookin' arms, all wavy like."

Tobias looked at John, who palmed the cross beneath his shirt in shocked disbelief.

Chapter 29

While Tobias found Quincy amusing, it was a stretch to say he trusted him. His tale of King Arthur gave him goose bumps, but it could have been some elaborately conceived trick of the devil. They hadn't been attacked in what Tobias considered a very long time. It would make sense to lull them into a false sense of security, give them the impression that things were going their way. Then, when the time was right, have Quincy tell his tale. John would whip out the Crux in a defining moment of realization, and then the attack would occur.

Tobias scanned the area. Everything seemed to be peaceful enough. On the other hand, what if Quincy's tale was a historical account and not some trap? If that was true, then John actually had the Holy Grail around his neck. It seemed surreal to even ponder such a question with such far reaching implications.

He looked towards John and gave him the slightest of head shakes. John removed his hand from his chest and let it fall back to his side. He understood. Keep the Crux hidden.

"So what became of Arthur?" Tobias asked, turning back to face Quincy.

Quincy blew a cloud of smoke from his mouth. The cigarette he'd just lit hung loosely in his shaky hand. "He eventually became king. That much of the popular myth is true. After his much-ballyhooed coronation, he marched his army to take over Camelot. Since he was king, he now had the legal power, and the manpower, to do it."

Rupert chimed in. "So the legend of King Arthur and Camelot is true."

Quincy inhaled a deep, satisfying puff of smoke and held it longer than normal. He looked at Rupert from the corners of his eyes. "Yes and no," he said amongst the cloud of exhaled smoke. "It's said that, when Arthur and his army approached this very hill, the castle that rested at its peak was no longer there."

"As in abandoned?" Tia asked.

Quincy shook his head. "No. Camelot was gone, every white brick of it. They say that Arthur, having looked from the ground up in shock, dismounted his steed and ran to the top in full armor. When he got there, he dropped to his knees, held his hands to the sky and cried like a little baby." Quincy laughed. "Boo hoo. The castle he sought by the name of Camelot no longer existed." Quincy violently coughed and held his chest. He then held the cigarette up in front of his face. "Blasted things are going to kill me."

"Does your legend tell anything else?" John asked.

"The tale ends there, I'm afraid, but some say that Arthur was so set on having Camelot and command of the knights who occupied it, that he built his own version of the castle elsewhere in the country. After years of construction, Arthur did indeed have Camelot and control of a group of knights-"

"Let me guess," Rupert interrupted, "the Knights of the Round Table?"

Quincy winked at Rupert and nodded.

"That sure is an interesting twist on the legend," John said.

The old man snickered. "Like I said, there isn't anything up there but rocks and grass."

"And one of those rocks has the Mark on it?" Tobias asked.

"That's what I said, isn't it?"

Gazing up the tiered hill, Tobias tried to envision a

massive castle resting upon the flat peak. He realized that this would have been an ideal spot to build a citadel. To attack the castle an enemy would have two choices — take the heavily guarded road and face almost certain death, or attempt to scale the tiered mounds of earth and give the castle's occupants time to fully prepare a counter-attack. It seemed like a lost cause either way.

"This way," Quincy said, waving the group on.

They followed him up what appeared to be the flattest part of the hill. He was slow, but careful, in his movements. The north side of Cadbury Castle was surrounded by thick trees that wound halfway around the hill. The front part, the one the group now traversed, were made up of hilly ramparts that Tobias could only assume were the castle's first line of defense back in the day.

The fog began to disperse, but as was the norm, the English sky remained grey and unwelcoming.

"Here we are," Quincy said as they reached the flat peak, "the great castle of Camelot." He laughed and looked around before taking a swig from his flask.

Just as the old man said, the summit was barren of anything other than grass, trees, and rocks. There was a small brick structure, about three feet in height, located in the center of the hill. When asked, Quincy explained that it had been erected for the new millennium, with its *2000 AD* carving.

"Where did you see the marking?" Tobias said.

Quincy pointed towards the trees on the opposite side of the hill. "Over here." He cut a path through the short grass, across the hill.

At the base of one of the many trees was a large stone, partially obstructed by some long grass. On the smooth, angled top of the rock was etched the Guardian's Mark, just as the old man had said. Tobias bent down and brushed away some scattered debris. The Mark was faded, but it was unquestionably that of the Guardian's. Tobias was surprised Quincy had seen this at all. From the distance it appeared to be just another ordinary rock. Tobias figured he probably used it as a pillow during one of his drunken nights.

With his index finger, Tobias traced the intersecting swords. He then traced the cross that lay inside the circle, which had held up better against the elements over the many years. Its carving seemed much more intact, especially in the center. He traced it again. It felt different than the other parts, deeper.

He stood and studied the rock from above. "Has this stone always been here?" he asked, pointing. "Beneath this tree?"

Quincy looked up at the tree and then back down to the rock. "That's where I found it, anyway. Can't say where it was before I set my eyes on it, though."

Sam bent down, resting her butt on the heels of her feet. She studied the rock for a moment in quiet contemplation before reaching out. Tobias watched her trace the Mark as he had, stopping at the center of the cross.

She looked up. "The center of the cross is deeper than the rest."

"That's what I felt, too," Tobias said, confirming both of their suspicions.

Sam angled all around, studying its symmetry. "I think there's a slit cut out."

Tobias bent down next to her.

"You think the weather did this?" she asked.

He shook his head. The slit was manmade. There was no question about it. And, if that was the case, then why was it there? It had to serve a purpose.

Quincy took a seat on the soft grass. He then fell onto his back and closed his eyes. Apparently being awake had made him tired.

"Do you think that rock has something to do with Camelot?" Rupert asked. He had Tia in the grasp of his right arm and held her tight to his body.

"It must. This mark is too rare to be a coincidence."

Tobias bent down again and tried to wedge his fingers under it, but he had no luck. The rock went too far beneath the surface. It occurred to him that maybe his brethren left something beneath it, like leaving a house key under the doormat. He didn't think it would be that obvious, but he knew they couldn't afford to overlook anything at that point.

"You need some help," Rupert asked, bending down next to him. He put his large shoulder against the rock and dug his feet into the soft soil. Closing his eyes, he took a deep breath and pushed with all his might. After less than ten seconds he began to slide in place. Rupert fell to the ground after a large exhale.

Tobias found it hard to believe there existed something in this universe that his giant friend was unable to move.

"It's no use," Rupert said. "This thing is buried way too deep."

Quincy lay still, but kept one eye open and trained on their doings.

Tobias had a feeling that Quincy had tried all of this before. Puzzles that lacked answers were the one thing that could drive a man to the brink of lunacy. Or possibly, as in Quincy's case, cause a man to drink.

Unsheathing his sword, Tobias walked past the rock and into the tall grass on the side of the hill. Quincy stared wondrously at the sword that appeared from thin air, shaking his head in disbelief. With a few powerful swipes, Tobias cleared the area of the tall grass and looked for anything that might be hidden behind it. He thought that maybe the rock pointed to something nearby. Finding nothing of interest, he walked back up the hill and drove his sword in the ground.

"It's at the base of this tree," John said, looking up. "Maybe something is up there?"

Tia shook her head. "It can't be. I'm no botanist, but I don't think these trees would've been around back then. I don't think they're more than one hundred years old or so."

Tobias agreed. "It has to be something more permanent—something that could stand the test of time." He again looked down at what he started mentally calling the Guardian's rock. "John, you have any answers in that head full of ancient knowledge?"

John shook his head. "Sorry. Like I said, the ghost wasn't around... ." He suddenly brought his hand up to his forehead.

Tia grabbed him at the shoulders. "Are you okay, hon?"

John grimaced in pain. After a brief moment of silence, the pain seemed to pass, and John stood up straight. "I was wrong, Tobias. ..."

At that moment, the ear bud beeped. "Tobias, are you there?" It was the Cardinal. *Of all times for him to call, why does it have to be now?* He pointed to his ear and then held up his index finger, signaling for the group to hold on. Reaching up, he pushed a small button on the ear bud, allowing him to have two-way communication with the Cardinal. "I'm here. Are you all right?"

Ruffling sounds took the place of an answer. Tobias figured the Cardinal, not a technologically savvy person, was still trying to secure the ear bud in his ear. He finally got it adjusted and continued. "I am fine, dear boy, but I fear the world is not faring as well."

Tobias glanced at Sam as she looked down and rubbed her stomach. She had the slightest of smiles on her face. Whatever the bad news was, her presence seemed to lessen its severity already.

The cardinal continued. "The number of chasms around the world is increasing at an alarming rate. Parts of Paris, France, have been completely enveloped by the shifting Earth. The same can be said of Tokyo, Madrid, Los Angeles... ."

It was progressing faster than Tobias thought it would. It wouldn't be long before the devil had gained enough power to rise and command his army against humanity.

"On top of that, a large number of volcanoes previously thought extinct have been born again. Plumes of smoke are being jettisoned from their cores, filling the sky. The world is collapsing upon itself, Tobias. Riots have broken out. Civilized behavior is now an afterthought. I have even heard mention of the word Armageddon on more than one occasion. The Holy See has called all the Cardinals back to the Vatican for an emergency session."

"Does that include you?"

"No. The Pope understands my worth lies here with you." Static burped on the line. "Have you found the third Sign yet?"

Tobias was relieved. Not only did he need a fast way out of the country, but the Cardinal's extensive religious knowledge might come in handy.

"No, we haven't found the Sign." More static interrupted their conversation. Tobias adjusted the earpiece, but it had no effect. "Cardinal...can you hear me?"

Static hissed back. He was gone.

The group looked at him for answers to the one-way conversation they'd just heard.

Tobias breathed deep. "Things are escalating." He paused. "Actually, things are spiraling out of control." He knew that with each riot, quake, and death, the devil grew in power. It had gotten to a point where he didn't know if it could be stopped. Their time may have already run out.

Chapter 30

While Tobias was thankful they hadn't been attacked in a while, the Cardinal's call let him know the rest of the world wasn't as lucky. The rough hands of immediacy nudged him on the back, yet there he stood, staring at a rock in the middle of the English countryside. He felt downright helpless. He knew it was significant. Its placement on top of Cadbury Castle wasn't a coincidence. It couldn't be. Somehow it pointed the way to Camelot, but everything they'd tried so far had failed.

"What happened to you before the Cardinal called?" Tobias asked, looking over to John.

John shook his head, apparently reliving the pain. "I don't know what it was, but I'm sure glad it's over." He rubbed the back of his neck. "I felt like my head was going to explode, like my eyes were going to pop out of my head from the pressure. It kept getting worse until my vision went black."

"And then it just stopped?"

He nodded. "But not before I saw a bunch of strange images. I couldn't actually make any of them out, though. They all just kind of blurred together." He grimaced again. "It was like watching a movie in super-fast forward."

Tobias doubted those images just happened to run through John's mind. For some reason, being at Cadbury Castle seemed to have unlocked something in his head. He had no doubt it had to do with the Brotherhood's knowledge.

"I need you to try and see the images again," Tobias said.

The look on John's face, wide-eyed and distraught, hinted at the pain he'd felt moments ago.

Tobias noticed his reluctance. "I wouldn't ask you to do this unless I thought it was absolutely necessary. I think those images may help us. Hopefully, they'll show us the way to Camelot."

John took a moment and then nodded in understanding. He closed his eyes and concentrated. A full minute passed with nothing. Then, spastically, he doubled over in pain again. He held his head with both of his hands. His jaw locked, confining his moans of agony. This time seemed worse. It seemed more painful than before.

Sam went to help, but Tobias held her back. For John's own good, he couldn't allow the process to be interrupted. Watching John writhe in pain was difficult, but necessary. It was Tobias' job to protect him, not guide him back into harm's way, but he knew it was the only way. They had run out of options and, more importantly, out of time.

Much to Tobias' relief, the wincing pain stopped a minute later. Taking his hands off his knees, John regained his composure and stood tall. His eyes remained closed, but they moved rapidly beneath their lids.

"The pain's gone," he sighed, "but it's still difficult to make anything out. There's one image that appears more often than any of the others, though." He squeezed his eyes tighter and focused. "It looks like a long, blurry cross."

"Like the Crux Signate?" Tobias asked.

John shook his head. "No. It's much longer and doesn't have the same wavy arms." With his eyes still shut tight, John cocked his head as he undoubtedly tried to understand the object's meaning. Deep wrinkles formed on his face from his unwavering concentration. "It kind of looks like a cross attached to a long metal pole."

Metal pole? A frightening thought crossed Tobias' mind.

What if they'd missed something along the way? What if they now stood only inches away from directions to Camelot and needed something they didn't have? His headache came thumping back.

"It's rounded at the top... ." John shook his head. "...And has a small green circle on each of its two arms." His face wrinkled more. "I think they're green, anyway. The colors seem to blur together."

Quincy stood behind Tobias with silver dollar-sized eyes. He took a long pull from his flask and wiped his lips with his sleeve.

Tobias teetered on John's words. He felt the answer was close by, almost like he already knew it, but it was just out of reach.

John opened his eyes and shook his head. "I'm sorry. It's gone."

Dammit. Tobias looked around at the group, stopping at Quincy. "What's wrong?"

Quincy stared through him, like he had seen a ghost. "I know where yer cross is—the one that crazy fella's talking about."

"Where?" Tobias asked. He prayed, for the old man's sake, that this wasn't some game. He didn't have time for the ramblings of a drunk. Not now. Not when they were finally getting somewhere.

Quincy raised his shaking hand and pointed over Tobias' shoulder, past the group. Rising from the ground was Tobias' sword, right where he had stuck it. The hilt was adorned with solid green circles, emeralds, like the cross that John described.

John gazed down and frantically nodded in agreement. "He's right." His eyes grew wide. "That's what I saw. It wasn't a long cross. It was your sword." He looked back at Tobias.

Tobias walked over and removed his sword from the ground next to the tree. Grasping the blade, so that the hilt was unobstructed, he held it out. The rest of the group crowded behind him and peered over his shoulder. The thought had never occurred to him, most likely because when he drew his sword it was to battle and not to admire, but it did resemble a cross. It was a subtlety he had missed until that moment.

At the speed of light his mind assembled the puzzle and brought an answer screaming to the forefront. He laughed out loud—not because he found it amusing, but because, if his hunch was correct, then its implications stretched across history.

"What's so funny?" Sam asked.

"I don't know why I didn't think of this before." He turned to the Guardian's rock. "Everything else associated with King Arthur appears to be a lie, so why not this, too?"

He dangled the blade over the rock, with the tip over the deep-grooved center. Eyeing it carefully, he pushed the sword in with conviction and stopped when it could go no further. When finished, the rock consumed more than half of the blade.

"*The Sword in the Stone*," Rupert said, snickering. "My mother used to read me that when I was a kid.

Tobias stepped back with the rest of the group and admired the legend becoming reality. He waited in eager anticipation for something to happen, but nothing appeared to have changed. That had to be it. The images in John's mind pointed directly to his sword, which fit perfectly into the Guardian's Rock.

"Did any of you notice anything?" he asked the rest of his team. They looked around and shook their heads. Nothing had caught their eyes.

"Any more images, by chance?" he asked, turning to

John.

John shook his head. "I was lucky to get that much, man. I'm telling you, it's a mess up here right now," he said, pointing to his head.

It was then, when Tobias looked to the sky in frustration, that he noticed it approaching. Past the trees in front of them, the sky burned red with Evil. He realized their luck had just run out. The next wave of the devil's minions was headed right for them.

He reached down to remove his blade from the rock, but it wouldn't budge. It felt like the sword had been fused within the stone. He stood with a foot on either side and heaved with all his might. The sword stayed firmly in place.

Quincy's flask burped whiskey down the front of his shirt as he, too, stared up at the fast-approaching army from hell.

A distant clicking filled the air. The thickly-filled sky swayed like a red-hot ocean wave as the creatures closed on their position. The clicking transformed into a terrible buzzing. Tobias' heart raced. He had never seen so much evil concentrated in one place.

Rupert, his eyes pointed skyward as well, gently pushed Tobias out of the way. He grasped the hilt of the sword and pulled with every ounce of strength he could muster. The blade didn't budge.

Tobias knew that, if the big man had no luck, then the sword was not coming out—not by normal means, anyhow. He would need to fight without it.

"Get ready," he yelled, sweeping a micro-shotgun from his leg and tossing it to Sam.

She picked it from the air with surprising ease and then caught the new bag of shells he also tossed her way, a replenishment the Cardinal had thankfully brought. He then reached down and tossed the second shotgun to John. John was not as graceful, but he thankfully caught it. Tobias only hoped he didn't have to use it.

Tobias turned around to give Quincy direction, but the old man was out cold on the ground. Of all the times to pass out, he sure chose a dandy.

With a quick pull, Sam released the two molten-fire rounds hurtling towards the buzzing evil. It ate up the immediate sky and continued for fifty more yards. The insects that were caught in the path immediately disintegrated. Several loose wings and charred, spiny legs drifted towards the ground.

The hole in the sky immediately filled, like a dry piece of land eaten by a ravaging flood.

It seemed endless. Looking at the swaying sky, Tobias wondered if the world had enough to stop this, let alone their small and under-armed group.

The insects closest to John suddenly swept down. Tobias noticed and plucked his Glocks from their holsters. He shot rapid fire at the bugs. Each precisely aimed bullet hit its mark, causing the ten incoming hellions to splatter in midair. Globules of black ooze rained down like a shower of tar.

Now much closer, Tobias could see they were all uniform in appearance. Their attackers all had the same blood red outer shells with what appeared to be dark green moss covering certain sections. Each of the bugs beat their six ragged wings feverishly. Two long pincers protruded from their oval-shaped heads. The three-foot-long, larvae-like beetles were able to stop and hover with ease. Luckily for Tobias, they seemed to drop in groups. He feared what would happen if they all came at once. He felt like lunch at a mosquito colony.

Sam reloaded the shotgun and released another blast. The fire cleared the nearby area, but it was immediately filled in, like before.

"It's no use," she said. "There're too many of them."

He looked to his left. Rupert and Tia fought as a team, beating down groups of the insects at a time. A small mound of carcasses circled their position. The clang of steel and the sound of ripping flesh accompanied their frenzy.

John raised the gun and fired, hitting the top of a nearby tree and setting it ablaze. The recourse knocked him back, and the shotgun fell from his hands. He fumbled to pick it up, but it was no use as the gun bounced down the hill and disappeared into the long grass.

Tobias rushed to his side as another swarm plummeted from above. Their numbers were overpowering and ever-increasing. He grabbed John and dragged him to the center of their group. He then reached into his pack and removed a blue, metallic cylinder.

"Get down," Tobias yelled.

The group dropped to the hill's grassy terrain in unison.

He tossed the cylinder into the air and fired as it reached the apex of its climb, twenty feet above their heads. The first bullet missed, but the second shot tore through the casing. A blanket of sparkling mist fell upon the group, protecting them for the time being.

The insects hovered around the outside of the misty bubble. Several of them, the ones closest, tested the particle-filled air, but they were met with a quick, disintegrating death. More globules of tar rained down.

"The particles are coated in holy water and a combination of other stuff," Tobias said, answering the unasked question, "but it won't last long." He was surprised it worked at all. He desperately searched within his pack for something else. It was beginning to look like his bag of tricks was running out.

John stared, mesmerized at the prismatic glow of the sword in the stone as the mist fell around it. He rose from the ground and closed in on the blade. Entranced, he reached out and gripped the hilt with both hands. With no more force than necessary, John succeeded where the others had failed. He removed the blade from its confines and held it aloft. A laser-like gleam ran its length.

The ground rumbled below them. John fell with the sword in hand. The trees that lined the north face of the hill began to topple and roll down its slope like they were no more than toothpicks.

"What's happening?" Tia screamed above the commotion.

Tobias looked over. He had no idea. Whatever John had done seemed to do the trick. A great upsurge in the earth began all around the tightly packed group, as the muddy ground ripped itself apart. Five massive stone turrets, each of them connected by a crenellated wall, rose from beneath the soil and surrounded the group.

Tobias couldn't believe what he was seeing. The horizon in every direction, once filled with Evil, was replaced by the rising white stone walls of what he assumed to be Camelot. It was beneath them all along. The sword in the stone didn't provide directions. It led to the castle itself.

Dirt trickled down from above, falling from the high-reaching walls. The hill had transformed from a mound of fabled dirt to the most legendary of castles in the blink of an eye. It was a glorious sight, one that Tobias welcomed with an awe-inspired smile.

Transparent figures blinked into sight from all around, first one and then a hundred. The translucent apparitions took their places along the upper walls and around the group. An overwhelming feeling of tranquility and brotherhood overtook Tobias. He realized the ghostly knights that now surrounded them where somehow, someway, his brethren from the past. These were Guardians.

He felt it deep in his heart.

From their right approached another ghost, but this one didn't wear the ghostly armor of the Guardians. He wore a simple brown robe.

John turned and nodded. The ghost smiled briefly and then brought his hand up. He pointed towards the blood red sky. John turned back to the group. "We're safe now."

Tobias' previous fear was realized, as the insect-filled sky collectively lunged at the group.

From high atop the walls shot brilliant white arrows— hundreds, if not thousands, of them at a time. The glowing projectiles cut through the air and seared clean through the diving minions. The Guardians were unrelenting in their defense. The bugs that made it through the volley tried to grab the Guardians within their clamping mandibles, but they were no longer of this life. They could never be harmed by the devil's minions again. Their penance had been paid, and today would be their long overdue retribution.

Another round of arrows shot into the sky from the castle's walls.

From behind the team came a surprising whoosh as huge stones hurled through the air. The volley of glowing giant rocks arched past the walls and exploded like an atomic bomb in a blinding white brilliance that swept over everything in sight.

The group shielded their eyes. The light's intensity, while somehow calming, was too blinding to view.

Millions of popping sounds were followed by muted and fading cheers.

With his eyes now open, Tobias looked around. His ghostly brethren were gone and, with them, every single spawn of hell that had filled the sky only moments ago.

Chapter 31

As the last of the Guardians vanished, the man in the brown robe approached from their left and solidified into the form he'd held one thousand years ago. He wore an ordinary brown robe, tied at the waist with a frayed white rope. A manicured beard, colored white and brown, painted his face. Tobias had no idea how it happened, but the ghost appeared to have once again become a living, breathing man.

Nearing to within a few feet, the robed man gracefully swept a hand down towards Sam. "Are you all right, my dear?" he asked, helping her up from the ground.

Tobias recognized the deep voice. It was the same one that had helped them beneath the Sahara. This was undoubtedly the leader of the Brotherhood that shared John and helped activate the second Sign.

She nodded, smiled. "Yes. Thank you."

The robed man then turned to John. "It appears this time I look into your eyes, rather than through them." John halfheartedly grinned.

"There's something I don't understand," Tobias said, drawing the robed man's attention. "Why didn't you just tell us about Camelot while we were in Egypt?" He couldn't help but be frustrated. He thought about all the time they'd wasted just staring at the rock. Time better spent moving forward, rather than standing still.

The robed man casually walked up next to him. Then, with the innocence of a child, he hopped in place a few times. "I have not felt my legs in one thousand years," he said, smirking. "And it appears the pain that afflicted them is gone." He expelled a breathy snicker and then looked back to Tobias. "I could not tell you how to raise Camelot, for the same reason I could not tell you where to find the final Trinity Sign."

Frustrated and angry, Tobias couldn't hold back anymore. "I'm tired of these games. Time is clearly not on our side, yet all we get are more riddles and roundabout answers."

The group uncomfortably shriveled back. Tobias instantly regretted his outburst. He had every right To feel the way he did, but he shouldn't take it out on someone who didn't deserve it. Losing his cool now wouldn't help them find the final Sign. Sometimes his emotions got the better of him.

The robed man's smile vanished, replaced by the face of a man well aware of the current situation. "I assure you, Guardian, this is no game. Everything has its purpose. Whether it is to your liking or not, that is just the way of things." He broke his stare and gazed at the rest of the team. "Come," he said, moving away from the center courtyard and towards a large set of doors behind them, "this way."

Sam walked up next to Tobias and brushed his back. She gave him a reassuring smile, as if to say that everything would be all right. If only he could live in a world filled with her smiles. That would be a world worth fighting for. He shrugged off the thought and followed the rest of the group through the large, towering doors.

The room they passed through was deeply charred from what must have been a fierce battle. The white bricks of Camelot were stained dark black and crumbling. Tobias looked from the floor up to the ceiling. Whatever had happened in here could not have ended well for either side.

"I cannot tell you where the final Trinity Sign is, Guardian because, as I said, I am not aware of its location," the robed man said, glancing over his shoulder while continuing forward. "The Sign was moved after my death for its protection. It was a secret they did not share with my ghost."

Tobias inferred that last part as a joke—one in which he failed to see the humor.

"I am, however, sure that either your brethren or the Brotherhood would have left something behind to indicate the Sign's new location. Please know that, if I knew where the Sign of the Holy Spirit was, you would already be there. Of that you can be sure."

Another set of large wooden doors parted open, as if by magic, when the robed man approached. The team followed him down a hallway with a low, arching ceiling that soon emptied into a sprawling room. Deep charring also darkened the walls of this room, but to a lesser extent than the last. Long tables—some upright, others upended—littered the white stone floor. A lengthy balcony traced the room's rectangular shape a floor above. Several of its wood planks hung down, grasping at their neighbor to remain part of the structure. The ceiling arched high above them. Exposed wood rafters, thick and untouched, cut horizontally at its peak. Hanging from each of the beams was a charred deep-purple banner, emblazoned with the Guardian's Mark in silver stitching.

The robed man motioned for the group to sit at the nearby table. "This room," he said, "was once filled with men like you." The robed man looked across at Tobias. "Men who fought for a cause that was greater than themselves." The robed man looked around at the walls, apparently soaking in that which he hadn't seen in over one thousand years. He stopped at the banner nearest them.

"I apologize for my temper," Tobias said. He felt bad, almost embarrassed, by his lack of emotional restraint. The robed man's shield of compassion worked perfectly in blocking his stabbing anger.

The robed man smiled. "You have nothing to apologize for, Guardian. Emotions are what truly make us human. They are what urge us forward in the bleakest of times. Without them this battle humanity now wages would have been lost long ago, well before my time."

The robed man sat down silently next to John. John seemed reluctant to look up, like he feared what was to come next. "Have you come to accept what must be done, my child?" the robed man asked, grasping John's right shoulder with the care of a teacher toward his pupil.

John stared at the ground for a moment, distraught. He nodded softly, almost unwillingly. Then, suddenly, in one fluid movement, he stood and walked past the group. A few long strides later, he disappeared through a nearby archway and into darkness. *What was that all about?*

"Guardian, may I have a word with you?" the robed man asked, rising from his chair and making his way through a small doorway to their right.

Tobias looked back at the room John had disappeared into, stood from the bench, and followed the man. Ducking beneath the small archway, Tobias made his way into a much smaller room. The walls were black as night, much darker than the rest of the castle. He reached out and rubbed his finger across the rough surface. A clean streak formed as the soot clung to his skin.

The robed man stood at the end of the room near the remnants of a long wood table. "This is where I met with my demise over one thousand years ago." He turned and pointed to the corner. "Right over there, in fact. I remember it like it was yesterday. The devil's monsters came within inches of succeeding when I activated the final Sign. Thankfully, the Holy Aura dispatched them back to their fiery home, but it all happened so quickly. So many men died that day." He mournfully shook his head. "Thanks to their courage, the devil was relegated to a thousand-year wait—a wait that is nearing its conclusion."

Tobias remained quiet and let the old ghost soak in the past.

"I remember a day when I was surrounded by your kind, Guardian. The world was a better place then." He smiled. "It was a safer place."

Pride swelled within Tobias. He tried to imagine what the world would be like if there were still Guardians. He wondered if the world would indeed be a better place. Would mankind accept a life free from Evil's grasp? Or would it need to feed the innate darkness within its soul? Tobias turned away from the man and looked out the small arching doorway. "What's going on with John?"

The robed man began to say something but caught himself. He started again. "I am truly sorry, Guardian. There are some things that cannot be discussed, even with the last of the protectors." He turned towards the corner. "That, like much of life, is just the way of things."

Curiosity itched from within. He wanted to know the secret, but Tobias chose not to pester the ghost. He had to have his reasons. And as long as it didn't interfere with finding the last Trinity Sign, Tobias decided to let secrets lie where they must. He knew that all secrets eventually become known. He would just wait it out.

A sudden ruckus echoed from behind them within the large room. Tobias spun around and caught sight of Quincy as he staggered through the large wood doors that led from the courtyard. Until that moment, he hadn't even realized the old man had gone missing. He hadn't really cared.

Quincy wore an armored chest-piece tattooed with the Guardian's Mark. The insignia was bright and inspiring. He also had on one leg piece, two gauntlets, and a helmet that was far too large. His head was nestled loosely in the helmet, and the face guard was propped open like a gate, revealing the drunken smile on his face.

"Look at all the stuff I found," Quincy said.

Tobias stormed out of the small room. "What are you doing, old man?" Tobias said, tearing the helmet off Quincy's head. He felt like the Guardians were being mocked, like he was being mocked.

Quincy cried in pain as the helmet ripped out some of his aging white hair. He brought his hand up and rubbed his scalp. "Watch it, why don't ya? At my age I can't afford to lose any more of that."

Sam covered her mouth to hide a giggle.

Tobias held the helmet in front of him. "Where did you get this?"

Quincy turned around and looked out the door, back into the courtyard.

"Out there," he said, pointing. "There's a room full of this stuff. I get first dibs, of course." Quincy took his flask and tipped his head back. He held it in the air above his open mouth. A single drop traced the flask's rim and then fell onto his waiting tongue. Licking his lips, he eyed the hole and made sure it was indeed empty.

"Did you see anything else...?" Tobias was about to say "strange," but then thought better of it. Everything around there was strange.

Quincy nodded. "Well, you'll be pleased to know I saw another one of these marks," he said, banging the metal chest armor he wore.

"Where?" Tobias asked.

"I'll show ya."

The group followed Quincy back into the courtyard. They veered to the right and through an open door. Just as he had said, the room was filled with Guardian armor and weapons. Everything was perfectly preserved. The polished gleam shone from every direction. *This had to have been their armory*, he thought. Each of the weapons must have held a story of some long ago adventure.

"This way," Quincy said from the other side of the room.

Something inside Tobias longed to feel a connection with his past. He let his hand gently glide over some of the room's items as he passed by. The metal was smooth, untarnished by time. He yearned for the family he'd never had.

Passing through another small doorway, they took a right and followed a long, door-lined hall.

"See," Quincy said, pointing to the door at the far end.

The robed man pushed his way to the front of the group. The ghost stood in front, surveying the old door with care. The Guardian's Mark was burned deep into the wood. He reached out and tried to open it, but the door wouldn't budge.

"I figured as much," the robed man said, turning to face the group. "This is what we are looking for. They must have put the clue to the Sign's whereabouts in here."

"How do you know?" Tobias asked. "Aside from the obvious Mark."

"This was my room while I walked the Earth. I can assure you that the Mark was not there when I passed."

He looked to Rupert. "Think you can break it down?"

Rupert walked up and pushed on the door. It gave nothing. He shrugged and removed his giant metal mallet. "I'll give it a shot," he said, pushing the group back with a wave.

John ran up. "Hold on." He removed the Crux, jiggling it in his hand. "It's worked so far."

249

"Hey…," Quincy said, seeing the Crux.

John ignored him and held the cross to the door. A quick snap, and the door nudged unlocked. John pushed it open and entered.

With a flick of the robed man's hands, the surrounding torches lit. The stark stone walls held court within a small, round room. The only object within the old living quarters was a raised block of stone in the center of the floor. On it, like everything else before, was the image of the Crux Signate.

At that moment, a haunting echo of trumpets sounded throughout the castle. The group turned to one another. They were all accounted for, except for Quincy. *Where has he run off to now?*

The trumpet sounded again. This time it was more sustained. The robed man turned and looked down the hallway. "I fear our time has run out. The alarm has been sounded. We are under attack."

Tobias shot into command mode. He knew the group needed direction if they were to survive. "John, Sam, work with the robed man to find whatever it is we're looking for."

They nodded and began to frantically investigate the barren room.

He knew leaving John's side was a risk, but it seemed the better of two bad options. Something told him that the robed man would protect one of his own with everything his ghostly presence could muster. He just prayed that was enough.

He looked at Rupert and Tia. A grin rested on each of their faces. He already knew his words would be wasted. Drawing their weapons, they left the confines of the small room and ran back down the hall.

Blood-chilling noises, those which could only come from something beyond dead, echoed throughout the noble castle.

There was something strange in the air—something more powerful than their past confrontations. The devil had to be close to full strength now, Tobias was sure of it. Whatever awaited them in the courtyard would not be easy to defeat, if they could defeat it at all.

As they reached the end of the hall, Tobias stopped and peered through the armory. Guardians once again lined the ramparts and fired their white-light arrows into the reddening sky. More of his ghostly brethren were already engaged on the ground, locked in battle with the nearest spawn. Tobias realized hell's army must have found a way to breach the walls. Even within an impenetrable castle they were vulnerable. The situation, having just started, was already out of control.

He looked back up the hall to the others. The robed man met his gaze and nodded. It went unspoken, but Tobias was sure they were on the same page. John must be protected at any and all cost. With a wave of his hand, the robed man shut the door.

"Grab anything from this room that you can use," Tobias said, looking around at the gear within the armory.

Reaching to his right, he grabbed an armored chest-piece and secured it tight. He expected to be weighed down, but he found the metal surprisingly light. In fact, it felt like he had on no more than a light coat. He removed his sword and swung it, marking an imaginary "X" in the air with no constrictions in his movements.

Rupert tossed his battle-mallet to the side. It hit with a large clang against the pile of armor. Tia followed her husband's lead. They both searched the room for the most suitable of armaments. These weapons, they all realized, would undoubtedly have more power in stopping what was coming for them.

Tobias turned his attention back to the courtyard. While

he was hesitant to go running out there, throwing himself into the middle of the fray, he knew there was little option in the matter. There was only one way into the battle, and that was head-on.

What had been open space minutes ago was now flooded with the clangs of swords, swinging with a thousand-year-old grudge. Seeing the Guardians battle with the devil's army forced the welling pride in him to shoot to the surface. He no longer felt alone. For the first time in a long time, Tobias felt a sense of family, and he would never let anyone, or anything, threaten it.

Nearing the door, he reached out and grabbed a second sword from the wall. This one was similar to his, but it had a smaller, thinner blade. He could move this one faster and hopefully bring an end to more than one of the spawns with its metal tip.

As Tobias ran through the stone archway, the severity of the battle became all too apparent. The air was filled with the same insects they had so recently defeated. Hell Hounds climbed down the inside of the castle walls like spiders. Gargoyles blinked in and out of the air. The wind carried with it a pungent smell of death.

They were vastly outnumbered, yet the Guardians fought on, thankfully impervious to what the devil threw at them. They battled with an intensity Tobias had never seen. Energized by pride, he charged into the heat of battle with both swords at the ready. Regardless of the form, be it ghost or flesh, the Guardian cause was unified. He resolved that if he were to die, here in Camelot, then that is what was destined to be. At least he would die fighting alongside his own.

Rupert and Tia hauled ass from within the armory and into the battle. Rupert was too big, and Tia was too small, for most of the armor, but what they lacked in protection they made up for in offensive power.

The armory afforded Tia a metal helmet. Artistically designed, the helmet flowed with sloping curves and carved features, the Guardian's Mark etched into the side. Her shifting eyes went unobstructed, searching for the nearest enemy to vanquish. She held two thin, short swords. She'd never met a blade she could not master. The devil's minions would learn that with the unprejudiced fury she was about to release.

Rupert elected for the longest blade he could find, coupled with the tallest shield Tobias had ever seen. The big man swung and blocked without so much as an afterthought. Already accustomed to his new weapon, he brought upon the demise of anything unlucky enough to approach him.

Fighting his way through the commotion, Tobias made his way to the stone stairs nearest him. The close quarters made it difficult to swing his blades with enough force to make a difference. His brethren, moving in packs, quickly dispatched several Hounds on the stairs and led the way up the flight and onto the wall.

Tobias followed their path-clearing lead as two more Hounds bore down on him from behind. He turned in time to see a Guardian, airborne, drive his blade deep into one of the beasts' necks. The fused lump of good and evil tumbled down the stairs and out of sight.

The second Hound, no more than fifteen feet away, leaned back to pounce, its hind legs contracted for the most spring. Tobias drew his right sidearm and fired until the chamber clicked empty. The dreadful beast shrieked in pain as the alkaline mixture mixed with its acidic blood. The beast melted from the inside out. A pool of liquid sloshed from its belly, followed by what was left of its intestines. Its carcass dropped to the ground with a wet thump and slid over the edge of the wall and out of sight.

Tobias breathed a sigh of relief. *That was way too close.*

He climbed the final few stairs, and ran through a recently cleared path and up to the front of Camelot. Everything was colored red with the Evil. The horizon, moving as a whole, strummed with ratty wings. The grass and rocks that composed the hill could no longer be seen beneath the swarming army.

Arching his brow, Tobias looked to the sky. Having never asked for it before, he figured now was as good a time as any to seek divine intervention.

Chapter 32

John stood frozen in place, listening to the muted, yet distinct, sounds of battle outside. To him the question wasn't *if* the evil got through, but *when*. *Maybe all of this was a bad dream,* John thought. At least, that's what he tried to tell himself. It was entirely possible that he'd drunk too much and was passed out on his porch in Connecticut. It wouldn't be the first time. That would be the more believable explanation.

"John," Sam said, "what are you doing?"

Then again, maybe this was now his reality. "Sorry," John said.

He shook the cobwebs from his head and held the Crux Signate out at arm's length. Like all the times before, he was mesmerized. Maybe it was the history behind it or, quite possibly, just the purple flecks that sparkled in even the dimmest of lights. Regardless, it held a power over him that he couldn't explain. He walked past Sam and bent down next to the robed man. Twisting the Crux around, he reached out and placed it in the carved block in the center of the room. Nothing happened.

He lifted the Crux and placed it back down. Again, nothing happened.

"What am I doing wrong?" he asked. "It worked all the other times."

The robed man looked on, perplexed, and shrugged.

A booming crash shook the entire room, like a comet had just collided with the castle. A single white brick fell from above, followed by a cloudy shower of dust.

John looked up. *Maybe they aren't coming through the door,* he thought. He quickly realized it was a stupid thought. They weren't dealing with people. These were creatures from hell. Just the thought caused a shiver to run down his spine. He had already seen more than he knew existed, but that had all been under the protection of Tobias. If something came to get him now…

Another pounding vibration resounded from above.

"There has to be something else," Sam said, trying to regroup. "Something we're missing."

They looked around. The room was still bare, except for the single block in the center of the floor and the one that had just fallen from the ceiling. John looked at the fallen brick, knowing it would not be the last if they didn't find the answers soon.

Chapter 33

From his position high atop the wall, Tobias watched as two large dragons landed across the courtyard. They came down with a crash, one after the other, right on top of John's location. He realized that it would only take a few swipes of their spiky tails, and all would be lost. While the walls of Camelot seemed strong, he doubted even they could remain standing after the onslaught of the two hell-born beasts.

Luckily, the dragons seemed more concerned with the platoon of ghostly Guardians rushing to attack them than what was inside the walls, but he knew that wouldn't last for long. Either John needed to find the information, or Tobias would have to deal with the dragons himself. He hoped it was not the latter.

He looked down into the courtyard in time to see teams of Guardians wheel several large catapults forward from the rear of the castle. With the devices in place, the soldiers released their payloads into the sky. The malformed blocks of brilliant white stone pummeled through the air, flipping end over end before crashing into whatever group of evil was closest. When the stones hit the earth, a blinding flash rippled from the impact.

Tobias knew this battle would be over soon. The devil had turned on the faucet, and a steady stream of hell flowed out. While the Guardians couldn't be hurt, he and the rest of the group could.

What was taking them so long in that room? The thought was rocked from his head as a tremendous crash rattled the entire castle. Tobias fell to his back, knocking the air from his lungs. He glanced to the front wall where the enormous wood gate and iron portcullis had rested, closed, only moments ago. In their place was the largest monstrosity Tobias had ever seen, much larger than the dragons that still continuously pounded on the castle walls. Loose bricks of the castle's walls tumbled into several piles.

The behemoth lumbered through the awning gateway like a wrecking ball, taking out the arch with the front of what Tobias assumed was its head. Each step from its six tree-like legs thumped the ground with the intensity of a small earthquake. From its mouth came a sweeping gush of black fire. Had he not been able to feel the heat from where he was, Tobias would have sworn it was liquid by the way it moved. The Guardians rushing towards the beast became engulfed within the anomalous flame. In an instant, they all vanished. Their ghostly forms were no longer immune to the devil's onslaught. As such, their situation had just become bleaker than it had ever been.

Chapter 34

Sam stared at the stone resting in the center of the room. Its cross-shaped carving taunted her silently, challenging her to figure it out. She watched as John tried the Crux to no avail, and then the robed man take on a look of desperation. She knew things weren't going in their direction. The rumblings and ungodly noises told her that much. The sense of progress she had felt suddenly dissipated, replaced by nervous anxiety.

Why would they make something this important so difficult to solve? Her thoughts drifted to Tobias. She wanted to tell him not to go back out into the courtyard, but she knew they would be wasted words. The feelings she felt for him were killing her. She wanted to pull him aside and tell him what she felt, but she knew that wasn't a possibility. Not now. Not with all hell literally breaking loose.

John violently pulled at his hair in frustration. "I don't know what else to do."

Sam scanned the walls. She looked for something — anything — to help, but they were all plain and uninteresting.

The robed man stood in deep thought and stared down at the white mystery block. "Wait," he said suddenly, turning to John.

John spun around. "You know what to do?" Hope filled his voice.

"I may," the robed man said. "I just may."

Sam sensed the hesitation in his voice. "If you are going to do it, now would be a good time."

The robed man nodded and literally vanished from the room. Sam and John looked at each other, confused. They didn't have enough time to question his actions before he returned.

"Give me your hand," the robed man said, holding out one of his one. His other hand held a five-inch dagger. Upon seeing it, Sam's eyes grew wide. She wondered what he was going to do.

John raised his hand between himself and the robed man, unaware of what Sam saw. With a precise swipe, like that of a surgeon, the robed man slashed a small gap in John's hand with the ultra-sharp blade he had fetched from the armory. John pulled back like a recoiling snake. "What the hell are you doing, man?" He grasped the wrist of his bloodied hand.

The robed man dropped the dagger and grabbed for the wound he had just made. John pulled away.

"Your blood must be the key, my son," the robed man said, rapidly trying to explain his actions. "They would never risk the location of the last Trinity Sign being revealed by happenstance. It has to be a combination of the Crux and the blood of its caretaker. There can be no other solution. Think to what has already happened. You know it to be true."

Sam felt like the robed man was right. She felt his sincerity. Sam watched as John's expression changed from doubt to acceptance.

John reached down and planted his bloodied palm on top of the cross-shaped carving. A small trickle of blood seeped over the block's sides, eventually dripping down the cracks into the dusty floor. A click sounded, and the block began to descend, with the Crux still resting on top. John pried it free from the carving before it disappeared below the ground. The wound on his palm healed in an instant.

The room shook once again as something pounded on the ceiling above. Sam felt like her ears were going to pop.

Something was clearly trying to get in, when all they wanted was to get out.

Chapter 35

Lumbering through the courtyard, the six-legged beast spewed its black flame in every direction. The Guardians nearest the monstrosity took cover behind anything they could find after watching their ghostly kin vanish. Tobias figured close to half their numbers had already fallen victim to the creature in the first minutes of its attack.

The dragons to his right, still perched atop John's location, began to wail on the white brick walls, using their spiky tails as wrecking balls. Each would take turns shrieking into the air. Reminiscent of a medieval factory, small puffs of flame shot through their elongated snouts and disappeared into smoke high above their heads.

Tobias knew it was only a matter of time before they found John, but there couldn't have been a worse time for it to happen. His path back through the courtyard was blocked by the lumbering hard-shelled behemoth.

Past the courtyard, atop the far wall, Rupert and Tia fought side by side. Tobias caught sight of them as they charged alongside a group of Guardians towards the dragons. They shifted in and out of sight as the semi-translucent Guardians rushed all around.

The dragons had also shifted their attention, preparing for the incoming raid. Tobias realized he needed to get over there and join the fight. He feared even their might would not be enough to down the giant, horned beasts.

The upper walls of the castle had been jammed solid in battle, but they were a far better option than the courtyard. He readied his swords and charged, powering down his mind and letting his emotions carry him forward. He made it twenty feet before being knocked off the wall by the swipe of the Tormentor he failed to notice to his left. After flipping through the air for what seemed like an eternity, he landed hard on the stairs. His armor clanged as he rolled side over side to the bottom of the flight and eventually into the courtyard, face-down.

Excruciating pain ripped through him as he lifted himself off the ground. He was sure he'd suffered another broken rib. His breathing became more difficult as the splintered bones pressed against his lungs. Adrenaline, however, his constant motivator, coursed through his body and pushed away the pain.

Looking back over his shoulder, Tobias watched as a legion of Tormentors crested the walls. The nearest group of Guardians immediately engaged, swiping with their brilliant white blades. The wall he'd stood on seconds ago became a mass of commotion. He knew it would be certain death to go back up. His only option now was to get through the courtyard and past the three-story monster that resided in the center.

He reached to his right side and released the straps holding the chest armor in place. The dented piece of metal clanked to the ground at his feet. It helped to ease his breathing a bit, but not enough for it to matter. The smaller sword was lost during the fall. His sword, the one that had seen him through many an encounter, was still grasped firmly in his hand. He knew it would be the deciding factor on whether he lived or died. Bullets would not make a difference in this waging battle.

His sense tingled. Something was wrong. Looking to his right, he had just enough time to dive out of the way from the incoming stream of black fire. The Guardian-killing beast had turned its attention on the last living Guardian.

Chapter 36

The shaking forced John to his knees. More of the white bricks fell from overhead, one of the blocks nearly crushing his skull. He feared, by the looks of thing, this might be the end of their journey.

He leaned over the spot in the floor where the stone block descended. He peered into the small square of darkness but couldn't make out a thing. He was sure he heard something, though—something he hoped would get them out of this situation. His hands were shaking, and his eyes jittered about. The anxiety was killing him. He wasn't cut out for this kind of stuff. Life was so much easier without responsibilities.

More dirt rained from the ceiling. Looking up, John realized it wasn't going to last much longer. Suddenly, the stone block slowly grinded its way back up from below. He breathed a sigh of relief. Maybe he would live to see another day. A small smile forced its way to his face. Atop the block's blood-stained surfaced rested a small gold tube.

Not waiting for it to finish its ascent, John swiped the tube up. He shook it in his hand and listened. His bloodied hand caused the surface to become murky and tarnished.

Sam, noticing this, grabbed the tube from him. "You might ruin a clue," she said. She rolled the tube on the bottom of her shirt and vigorously wiped it clean.

The tube itself was simple in appearance. Its gold shell was smooth and uninteresting. She twisted the end with all her might, but it didn't budge.

"Wouldn't it make sense that only I could open it?" John said with his hand held out in front of him, unintentionally smug. Sam nodded and humbly handed it back.

John took the golden cylinder in his bloodied hand and twisted with his other. The tube's cap popped off with ease and fell to the ground. It bounced until eventually coming to rest at the far wall.

John motioned to Sam. She held her palms out as he tilted the gold tube. A small rolled parchment fell free from within. It was well-preserved, but showed obvious signs of its age. Holding the tube above his head, he peered inside. Satisfied that there was nothing left, he dropped it without a second thought.

Sam broke the purple wax seal bearing the Guardian's Mark. She hastily, yet carefully, unfolded the paper.

Another tremendous boom reverberated from above. The door leading to the hallway became blocked by a large pile of falling stones. They were now trapped in the small, deteriorating room.

Sam held the yellowing parchment out for John and the robed man to see as she read.

The final sign is hidden on a distant dot of land
To find it you must look for the guardians where water meets the sand
For they alone hold the secret and are ultimately the tool
The Brotherhood of the Sealed must ensure the devil will never rule

Brother Iunapar

They stared at the writing in confusion.

The robed man spoke. "Brother Iunapar was next in the line of succession for leader of the Brotherhood of the Sealed. After I passed, he would have taken over. His priority would have been to hide the final Sign."

"Why a poem?" John asked, frustrated. "Why not just tell us where it is?" He knew Tobias would be pissed it was another riddle.

The room filled with dust as the hall outside collapsed upon itself. John was momentarily blinded, but his ears picked up a familiar giggling from somewhere close.

Chapter 37

Flames, black as night, shot past Tobias on either side. If it wasn't for the large stone pillar—a support for the flight of stairs above him—he would surely have faced a crispy death. While he was protected from the ominous black flame, he knew it wouldn't be for long. The cool stone was heating up. He needed a plan, a way past the colossal beast blocking his path. Nothing, unfortunately, came to mind.

The flames stopped as they had before as the beast prepared the next wave of fire. Tobias knew the respite would be short, but he was thankful one existed at all. He took the opportunity to get his bearings on their situation.

On the opposite side of the castle, Rupert and Tia fought feverishly alongside the remaining Guardians. They hacked enemies apart like a wood chipper, scaly limbs and charred flesh flying everywhere. The fact that they were surrounded by a small legion of vengeful ghosts only helped.

The dragon nearest to Tia, less than fifty yards away, had destroyed the hall leading to John's location. Tobias, with his back against the pillar at the time, knew something large had fallen. The crashing sound of stone echoed over the pangs of battle. He prayed, for humanity's sake, that John and company were not beneath the roof when it collapsed.

A large group of Guardians fought with the dragon closest to them. Their swords bounced off the beast's impenetrably scaly hide. The dragon swatted at the Guardians, but it was as equally ill-prepared, as its swipes passed through their misty figures without causing any damage. The stalemate continued as Rupert and Tia stood back, taking stock of the situation.

Tobias ducked back behind the pillar as the next wave of flames engulfed his position. He leaned forward some, taking his back off the increasingly heated stone. He couldn't stay in that position much longer. He knew the beast would eventually tire of the game and charge his position. When that happened, all bets on his survival were off. He needed to come up with something—anything—and it needed to be quick.

A few minutes passed, and the flames stopped once again. Thankfully, that thing had an off switch.

Tobias peered from behind the pillar.

Rupert, along with five or six Guardians, was engaged with a Tormentor that had approached from behind him. The group made easy work of it, and the beast plummeted to the courtyard, dead.

Tia dashed from her position and followed a second round of Guardians as they charged the dragon. The knights stopped at the beast's neck, but Tia continued to its underbelly, stopping beneath its left front leg. She gazed up, looking for something, as the beast's hide swayed like a protected ocean of scaly flesh.

Tobias watched her, eventually figuring out what she was doing. Scale plating lined the dragon's underside, just like it had the rest of the gargantuan beast, except for a few exposed spots where its legs protruded. It was the beast's only noticeable weak spot aside from its head, a place where a blade could do the most damage.

Tia stood dwarfed beneath the huge dragon, yet she valiantly waited for the right time to strike. She dropped her swords and picked up a pole arm from a pile nearby. Tobias felt like he was in her mind, reading her thoughts. The pole arm, being long and sharp like a spear, would cause the most damage with only a single blow; hopefully, one powerful enough to down the flaming beast.

The devil's army packed every square inch of the castle like an army of ants. The time when they were outnumbered had long since passed. Now, it was a fight for survival and not victory.

Before the next wave of flames erupted, Tobias made an impulsive decision to move. He dove to his right, and rolled behind a broken wall. No flames. Carried by adrenaline, he sprinted until coming to rest in the middle of the courtyard. He used the back wall of a small, crumbling structure as a shield.

The large Guardian-killing beast followed his progress, yet was too slow to move at his pace. The ground shook as the monster repositioned itself. Tobias looked around. There was no other cover nearby. He realized this was as far as he was going. A decision, other than where to run to next, would need to be made there.

His view of Rupert and Tia went unobstructed through a small hole in the wall. Rupert danced from side to side like a boxer, carving anything in his way. He was in rhythm now. It was something Tobias hadn't seen in years. He then peered over to Tia in time to see something bounce off her helmet, knocking it off. She fell with a thud next to the dragon's thick leg.

Tia pushed herself off the ground and brought her hand up to her head. A small laceration caused a stream of blood to drip down her cheek. She wiped a small bit off and eyed it with disdain. Tobias knew from her expression that it only pissed her off. *Hell hath no fury like a woman scorned*, echoed through his mind. And hell was about to find that out the hard way.

The gargantuan beast covered the wall Tobias hid behind in another round of black flames. The hole in the wall succumbed to the heat and fell apart even more as a column of flames shot through it. His protection was crumbling to the ground all around him.

A raucous collection of shouts sounded from the other side of his hiding place and the flames stopped. A group of Guardians rushed the beast from below and gave Tobias enough time to search for a way out; one that didn't involve continually running and hiding.

On the wall above, Tia grabbed the pole arm tightly in her grasp. The dragon swayed, revealing the sought after sweet spot. With a powerful thrust, she rammed the sharp metal tip of the pole arm into the exposed patch of flesh. The medieval weapon continued under her force until almost completely disappearing from sight. A dark black liquid poured from the open wound, covering her right arm.

The dragon reared back and screeched in pain. Pillars of flame escaped from its mouth and nose. It lifted its front two legs from atop the stone wall high into the air. The higher it rose, the more fearsome it became. Its enormous wings beat large gusts of wind that knocked Rupert from his feet.

The ghostly Guardians shot into action. Taking a cue from Tia, they collectively charged the beast and drove their blades deep into the exposed portions of the dragon's underbelly. It wailed in pain and reared back farther, losing its already uneven footing. Its balance failed, and the dying beast fell. The ground shook as it hit the grassy terrain outside the castle's walls.

Tia looked back to Rupert and raised a fist to the air. A smile cut her face. Tobias smiled, too. It was good to see them in action again. The group of Guardian dragon-slayers cheered the small victory.

With all the commotion, Tia failed to notice the second dragon's tail as it plunged towards her. With flesh-tearing penetration, a large spike from its tail punched through her back. Blood oozed from her mouth and sprayed from the gaping wound in her chest. She shockingly looked to Rupert, who stood in disbelief thirty feet away. Tia tried to scream, but her lungs lacked the air to do so, having been devastated by the spike.

"Tia!" Tobias screamed. He broke from the wall but was pinned back by the beast's black flame once again. With his back to the wall, his mind numbed. Tia was dying, and there was nothing he could do about it. Rage took over. He waited for the flames to subside. Seconds seemed like years. Finally, the flames ceased. He looked at the beast. It was once again occupied by a group of ghostly knights.

Rupert had dropped both his sword and shield by his side, leaving him exposed to attack. Tobias wanted to charge, to rush to Tia's aid, but his feet wouldn't move. His brain had trumped his emotions. If he darted from cover now he would surely perish. He hated himself at that moment. He felt like a coward, but he knew there were no alternatives.

The dragon raised its tail from the top of the wall, taking Tia with it. Her arms and legs were limp. Blood trickled down her body and fell back to the stone wall.

Rupert's shock turned into unbridled rage. He charged the dragon with fire in his eyes, careening over the path of the dead with an unflinching stare locked on his prey. His muscles were flexed tight. Veins shot to the surface of his skin. He grabbed a broadsword from the ground while in stride. A fierce cry of hatred shot from his mouth.

The dragon roared as if taunting him closer. Rupert continued, unflinching.

The dragon snapped, baring its razor-sharp teeth. Rupert sidestepped its attack and spun out of harm's way. Several of the dragon's protective plates had ripped off its hide during the fight. It was a battle scar that Rupert sought to exploit. One such area resided on its ever-shifting,

271

snakelike neck. He wasted no time driving the large sword deep into the exposed flesh.

A gush of black ooze sprayed from the wound opening. The dragon flinched back and raised its head and neck high above the castle wall. Rupert hung on with one hand and rose with it, while ripping at the plates with his other hand like a man possessed.

Tobias watched from afar. *How did things get so bad?* He looked at Tia as she dangled from the dragon's tail. Her chin rested against her chest, and her eyes were closed. His eyes welled with emotion. A numbing sensation shot from his head down to his toes. For the first time in a long time he was uncertain of what to do.

Black flame forced him to take cover again. He swore that would be the last time he ducked for cover. Either he would prevail, or he would die trying.

Chapter 38

John rubbed the dirt from his eyes and tried to clear his vision. The giggling of the Imps had vanished and was replaced by a tree-toppling crash just outside the wall. The ground vibrated beneath his feet, but thankfully, the ceiling above them had stopped falling. He knew something bad was happening, but because he was locked away in the tiny room, he was unaware of what that could be.

"Let's get out of here." Sam said, coughing. "We have what we need."

John nodded and looked around. He, too, wanted out.

The robed man stood with his back to them, facing the wall to their right. "What's wrong?" John asked, tucking the parchment into this waistband and covering the end with his shirt.

The robed man spun around. "Something is coming. Quickly," he said, pushing both John and Sam near the caved-in doorway through which they had entered.

As they stumbled back on the robed man's command, blocks of the far wall began to jettison outwards, as if magnetically pulled away. Stone after stone vanished and was replaced by a continually growing view of the dusty courtyard outside. Seconds passed before a human-sized hole was ripped into the white stone. Standing there, in a zombie-like trance, was Quincy.

"Thank God," Sam said. She moved towards the hole.

The robed man held out his arm to stop her advance. "I believe we owe our thanks to something else for what stands between us and freedom, child."

Quincy stepped over the remaining stones at the base of

the wall and entered the room. His glowing red eyes cut through the darkness. Before John realized what had happened, Quincy lunged and grabbed his neck.

Not again. John's neck throbbed, and his eyes watered. He tried to break the old man's grasp, but failed. He was too strong. White mist began to float from John's parted lips, like it had when he was in the phantom's grasp at Sam's cabin. He felt lightheaded from the loss of air. The sounds of the battle around him became hushed.

The robed man reached out and grabbed Quincy by the waist. Without any noticeable exertion, he lifted him off the ground and broke his grasp on John. He then flung Quincy headfirst into the rubble near Sam, causing his possessed body to scrape to a stop.

Sam jumped out of the way and took a position behind the robed man.

"There is another exit from Camelot," the man said. Quincy lay stunned on the ground, shaking his head. "Within the sanctuary, there is a table burned with a Guardian's mark. Beneath it you will find your escape." The robed man looked back to Quincy, who was now up and hovering towards them. "Go now. I will deal with this abomination."

"But, Quincy…," Sam said.

"He is beyond any help you could render," the robed man said, as if reading Sam's mind. "The devil has him now. His weak soul made him easy prey. Now go before it is too late." He looked caringly. "And Godspeed to you both."

With Sam in tow, John darted through the opening and into the commotion of the courtyard. The robed man locked up with Quincy once again as they left.

Directly to their right was Tobias, taking shelter behind a crumbling structure from an unfathomably large creature. Tobias looked past the creature and up to the top of the nearby wall. His face was expressionless and unnaturally pale.

John followed his gaze but was unprepared for what he saw. He stared hollowly at Tia, pierced by the dragon's tail. Rupert hung from its neck, covered in black blood. John's emotions shut down, all except one. A driving rage drove him past Sam and towards a set of stairs that led up to the dragon above.

Chapter 39

From his position behind the wall, Tobias noticed out of the corner of his eye when John and Sam exited into the courtyard. A sense of relief quickly mingled with his anger. They hadn't been buried when the hall collapsed. It was only a small glimmer of hope shining from within the darkness, but it was something. He struggled with their salvation and Tia's pain at the same time. His emotions rammed into each other, vying for the right to be felt. It was too much. He needed to be clear, emotionless, and he needed to act quickly.

John reached the nearby stairs without incident. Why John was running into danger, rather than away from it, was something Tobias didn't have time to answer. Tobias scouted John's intended climb. On top of the wall lingered a pair of Hell Hounds waiting for their next victim. Tobias realized it would be John unless he intervened. It was now or never.

He peeked to his right around the edge of the wall. The monster released a quick burst of flame before being subdued by the Guardians once again. This was his chance. The moment the flames subsided, he broke from behind the crumbling wall and bolted into the open. The monster could no longer be avoided. It needed to be dealt with, and Tobias had more than enough rage to drive him through the process.

Using his unnatural speed, he covered the ground between the gargantuan beast and himself before it could spray its dark flames. He took the anomaly by surprise and strafed down its left side. Adrenaline rushed into his arms and legs. More strength than he had ever felt pumped through his body. He would not be stopped. He could not be stopped.

With his glimmering sword held firmly in both hands, Tobias wound up like a batter and swung the blade with every ounce of strength he could muster. It cleaved through three-quarters of the monster's heavy leg in one swipe. He pulled back and wound up again, not feeling anything but hate pushing his swing. He exuded more force than necessary, and the blade cut clean through, severing the leg and causing the beast to shriek in pain. It echoed throughout the entirety of the castle. The bottom stump toppled over and sloshed to the ground. More of the same black ooze pooled at Tobias' feet.

The mammoth tried to reposition itself, but Tobias had already moved on to the next leg. This time, more accustomed to the force needed, he slashed through the leg with only one cut. Again, the monster cried out. It lost its balance, trying to stay upright with only one leg left for support on the left side. Black flames spewed into the air from its open mouth and mixed with the red sky.

One left, Tobias thought. A plan began to form in his head.

A new wave of Guardians rushed the toppling beast and followed his lead. They slashed at the monster's right legs, cutting off one before Tobias finished what he had started. With all the energy his anger could manifest, he brought the sword back until the blade touched his back. With an angry yell, he swiped the rearmost leg in half.

The Guardians cheered as the beast tipped to the left on its three oozing stumps.

Tobias, not wasting any time, rushed up the angled side of the downed beast and onto its hard-shelled back. The creature tried to stand, but it fell back down with a crash, kicking up a cloud of dust. Tobias fell onto his back and slid down the slippery shell. Instinctively, he dug his sword deep into the beast's body, anchoring himself in place.

He regained his footing and sprinted the final ten feet to the creature's head. Bringing the sword around, he positioned it chest-high with the blade facing down. He caught sight of the cross-shaped hilt before ramming the sword between the creature's bulbous eyes. It roared in agony and tried to shake him off. Tobias clung to his embedded sword until it stopped, like a cowboy trying to remain on a bucking bull.

The beast's head fell to the ground with a thump. It would not kill another Guardian today. Tobias then immediately turned and bolted towards John, who unwittingly climbed closer to his waiting death.

"John," Tobias yelled, his words lost in the sounds of battle. *It's never easy.*

The Hounds noticed John before Tobias could clear them out. He sheathed his sword in one graceful stroke and removed his guns from his waist. The Hounds went airborne, both ready to pounce on the last of the Brotherhood of the Sealed. Without breaking stride, Tobias emptied both guns into the sides of the Hounds. The bullets hit their marks. The beasts dropped like bricks from the air and skidded over the wall's edge into the courtyard below.

Tobias holstered his guns and leapt from the back of the creature onto the stairs. He tackled John at the waist and rolled onto the ground. In a fit of anger, he grabbed John by his shirt and lifted him off the ground.

"What the hell do you think you're doing?" He didn't know if he could control the rage that now coursed through him. The emotions he needed to defeat the beast were hard to push back. A victim of circumstance, he felt controlled by them now, almost wanting to allow his rage out and into the open.

"The dragon… It has Rupert and Tia," John said, stuttering, frightened.

Tobias kept his unflinching stare locked on John. The thought of his friends never left his mind, but he'd chosen not to deal with that. Now he had no choice. He looked up at Tia's motionless body and Rupert struggling to find a way to slay the dragon and save his seemingly already dead wife.

He looked back to John. "What are you going to do, huh?" Tobias said, shaking him, trying to get his point across.

John tried to shrivel back, but Tobias' unfaltering grip was too tight. There was nowhere for him to go.

"The world needs you alive, John. You won't stay that way for long if you go charging around armed with only your good intentions."

John nodded. He focused on the ground.

"If you want to help, then go watch out for Sam." They both looked at the emotionally paralyzed woman, left alone in the courtyard. "I'll deal with this." He released his grip.

John trudged down the stairs and back to Sam as Tobias bolted up the stairs.

The dragon tried to fend off a relentless wave of attacking ghosts. Tia's body dangled limply from its tail. Her eyes were closed, and blood seeped from her nose and mouth. Tobias fought back the tears. He let rage take their place.

One final push, and the Guardians finally toppled the dragon. Rupert fell from the sword lodged in the beast's neck and onto the broken castle wall. Tia slid from the tail and fell to the ground like a wet sponge. She remained motionless upon impact, her arms contorted by her sides. A giant thump shook the ground as the dragon fell off the wall and joined the other one, dead.

Hurtling everything in his path, Tobias hurried to Rupert's side. He pried the big man off the ground. Rupert shrugged him off and wobbled to his feet. No doubt carried by emotion, he ran towards Tia in desperation. He pushed through the commotion, breaking anything in his way with his bare hands.

Upon reaching his wife, he slid down next to her. Tears ran down his cheeks. Cupping her head in his massive hands, Rupert put his head down to hers and cried. He rocked her gently.

Tobias knew that she was already dead. There was nothing any of them could do to change that now. He closed his welling eyes. Everything moved in slow motion—the battle, the grieving, and the pain. If he had never gone to get them, then Tia would still be alive. They would still be together, happy. He might as well have killed her himself. Tobias had never felt so helpless in all his life.

Rupert looked to the sky. "Tia!" he yelled with all the force his lungs would allow before laying his head on her still chest. His watery eyes were filled with the redness of anger, hate, and loss.

Sniffling, Rupert gently placed his wife's head back to the ground and closed her eyes. He lovingly placed a kiss on her bloodied lips and held it for a moment before standing back up. Rupert turned back around, and the look on his face sent chills coursing through Tobias' body. Anger had doused the flame of sadness. Pure, unadulterated hatred possessed him now. He picked up a broadsword to his left and swung wildly at any enemy within reach. He felled three of the flying insects and a Gargoyle before Tobias and a small group of Guardians carefully intervened.

Grasping Rupert from behind, Tobias tried to secure his two enormous arms. "Rupert," Tobias said, not knowing if what he was about to say was right. "We need to go. There's nothing we can do for Tia now." Rupert tried to break out of his grasp. Tobias didn't know if this would end well. "Rupert, listen to me. Please." He turned him around. "I love Tia, too, but we will all share her fate if we stay here for one minute longer. The only way to avenge her is to leave right now." Guilt flowed freely throughout his body, but it was a feeling he couldn't deal with now. He needed to get the group of out of here first. Then he could hate himself. But he swore he would not lose another member of his dwindling team.

Rupert gazed down at the lifeless body of his wife one last time before barging by Tobias and down the flight of stairs. Sam, gushing tears, hugged Rupert's large arm when he approached. He looked down at her, but stayed catatonically still.

Tobias tried to shake off what had just happened, at least for the few moments he needed to get them the hell out of there."Do we have what we came for?" Tobias asked John.

John nodded softly, sympathetically.

A roar bellowed through the air. What was left of the front wall of the castle came crashing down. Three more Guardian-killing beasts lumbered into the courtyard and destroyed everything in their path. Continuous sheets of black flame gushed across the castle courtyard like waves of oil.

"Follow me," John said, running across the wall and back into the sanctuary.

Left with little choice, Tobias did exactly as John said. He ushered Rupert and Sam first and then followed behind.

They slipped through the fractured stone doorway leading to the sanctuary. John ran around the room, frantically searching for the mark the robed man had told him about.

Tobias turned to Sam. "What is he doing?"

"The ghost said there was another way out of the castle, some kind of secret exit."

"Over here," John said, pointing to one of the elongated tables. On it was carved the Guardian's Mark just as the robed man said it would be. They rushed to his side.

"There's a trap door down there," John said, pointing.

Rupert bent down and heaved the enormous table into the air. It hurtled across the room before finally coming to rest upside down against the far wall. He then reached down and pulled the trap door up by its large brass ring with such force that the hinges holding it firm broke apart and fell.

Darkness and uncertainty filled the square opening in the floor. Tobias would take his chances with the unknown below rather than deal with what chased them. He hustled the team into the hole in the floor and followed. As had happened in Egypt, torchlight spread as John passed by. The escape tunnel ran straight with a downward slope.

The group ran until they reached the end of the escape tunnel. Just like in Egypt, the path was blocked by a large stone. With the touch of John's hand, the block slid out of the way and opened to the outside.

The failing rays of daylight blanketed the English countryside. Tobias turned around and looked back towards Camelot. The battle continued, but the castle was nearly destroyed. It would not be long before the devil realized they were no longer there. Tobias hoped that, by that time, he would be out of his reach for good.

Chapter 40

Tobias figured they had put close to four miles between the devil's army and themselves. They walked quickly in a single file line off to the side of the road. The red sky faded behind them, replaced by the ambiance of a half-moon night. A heavy silence blanketed the countryside, occasionally interrupted by a breezy whistle across the tops of the long blades of grass. With the sounds of battle far behind, they crept along the side of the road enveloped in their own thoughts. Tia's death weighed heavily on everyone's mind, almost numbing them to a stop, but Tobias knew that one of them screamed exponentially louder than everyone else on the inside.

He wanted to console Rupert and tell him the pain would pass, but each time he went to speak nothing came out. The words didn't exist that could convey what Tobias actually felt. In his mind, he was solely to blame for her death. He alone sentenced Rupert to a lifetime of lonely regret. Tobias knew that the loss of Tia had doomed Rupert to a future of horrific nightmares and endless "what-ifs".

Guilt tore apart his insides like a caged animal trying to escape. He would never let it loose—never allow it to run away and be forgotten. Tobias would carry the pain with him for the rest of his life as his own scarlet letter. That was his unspoken pledge. It would be that pain that pushed him furiously to enact his revenge—to defeat the Evil that took Tia away from them, no matter how bleak their situation seemed. *We will prevail*, the thought. And he would give every last drop of his blood to ensure it.

A pair of approaching headlights from behind

illuminated the road and snapped Tobias from his thoughts. He turned and squinted. It was the first hint of civilization in over an hour, if he could call it that. The whining of the overtaxed engine increased in volume until it was within twenty feet. With his hand out, palm facing the decrepit pickup truck, Tobias stood his ground in the middle of the road. His primal instincts pushed away any semblance of civilized behavior. They were in the middle of a war. There was no longer a place for the nice Tobias. If he needed to, he would commandeer this truck by any means necessary.

The brakes squealed, and the driver slowed the truck to a stop. The rest of the group stood confused in the headlight's fading yellow glow.

An elderly couple sat in the front seat. The old man peered at Tobias from the driver's side as the woman fearfully glanced from the passenger side. Seeing their faces made Tobias rethink his newfound primal urges. Their aged, doe-like eyes stared at him innocently, curiously.

The driver rolled down the window as the engine sputtered and burped. While the old woman looked frightened, the old man seemed indifferent, like this happened to him all the time.

"I don't know what you're trying to do," the elderly man said, "scaring us half to death like that. Nobody walks out here at night. We thought you were a ghost." He looked to his wife and then back to Tobias.

"I'm sorry about that," Tobias said. "I had a little too much to drink today, and…well, you know." He couldn't bring himself to use force on the old couple. He hoped the ridiculous excuse worked in its place and that the darkness hid the weapons well enough. His thoughts were swirling like a vortex, making it impossible to create a truly believable lie.

The old man peered deep into his eyes and nodded.

"We're trying to find the airport," Tobias said, pointing further down the road. "Are we headed the right way?"

"Bristol Airport?"

Tobias nodded.

"If you keep walking straight, you'll eventually bump into it. You can't miss all the lights and such." He began to roll up the window. "Goodnight... ."

The elderly woman stopped him in mid-sentence. "Henry, how would we sleep tonight knowing we left them to wander out here? Especially with all those giant swarming bugs the news keeps getting on about."

Henry turned to his wife and returned her sweet smile. He patted her folded hands and turned back to Tobias. "Hop in the back," he said pointing his thumb to the bed of the pickup. "As it turns out, we're going that way."

Tobias flashed a quick smile of thanks and nodded to the others. He didn't know why the elderly couple chose to trust them. If Tobias had been in their position, he doubted he would do the same. It reassured him that they were fighting, and dying, for a just cause—the protection of people like these. Again his thoughts went to Tia and her bright smile and glowing personality. It was an overwhelming, and inescapable, feeling of loss. *I'm so sorry, Tia.*

As Sam walked by on her way to the truck bed, the old man stopped her with a look of concern. "You can ride up front with us, lovey."

The elderly woman nodded in agreement and then scooted to the center of the bench seat, a smile on her face. Sam, not one to take the bed of the truck over comfort, walked in front of the truck and entered through the passenger door. The rest of the team piled in back. A few small rusted-out holes ate away at the weathered metal truck bed, but they found room where they could.

"Thank you," Sam said, closing the door.

"You're quite welcome. My name is Margaret, but my friends call me Maggie. And this...," she said, turning her head, "...is my husband, Henry."

Henry nodded with a smile and then moved the truck forward down the quiet road.

"I'm Sam," she said. "Thanks for the ride."

"Short for Samantha, I take it?" inquired Margaret.

Sam nodded.

"That's a lovely name, dear. I knew a Samantha once. She was a duchess, believe it or not." Margaret looked away, pleased, like she was royalty herself.

In the back of the truck, John sat across from Tobias and stared out at the passing fields of tall grass. Tobias knew from his withdrawn body language that something more than the loss of Tia was bothering him. It had to be his secret, but it was getting to a point where Tobias might have to pry for the sake of John's health. This was not how Tobias had envisioned this would go when he'd taken that folder from Father Fenn in Africa. The devil was believable then, but not tangible. Now that Tia was gone, Tobias couldn't help but second guess every decision he had made up until that point.

Rupert sat hunched over his knees, his head buried in his hands. His back pulsed now and again. He was quiet— no sobs or sniffles—but Tobias didn't need them to know that Rupert was crying. Tobias had known Tia for a good portion of his life. She always found a way to comfort him when he needed it most. She accepted not only Tobias, but his bizarre life without question. In time, she'd become one of the few people he actually considered family. But, like the rest of his family, she, too, had been taken from him much too early. While Tobias fought for the Church out of obligation, the more people he loved around him died, the more he found the idea of God implausible. How could some benevolent being allow such good to perish while leaving such evil to prosper?

While Tobias was no stranger to death, he could not even begin to understand what Rupert felt. Rupert and Tia had known each other for over twenty years. Fifteen of them were spent married, most of them in love. He had just lost the one person he cared for most in this world, the one person that was his ideal match in life. Tobias feared Rupert would fly off the handle—lose his connection to the world—and Tobias knew, if that happened, there was nothing he could do to stop it. Tobias didn't know if he would even try.

He sat down next to Rupert with a sigh. No words or gestures were needed. He just wanted his friend to know he was there, sharing the pain, and that he wasn't alone. If and when Rupert chose to talk, Tobias would be there to listen with a weighed-down and guilty heart. Until then, he would sit in the numbness with Rupert by his side.

The old man slid the rear window open. "You fellas all right back there?"

"Yes. Thanks again for the ride," Tobias said.

Sam looked back at Tobias and smiled before having to redirect her attention.

"You don't look too far along, dear?" Maggie said from within the heated cabin, gazing at Sam's belly.

Sam turned in surprise. She cocked her head to the side and furrowed her brow. "I'm sorry?"

Maggie smiled. "I don't mean to pry, but you are pregnant, are you not?"

Sam nodded slowly. "How did you know?"

The elderly woman grinned. "I was a midwife for most of my life."

"A darn good one, too," Henry interrupted.

"Thank you, dear," Maggie said, patting Henry's knee.

She turned back to Sam. "I've seen many a mother-to-be, and the glow is particularly strong on you."

"Glow?"

"If you know what you're looking for, and I do after all the years, then it's as obvious as your belly will be later on. The glow is in your eyes—can't mistake it."

Sam blushed and made small, soft circles on her stomach.

Maggie nodded with a smile. "The best days are ahead of you." She turned to her husband. "Henry and I have five children. They are all grown and moved away, but you never lose the connected feeling you have with them."

Sam smiled.

Maggie glanced over her shoulder to the bed of the truck. Tobias and Rupert sat beside each other, swaying with the ride. She looked back to Sam. "I don't mean to be nosy, dear, but is one of those gentlemen the father-to-be?"

"Maggie," Henry said, embarrassed, "that's none of our business."

"Oh shush, Henry. It's just a question."

Sam blushed and cleared her throat. "Uh, well... ."

They rounded a bend in the road, and the airport came into view.

"Here we are," Henry said. He looked over to Sam and winked. The timing of their arrival couldn't have been better for Sam's sake.

Tobias hoped from the back of the truck, followed by Rupert and John.

"Thanks again," Tobias said, walking up to the driver's door and shaking Henry's hand.

Henry grinned. "Not a problem at all. I'm glad we could help."

Sam walked over to join the rest of the group.

"Bye-bye, dear," Maggie said. "Take good care of

yourself." She smiled and glanced at Sam's belly once again.

The elderly couple drove off slowly down the road. A single backfire broke the silence. The group walked the short way into the airport proper. Fire burned within several of the hangars in the far distance and gave the immediate sky an amber glow.

Camelot appeared to have been the evil army's second stop.

Chapter 41

An aviation graveyard spanned the horizon as far as Tobias could see. Burning and twisted pieces of jet carcasses lined the ground. Every one of the large private hangars had been reduced to piles of ash, except for one. Tobias felt absolute relief upon seeing the one building spared, but that feeling quickly gave way to caution. Of all the hangars to remain, this one happened to be the Cardinal's. He wondered how that could be. If the devil wanted to deal them a severe blow, then he surely would have dispatched the Cardinal and their only exit at the same time, yet Tobias now stood in front of Rathady's hangar, staring at its mostly untouched, but slightly charred, metal exterior. Whatever the reason, he knew to approach it carefully.

The hangar door was open, but the darkness inside made it difficult to see. Tobias inched a couple of feet forward and then stopped. It would be too difficult to protect the group if they entered through there. The opening was far too large. The group needed to stay bunched. It would make protection easier.

Looking through the rising smoke, he noticed a small open side door to their right. Cautiously, he led the team over. Drifting particles of ash piggybacked on the wind, carrying with them the malodorous scent of death. More charred bodies—airline personnel, he assumed—obstructed their path like limbs from trees downed after a heavy storm. All the bodies had an agonized expression frozen on their burnt faces. Several of them had only one arm or leg, likely torn off by the bugs, but most had neither. Respectfully, Tobias took an extra amount of care to avoid each of them.

They probably died on the spot, victims of a soulless enemy. They were not the first, and unfortunately would not be the last.

Tobias peered into the darkness through the side doorway. The jet's stairs were extended, and on them sat the Cardinal, staring down at the ground with his head in his hands. His flowing crimson robe dangled to either side, like a spill of cranberry juice. The open hangar door allowed much of the floating ash inside and, coupled with the minimal light, it created an apocalyptic feel within.

The sounds of the approaching group startled Rathady back to attention. He leapt from the stairs. "Thank heaven you are back," he said, surprised. "I take it the last Trinity Sign's location is no longer a mystery?"

Nice to see you too, Cardinal.

The whole situation stunk. The pieces weren't falling together the way they should. The Cardinal's demeanor was not of the man he had known for so long. The Cardinal he knew would wonder why their group was now one member short. He would want to know about Tia. He would mourn her loss and pray for her soul. He would ask about their welfare before asking about the Sign.

"What happened here?" Tobias asked. He watched carefully as the Cardinal answered, looking for any telltale signs of deceit. He felt guilty even resorting to such tactics, especially with someone like Rathady, but he knew there would be no second chance if he were to miss something.

The Cardinal looked to the ground and shook his head. "Hell came looking for you, I can only assume." He paced away, slowly, and recounted what happened. "Ashamedly, I was too fearful of what approached to get a good look. The air and ground hummed with the sound of evil. I was alone and no match for anything more than a good mental debate, so I hid inside the jet and prayed for it to pass." He looked around at the untouched hangar. "I can only assume my prayers were answered. Thank the Lord."

Tobias continued to watch the holy man. "Go on."

"The onslaught began as I was speaking with you over the communication device you gave me. Then my ear filled with static, and you were gone."

Tobias nodded. He remembered that happening. soon after the devil's army attacked them at Camelot.

"The next thing I knew the whole hangar was vibrating. The metal siding was pulled outwards, like a tornado hovered overhead. Then, and this part I remember clearly, the air filled with this horrific buzzing sound. It was sinister in some way, like one collective voice scattered among millions of wings. Thankfully they failed to notice me. I would have been no challenge for them. I fear my old skin would have been quite easy for their pincers to skewer through."

Something snapped in Tobias' mind. He peered at the Cardinal.

The Cardinal looked back. "What is it, Tobias?"

"You said that you hid inside the jet during the onslaught?"

The Cardinal nodded and mentally rechecked what he had said. A bead of sweat formed on his brow. It was one of the telltale signs Tobias was looking for—one he wished he hadn't seen. No sweat meant the Cardinal was the honest man he had grown to respect and trust. Sweat…well, that could only mean one thing. The man that stood before them was not who he thought him to be.

"So how is it you know so much detail? How did you know the bugs had pincers?" Tobias shifted his balled fist into an open palm. He felt a trap about to be sprung. Of all the people Tobias would believe could betray him, Rathady would have been at the bottom of the suspect list.

292

The Cardinal shifted nervously in place. The sweat grew worse, and then the white-haired man looked up with a grin on his face, confident.

"I should have known, Tobias." Rathady's expression changed from timid fright to knowing arrogance. "You are far too perceptive to fall for anything less than the truth. I'm sorry you had to find out this way. I had planned on discussing this with you later."

Tobias' suspicions were right. For whatever reason, the Cardinal had betrayed them.

"Why?" Tobias asked, scanning the immediate area. There were too many dark spots inside the hangar. Something lurked nearby. He felt it.

A snicker slithered from between the Cardinal's cracked lips. "Why would I help the devil?" The Cardinal looked around at the group. "The answer is quite simple, actually. I was shown the truth hidden amongst the lies." He took a small handkerchief out and dabbed the sweat from his brow. "During my countless years of devout worship," he rolled his eyes, "I acquired a certain amount of knowledge not available to the masses. Within those words was hidden a realization that changed my beliefs. The devil wants the same thing that God does—mankind's devotion. The only difference is that the devil will reward our devotion, while God—if there is one at all—continues to use us as his playthings."

Tobias couldn't believe what he was hearing. While he found his own faith dwindling as the years went by, he could never envision allowing his soul to blacken. God or not, good still needed to thrive; otherwise, humanity was already doomed.

"So, what, you think the devil is going to spare you if he succeeds? Make you some kind of prince of the damned?"

"That's the thing, Tobias. It is not a matter of *if* the devil

293

succeeds, but *when*. And when he does, I want to see what life has to offer. I will no longer be a puppet, but a puppet master with far reaching strings."

"There won't be any life," Tobias said, "only death. How can you believe any of what you're saying? What happened to the noble, honest man I've known for so long?"

The Cardinal laughed. "That man died a long time ago, along with his misguided ideologies. However, I couldn't just go around proclaiming my new beliefs, especially a man of my stature within the Church. So, in the interest of what was to come, I remained silent, but ever listening. I have helped you along the way in the hope that you would discover the location of the final Trinity Sign, and it appears that you have. Its destruction will ensure the devil's rule and, with it, my new life."

Anger boiled to the surface. Any feelings Tobias had for the Cardinal vanished in an instant. To find out they had been shadowed the whole time by someone he trusted— someone he would have given his life for—made his vision blur with rage. He was forced to trust Rathady out of need, not to mention the years of help Rathady had given him. Tobias couldn't help but think of other missions he was sent on to which Rathady leant his knowledge. Were lives lost then because of the Cardinal's deceit? Had Tobias been played for a fool then, too?

"And if you find the final Trinity Sign, what then?" Tobias asked. He already knew the answer.

The Cardinal smiled. "Then, my dear boy, the devil will send his army to the Sign's location and destroy it before John here… .," He pointed. "…Can activate it."

Rupert's broadsword clanged on the concrete floor of the hangar. Tobias turned to see his bloodshot eyes staring at the Cardinal. His lip was curled, and his nose flared. Rupert had found the appropriate outlet for his rage. Tia's death now rested on the back of one man, the Cardinal, and Rupert would see to it that he paid.

The Cardinal lifted his right arm above his head, surprisingly quickly for a man of his age. With the sound of tearing metal, the wall in the rear of the hangar burst apart, and a pack of five Tormentors stormed in. They stopped their rampage when they got to within a few feet of the group and stood behind the Cardinal, waiting. Their partially armored bodies pulsed with every raspy breath they took. Their animalistic twitches and jerks made them all the more unpredictable. Hatred flowed from them—hatred for anything good. It was a hatred matched by Tobias for them and for Rathady.

"I am giving you," he waved his hands out at the group, "all of you, the chance to see what I've seen—a chance to stop your pursuit of something that will never be. You will never make it to the final Trinity Sign. I am giving you a chance to not only spare your lives, but to enhance them." He took a step towards Tobias and lowered his voice. "I've known you for a long time, Tobias, and I have always enjoyed our talks. Please, take what I am offering you. Tell me the location of the third Trinity Sign, and you will all be spared and allowed to prosper when the new world comes to be. Don't continue to follow a path that leads to no reward. Join me and see what life can really be like."

Tobias' lip twitched. He wanted to lop off the Cardinal's head right there. The audacity of his words was like a slap to the face. The devil finding them was made that much easier by the mouth of the man that stood before him. Tia's death may have been prevented. Then, in an instant, he remembered. "I take it you killed Vene?"

The Cardinal shook his head. "I have never killed a soul, Tobias. Vene is dead, yes, but not by my hands. The devil's helpers saw to it." He looked over his shoulder at the

Tormentors. "After you left for Egypt, he became too nosy. He was starting to suspect things, and… well, we just couldn't have that."

That made two deaths. Two deaths caused by the man he'd once considered a friend. *How could I be so blind?*

"If you are so determined to find the final Trinity Sign, why make an attempt on our lives above the skies of Egypt?" It would only make sense that those pilots were also part of the Cardinal's misguided plan.

After a moment of silence, the Cardinal answered. "That was not my doing."

Tobias looked back in disbelief.

"Why would I lie at this point?" the Cardinal said. "The devil is magnificently powerful. However, when he wants to do something, he does it without thought of future consequences, and he certainly did not care what I thought. He wanted you all dead and set the wheels of hell in motion, but perseverance is one of your greatest qualities, Tobias. Now I, for one, am glad to see that you somehow survived that ordeal, as did you the attack on Camelot. If not for any other reason than I will be rewarded for your capture, but now you must make a choice to further your lives."

"You already know my answer."

"Tobias, I beg you to reconsider—not only for your life, but those you are tasked with protecting." Rathady leaned in closer. "Just tell me the final Trinity Sign's location, and we can move onto a better world. Together."

One of the Tormentors roared and then pounded on the concrete floor. A spider web of fissures cracked their way out from its fists. The ground beneath them vibrated. Tobias knew they only had a few minutes left before this all went down, one way or the other, but the cracks gave him an idea.

The Cardinal lifted his hand casually, and the beast backed away.

Tobias suspected the five Tormentors were only the start. With another wave of the Cardinal's hand, more would come. This was a situation that couldn't be won by brute force, as they were on the losing end of that fight. Unfortunately, this was one time he had no backup plan.

"So, Tobias, what is your answer? We will locate the third Trinity Sign either way. This way, however, makes much more sense for you. You all live—well, except for John, of course. We can't have him running around with all that knowledge in his head." He turned to John with a crooked smile. "You understand, of course."

"And what's in it for me?" Tobias asked, stalling.

A curious smile arched across the Cardinal's face. "You live, Tobias."

"I'm going to need more than that, I'm afraid. I want whatever it is you're getting."

"Tobias," Sam said, surprised.

He glanced at her quickly before turning his attention back to Rathady.

The Cardinal laughed. "I don't think you are in any position to make demands."

"And I don't think you are as confident as you pretend to be. You won't find the third Trinity Sign without us. If you knew where it was, you'd already be there. If you kill us, then the devil wins for now, but later, when another rises, he will be faced with banishment once again. Therefore, I think the location of the final Sign is worth a bit more than safe passage." Tobias was winging it. He knew that if both John and Sam died, then the world was lost forever. He prayed that Rathady wasn't as informed as he thought he was.

"Come now, Tobias. I know as well as you do that John is the end of the line for the Brotherhood of the Sealed. There are no others."

297

Tobias smiled but said nothing. He hoped that slight gesture was enough to plant a bit of doubt in the Cardinal's mind. Even if John did die, and the devil won, there was still hope growing in Sam's belly. It was a long shot, but a shot, nonetheless.

The Tormentors stared at them, seething behind the frail old man. They wanted blood, and Tobias knew they were going to get it either way. His act had reached its conclusion, and there would be no encore today.

"Very well," the Cardinal said. "You win, Tobias. I will see to it that you are appointed to a high position within the new world. We will reign together and help the devil rule over those…less fortunate." An evil smile formed on his wrinkled face. "Now, tell me the location of the final Sign."

Tobias nodded. "Fair enough," he said, reaching over his shoulder. "We have a map… ." Removing his sword, Tobias brought it down and sliced clear through the Cardinal's head and into the upper part of his chest. The look of shock, sliced in two, was frozen on the holy man's face.

Tobias had just given him his answer. Rathady sloshed to the floor, dead. A large pool of blood poured from the open gash and stained the dark concrete floor. Deafening roars bellowed from the Tormentors. They seemed shocked by what had just happened, even with their pea-sized brains.

Tobias removed the only micro-shotgun he had left and clicked the trigger. He couldn't remember if he'd reloaded or not, but there was no time to check. His answer came in the form of two molten-fire rounds bursting from the barrel. The webbed circles, like those created by the Tormentor's pounding, arched out and cut down all five of the looming beasts. Their body pieces thumped to the ground.

"Get on the jet," he said, pushing Sam from the back. John and Rupert followed.

Tobias ran to the cockpit and powered up the controls. The turbines whirred into existence after he flipped a few switches. He flipped a few more and then pushed the stick forward. He throttled the jet up slowly, trying to get out through the large bay doors and around the littered floor.

A massive crash rattled what was left of the hangar.

Behind them, and rapidly gaining, were ten or more Tormentors, by Tobias' quick count. While Tobias knew he needed a quick exit to the runway, it would be hopeless to try and outrun the beasts. They were too fast for his little group, and any damage to the jet would surely seal their demises.

Rupert looked back at Tobias and then out the door. He wasn't the only one that had figured it out, apparently. He closed his eyes and nodded softly to himself. "Tobias," Rupert said. "Tia's death wasn't your fault. She died for a belief, the same belief all of us share." He looked back out the door. The Tormentors were close. "The world needs good in it. Make sure it stays that way." Rupert picked the broadsword up from the ground. "You're a good man, Tobias, and a great friend. I'll keep my eyes on you. See you on the other side," he said, hopping from the slowly moving jet.

On his way out, Rupert engaged the door mechanism. The stairs retracted, and then the jet's door closed. Sam ran to the door with tears in her eyes, banging for Rupert to come back in. She held her hand to the small glass window as Rupert waved goodbye with a smile. He then turned towards the incoming Tormentors, disappearing out of sight.

Tobias went numb. *What the hell just happened?*

The jet lurched to the left as one of the beasts swiped at the tail. It wasn't enough to knock them off course, but Tobias realized that the next one might be. He couldn't afford to have that happen. He gave it more power than he could comfortably control. This was their only chance.

Outside, the obstructed runway made for a daunting takeoff attempt. He turned the jet straight and pointed it down the clearest part of the strip. To the jet's right was the hangar they'd just departed. Rupert was swinging widely with the enormous broadsword. He had already downed two of the Tormentors and was working on a third. From the rear of the hangar stormed a line of Hell Hounds.

Tobias looked back and pushed the jet to full throttle. Its muted engines created a constant hum within the cabin. It was not, however, enough to drown out Sam, who wept uncontrollably next to the closed door, tears streaming down her face. Thinking back to when he'd first met her in her Connecticut cabin, Tobias remembered that she left nursing because of the death—because of the people that couldn't be saved. Now she had seen more death in the past day than she'd probably witnessed in her entire life. He couldn't comprehend what she was going through. Hell, he didn't know what to expect from his own emotions if they survived this.

John helped Sam back to her feet and into the nearby leather seat. Tobias checked the gauges as the jet approached takeoff velocity. Before him on the runway were the burning shells of other jets.

He pulled back on the controls with all he had left, and the jet lifted off the scarred runway and barely cleared the wreckage in their way. Once airborne, he circled back over the hangar. The remaining walls and roof had been ripped away, revealing the battle below. Rupert swung his sword with the might of a Titan and the rage of a widower. However, it soon became too much for the big man to handle. A Tormentor grabbed hold of Rupert's back and picked him off the ground, throwing him a good way across the hangar like he was made of papier-mâché. The mass of Evil piled on top of him, and he vanished from sight forever.

Tobias fought back the tears. He would never forget Tia and Rupert. He would avenge them.

Chapter 42

Tobias stared out the cockpit window in a numb haze. He'd flown the jet for the past hour on instinct alone. His mind was elsewhere. A lifetime of pain could never prepare him for what had happened in England. Over the years, he had seen countless people die—some good, others not—but watching death steal two people he considered family was something he would never forget. The sense of guilt would be forever forged into his life as a permanent reminder of their selfless acts. In the beginning, he was driven by a sense of obligation, but now it was much more than that. Now it was an unspoken commitment to his dead friends to triumph when all that faced them was defeat.

What worried him the most was the mental wellbeing of John and Sam. Sam had stopped crying, but now she and John sat silent in the cabin. He wondered what, if anything, was going through their minds. Maybe they were numb like he was. They were quite possibly driven over that imaginary line separating the sane and insane. Or maybe their minds were empty, as they too wrestled with the emotional overload. Regardless of their mental states, he hoped they would be able to stick it out for just a little longer. He sensed the end was near, for better or worse.

The sky was surprisingly calm and quiet. He expected to be chased, but their flight had been, so far, uneventful. Tobias bounced from cloud to cloud like he was playing a skyward game of connect the dots. He figured that, if the devil sent his army in pursuit, he would use the grayish puffs as cover the best he could. It was a half-baked idea, but it was all he had at the moment. He was also surprised to find the skies absent of a military presence. If the world was in such a panic, which it appeared to be, then every military in the world should be protecting their space, but they were so far removed from major civilization that they were probably not viewed as a threat. Or maybe they had already succumbed to the Evil that now seemed to flow freely across the planet.

He looked back over his shoulder at John. "You said you found something at Camelot?"

John tiredly lifted the aging parchment. A small rip cut through the upper portion of the dry paper, an effect of what transpired since he took possession of it.

"It's another riddle," he said, annoyed.

"Can you make any sense of it?"

John shook his head. "Not really." He looked down and read it aloud, garnering Sam's attention as well. *"The final sign is hidden on a distant dot of land. To find it you must look for the Guardians where water meets the sand, for they alone hold the secret and are ultimately the tool. The Brotherhood of the Sealed must ensure the devil will never rule.'* John looked up from the parchment. "It's signed by a Brother Iunapar. The ghost said he was the next in the line of succession in the Brotherhood."

From within the cabin he heard the laptop run through its boot-up sequence. Sam had moved a row back to the small table. Her face glowed in the iridescent light given off by the laptop's LCD. She looked up. "It's not doing us any good for me to just sit here, depressed. It will help get my mind off things for a few minutes."

Sam searched the Internet, trying each line of the poetic riddle. The searches came back with nothing useful. She then broke the lines down to keywords. She tried *distant dot of land,* followed by, *guardians where water meets the sand.* All returned digital garbage.

"I'm not getting much, if anything," she said.

"It wouldn't be something that easy," Tobias said. "We need to break this down so that it would make sense back when they wrote it. The Brotherhood probably described it the best they could at the time. Governments change, people change, but land, for the most part, stays the same."

Sam gazed out through the jet's window and attempted to put a new, logical spin on the words. "A distant dot of land must be an island, right?" she said.

John looked up from the parchment. "That would make sense, but that leaves, like, a million possibilities."

Sam sank back into her leather seat in frustration. With a heavy sigh, she pondered the riddle once again. "Can I see that for a second?" She looked across at John, who nodded and handed the parchment over. "Okay, if we assume we're looking for an island, the second line makes more sense. *Where water meets the sand* could be a description of a beach, right?"

Sam keyed *island guardians* into the search engine. That, too, met with minimal results and certainly nothing the group could go on.

Tobias banked the jet to the left into a grouping of thick clouds.

"Try Brother Iunapar. Or, better yet, just try Iunapar," John said, looking over at Sam. She tried what John suggested and looked up, surprised. "What is it?" John asked. "Did that actually work?"

Sam shook her head. "No, but the search came back with zero results. I've never seen that happen."

"Try different combinations of the word Iunapar," Tobias suggested. "Can you make any other words out of it?"

"Like an anagram. Gotcha," Sam said.

With a few keystrokes, Sam broke the word down and tried different combinations. Each of her new words, most of which made no sense, met with minimal results. She sat back, more frustrated than before.

Then it occurred to Tobias. "Try it backwards." It seemed so many other things were backwards along this journey, so why not this?

Sam furrowed her brow and leaned forward in her chair. She typed *rapanui* into the search engine, and let it do its thing. Over a million links were returned, the first of which piqued her interest. "I think we may have something here," she said, surprised.

Tobias turned. "What is it?"

"Easter Island is mentioned all over the place." She clicked one of the resultant search links and read the screen in silence for a few minutes.

"You mind sharing?" Tobias quipped.

"Sorry," she said, looking up from the LCD. "Easter Island has to be what we're looking for." She scrolled further down the website. "It mentions the Rapa Nui on almost every page. They were said to be the first inhabitants of the island. The exact settlement date seems to be debated, but it looks like the dates range from 300AD to 1200AD."

Tobias' mind went racing. Quincy's story about the Guardians leaving Camelot would give some truth to Sam's idea. The ghost said he didn't know the whereabouts of the final Sign because it was moved after his death, which happened after the devil's previous attack. Brother Iunapar was said to be the next in line of succession; therefore, he would have been the one who would have moved the final Trinity Sign to someplace more secure. What was more secure than one of the most remote islands on the planet?

"That has to be it," he said, almost willing it to be true. "Everything seems to converge on that idea. The final Trinity Sign must be somewhere on Easter Island."

Sam scrolled further down and then checked the

parchment again.

"I think we're onto something here. The third line, *Guardians where water meets the sand*, has to be in regards to those giant faces all over the island." She scrolled some more. "They're called Moai statues." She read some more. "Seems that nobody really knows how the statues got there or what their purpose is."

Tobias was certain of it now. "Sam, can you get me the coordinates of Easter Island?"

"Way ahead of you," she said. "27° 07 south, 109° 22 west."

Tobias punched the coordinates into the jet's navigation system and checked the main gauges.

"We don't have enough fuel to make it the whole way." He wished the Cardinal had been kind enough to fuel up the jet, but he obviously had other things on his mind, like turning evil. He checked the GPS. "The closest I can get us is San Antonio, Chile. We'll try and refuel there."

Chapter 43

Tobias felt a sense of relief when he saw Chile in the distance. While he knew they would have enough fuel to make it, the glowing—almost searing—low-fuel light started to make him think differently. He circled the jet once before being cleared to land by a deep voice from the tower. Having no manifest or flight plan, Tobias thought for sure they would be in for some kind of hassle, but he was cleared to land without a single qualm on the part of the tower officials. In fact, they seemed a little overeager to get him out of the sky. Whether it was actually good fortune or another trap remained to be seen.

After gently touching down, Tobias followed the guidance of the runway technician, slowed the jet to a stop off to the right and powered off the controls. The instant he stood from the pilot's chair, his lower back ached, and his right knee popped. The whole ordeal hadn't been very forgiving on his body. He was starting to feel like an old man. It was an embarrassing feeling, one which he would hide to the best of his ability.

"Okay," he said, walking into the cabin. "We need to fuel-up quick. The sooner we're back in the air, the better."

John and Sam nodded.

He walked past them and opened the cabin door. The backsplash of the Pacific Ocean was interrupted by the same gangly technician that had just parked them.

"Are you the pilot, señor?" the tech asked, glancing casually at the weapons protruding from beneath Tobias' unneeded overcoat.

Tobias nodded. He saw the look in the technician's eyes.

He knew it well, the look of indifference. He figured this wasn't the first time a jet full of armed strangers happened to land unannounced. He had been around the world more than once. Because of that, he knew drug lords sometimes paid off workers at smaller airports to look the other way. He'd used that very trick to smuggle himself into some less-than-hospitable areas over the years.

"We are forced to ground your jet for the time being, señor." He smiled an apology. "You are lucky to even be alive. Have you not heard?"

Tobias wondered what the hell he was talking about. "Listen, if this is about having no manifest, I can explain. ..."

The technician shook his head. "I do not think you understand, señor. All air travel across the globe has been halted. The skies are no longer safe." The technician appeared anxious. He leaned in closer, as not to shout. "They say it is the end of the world."

It was worse than Tobias had thought. The devil's reach knew no boundaries. It now stretched across every continent and body of water. Grounding all aviation was sure to cause panic on a global level, and where there was panic, there was rioting, and eventually death. All of that fed the devil and his drive for domination. The more unstable mankind became, the more powerful the devil was. Tobias wondered if the world knew what was actually at stake. No doubt the greatest scientific minds were congregating to explain the events and were failing miserably.

The team's only other means of reaching the desolate Easter Island would be to sail across the Pacific. It was a thought that Tobias quickly dismissed. Even if that was an option, a sea journey would take days, and he knew they were lucky to have hours, or maybe even just minutes. Commandeering the fuel they needed was the only way. The question was how to do so in the least invasive manner. The

Chilean people meant them no harm. A compromise needed to be made—one that didn't involve unneeded hostility.

"It looks like we'll be staying for a bit." Tobias lied.

"There is lodging just outside the airport," the technician said with a smile, pointing. "We will look after your jet for you in the meantime, not to worry." He then turned and walked back towards the main terminal building, towards a grouping of his fellow technicians, who were playing cards.

"Okay, so what's the plan?" John whispered. "We're obviously not staying."

Tobias waited for the technician to walk out of earshot. "There's a fuel truck over there," he said, nodding to his right. "If we can fill the jet up with that, it should be enough to get us to Easter Island."

"So, let's just take the fuel."

"That's the plan, but we need to create a distraction first, something to occupy those workers. The last thing we need is a battle with local law enforcement."

John nodded in agreement.

While they thought, Sam acted. "I'll take care of this," she said, gently pushing her way past them. Undoing her hair from the ponytail and playfully twisting the ends, she purposefully strutted towards the terminal with a teasing smile. The technicians puffed out their chests and sucked in their bellies as soon as they saw her approach. Their faces beamed with the grins of overworked and undersexed men. The power of seduction was nearly invincible when applied properly, and Sam was working it to perfection. Tobias knew it was exactly the reaction she was hoping for.

"Hi guys," she said with a smile. "Anyplace around here that…?"

Her distraction was cut short by a sudden and harsh rumbling. The ground tore apart as if constructed from wet paper. A fissure sliced beneath her feet like the ones all

309

around the world, like the one they had seen in Cyprus.

Tobias ran to the fuel tank on the jet and spun it open. He knew this was going too smoothly. He turned to John. "There should be a lever on the truck to open the fuel line. Connect the line to here," he said, pointing, "and then pull that lever. And do it quick."

John nodded and then bolted for the fuel truck as Tobias sprinted towards Sam.

The ground ripped apart beneath the terminal building, splitting it in two and sending the technicians running for cover. Walls of glass and metal came crashing down upon each other. A large water main burst where the building had stood moments before, shooting a geyser of foaming liquid high into the air.

Already running, Tobias watched as Sam lost her balance over the widening crevice. She teetered on the chasm's edge, swaying with her hands before falling forward with a scream.

"Sam!"

She fell, face-down, across the lip of the crevice. As if she was in some old black-and-white comedy, her boots stretched out at the toe, and her hands palmed the opposite side. Tobias realized that, if the divide opened much further—inches, even—she would be lost. And, with her, would go what remained of his heart.

"Hang on," he yelled, almost to her.

The crevice inched farther out. Her body was running out of length.

If he bent over to grab her, he knew they would both undoubtedly fall in. The footing was ever changing, and one wrong move meant death. He needed to think, but his mind was a jumble. *Concentrate.*

Focused and determined, Tobias bounded over the crevice and ran to the conveniently placed fire hose on the side of the maintenance building to his right. The plume of water from the main crashed down onto him. Then, like some kind of cliché action hero, he wasted no time in tying the hose around his waist and sprinting back towards the gap. He had no idea if this would work, but the time for thinking before acting had past. Now, it was all about instincts.

Sam held on with the tips of her fingers as Tobias dropped and slid along the rubble-strewn ground, his right leg pointing the way. The concrete burned, but he continued, oblivious to the pain. Like a hawk catching its prey, he met Sam in midair as her grip failed. Their bodies collided above the newly-opened steaming pit. He held her with everything he had as the thick hose unwound rapidly behind them.

She clung to his strained body. He hoped his improvisation worked. It had to work.

Their descent ended as abruptly as it began as the hose ran out of length. They jerked to a stop. It knocked the wind out of him, but his grip remained viselike. The momentum caused them to swing from side to side. Tobias became a human bell, while Sam was the unfortunate pendulum. The fibers of the hose creaked under their weight.

Tobias looked at Sam as the world crumbled around them. Even with all that was going on, he felt disarmed by her beauty. His hardened physique did nothing to protect his softening heart as he felt her grip him tight. He slowly ran his fingers along her cheek and wiped away several of her tears as their swinging slowed.

She sniffled softly and peered up at him. "I can't take much more of this."

His throat felt tight and dry. If this was it, he was sure as hell going out happy. Without thinking, he leaned in close and kissed her passionately, if only for this one moment. Evil, be damned.

311

Sam kissed him back. Her grip tightened.

"Are you guys all right?" John yelled from above followed by a loud explosion. "We have to get out of here. This place is falling apart."

The ground shook again. The crevice grew wider. Several small chunks of the runway tumbled down to either side.

Tobias leaned away from Sam. For an instant, he forgot their situation. It was a nice feeling he hoped to duplicate later—hopefully in a more private, less hellish place.

Sam's eyes were closed, her lips still puckered.

He looked up to John. "Can you get us out of here?" Smoke wafted across the top of the crevice and obstructed Tobias' view. He knew John wouldn't be able to pull them up, and Tobias had nothing to climb up, even if he had been able to.

John studied the situation and leaped the pit. It didn't take long before they began their journey back to the surface. They rose several inches and then jerked to a stop.

"Sorry!" John shouted from up top. "Hold on a second."

A few seconds later, they began to rise again. This time, it was a much smoother ride. Ten more seconds, and they were within John's reach. He helped them from within the crevice and back onto the shaky runway.

Tobias removed the hose from around his waist and let it fall to the ground. He looked over John's shoulder curiously and followed the hose to the other end. There, attached to the back of the large tow truck, was a motorized winch. John had secured the metal line around the hose.

"Great job," Tobias said, patting John's arm. It was fast thinking Tobias didn't know John was capable of. He was proud of him.

"Thanks." John nervously smiled. "Can we get out of here now?"

That was the best idea Tobias had heard all day.

They ran across the rumbling ground on their way to the jet. The entire airport was coming down around them. The fissure extended by the second and engulfed more and more of the runway as it grew. Tobias reached the stairs first and helped Sam up. Then he motioned for John to follow. With both of them safely onboard, he ran to the fuel line and detached it while it was still pumping, causing fuel to gush from the hose. There was no time for procedures.

John sealed the door behind them, and Tobias jumped into the pilot's seat. Sam took the copilot's. He flipped on switch after switch, gearing the jet for takeoff. Lights and indicators lit the cockpit, but only one mattered. The fuel tank was a little less than half-full. He hoped that was enough. It needed to be enough.

As he turned the jet around, pointing it for takeoff, a spiral of fire shot from the crevice. It spun like a drill bit, cutting a hole in the sky in front of them. When the spinning stopped, it revealed a towering, snakelike creature. Whirling halos of fire surrounded its tubular, glowing-red body.

"I don't even want to know," Tobias said out loud.

He turned the jet around and gunned it down the runway with the beast towering in the air. The crevice swallowed the ground behind them at an increasing rate. The rumbling of the runway made his vision blur and the jet shake. The pavement seemed to wave as the beast plunged down to the ground on the right of the jet. The looming Firesnake stretched from the crevice to well beyond the jet. Its body blocked the view of the entire ocean to their right, burning and seemingly never-ending.

Rocketing forward, Tobias noticed the runway split apart in front of the jet. A new crevice divided the ground. "Hang on," he yelled.

He pushed the engines to their limits. The Firesnake

swayed far right and prepared to swipe with its titanic body. The runway disappeared before them, parts of it falling into the ocean far below. The three forces met at the same point in time. The creature swung its enormous body towards the jet as the runway deteriorated in front of them and the crevice met them from behind. In what Tobias could only assume was the answer to his previous prayer for divine intervention, the jet missed everything and soared into the air, untouched. As the Firesnake wafted beneath the jet, it brushed over the spilled fuel, igniting a fiery explosion of thick black smoke. He felt the push of air beneath the jet from the explosion.

Tobias kept the controls pulled back, trying to put as much elevation as he could between them and the terrors below. With a mountain range too close ahead, he was forced to bank hard left and back into the newly-created war zone.

A second Firesnake erupted from within the crevice. This one wasted no time in attacking. Its gaping, cavernous mouth snapped at the air and tried to swallow them whole. Each of its tree-sized teeth jutted out like giant stalagmites, signaling a sure end to anything that got within reach.

Tobias pushed the controls forward and dropped the plane in between the two beasts. His stomach climbed into his throat. Banking the jet hard left again, he swept an arching trajectory around the creature's tubular body. The halo of fire radiated outside the jet's windshield as they passed. The Firesnake was far larger up close than he'd expected. The side of his face burned like it did on the hottest of summer days, even while inside the protection of the jet. It was like the fingers of hell had reached up through the crack, trying to pry open an entryway.

He brought the jet down close to the ground as the creatures positioned for another strike, but he flew off the cliff side before they could. He hovered close to the ocean's wave-strewn surface until he put a safe distance between them and the monsters. Pulling back on the controls, he brought the jet back into the sky and keyed in Easter Island's coordinates. He prayed the last Trinity Sign, and an end to this nightmarish ordeal awaited them.

Chapter 44

Sam was quiet. She sat in the back of the jet with her knees up against her chest and stared fixedly at the laptop. Once in a while she would quietly gasp, or give a muted "hmm" to nobody in particular. Tobias had asked her to soak in as much information as she could about Easter Island. He wanted to know its history, legends, topography, and anything else that may have been of use to them. They would have to hit the ground running, and the more prepared they were, the better off they'd be.

He turned to John, who sat in the copilot's seat. "Are you all right?" he asked, worried by his silence.

John rolled his head to the left and glanced back, drained. He grinned and nodded, seemingly enveloped in thought. Dark bags had formed beneath his bloodshot eyes. His lips were dry and cracking. Tobias didn't know if John was getting worse, or if he failed to notice just how bad he looked. Either way, he knew it wasn't just the physical challenge of their journey affecting him. The moments of action most likely helped him to forget what chewed at him from within—the secret hinted at by the robed man, the ghost. But the downtime, like the flight, was when John most likely dealt with whatever was troubling him.

Beneath the jet, the water of the Pacific Ocean spanned from horizon to horizon. From their altitude, it looked calm, motionless, save for the thin lines of the windswept waves. The sun cast a reflective band on the water that followed their progress and eventually fell upon the only parcel of land in sight.

Cresting from the dark blue water, the desolate Easter

316

Island emerged triumphantly as if proclaiming its right to exist in the middle of nowhere. Its unimpressive size was highlighted by the nothingness that surrounded it. According to one of Sam's few outbursts of information, the island was a mere sixty-three square miles around. Its triangular shape held a volcano in each of its three corners. The word trinity rang true in more ways than one.

The face-like statues—the Moais—littering the island were said to have been carved by the island's first inhabitants, the Rapa Nui, or, as they now understood it, the Brotherhood of the Sealed. Were the statues only a marker leading to the Trinity Sign, or did they have some other, unknown meaning?, Tobias wondered. Brother Iunapar was intelligent enough to realize that history would record the Rapa Nui's civilization and, therefore, the clue to the Sign's whereabouts. It was a gamble on the Brotherhood's part, but one that was hopefully about to pay dividends.

Assembling the pieces of the fragmented puzzle wasn't easy, given the information they had, but Tobias gave it his best shot. He deduced that the Brotherhood of the Sealed departed Camelot some one thousand years prior and after the devil's last attack with the final Trinity Sign in tow. They must have embarked on a journey to find a place where evil would be much less likely to flourish—to find a place that would escape most travelers' journeys and could, therefore, remain undetected. He surmised that Brother Iunapar, the Brotherhood, and the Guardians set sail for an island they had already scouted. The very island they now approached for a landing, Easter Island.

Much like those in Chile, the airport controllers were surprised to have anyone requesting permission to land, and they advised him to do so immediately. He heard the same chatter as before—global halt on air traffic, not safe, etc. ... *If they only knew the truth,* he thought, removing the headset and setting it down on the center console, the inaudible and muted squawks of the airport personnel still present.

He landed effortlessly on the single runway at Mataveri International Airport. Slowly guiding the jet off to the left, Tobias stopped next to two others and powered down the controls. A sudden feeling of finality overcame him. Every step since their journey began was a move towards Easter Island. Now they were there, and the end was within sight, but would it end well?

John stood from his seat, stretched briefly, and walked into the cabin without uttering a word. Tobias followed him out and sat across from Sam. She looked up from the laptop.

"What's the name of that town you were talking about?" Tobias asked.

Sam brushed the touchpad and scanned the page. "Hanga Roa. It's just northwest of here," she said. "And it's actually the only town on Easter Island."

"Okay, then that's where we start looking. Someone on the island may know something. But let's keep as low a profile as possible. At this point, we can't trust anyone." He knew he sounded paranoid, but it was for good reason. They had come this far. He wasn't about to let slip a few words that could possibly hurt them.

Sam grabbed a small pile of printouts from her web travels and exited the jet. John followed with his head down, buried in turmoil. Tobias brought up the rear. They headed northwest, as Sam had suggested. It was an easy call to make, as the town was within sight.

"There's a church in town," Sam said, spinning around with one of the printouts in hand. "Maybe we could start there?" She scanned the page. "Church of the Holy Cross," she said with a snicker. "Go figure."

Conveniently named. "Let's start there, then."

It didn't take long to arrive at the outskirts of the island's only town. The residents of Hanga Roa moved slowly about and tended to their everyday chores. Two small motor boats—one painted a faded blue, the other a bright red—sat moored on the waterside to their left, rocking gently atop the ripples of the waves coming ashore. The delicious smell of fresh bread wafted through the air, reminding Tobias of how hungry he was. A soft ringing bell sounded from somewhere, almost like a shifting buoy in the water. Several older women sat on a nearby porch, huddled in a semi-circle, and rocked away the daylight. Their wrinkled faces watched curiously as the team passed. One pointed at them and then turned to the others and whispered.

A few shouts of playing children echoed about as they made their way farther down the main road in town. Most of the villagers went about their business, uncaring. A few stared. One person actually yelled at them in some other language. Tobias ignored him. There was no time to deal with more crazies.

Eventually, they arrived at the Church of the Holy Cross and what, Tobias hoped, was a clue to finding the final Trinity Sign. The structure was very "unchurchly" in appearance. Tall white pillars, ornamented with grey figures, stood guard at the building's front entrance. The exterior walls consisted of brown patches of stone, mortared by white cement. A simple frieze of the Lord hung above the front door in understated beauty. There was no grand entrance or overdone features. It was a simple building with a defined purpose. It was the way Tobias thought all churches should be. And, because of that, he liked this one.

He pulled open the front door and cautiously entered. Before him spanned several rows of simple wooden pews, each of which were empty. The sun spilled in through a few large windows and bathed the interior in light.

"'*Iorana!*" blurted the priest to their left, taking the group by surprise. *"Pehe korua?"*

Tobias turned to the priest. He was a short man, but he closed the gap between them more quickly than expected. What was left of his hair made a horseshoe around his head. A curious smile crossed his pale face, showcasing teeth in dire need of a dentist.

"I apologize," the priest said. "I asked how you are doing in our native tongue of Rapa Nui. I find it adds to the Easter Island experience for the tourists."

"We're fine, thank you." Tobias eyed the man curiously. "We're sorry to barge into your church like this... ." He felt a "but" was necessary, but what could he say? That they were in search of the last of three mystical Trinity Signs in order to prevent the devil from enslaving the world? It seemed to go against their whole "low profile" approach.

"It is not my church," the priest said, dramatically reaching his arms up to the ceiling. "This house belongs to the Heavenly Father, and it openly welcomes visitors."

Tobias wanted to ask the priest some questions—find out any information he could—but, again, how could he ask without being obvious?

"Father, may we speak with you for a moment?" Tobias looked around. They were still alone.

"Indeed," he said, turning his back to the group and walking away down the center aisle. "Indeed, indeed."

Sam whispered in Tobias' ear. "He's a strange little man, isn't he?"

Tobias nodded in agreement. *Strange was an understatement.*

They followed the traipsing priest farther into the church, towards the back. He glanced over his shoulder with a strange smirk, mumbling softly to nobody but himself.

"A private matter?" the priest muttered, taking a sharp left at the back wall of the church and towards a side room.

"Hopefully, I can be of assistance." He suddenly stopped dead in his tracks and spun around. He reached up and held up his right index finger to Tobias' nose. "You aren't here for my cocoa, are you?"

Tobias wanted to laugh, but the serious nature of the priest's face made him hold back. "No, we're not here for your cocoa."

A smile once again brimmed on the short man's face. "Good." He spun back around and opened the door to the side room. "Keeps me warm on the cold nights, my cocoa does."

They followed him into the deceivingly large space and closed the door.

"So then," the man said. "Tell me the questions you have, and I'll see if I can provide you with the answers you seek." He moved his head from side to side, scanning the group. He stopped at John. His eyes grew wide, and he shuffled closer. "There's something different about you, isn't there?"

John looked at Tobias and then back down at the priest before shaking his head, confused.

The priest stared for another minute. "I thought so." He then shuffled away, back towards Tobias.

Behind them, the door creaked open. Another priest entered the room. He was taller than the first and, upon seeing them, his face grew red with anger.

"What are you doing in here, yet again?" He stormed closer. "Are those my clothes you are wearing?" The new priest took the other one's arm. "This is your last warning, hermit. The next time I find you in here, you will spend a considerable amount of time in the jail." He brought his face in closer to the old man. "Or worse. Do we understand each other?"

The funny old man nodded, and the scolding priest let

go of his arm. He brushed the spot where he was held, shuffled next to Tobias, and paused. He motioned for Tobias to bend down closer to him. Tobias cautiously leaned in closer. "The devil's ears listen in places you would not expect," the crazy priest whispered. With that, he bolted from the office, laughing his way out of the church.

"I'm sorry," the new priest said, turning to Tobias. "He is a harmless old man that lives in the Orongo Village on the volcano's side, but he works my very last nerve." He shook his head. "Father Horat," he said, holding his hand out in introduction.

"Tobias," he said, obliging the Father and shaking his hand.

The Father nodded to John and Sam with a silent, "Hello". "So, what brings you to my humble church?"

Tobias thought he would use the same restrained explanation he planned to use with the first priest, or at least the person he'd thought was a priest. The less anyone outside his group knew, the safer he felt they would be, but after the crazy man's words, he didn't feel a need to dig any deeper.

"We're sorry to disturb you," Tobias said. "We're just passing tourists who happened upon your church." Tobias smiled and nodded for the group to follow him back out the way they'd come.

"Very well then," the priest said with a smile, following them. "Have a pleasant visit to our little island."

As soon as they got outside, Tobias turned to justify their quick exit. "That crazy guy whispered something to me before he left. I think he might be what we're looking for."

"What did he say?" John asked.

"He said the devil has ears in places we wouldn't expect."

"A little too familiar to be coincidence," Sam said.

"I agree." Tobias looked up to the darkening sky in the distance. He hoped it was only an incoming storm, but he feared it could be worse. "We need to hurry. The priest said the old man lived in Orongo Village."

"Got it," Sam blurted. She flipped through her printouts and pulled one of the pages free. "Orongo Village is on the rim of one of the three extinct volcanoes on the island, Rano Kau. It's South of here, not too far."

Tobias had noticed a large crater near the airport before they landed. That had to be the place. They walked back through the small town on their way to Orongo Village. The same group of old women watched the group as they passed, knowing smiles on their faces.

Chapter 45

The bodiless Moai statues dotted the landscape like giant chess pieces in some long forgotten game. Most of them stood erect, firmly rooted in the rocky soil, while some less fortunate ones lay toppled on the ground. According to Sam and her printouts, they weighed close to fourteen tons. Each of their similarly frozen expressions held an untold story from long ago. Looking around, Tobias realized there were many more than he had originally thought—hundreds of them, in fact. He wondered how the Brotherhood and Guardians managed to not only create, but also move these huge anomalies. Then again, he realized it was probably a small feat compared to what they had already accomplished at that point in time.

The sculpted stone face had humanistic features but in an exaggerated, almost cartoon-like, way. Their tightly pursed lips, chiseled below their elongated noses, looked as if they held secrets back from the world. The sun hit them in such a way that a long shadow cast the majority of their eye sockets in darkness. He wondered what their dark pupils had seen over all these years—if they somehow already knew the outcome of this day.

A short walk later, they arrived at the base of the Rano Kau crater. It seemed like an afterthought of nature, placed in the middle of the grassy rise. Tobias stared up its sides and took in the view as the trade winds battered them from the Pacific Ocean. He couldn't put his finger on it, but something felt different about this place. It felt like the right place to be.

Weary legs and hardened wills carried the group up the

sloping side. Only when they reached the top did the true magnitude of nature reveal itself. The mighty Pacific Ocean, a dark blue expanse far below, engulfed the world outside of the volcano's steep sides. Before them, inside the dormant crater, was a soupy mess of stagnant black water. What used to be a mighty volcano was now a dirty pool. While less imposing in its current condition, the sight was no less awe-inspiring from their current vantage point.

Fifty feet ahead stood the remnants of Orongo Village, or what they assumed was the village, anyway. Thin stone blocks of varying sizes sat atop one another, forming the walls of the ceremonial huts. Most of the structures were carved within the grassy terrain near the cliff side, capped by an earthen roof. The outer walls opened towards the ocean through a smallish doorway.

Little rock igloos, Tobias thought.

He approached the village cautiously. Using the fading daylight, he looked around the desolate area in search of the old man from the church. Strangely, they appeared to be the only people there. For such a touristy destination, the island seemed rather subdued—empty. He figured it had to do with the flight ban. That, and maybe people were starting to catch on that the world was not experiencing some form of super-global warming, as the governments would have them believe.

He swept aside his trench coat with his left hand, resting it atop his gun. Now was not the time to push caution aside.

As Tobias inched closer, the crazy old man from the church appeared from within one of the Orongo huts. He failed to notice the group, as they were to his back, and walked to the edge of the cliff to stare out at the ocean. The sun had set in motion a barrage of colors that gleamed beautifully off the rippling water. Purples, reds, yellows, and oranges all filled the sky like they were painted in one giant,

325

colorful brushstroke. Continuing to take in the view, the hermit placed his hands on his lower back and leaned back with a forceful sigh. Tobias figured that the hunching over to go in and out of the small doors must have taken its toll on his aging spine.

When Tobias took a few steps closer, the old man spun around expectantly. He had both hands out in front, like a wrestler waiting to grapple. Upon seeing them, his demeanor changed. His hands fell to his sides, and the same crazy smile he'd had at the church grew on his face. A strong wind gusted, causing the back of the man's white hair to stick straight up like a patch of weeds.

"I knew you would come," the crazy man said.

Tobias approached carefully, his hand still resting on his gun. He inched closer to the man, but not too close. The edge of the cliff was a mistake that couldn't be corrected.

"And how did you know that?"

"Because, Guardian, it is your destiny," he said with a smile.

The sound of the whipping winds cut through the silence.

A moment passed before Tobias spoke. "How is it you know of the Guardians, old man?"

The hermit laughed. "Because it is my job to know. Just like it is your job to protect the last of the Sealed." He squinted and studied John for a moment. Seconds later, he returned his attention to Tobias. "You have done well to help bring him this far."

"Hold on," Tobias said, holding up his hand. "How exactly do you know all of this?" He wondered if the insanity was ever going to end. It was one farfetched thing after another.

"Like I said, it is my job to know." He turned around towards the stone and earthen structures. "Follow me," he said, walking away. "When the sun sets, the wind develops quite a bite."

Crouching through the doorway, the hermit disappeared into the largest of the stone igloo structures.

Tobias felt the chill of the wind as it battered against the cliff side. Sam had already made her way in, and John had followed her. Tobias followed their lead and ducked beneath the tiny arch of the doorway. His hidden sword scraped slightly against the keystone.

Inside, a fire burned in the center of the earthen floor. Its warmth pushed outwards to meet the colder air at the door. He felt the heat penetrate deep within his body, seeping into his tired bones. It was the first time in a long time that he felt comfortable, if only for a moment. To curl up and sleep right now would be better than anything in the world.

Roughly-carved stone slabs were positioned around the fire. Tobias figured they were improvised furniture, as the hermit sat down on the one farthest from him.

"Sit, sit," the hermit said, motioning for them to follow his lead.

Sam and John sat near the old man. They put their hands up to the flames to warm the chill the outside had put on them. Tobias sat on the bench nearest the door. He wanted to be ready for anything that might try and take them by surprise.

"I am like you in some ways, but differ in most," the old man said, looking straight at Tobias. The smile on his face had been replaced by a more serious expression.

"How is that?"

"I am the Keeper of the Records. I am neither Guardian nor Sealed, but I have an obligation to humanity like both of you. It is my duty to record and maintain the accounts of the Brotherhood of the Sealed and their protectors, the Guardians. Their combined history is something the masses can never be told, yet it can never be allowed to fade with time."

"So you're not crazy?" Sam asked.

The hermit laughed. "Not entirely, anyway," he said in a raspy voice. "My craziness is nothing more than a simple show. It keeps the villagers at a safe distance. Very rarely does anyone venture into Orongo Village, and when they do, I ensure their first visit is also their last."

"So, you live here?" John asked, looking around at the stark walls.

He nodded. "I have lived here for the better part of my life, yes. Before me, another resided within this ancient village and kept the knowledge that I now keep. The legacy of the crazy old man in Orongo Village is something that has passed through many a generation."

"You said you were expecting us?" Sam said, questioning.

"Yes." He smiled warmly at her. It was the same smile the robed man had given her when he came to visit them at the cavernous Sign in Egypt. "I have been expecting all of this for quite some time."

Tobias furrowed his brow. "If you're some kind of seer, then why allow so many to die?" He thought of Rupert and Tia. He thought of the countless other lives lost around the world from the terror that was spreading.

The hermit looked down at the raging fire and poked the center with a stick. "When I said I knew all of this was coming, I meant it in a much broader sense. I am no fortune teller, Guardian. It was written that you would come, the last Guardian, with two under your protection—the last Brother and the Matron of the Sealed. The events of your journey will culminate in a final showdown atop this dormant volcano."

"Where is the third Trinity Sign?" Tobias asked. No

more riddles. No more delaying.

"It is near."

Tobias stood and leaned towards the open doorway. The end was within sight, yet seemed so far away. "Then let's go finish this."

The old man motioned for Tobias to sit back down. "Your rush will get you no closer to the end, Guardian. The Sign is inaccessible at the moment."

"What do you mean, inaccessible?"

"The Sign will not reveal itself until the devil is at full strength."

What? Tobias had a hard time believing what he was hearing. "We finally seem to have the upper hand in all of this, and now we have to wait for the devil to catch up?"

The old man's gaze remained fixed on Tobias. "I assure you everything has a purpose."

Tobias wanted to pull his hair out in frustration. To reach their goal, and then be kept from it over some kind of formality, was absurd. He took a deep breath and tried to calm himself down. His anger was directed in the wrong place. He needed to remain focused, if just for a little longer.

Outside, far in the distance, he noticed the pitch-black sky began to take on a familiar blood-red glow. His worst fears had been realized. They were unprepared for an attack now. Even when they had both Rupert and Tia, they were lucky to escape alive. He hoped they could activate the last Sign and close the proverbial book on this whole mess. Now, according to the hermit, they needed to wait until the devil was upon them. It seemed the farthest thing from logical.

He turned to the hermit. "Does this scripture of yours tell who wins the battle?"

"I'm afraid not," he said, shaking his head. "That part has yet to be written."

Anger rampaged through Tobias. Enough was enough.

If this was where they made their final stand, then he would make sure it was a good one.

"How will we know when the devil is at full strength?" Tobias asked, turning his attention back to the old man. He needed to know the exact moment. He realized that even a second of delay could make the difference once this started.

"When the Sign reveals itself, we will know. The devil is directly linked to his own expulsion by forces we could never understand." The hermit walked out of the hut and into the darkness. "It is just the way of things," he said, fading into the night.

Tobias heard that expression far too much for his liking. It would be nice to understand some things instead of just having to blindly accept them.

The pounding waves alerted him to the cliff side hidden somewhere close ahead. The old man stopped and looked up at the distant redness.

"Can we at least make our way to the Sign's location?" Tobias asked. He wanted to get everything ready. There could be no slipups. There would be no second chances this time.

"There is no need to go anywhere, Guardian," the hermit said, grinning. "We are already where we need to be." The old man turned towards the caldera. "Buried within the dark water of this volcano is the final Trinity Sign. However, as I said before, it will not reveal itself until the devil is at full strength."

Tobias became noticeably irritated. It was unlike him to lose his cool, especially after everything they had been through, but the rules now governing humanity's future needed to be somehow broken.

"Why would they do that? Why limit our chances of success?" He felt like punching something.

The old man looked calmly into his eyes. "I do not think

you fully understand the third Sign, Guardian." He looked briefly at both Sam and John to ensure they were listening. "The final Trinity Sign can only be used once every one thousand years, when the devil himself appears. The third Sign's source of power is the most unique in the world. To waste it prematurely would mean certain failure. Therefore, it must be activated at the most opportune time."

An idea popped into Tobias' head. "Can't we go down into the water and find the damn thing?"

"It will do you no good," the hermit said. "Even if you were to find the Sign, which I doubt you would, it would not activate until the right time. And even then, only one can ensure humanity's future." He looked sorrowfully at John and then back to Tobias. "And you are not that one, Guardian."

John sighed and looked down dejectedly.

"Don't worry, John," Tobias said with confidence. "We'll make it out of this. We've come this far." He had to lie. To break down his team's confidence when they needed it the most would be counterproductive.

John turned to the group. "The thing about that is... ." He paused. His emotions came rushing to the surface. A single captive tear made its break down his cheek. He looked towards the rapidly approaching Evil in the sky and then let his sight drift to the ground.

Sam laughed nervously and took his hand. "Don't worry. Tobias will figure it out." She looked at Tobias, begging him silently for reassurance. "Right?"

John looked up. "I'm going to die, Sam. Here, on top of this volcano."

"I won't let that happen, John," Tobias said.

"I'm sorry, Tobias, but I don't think you have a choice in this."

"What are you talking about?" Tobias asked John. When

John gave no response, he turned to the hermit. "What is he talking about?"

The hermit walked over to John and gently patted him on the back. "As I said, Guardian, the final Trinity Sign uses a power source that is absolutely unique. It is activated by a combination of the Crux Signate and the activator's spirit. The human soul is the only thing powerful enough to stop the purest form of evil. John must willingly give his life to save the rest of humanity's. That is the sacrifice the Keeper of the Crux Signate must make when the time comes."

Sam shook her head in disbelief. "No, there has to be another way." She turned to the old man. "There has to be another way. Something. Anything." Her eyes began to well up with tears.

"I'm sorry," the hermit said compassionately. "There is only one way."

That was the secret the robed man shared with John that John couldn't tell him. That was the knowledge that had burned inside of John since Egypt. The more they triumphed in their quest, the closer John came to his death, and he'd known it all along. Tobias' mind was scattered, yet focused. That must have been how the robed man died. He was the last to activate the Trinity Sign one thousand years ago. He gave his life and his spirit to ensure another one thousand years of humanity's freedom, just as John must do today.

John slumped to the ground and leaned back against the wall of stones. He stared out at the red sky. Tobias looked on, unsure of what, if anything, to say. Sam's crying sank his heart further.

"This is what I am destined to do." John said, laughing through a sniffle. "Hell, I'd rather go out saving the world than dying slowly on my front porch drunk in Connecticut. At least this way I know my life was worth something."

"But if John dies today," Tobias said, finding the words

lingered too long, "then so does any hope for future generations to ward off an attack."

The hermit nodded softly, and then answered. "You are forgetting something, Guardian. The second Sign ensured that the lineage of the Brotherhood would not end with John's sacrifice. The child that the Matron carries within her will begin a new line of the Brotherhood. Hopefully, if we survive this, that child will have children of his own one day. And they will have children, and so on. The legacy of the Brotherhood will not be snuffed out like a candle's flame. It will burn more fiercely than the sun, given enough time. With John's sacrifice comes the rebirth of hope."

Sam fell to her knees and hugged John. "There has to be another way." Her sobs were muffled against his shirt.

John squeezed her tight and closed his eyes, forcing the last of his tears out.

Tobias watched as the two friends said goodbye in their own way. Their ever-tightening grips exuded emotions that words could never properly convey. Tobias lacked the words to express his own emotions at the time. Even though he was numb, he was thankful for what John was about to do, but he was sorry that he had to do it. When they'd first met, Tobias thought John would be an impossible annoyance. But, after all they had been through, he considered him more of a brother. That may have doomed John, as any family member of Tobias' suffered a cursed life that would, no doubt, end in death. If given the chance, he would switch places with John, but he knew now that wasn't an option.

John pushed Sam away slowly and held her for a moment at arm's length. He gently wiped her tears away. "Thanks for always being there for me, Samantha. You were the only one to actually give me the time of day, even when I was a drunken jerk."

Sam nodded and hugged him again.

John smiled at her and then stood. Reaching down, he helped the Matron of the Sealed off the ground. His demeanor had changed. It appeared that John accepted his fate, and with it, he accepted his death.

Chapter 46

Behind them, over the cliff, the ocean began to boil. The final battle was upon them.

"Inside. Now," Tobias yelled, pushing John and Sam back into the Orongo hut. "You too," he said, looking at the hermit.

The Keeper of the Records snickered. "I may be old, Guardian, but I assure you it is only in appearance." He scampered into the small doorway to the right of where Sam and John now hid. Within seconds, he returned back into the night with a Guardian's sword. "It's been passed down from Keeper to Keeper over the years. It was a gift from the Guardians of the past. I assure you, I know perfectly well how to use it." The hermit cut an "X" through the air with the ease of a much larger man. Any other blade of that size would have surely weighed him down, but not the blessed sword he now held. It was light as a feather and sharper than anything else in existence, save for Tobias' own.

So be it. Tobias could use the help. Reaching back, he, too, removed his sword from the sheath that hid it from the world. The two matching blades gleamed red from the sky above. It would be them against a seemingly infinite army of evil. He would make his brethren proud for as long as he was able to.

Both he and the hermit stood deathly still and watched the last of the night sky burn red. There was no preparation that could be done. All they could do was focus on what was to come next. Tobias turned his attention from the sky to inside the stone hut, which was now splashed with an ominous red hue. Sam and John sat huddled together against the back wall. Their eyes stared out in horror.

The hermit looked over at him, this time with hope in his eyes. "Fear not, Guardian. We are not alone in this battle. If the scripture is accurate, which it has so far proven to be, then help will arrive when we need it most."

"And I assume that scripture doesn't say when this help will arrive, right?"

The old man's face soured. He shook his head.

Of course it doesn't.

The wind carried with it a heavy thumping from the millions of beating wings approaching over the Pacific. The sound was much louder than it had been at Camelot. This would be the devil's army at full force, Tobias realized. This was it, and he was ready for it. Like John, he had accepted his fate. He would protect humanity's only hope, or die trying.

A small band of Gargoyles led the charge ahead of the army proper. Their humanoid bodies vanished and reappeared, just like they had in Boston. The same ghastly screech that echoed against the walls of the Trinity Church now filled the entirety of the sky like a chorus of banshees. Trails of black smoke wafted on the strong winds.

Sam screamed. Tobias turned.

Both Sam and John were locked up with what he assumed were Imps. Their clothes were pulled out at different places by the invisible annoyances. He darted forward and slid through the low door of the stone hut. Using his momentum, he planted his foot on the ground and rose in one fluid motion like a base runner successfully stealing second. He swiped quickly where he thought the Imps to be. The second of resistance he felt on the blade verified that he struck correctly. The slop of creatures' bodies hitting the wall confirmed it. With one strong thrust, Tobias skewered the other two and freed Sam.

336

He held his sword in his right hand and swept his gun from the left of his waist. Two rounds, and John was free.

"Take this," he said, handing the gun to John. He then looked at Sam and handed her his other sidearm. "Protect yourself at all costs."

She stared with a look that couldn't be confused. He, too, would be careful, if only to see her again.

"Incoming!" screamed the hermit from outside.

Several of the nearest Gargoyles, the ones forming the tip of the evil spear, dove from the sky. Tobias dashed back out into the thick of the incoming battle.

The hermit swung the sword with the grace of a trained fencer as the sky fell upon him. He downed three Gargoyles before Tobias could figure out the best plan of attack. Their unholy carcasses careened over the side of the cliff into the boiling ocean below. With each swipe, he laughed crazily, seemingly enjoying something other than being a crazy old hermit.

Tobias shot him a look. The old man looked back and shrugged.

What looked to be a hopeless battle turned exponentially worse as the second line of Gargoyles dropped Hell Hounds from their within their grasps. Running on instinct, Tobias reached into his bag and pulled free his last two bullet clips. He threw them into the hut. "Hell Hounds."

John nodded. Picking up the bullets, he fumbled to load them. Sam, not waiting for the outcome, took his gun and did the task for him before doing the same for hers. Whatever came through that door next was in for a rude surprise.

Large pieces of the cliff broke off and plummeted down into the Pacific Ocean. The musty smell of saltwater, a result of the odd boiling, permeated the air.

From Tobias' right galloped a pair of Hounds intent on

finishing him off. He immediately rushed towards them and tried to close the gap. In mid-stride, he removed the micro-shotgun from his leg and flipped open the chamber. One shell remained, and there were no others to speak of. He knew he needed to make this shot.

The Hounds leaped from the top of a nearby embankment and were now gaining speed. Thirty yards divided them from him. He stopped in his tracks, pulled the trigger, and let the molten-fire round fly. The Hounds took to the air, now a mere ten yards away. Tobias brought his arm up and shielded his face. He braced for an impact, but he heard the splat of their grisly body pieces hit the ground and felt a few smaller pieces brush by him.

He was met with a glorious sight when he opened his eyes. The last of his shells, as if set aside by some unforeseen force, had done its job impeccably. A mound of mushy, circular Hound pieces lay before him, spastically flopping around as if still attached.

"Guardian!" yelled the hermit.

Tobias spun around to find each of the Keeper's arms held tightly by a Gargoyle with a Hell Hound bearing down on him fast. Tobias sprinted towards the old man. He realized that the Hound would reach him first. He needed to improvise. With a mighty thrust, he hurled his sword through the air. Four airy revolutions later, the blade found its mark. It impaled the Hound's neck, dropping it dead to the ground.

The old man struggled to break free as Tobias continued in full stride. Tobias passed the Hound's body and removed his sword with one swift motion, its acidic blood dripping down the blade.

The Gargoyle on the hermit's left relinquished his grasp and bore down on the sprinting Tobias. He wound up and swung at the beast, but it vanished before the two met.

Reappearing behind him, Tobias didn't have enough time to react before the force of the monster's sharp talons dug through his jacket and deep into his back, right below his shoulder blades.

Tobias fell to his knees. The blinding pain caused white flashes to race across his eyes the more the Gargoyle dug into his back. It had pierced just the right place to make his arms fall numb. He felt its hot, rank breath waft against the side of his face. He was, unfortunately, at its mercy.

With one hand now free, the hermit picked his sword from the ground and swung at the remaining Gargoyle holding him captive. Before the monster could react, he sliced its clawed feet clean off its body. The beast shrieked in pain and flapped back on its wings. The old man, anger in his eyes, then drove his blade deep into the beast's belly, instantly knocking it from the air and into the boiling water below. He then turned his attention to Tobias. With a well-placed swing of his sword, the hermit freed Tobias from the Gargoyle's grasp. The beast's head rolled away, and its body fell with a thump before disappearing into a pile of dust.

Before Tobias could give thanks, gunfire rang into the air behind them. He turned to find several more Hell Hounds snapping their grisly jaws at the entrance to the hut. One Hound was dead and spewing smoke. Tobias knew Sam and John had little, if any, ammo left.

Bang. A second Hound fell dead. The third fought its way in and dragged Sam out by her leg. John fired once, and the gun clicked empty, the bullet not hitting its target. He then threw the gun in frustration. Despite her attempts at freeing herself, the Hound dragged Sam closer to the cliff. Tobias realized the beast knew what it was doing. It was intent on killing her—right then, right there.

Driven by rage, Tobias stood, but he quickly fell back down to his knees. The wounds to his back were greater than he had thought. The loss of blood caused his head to swim and his body to ache. He dug his sword into the ground and helped himself up. He would have plenty of time to hurt later, or at least he hoped he would.

The hermit, already sprinting towards Sam, left Tobias to catch up when he could.

Sam's scream pierced the air. Her foot dangled over the edge. She dug her fingers into the grassy earth and tried to slow her momentum, but it was no use. Her strength was no match for that of the Hound.

Tobias' stomach churned as he painfully hobbled closer. The unimaginable became real. Sam was seconds from death.

From the corner of his eye, Tobias noticed the blur of John go shooting from the hut. Firmly grasped in his hand was a burning piece of wood from the fire. With unexpected heroism, John struck at the beast's eye, ramming the fiery torch into its pus-filled flesh, which ended with a wet popping sound. The Hound relented, letting go of Sam. She grasped for safety, but the beast had pulled her too far. Momentum now carried her over the edge.

The Hound turned to John, the flaming shrapnel still in its eye, and lunged.

The hermit seemed to be in two places at once. He sliced through the air at just the right time and cut the Hound in two. The front half of the beast careened off to the right. Its rear section sloshed to the ground. Black, malformed organs slipped out like a slow moving mudslide and burned the ground beneath the Hound.

Both of Sam's feet dangled over the edge. Gravity was now her greatest enemy.

Tobias reached the edge and dug his sword deep into the ground. It would be his anchor. He swung his legs over the side and held onto the hilt for dear life. With his free hand, he reached out and grabbed Sam. The holes in his back burned hot with pain. The salty steam that rose from the boiling ocean intensified the hurt. More than anything, he prayed the sword held their weight.

It didn't take long before the hermit ran over and reached out for Sam, taking one of her arms in his. She climbed over the edge and dropped to the ground on her back, breathing rapidly. After he secured Sam, the hermit helped to lift Tobias back to the top.

Tobias, battered but not beaten, rotated with his blade in hand. He bellowed a throaty roar and swiped with all his might, halving the two incoming Gargoyles in midair. The overly-forceful swing caused the blade to crash off the stone wall of the hut nearest them and set a small patch of sparks flying.

Out of breath, Tobias looked up into the sky. Red eyes hovered all around like evil fireflies. Circling above them were millions of the devil's spawn. On the ground lumbered not only Hounds, but also legions of Tormentors that scaled the cliff side. This was the beginning of things to come. He soon realized that the army was only toying with them. Its fury had not even been unleashed. They had not been given the final order yet. If they had, it would already be over. Tobias couldn't possibly defeat them all. He didn't know if he had the strength to beat even one more.

As hope fled, the ground shook once again, but far more forcefully than before. Several of the stone huts crumbled in upon themselves. Tobias and the hermit surrounded John and Sam the best they could. It was difficult to remain standing. Then the rumbling stopped, and a low hum started.

"Look!" screamed the old man, pointing.

The darkened water within the caldera churned and bubbled. Something rose from within its murky depths. He

341

knew it could only be one thing, and that meant the devil was now at full strength.

With no time to react, a majority of the Evil in the sky darted towards them. They were so close to salvation. Tobias tightened his grip with both his hands on the hilt of his blade. He was lightheaded and weak, but he had never been more determined in his life.

He attributed the sudden visions he had to the blood loss, but the closer he looked, the more he realized it was no mirage. From every direction rose the Moai statues. Their massive tonnage floated gracefully in the air as if lighter than the air itself.

A strange feeling of serenity washed over him. *How is that possible?*, he thought.

The rising Moais cracked down the center, ripping through their chiseled faces. A blinding white light shone from within, like the brightest light turned on in the darkest room. The air felt warm and pure in an instant.

Tobias looked on in amazement as the stone pieces fell back to the ground. What had come from within them was something he lacked the words to properly describe. Each aurorally white figure rose with large wings. They had no face or any defining characteristics, just a humanistic figure made out of the purest of lights. Hundreds of them, now loose from their rocky confines, rose unimpeded into the enemy-infested sky.

The hermit laughed. "Like I said, Guardian, help will come when we need it most." The hermit watched the sky with giddy excitement.

"What are they?" Tobias asked.

"Angels," Sam said. Her mouth hinged wide open. "I don't know how, but those have to be angels. I can just feel it."

Breaking from their dive, the devil's army turned their

attention to the brilliant white beings as they rose further into the sky. As the swarm of Evil approached, a white globe of light shot from each glowing entity like a sonic wave. It flashed through the sky, ripping apart anything in its path. Ashes from the thousands of creatures that were just killed rained down.

The angels continued their ascent, bursting light as they went.

Fitting, Tobias thought, as the ash rained down, considering they were on a volcano. He couldn't help but smile at their unbelievable salvation. Wave after wave of Evil-clearing light lit the night sky. Hell's minions appeared to be no match. Even the ground forces were devoured by the flowing light.

Tobias lowered his sword and watched the battle sway in their favor. "Where's John?" he asked, looking around.

Sam looked to her left and shrugged. "He was just here."

Tobias ran to the edge of the extinct volcano. There, rising from the murky water like a beacon of hope, was the Sign of the Holy Spirit, the last of the Trinity Signs. John had slid down into the caldera and was now wading towards it. Black water arched out in front of him as his legs pushed with everything they had left. Behind him, more than twenty Hell Hounds gained on his position. Within the submerged crater, the Hounds were out of reach of the Angel's light.

Tobias realized there was nothing he could do for John now. He was on his own. He would never be able to reach him in time, and he was out of ammunition. He watched as John ran from one death towards another.

Over the cliff side, the ocean exploded upwards. Thick walls of water plumed high into the air. It hung there precariously before falling back seconds later with a Niagara Falls-like crash. A searing wave of fire filled the entire sky, in every direction. The very black of the night seemed to shy

343

away, as a whole.

As the wave of orange and red flames reached the rising angels, they burst into flames. Their glowing white bodies fell from the sky like comets racing towards the Earth, disintegrating as they went. Where the wall of water had stood only seconds ago loomed a sight that caused Tobias to drop his sword from his grasp and exhale all his breath in one big whoosh.

In that instant of fear, he realized that they were too late.

Three hundred feet or more in the sky stood what Tobias could only assume was the devil himself. As tall as a skyscraper, the purest form of Evil's pitch black eyes surveyed the area with disregard. His massive body stood packed with exposed muscles where its charred skin had ripped off. Two giant horns protruded from its head and vanished into the low hanging clouds. From its bottom jaw jutted two dark brown tusks.

It stretched its arms out to the sides and roared a sound so horrifying Tobias felt the grass die beneath his feet. It was as if a thousand lions roared at once. Tobias felt the urge to die. For some reason, he wanted to die. *Focus.*

Tobias forced his eyes away from the monstrosity and looked down at John. He had, thankfully, made it to the sign, but the Hounds were closing in. Fate would run its course now, and he would watch as it did.

John grabbed hold of the Sign's landing, a couple feet over his head, and hoisted himself up. The third Trinity Sign appeared to be the shape of the Crux from overhead. A small monument, like the one John had used within the limestone tunnels in Egypt, jutted out. He reached into his shirt and removed the Crux Signate. It dangled on the chain in front of him for a moment.

The Hounds were twenty yards away from the Sign and gaining.

The devil pushed tsunami-sized waves out in front of himself as he lumbered towards the island. The ground shook under each step of his massive weight. More of the cliff broke free and plummeted below as the waves hit the island. With the wave of his fist, the devil summoned his minions to attack. The sky fell.

"Here they come," Tobias said.

John looked back from atop the Trinity Sign. Water dripped from his body. Blood seeped from a gouge in his forehead, but a smile appeared on his face. He raised his left hand up and waved goodbye.

Sam threw herself into Tobias' beaten form. She shielded her eyes on his bloodied shirt and cried so hard that she forgot to breathe.

Tobias held her tight, but he kept his eyes on John. He nodded softly, remorsefully. All this time he'd tried to save John, but in the end, it was John who'd ended up saving him—saving the rest of the world.

The Hounds leapt into the air as John thrust the Crux into the protruding monument. The Hell Hounds all instantly disintegrated, turning to ash on the wind. A hollow boom sounded from deep within the caldera.

The devil, having arrived at the banks of Easter Island, lunged towards John. Its enormous, pulsing hand swept by Tobias like a train car in mid-air. It reached for John but was seared clean off by an unseen aura now protecting the Sign. It roared again and pounded the ground with its other hand, knocking a section of the island clean off and everyone except for John to the ground.

John rose into the air, carried on a thick beam of white light that disappeared far into the clouds overhead. The Sign hummed and vibrated like an overloaded nuclear bomb. A brilliant pulse of light haloed upwards, along the beam. As it hit John, the sky burst into radiant illumination like a sun going supernova, a trillion points of light all brighter than anything mankind has ever seen.

The overpowering light blinded Tobias and forced him to shield his eyes. He heard pops and bursts from all around like he had at Camelot. The devil roared in agony, a sound so terrible it shook the entire island. Tobias held Sam tight.

Moments later, the light faded, and Tobias opened his eyes. He hesitantly looked to the sky, towards the devil. It was clear, save for a fizzling white glow. Where the devil and his army had loomed moments ago was now just empty space filled in by the dark, cloudless horizon.

He peered down into the caldera. The Trinity Sign was gone, and so was John.

Sam still clung tightly to Tobias' shirt, her remorseful sobs buried in his chest. He reached his arm around her, wincing in pain as he did, and stroked her back. He gently kissed the top of her head and closed his eyes. Somehow, someway, this whole ordeal appeared to finally be over. He figured now was as good a time as any to retire and write that book of his. The ending, however, would need to wait, as only time would be able to fill in the blank pages. He hoped they would one day tell of a happy ending—one spent with Sam.

Chapter 47

Seven months had passed.

The images of what had transpired seemed to fade from the collective mind of the world. Scientists had their theories. They explained away the different occurrences with tangible explanations—super-earthquake, massive global warming, subduction of tectonic plates, thriving super bug colonies. ... The list went on. Tobias found all their explanations to be comical, but amidst the ignorance was where the truth would remain hidden.

The trade winds were not as strong this time, as Tobias, with Sam by his side, walked up the slope of Rano Kau. They had come back to Easter Island for a different purpose than before. This time he was without the lingering feelings of doom or the drive to save the world. Instead, the very pregnant Sam held his hand. They were in no rush to get to the top this time.

Rounding the top of the path, they were greeted by a group of tourists scurrying away. The eldest of the group kept looking back over his shoulder towards a crazy old man, waving his arms frantically about. Sam looked at Tobias, and they smiled.

The hermit turned his attention to them. After the tourists were out of sight, he hobbled over. "Welcome back, Guardian," the hermit said. "And you, Matron. I see you are progressing nicely." He looked at her belly and smiled.

Tobias glanced around at the scenery. It was much different in the daylight than it was in the darkness.

"What brings you back?" the hermit asked.

Tobias knelt down and removed his backpack. Reaching

in, he removed a small, flat stone.

"We thought a memorial was only fitting." Tobias turned the stone towards the hermit.

The hermit smiled and nodded. He understood. "I know the perfect place for that." He walked towards the edge of the caldera on the ocean side. Sam and Tobias followed.

The old man scurried over to an outcropping of large stones at the edge of the watery pit. Ghostly visions of John climbing the Sign filled Tobias' mind. While this place was the epicenter of man's salvation, it was also the location of deep sorrow, but he hadn't come to dwell in those feelings. Not today.

The hermit stopped next to what appeared to be a brownish tree trunk sticking out of the ground, some five feet high.

"I think this would be a fitting place for such a memorial."

"What is it?" Sam asked.

The old man smiled. "This would be a token unwillingly left behind by the devil."

Tobias gazed upon it further. Seconds later, it hit him. A tree had never resided there. This was the tip of one of the devil's tusks. It must have broken off and fallen to the ground before he was sent back to hell.

"I think this is a perfect place," Tobias said, laying the memorial stone down.

The three gazed upon its simplistic beauty. Two lines were etched within a carving of the Crux:

For Those Who Fell at the Guardian's Side,
Saviors and Friends to all Mankind

Sam reached down and traced the words.

"How are you feeling?" the old man asked Sam while

looking towards her belly.

She rubbed the outside of her shirt in a circular motion. "It took a little getting used to, but I wouldn't change it for anything in the world."

He smiled and turned to Tobias. "And you, Guardian? What will you do now that Evil's master has been struck down for another one thousand years?"

Tobias looked at Sam. "I'm going to take a shot at fatherhood."

Sam chimed in. "We figured, who better to protect the last of the Brotherhood of the Sealed than his Guardian father?"

The old man nodded, beamed a smile, and soaked in the ramifications.

"So, what of the Guardian bloodline? The child will need protection when you have passed to the next life." A playful smile arched his face. He looked from Sam to Tobias and back again.

"One child at a time, Keeper."

Sam blushed and turned away in embarrassment.

"Ooh," the old man said, remembering something. He held up his finger for them to wait. Rushing away, he entered into the last standing Orongo huts. When he returned, he held out his arm. Dangling from within his grasp was the Crux Signate. "I had a feeling I would see you again, Guardian. I think this would be best suited in your hands."

Tobias took the cross and stared at its purple-tinted metal. He gave it one final look before slipping it around his neck and under his shirt. Everything felt complete now.

"Take care, old man," he said, turning to walk away back down the hill and into his future with Sam.

"Wait!" the hermit shouted as they continued down the hill. "One last thing. What will you name the baby, so that I can mark it in the records?"

Sam turned and smiled. "John. We're naming the baby John."

THE END

www.ingramcontent.com/pod-product-compliance
Lightning Source LLC
Chambersburg PA
CBHW061318170626
46817CB00001B/227